NEW YORK TIMES BESTSELLING AUTHOR

DIANA PALMER

TEXAS HONOR

Previously published as *Unlikely Lover* and *Rage of Passion*

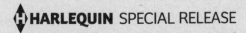

HARLEQUIN SPECIAL RELEASE

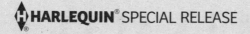 HARLEQUIN® SPECIAL RELEASE

Recycling programs
for this product may
not exist in your area.

ISBN-13: 978-1-335-47694-4

Texas Honor

Copyright © 2021 by Harlequin Books S.A.

Unlikely Lover
First published in 1986. This edition published in 2021.
Copyright © 1986 by Diana Palmer

Rage of Passion
First published in 1986. This edition published in 2021.
Copyright © 1986 by Diana Palmer

This edition published by arrangement with Harlequin Books S.A.

For questions and comments about the quality of this book, please contact us at CustomerService@Harlequin.com.

Harlequin Enterprises ULC
22 Adelaide St. West, 40th Floor
Toronto, Ontario M5H 4E3, Canada
www.Harlequin.com

Printed in U.S.A.

CONTENTS

A prolific author of more than one hundred books, **Diana Palmer** got her start as a newspaper reporter. A *New York Times* bestselling author and voted one of the top ten romance writers in America, she has a gift for telling the most sensual tales with charm and humor. Diana lives with her family in Cornelia, Georgia. Visit her website at dianapalmer.com.

Books by Diana Palmer

Long, Tall Texans

Fearless
Heartless
Dangerous
Merciless
Courageous
Protector
Invincible
Untamed
Defender
Undaunted

The Wyoming Men

Wyoming Tough
Wyoming Fierce
Wyoming Bold
Wyoming Strong
Wyoming Rugged
Wyoming Brave

Morcai Battalion

The Morcai Battalion
The Morcai Battalion: The Recruit
The Morcai Battalion: Invictus
The Morcai Battalion: The Rescue

Visit the Author Profile page
at Harlequin.com for more titles.

UNLIKELY LOVER

CHAPTER ONE

WARD JESSUP WENT to the supper table rubbing his big hands together, his green eyes like dark emeralds in a face like a Roman's, perfectly sculpted under hair as thick and black as crow feathers. He was enormously tall, big and rangy looking, with an inborn elegance and grace that came from his British ancestors. But Ward himself was all-American. All Oklahoman, with a trace of Cherokee and a sprinkling of Irish that gave him his taciturn stubbornness and his cutting temper, respectively.

"You look mighty proud of yourself," Lillian huffed, bringing in platters of beef and potatoes and yeast rolls.

"Why shouldn't I?" he asked. "Things are going pretty well. Grandmother's leaving, did she tell you? She's going to stay with my sister. Lucky, lucky Belinda!"

Lillian lifted her eyes to the ceiling. "I must have pleased you, Lord, for all my prayers to be so suddenly answered," she said.

Ward chuckled as he reached for the platter of sliced roast beef. "I thought you two were great buddies."

"And we stay that way as long as I run fast, keep my mouth shut and pretend that I like cooking five meals at a time."

"She may come back."

"I'll quit," was the gruff reply. "She's only been here

four months, and I'm ready to apply for that cookhouse job over at Wade's."

"You'd wind up in the house with Conchita, helping to look after the twins," he returned.

She grinned, just for an instant. Could have been a muscle spasm, he thought.

"I like kids." Lillian glared at him, brushing back wiry strands of gray hair that seemed to match her hatchet nose, long chin and beady little black eyes. "Why don't you get married and have some?" she added.

His thick eyebrows raised a little. They were perfect like his nose, even his mouth. He was handsome. He could have had a dozen women by crooking his finger, but he dated only occasionally, and he never brought women home. He never got serious, either. He hadn't since that Caroline person had almost led him to the altar, only to turn around at the last minute and marry his cousin Bud, thinking that, because Bud's last name was Jessup, he'd do as well as Ward. Besides, Bud was much easier to manage. The marriage had only lasted a few weeks, however, just until Bud had discovered that Caroline's main interest was in how much of his small inheritance she could spend on herself. He had divorced her, and she had come rushing back to Ward, all in tears. But somewhere along the way Ward had opened his eyes. He'd shown her the door, tears and all, and that was the last time he'd shown any warmth toward anything in skirts.

"What would I do with kids?" he asked. "Look what it's done to Tyson Wade, for God's sake. There he was, a contented bachelor making money hand over fist. He married that model and lost everything—"

"He got everything back, with interest," Lillian interrupted, "and you say one more word about Miss Erin and I'll scald you, so help me!"

He shrugged. "Well, she is pretty. Nice twins, too. They look a little like Ty."

"Poor old thing," Lillian said gently. "He was homely as sin and all alone and meaner than a tickled rattlesnake. And now here he's made his peace with you and even let you have those oil leases you've been after for ten years. Yes sir, love sure is a miracle," she added with a purely calculating look.

He shivered. "Talking about it gives me hives. Talk about something else." He was filling his plate and nibbling between comments.

Lillian folded her hands in front of her, hesitating, but only for an instant. "I've got a problem."

"I know. Grandmother."

"A bigger one."

He stopped eating and looked up. She did seem to be worried. He laid down his fork. "Well? What's the problem?"

She shifted from one foot to the other. "My brother's eldest girl, Marianne," she said. "Ben died last year, you remember."

"Yes. You went to his funeral. His wife died years earlier, didn't she?"

Lillian nodded. "Well, Marianne and her best friend, Beth, went shopping at one of those all-night department store sales. On their way out, as they crossed the parking lot, a man tried to attack them. It was terrible," she continued huskily. "Terrible! The girls were just sickened by the whole experience!" She lowered her voice just enough to sound dramatic. "It left deep scars. Deep emotional scars," she added meaningfully, watching to see how he was re-acting. *So far, so good.*

He sat up straighter, listening. "Your niece will be all right, won't she?" he asked hesitantly.

"Yes. She's all right physically." She twisted her skirt. "But it's her state of mind that I'm worried about."

"Marianne..." He nodded, remembering a photograph he'd seen of Lillian's favorite niece. A vivid impression of long dark hair and soft blue eyes and an oval, vulnerable young face brought a momentary smile to his lips.

"She's no raving beauty, and frankly, she hasn't dated very much. Her father was one of those domineering types whose reputation kept the boys away from her when she lived at home. But now..." She sighed even more dramati-cally. "Poor little Mari." She glanced up. "She's been keep-ing the books for a big garage. Mostly men. She said it's gotten to the point that if a man comes close enough to open a door for her, she breaks out in a cold sweat. She needs to get away for a little while, out of the city, and get her life back together."

"Poor kid," he said, sincere yet cautious.

"She's almost twenty-two," Lillian said. "What's going to become of her?" she asked loudly, peeking out the cor-ner of her eye at him.

He whistled softly. "Therapy would be her best bet."

"She won't talk to anyone," she said quickly, cocking her head to one side. "Now, I know how you feel about women. I don't even blame you. But I can't turn my back on my own niece." She straightened, playing her trump card. "Now, I'm fully prepared to give up my job and go to her—"

"Oh, for God's sake, you know me better than that

after fifteen years," he returned curtly. "Send her an airline ticket."

"She's in Georgia—"

"So what?"

Lillian toyed with a pan of rolls. "Well, thanks. I'll make it up to you somehow," she said with a secretive grin.

"If you're feeling that generous, how about an apple pie?"

The older woman chuckled. "Thirty minutes," she said and dashed off to the kitchen like a woman half her age. She could have danced with glee. He'd fallen for it! Stage one was about to take off! *Forgive me, Mari,* she thought silently and began planning again.

Ward stared after her with confused emotions. He hoped that he'd made the right decision. Maybe he was just going soft in his old age. Maybe…

"My bed was more uncomfortable than a sheet filled with cacti," came a harsh, angry old voice from the doorway. He turned as his grandmother ambled in using her cane, broad as a beam and as formidable as a raiding party, all cold green eyes and sagging jowls and champagne-tinted hair that waved around her wide face.

"Why don't you sleep in the stable?" he asked her pleasantly. "Hay's comfortable."

She glared at him and waved her cane. "Shame on you, talking like that to a pitiful old woman!"

"I pity anyone who stands within striking distance of that cane," he assured her. "When do you leave for Galveston?"

"Can't wait to get rid of me, can you?" she demanded as she slid warily into a chair beside him.

"Oh, no," he assured her. "I'll miss you like the plague."

"You cowhand," she grumbled, glaring at him. "Just like your father. He was hell to live with, too."

"You sweet-tempered little woman," he taunted.

"I guess you get that wit from your father. And he got it from me," she confessed. She poured herself a cup of coffee. "I hope Belinda is easier to get along with than you and your saber-toothed housekeeper."

"I am not saber-toothed," Lillian assured her as she brought in more rolls.

"You are so," Mrs. Jessup replied curtly.

Lillian snorted and walked out.

"Are you going to let her talk to me like that?" Mrs. Jessup demanded of her grandson.

"You surely don't want me to walk into that kitchen alone?" he asked her. "She keeps knives in there." He lowered his voice and leaned toward her. "And a sausage grinder. I've seen it with my own eyes."

Mrs. Jessup tried not to laugh, but she couldn't help herself. She hit at him affectionately. "Reprobate. Why do I put up with you?"

"You can't help yourself," he said with a chuckle. "Eat. You can't travel halfway across Texas on an empty stomach."

She put down her coffee cup. "Are you sure this night flight is a good idea?"

"It's less crowded. Besides, Belinda and her newest boyfriend are going to meet you at the airport," he said. "You'll be safe."

"I guess so." She stared at the platter of beef that was slowly being emptied. "Give me some of that before you gorge yourself!"

"It's my cow," he muttered, green eyes glittering.

"It descended from one of mine. Give it here!"

Ward sighed, defeated. Handing the platter to her with a resigned expression, he watched her beam with the tiny triumph. He had to humor her just a little occasionally. It kept her from getting too crotchety.

Later he drove her to the airport and put her on a plane. As he went back toward his ranch, he wondered about Marianne Raymond and how it was going to be with a young woman around the place getting in his hair. Of course, she was just twenty-two, much too young for him. He was thirty-five now, too old for that kind of child-woman. He shook his head. He only hoped that he'd done the right thing. If he hadn't, things were sure going to be complicated from now on. At one time Lillian's incessant matchmaking had driven him nuts before he'd managed to stop her, though she still harped on his unnatural attitude toward marriage. If only she'd let him alone and stop mothering him! That was the trouble with people who'd worked for you almost half your life, he muttered to himself. They felt obliged to take care of you in spite of your own wishes.

He stared across the pastures at the oil rigs as he eased his elegant white Chrysler onto the highway near Ravine, Texas. His rigs. He'd come a long damned way from the old days spent working on those rigs. His father had dreamed of finding that one big well, but it was Ward who'd done it. He'd borrowed as much as he could and put everything on one big gamble with a friend. And his well had come in. He and the friend had equal shares in it, and they'd long since split up and gone in different directions. When it came to business, Ward Jessup could be ruthless and calculating. He had a shrewd mind and a hard heart, and some of

his enemies had been heard to say that he'd foreclose on a
starving widow if she owed him money.

That wasn't quite true, but it was close. He'd grown up
poor, dirt poor, as his grandmother had good reason to remember. The family had been looked down on for a long
time because of Ward's mother. She'd tired of her boring
life on the ranch with her two children and had run off with
a neighbor's husband, leaving the children for her stunned
husband and mother-in-law to raise. Later she'd divorced
Ward's father and remarried, but the children had never
heard from her again. In a small community like Ravine the
scandal had been hard to live down. Worse, just a little later,
Ward's father had gone out into the south forty one autumn
day with a rifle in his hand and hadn't come home again.

He hadn't left a note or even seemed depressed. They'd
found him slumped beside his pickup truck, clutching a
piece of ribbon that had belonged to his wife. Ward had
never forgotten his father's death, had never forgiven his
mother for causing it.

Later, when he'd fallen into Caroline's sweet trap, Ward
Jessup had learned the final lesson. These days he had
a reputation for breaking hearts, and it wasn't far from
the mark. He had come to hate women. Every time he
felt tempted to let his emotions show, he remembered his
mother and Caroline. And day by day he became even
more embittered.

He liked to remember Caroline's face when he'd told her
he didn't want her anymore, that he could go on happily
all by himself. She'd curled against him with her big black
eyes so loving in that face like rice paper and her blond
hair cascading like yellow silk down her back. But he'd
seen past the beauty to the ugliness, and he never wanted
to get that close to a woman again. He'd seen graphically

how big a fool the most sensible man could become when a shrewd woman got hold of him. Nope, he told himself. Never again. He'd learned from his mistake. He wouldn't be that stupid a second time.

He pulled into the long driveway of Three Forks and smiled at the live oaks that lined it, thinking of all the history there was in this big, lusty spread of land. He might live and die without an heir, but he'd sure enjoy himself until that time came.

He wondered if Tyson Wade was regretting his decision to lease the pastureland so that Ward could look for the oil that he sensed was there. He and Ty had been enemies for so many years—almost since boyhood—although the reason for all the animosity had long been forgotten in the heat of the continuing battle over property lines, oil rigs and just about everything else.

Ty Wade had changed since his marriage. He'd mellowed, becoming a far cry from the renegade who'd just as soon have started a brawl as talk business. Amazing that a beautiful woman like Erin had agreed to marry the man in the first place. Ty was no pretty boy. In fact, to Ward Jessup, the man looked downright homely. But maybe he had hidden qualities.

Ward grinned at that thought. He wouldn't begrudge his old enemy a little happiness, not since he'd picked up those oil leases that he'd wanted so desperately. It was like a new beginning: making a peace treaty with Tyson Wade and getting his crotchety grandmother out of his hair and off the ranch without bloodshed. He chuckled aloud as he drove back to the house, and it wasn't until he heard the sound that he realized how rarely he laughed these days.

CHAPTER TWO

MARIANNE RAYMOND DIDN'T know what to expect when she landed at the San Antonio airport. She knew that Ravine was quite a distance away, and her Aunt Lillian had said that someone would meet her. But what if no one did? Her blue eyes curiously searched the interior of the airport. Aunt Lillian's plea for her to visit had been so unusual, so...odd. Poor old Mr. Jessup, she thought, shaking her head. Poor brave man. Dying of that incurable disease, and Aunt Lillian so determined to make his last days happy. Mari had been delighted to come, to help out. Her vacation was overdue, and the manager of the big garage where she kept the books and wrote the occasional letter had promised that they could do without her for a week or so. Mr. Jessup wanted young people around, he'd told Lillian. Some cheerful company and someone to help him write his memoirs. That would be right up Mari's alley. She'd actually done some feature articles for a local newspaper, and she had literary ambitions, too.

Someday Mari was going to be a novelist. She'd promised herself that. She wrote a portion of her book every night. The story involved a poor city girl who was assaulted by a vicious gang leader and had nightmares about her horrible assailant. She'd told Aunt Lillian the plot over the phone just recently, and the older woman had been delighted with it. Mari wondered about her aunt's sudden enthusiasm because Lillian had never been particularly interested in anything except getting her married off to any likely candidate who came along. After her father's death, especially. The only reason she'd agreed to come down to Ravine was because of poor old Mr. Jessup. At least she could be sure that Aunt Lillian wasn't trying to marry her off to him!

Mari pushed back her hair. It was short now, a twenties-style pageboy with bangs, and it emphasized the rosy oval of her face. She was wearing a simple dropped-waist dress in blue-and-white stripes and carrying only a roly-poly piece of luggage, which contained barely enough clothes to get her through one week.

A tall man attracted her interest, and despite the shyness she felt with most men, she studied him blatantly. He was as big as the side of a barn, tall with rippling muscles and bristling with backcountry masculinity. Wearing a gray suit, an open-necked white shirt and a pearly gray Stetson and boots, he looked big and mean and sexy. The angle of that hat over his black hair was as arrogant as the look on his deeply tanned face, as intimidating as that confident stride that made people get out of his way. He would have made the perfect hero for Mari's book. The strong, tender man who would lead her damaged heroine back to happiness again…

He didn't look at anyone except Mari, and after a few seconds she realized that he was coming toward her. She clutched the little carryall tightly as he stopped just in front of her, and in spite of her height she had to look up to see his eyes. They were green and cold. Ice-cold.

"Marianne Raymond," he said as if she'd damned well

better be. He set her temper smoldering with that confident drawl.

She lifted her chin. "That's right," she replied just as quietly. "Are you from Three Forks Ranch?"

"I *am* Three Forks Ranch," he informed her, reaching for the carryall. "Let's go."

"Not one step," she said, refusing to release it and glaring at him. "Not one single step until you tell me who you are and where we're going."

His eyebrows lifted. They were straight and thick like the lashes over his green eyes. "I'm Ward Jessup," he said. "I'm taking you to your Aunt Lillian." He controlled his temper with a visible effort as he registered her shocked expression and reached for his wallet, flashing it open to reveal his driver's license. "Satisfied?" he drawled and then felt ashamed of himself when he knew why she had reason to be so cautious and nervous of him.

"Yes, thank you," she said. *That* was Ward Jessup? *That* was a dying man? Dazed, she let him take the carryall and followed him out of the airport.

He had a car—a big Chrysler with burgundy leather seats and controls that seemed to do everything, right up to speaking firmly to the passengers about fastening their seat belts.

"I've never seen such an animal," she commented absently as she fastened her seat belt, trying to be a little less hostile. He'd asked for it, but she had to remember the terrible condition that the poor man was in. She felt guilty about her bad manners.

"It's a honey," he remarked, starting the engine. "Have you eaten?"

"Yes, on the plane, thank you," she replied. She folded

her hands in her lap and was quiet until they reached the straight open road. The meadows were alive with colorful wildflowers of orange and red and blue, and prickly pear cacti. Mari also noticed long stretches of land where there were no houses and few trees, but endless fences and cattle everywhere.

"I thought there was oil everywhere in Texas," she murmured, staring out at the landscape and the sparse houses.

"What do you think those big metal grasshoppers are?" he asked, glancing at her as he sped down the road.

She frowned. "Oil wells? But where are the big metal things that look like the Eiffel Tower?"

He laughed softly to himself. "My God. Eastern tenderfoot," he chided. "You put up a derrick when you're hunting oil, honey, you don't keep it on stripper wells. Those damned things cost money."

She smiled at him. "I'll bet you weren't born knowing that, either, Mr. Jessup," she said.

"I wasn't." He leaned back and settled his huge frame comfortably.

He sure does look healthy for a dying man, Mari thought absently.

"I worked on rigs for years before I ever owned one."

"That's very dangerous work, isn't it?" she asked conversationally.

"So they say."

She studied his very Roman profile, wondering if anyone had ever painted him. Then she realized that she was staring and turned her attention to the landscape. It was spring and the trees looked misshapen and gloriously soft feathered with leaves.

"What kind of trees are those, anyway?" she asked.

"Mesquite," he said. "It's all over the place at the ranch, but don't ever go grabbing at its fronds. It's got long thorns everywhere."

"Oh, we don't have mesquite in Georgia," she commented, clasping her purse.

"No, just peach trees and magnolia blossoms and dainty little cattle farms."

She glared at him. "In Atlanta we don't have dainty little cattle farms, but we do have a very sophisticated tourism business and quite a lot of foreign investors."

"Don't tangle with me, honey," he advised with a sharp glance. "I've had a hard morning, and I'm just not in the mood for verbal fencing."

"I gave up obeying adults when I became one," she replied.

His eyes swept over her dismissively. "You haven't. Not yet."

"I'll be twenty-two this month," she told him shortly.

"I was thirty-five last month," he replied without looking her way. "And, to me, you'd still be a kid if you were four years older."

"You poor, old, decrepit thing," she murmured under her breath. It was getting harder and harder to feel sorry for him.

"What an interesting houseguest you're going to make, Miss Raymond," he observed as he drove down the interstate. "I'll have to arrange some razor-blade soup to keep your tongue properly sharpened."

"I don't think I like you," she said shortly.

He glared back. "I don't like women," he replied and his voice was as cold as his eyes.

She wondered if he knew why she'd come and decided

that Aunt Lillian had probably told him everything. She averted her face to the window and gnawed on her lower lip. She was being deliberately antagonistic, and her upbringing bristled at her lack of manners. He'd asked Lillian to bring her out to Texas; he'd even paid for her ticket. She was supposed to cheer him up, to help him write his memoirs, to make his last days happier. And here she was being rude and unkind and treating him like a bad-tempered old tyrant.

"I'm sorry," she said after a minute.

"What?"

"I'm sorry," she repeated, unable to look at him. "You let me come here, you bought my ticket, and all I've done since I got off the plane is be sarcastic to you. Aunt Lillian told me all about it, you know," she added enigmatically, ignoring the puzzled expression on his face. "I'll do everything I can to make you glad you've brought me here. I'll help you out in every way I can. Well," she amended, "in most ways. I'm not really very comfortable around men," she added with a shy smile.

He relaxed a little, although he didn't smile. His hand caressed the steering wheel as he drove. "That's not hard to understand," he said after a minute, and she guessed that her aunt had told him about her strict upbringing. "But I'm the last man on earth you'd have to worry about in that particular respect. My women know the score, and they aren't that prolific these days. I don't have any interest in girls your age. You're just a baby."

Annoying, unnerving, infuriating man, she thought uncharitably, surprised by his statement. She looked toward him hesitantly, her eyes quiet and steady on his dark face. "Well, I've never had any interest in bad-tempered old men with oil wells," she said with dry humor. "That ought to reassure you as well, Mr. Jessup, sir."

"Don't be cheeky," he murmured with an amused glance. "I'm not that old."

"I'll bet your joints creak," she said under her breath.

He laughed. "Only on cold mornings," he returned. He pulled into the road that led to Three Forks and slowed down long enough to turn and stare into her soft blue eyes. "Tell you what, kid, you be civil to me and I'll be civil to you, and we'll never let people guess what we really think of each other. Okay?"

"Okay," she returned, eager to humor him. Poor man!

His green eyes narrowed. "Pity, about your age and that experience," he commented, letting his gaze wander over her face. "You're uncommon. Like your aunt."

"My aunt is the reincarnation of General Patton," she said. She wondered what experience he meant. "She could win wars if they'd give her a uniform."

"I'll amen that," he said.

"Thanks for driving up to get me," she added. "I appreciate it."

"I didn't know how you'd feel about a strange cowboy," he said gently. "Although we don't know each other exactly, I knew that Lillian's surely mentioned me and figured you'd be a bit more comfortable."

"I was." She didn't tell him how Lillian had described him as Attila the Hun in denim and leather.

"Don't tell her we've been arguing," he said unexpectedly as he put the car back in gear and drove up to the house. "It'll upset her. She stammered around for a half hour and even threatened to quit before she got up the nerve to suggest your visit."

"Bless her old heart." Mari sighed, feeling touched. "She's quite a lady, my aunt. She really cares about people."

"Next to my grandmother, she's the only woman that I can tolerate under my roof."

"Is your grandmother here?" she asked as they reached a huge cedarwood house with acres of windows and balconies.

"She left last week, thank God," he said heavily. "One more day of her and I'd have left and so would Lillian. She's too much like me. We only get along for short stretches."

"I like your house," she remarked as he opened the door for her.

"I don't, but when the old one burned down, my sister was going with an architect who gave us a good bid." He glared at the house. "I thought he was a smart boy. He turned out to be one of those innovative New Wave builders who like to experiment. The damned bathrooms have sunken tubs and Jacuzzis, and there's an indoor stream... Oh, God, what a nightmare of a house if you sleepwalk! You could drown in the living room or be swept off into the river."

She couldn't help laughing. He sounded horrified. "Why didn't you stop him?" she asked.

"I was in Canada for several months," he returned. He didn't elaborate. This strange woman didn't need to know that he'd gone into the wilderness to heal after Caroline's betrayal and that he hadn't cared what replaced the old house after lightning had struck and set it afire during a storm.

"Well, it's not so bad," she began but was interrupted when Lillian exploded out of the house, arms outstretched. Mari ran into them, feeling safe for the first time in weeks.

"Oh, you look wonderful," Lillian said with a sigh. "How are you? How was the trip?"

"I'm fine, and it was very nice of Mr. Jessup to come and meet me," she said politely. She turned, nodding toward him. "Thanks again. I hope the trip didn't tire you too much?"

"What?" he asked blankly.

"I told Mari how hard you'd been working lately, boss," Lillian said quickly. "Come on, honey, let's go inside!"

"I'll bring the bag," Ward said curiously and followed them into the rustic but modern house.

Mari loved it. It was big and rambling and there was plenty of room everywhere. It was just the house for an outdoorsman, right down to the decks that overlooked the shade trees around the house.

"I think this place is perfect for Ward, but for heaven's sake, don't tell him that! And please don't let on that you know about his condition," Lillian added, her eyes wary. "You didn't say anything about it?" she asked, showing Mari through the ultramodern upstairs where her bedroom overlooked the big pool below and the flat landscape beyond, fenced and cross-fenced with milling cattle.

"Oh, no, Scout's honor," Mari said. "But how am I going to help him write his memoirs?"

"We'll work up to it in good time," Lillian assured her. "He, uh, didn't ask why you came?"

Mari sighed. "He seemed to think I'd asked to come. Odd man, he thought I was afraid of him. Me, afraid of men, isn't that a scream? Especially after what Beth and I did at that all-night department store."

"Don't ever tell him, please," Lillian pleaded. "It

would…upset him. We mustn't do that," she added darkly. "It could be fatal!"

"I won't, truly I won't," Mari promised. "He sure is healthy looking for a dying man, isn't he?"

"Rugged," Lillian said. "Real rugged. He'd never let on that he was in pain."

"Poor brave man," Mari said with a sigh. "He's so tough."

Lillian grinned as she turned away.

"Did his sister like this house?" Mari asked later after she'd unpacked and was helping Lillian in the kitchen.

"Oh, yes," Lillian confided to her niece. "But the boss hates it!"

"Is his sister like him?" Mari asked.

"To look at, no. But in temperament, definitely," the older woman told her. "They're both high-strung and mean tempered."

"You mentioned that he had a male secretary," Mari reminded her as she rolled out a piecrust.

"Yes. David Meadows. He's young and very efficient, but he doesn't like being called a secretary." Lillian grinned. "He thinks he's an administrative assistant."

"I'll have to remember that."

"I don't know what the boss would do without him, either," Lillian continued as she finished quartering the apples for the pie. Another apple pie might soften him up a little, she was thinking. "David keeps everything running smoothly around here, from paying the accounts to answering the phone and scheduling appointments. The boss stays on the road most of the time, closing deals. The oil business is vast these days. Last week he was in Saudi Arabia. Next week he's off to South America."

"All that traveling must get tiresome," Mari said, her blue eyes curious. "Isn't it dangerous for him in his condition?"

For a moment Lillian looked hunted. Then she brightened. "Oh, no, the doctor says it's actually good for him. He takes it easy, and it keeps his mind off things. He never talks about it, though. He's a very private person."

"He seems terribly cold," Mari remarked thoughtfully.

"Camouflage," Lillian assured her. "He's warm and gentle and a prince of a man," she added. "A prince! Now, get this pie fixed, girl. You make the best pies I've ever tasted, even better than my own."

"Mama taught me," Mari said gently. "I really miss her sometimes. Especially in the autumn. We used to go up into the mountains to see the leaves. Dad was always too busy, but Mama and I were adventurous. It's been eight years since she died. And only one since Dad went. I'm glad I still have you."

Lillian tried not to look touched, but she was. "Get busy," she said gruffly, turning away. "It isn't good to look back."

That was true, Mari thought, keeping her own thoughts on the present instead of the past. She felt sad about Ward Jessup—even if he was a dreadful oilman. She'd heard her aunt talk about him for so many years that she felt as if she knew him already. If only she could make it through the week without making him angry or adding to his problems. She just wanted to help him, if he'd let her.

Mari was just going into the other room to call him when her attention was caught by the stream running through the room, lit by underwater colored lights. It was eerie and beautiful indoor "landscaping," with plants everywhere and literally a stream running through the middle of the living room, wide enough to swim in.

Not paying much attention to where she was going, Mari backed along the carpet, only half aware of footsteps, and suddenly collided with something warm and solid.

There was a terribly big splash and a furious curse. When she turned around, she felt herself go pale.

"Oh, Mr. Jessup, I'm sorry," she wailed, burying her cheeks in her hands.

He was very wet. Not only was he soaked, but there was a lily pad on top of his straight black hair that had been slicked down by all the water. He was standing, and though the water came to his chin, he looked very big and very angry. As he sputtered and blinked, Mari noticed that his green eyes were exactly the shade of the lily pad.

"Damn you…" he began as he moved toward the carpeted "shore" with a dangerous look on his dark face. At that moment nobody would have guessed that he was a dying man. As quick as lightning he was out of the water, dripping on the carpet. Suddenly Mari forgot his delicate condition and ran like hell.

"Aunt Lillian!"

Mari ran for the kitchen as fast as her slender legs could carry her, a blur in jeans and a white sweatshirt as she darted down the long hall toward the relative safety of the kitchen.

Behind her, soggy footsteps and curses followed closely.

"Aunt Lillian, help!" she cried as she dashed through the swing door.

She forgot that swing doors tend to swing back when forcibly opened by hysterical people. It slammed back into a tall, wet, cursing man. There was an ominous thud and the sound of shattering ceramic pieces.

Lillian looked at her niece in wide-eyed shock. "Oh, Mari," she said. Her ears told her more than she wanted to know as she stared at the horrified face of her niece. "Oh, Mari."

"I think Mr. Jessup may need a little help, Aunt Lillian," Mari began hesitantly.

"Prayer might be more beneficial at the moment, dear," Aunt Lillian murmured nervously. She wiped her hands on her printed apron and cautiously opened the swing door to peer into the dining room.

Ward Jessup was just sitting up among the ruins of his table setting, china shards surrounding him. His suit was wet, and there was a puddle of water under him as he tugged his enormous frame off the floor. His eyes were blazing in a face that had gone ruddy in anger. He held on to a chair and rose slowly, glaring at Lillian's half-hidden face with an expression that told her there was worse to come.

"She's really a nice girl, boss," Lillian began, "once you get to know her."

He brushed back his soaked hair with a lean, angry hand, and his chest rose and fell heavily. "I have a meeting just after supper," he said. "I sent the rest of my suits to the cleaner's this afternoon. This is the last suit I had. I didn't expect to go swimming in it."

"We could dry it and I could...press it," Lillian suggested halfheartedly, pretty sure that she couldn't do either.

"I could forget the whole damned thing, too," he said curtly. He glared at Lillian. "Nothing is going to make up for this, you know."

She swallowed. "How about a nice freshly baked apple pie with ice cream?"

He tilted his head to one side and pursed his lips. "Freshly baked?"

"Freshly baked."

"With ice cream?"

"That's right," she promised.

He shrugged his wet shoulders. "I'll think about it." He turned and sloshed off down the hall.

Lillian leaned back against the wall and stared at her transfixed niece. "Honey," she said gently, "would you like to tell me what happened?"

"I don't know," Mari burst out. "I went in to call him to the table, and I started looking at that beautiful artificial stream, and the next thing I knew, he'd fallen into it. I must have, well, backed into him."

"How you could miss a man his size is beyond me." Lillian shook her head and grabbed a broom and dustpan from the closet.

"I had my back to him, you know."

"I wouldn't ever do that again after this if I were you," the older woman advised. "If it wasn't for that apple pie, even I couldn't save you!"

"Yes, ma'am," Mari said apologetically. "Oh, Aunt Lillian, that poor, brave man." She sighed. "I hope he doesn't get a chill because of me. I'd never be able to live with myself!"

"There, there," Lillian assured her, "he's tough, you know. He'll be fine. For now, I mean," she added quickly.

Mari covered her face with her hands in mingled relief and suppressed amusement. Ward Jessup was quite a man. How sad that he had such little time left. She didn't think she'd ever forget the look on his face when he climbed out of the indoor stream, or the excited beat of her heart as she'd run from him. It was new to be chased by a man, even an ill one, and exhilarating to be uninhibited in one's company. She'd been shy with men all her life, but she didn't feel shy with Ward. She felt...*feminine*. And that was as new to her as the rapid beat of her heart.

CHAPTER THREE

"I DIDN'T MEAN to knock you into the pool," Mari told Ward the minute he entered the dining room.

He stopped in the doorway and stared at her from his great height. His hair was dry now, thick and straight against his broad forehead, and his wet clothes had been exchanged for dry jeans and a blue plaid shirt. His green eyes were a little less hostile than they had been minutes before.

"It isn't a pool," he informed her. "It's an indoor stream. And next time, Miss Raymond, I'd appreciate it if you'd watch where the hell you're going."

"Yes, sir," she said quickly.

"I told you not to let him put that stream in the living room," Lillian gloated.

He glared at her. "Keep talking and I'll give you an impromptu swimming lesson."

"Yes, boss." She turned on her heel and went back into the kitchen to fetch the rest of the food.

"I really am sorry," Mari murmured.

"So am I," he said unexpectedly, and his green eyes searched hers quietly. "I hope I didn't frighten you."

She glanced down at her shoes, nervous of the sensations that his level gaze prompted. "It's hard to be afraid of a man with a lily pad on his head."

"Stop that," he grumbled, jerking out a chair.

"You might consider putting up guardrails," she suggested dryly as she sat down across from him, her blue eyes twinkling with the first humor she'd felt in days.

"You'd better keep a life jacket handy," he returned.

She stuck her tongue out at him impulsively and watched his thick eyebrows arch.

He shook out his napkin with unnecessary force and laid it across his powerful thighs. "My God, you're living dangerously," he told her.

"I'm not afraid of you," she said smartly and meant it.

"That isn't what your Aunt Lillian says," he observed with narrowed eyes.

She stared at him blankly. "I beg your pardon?"

"She says you're afraid of men," he continued. He scowled at her puzzled expression. "Because of what happened to you and your friend," he prompted.

She blinked, wondering what her aunt had told him about that. After all, having your purse pinched by an overweight juvenile delinquent wasn't really enough to terrify most women. Especially when she and Beth had run the offender down, beaten the stuffing out of him, recovered the purse and sat on him until the police got there.

"You know, dear," Lillian blustered as she came through the door, shaking her head and smiling all at once. She looked as red as a beet, too. "The horrible experience you had!"

"Horrible?" Mari asked.

"Horrible!" Lillian cried. "We can't talk about it now!"

"We can't?" Mari parroted blankly.

"Not at the table. Not in front of the boss!" She jerked her head curtly toward him two or three times.

"Have you got a crick in your neck, Aunt Lillian?" her niece asked with some concern.

"No, dear, why do you ask? Here! Have some fried chicken and some mashed potatoes!" She shoved dishes toward her niece and began a monologue that only ended when it was time for dessert.

"I think something's wrong with Aunt Lillian," Mari confided to Ward the moment Lillian started back into the kitchen for the coffeepot.

"Yes, so do I," he replied. "She's been acting strangely for the past few days. Don't let on you know. We'll talk later."

She nodded, concerned. Lillian was back seconds later, almost as if she was afraid to leave them alone together. How strange.

"Well, I think I'll go up to bed," Mari said after she finished her coffee, glancing quickly at Aunt Lillian. "I'm very tired."

"Good idea," Ward said. "You get some rest."

"Yes," Lillian agreed warmly. "Good night, dear."

She bent to kiss her aunt. "See you in the morning, Aunt Lillian," she murmured and glanced at Ward. "Good night, Mr. Jessup."

"Good night, Miss Raymond," he said politely.

Mari went quietly upstairs and into her bedroom. She sat by the window and looked down at the empty swimming pool with its wooden privacy fence and the gently rolling, brush-laden landscape, where cattle moved lazily and a green haze heralded spring. Minutes later there was a stealthy knock at the door, and Ward Jessup came into the room, scowling.

"Want me to leave the door open?" he asked hesitantly.

She stared at him blankly. "Why? Are you afraid I might attack you?"

He stared back. "Well, after the experience you had, I thought…"

"What experience?" she asked politely.

"The man at the shopping center," he said, his green eyes level and frankly puzzled as he closed the door behind him.

"Are you afraid of me because of that?" she burst out. "I do realize you may be a little weak, Mr. Jessup, but I promise I won't hurt you!"

He gaped at her. "What?"

"You don't have to be afraid of me," she assured him. "I'm not really as bad as Aunt Lillian made me sound, I'm sure. And it's only a red belt, after all, not a black one. I only sat on him until the police came. I hardly even bruised him—"

"Whoa," he said curtly. He cocked his dark head and peered at her. "You sat on him?"

"Sure," she agreed, pushing her hair out of her eyes. "Didn't she tell you that Beth and I ran the little weasel down to get my purse back and beat the stuffing out of him? Overweight little juvenile delinquent, he was lucky I didn't skin him alive."

"You weren't attacked?" he persisted.

"Well, sort of." She shrugged. "He stole my purse. He couldn't have known I was a karate student."

"Oh, my God," he burst out. His eyes narrowed, his jaw tautened. "That lying old turkey!"

"How dare you call my aunt a turkey!" she returned hotly. "After all she's doing for you?"

"What, exactly, is she doing for me?"

"Well, bringing me here, to help you write your memoirs before…the end," she faltered. "She told me all about your incurable illness—"

"Incurable illness?" he bellowed.

"You're dying," she told him.

"Like hell I am," he said fiercely.

"You don't have to act brave and deny it," she replied hesitantly. "She told me that you wanted young people around to cheer you up. And somebody to help you write your memoirs. I'm going to be a novelist one day," she added. "I want to be a writer."

"Good. You can practice with your aunt's obituary," he muttered, glaring toward the door.

"You can't do that to a helpless old lady," she began.

"Watch me." He was heading for the door, his very stride frightening.

"Oh, no! You can't!" She ran after him, got in front of him and plastered herself against the door. "You'll have to go through me."

"Suits me, Joan of Arc," he grumbled, catching her by the waist. He lifted her clear off the floor until she was unnervingly at eye level with him. "You sweet little angel of mercy, you."

"Put me down or I'll… I'll put you down," she threatened.

He stared amusedly into her blue eyes under impossibly thick lashes. "Will you? Go ahead. Show me how you earned that red belt."

She tried. She used every trick her instructor had taught her, and all it accomplished was to leave her dangling from his powerful hands, panting into his mocking smile.

"Had enough?" she huffed.

"Not at all. Aren't you finished yet?" he asked politely.

She aimed one more kick, which he blocked effortlessly. She sagged in his powerful hold. Lord, he was strong! "Okay," she said, sighing wearily. "Now I'm finished."

"Next time," he told her as he put her back on her feet, leaving his hands tightly around her waist, "make sure your intended victim didn't take the same course of study. My belt is black. Tenth degree."

"Damn you!" she cursed sharply.

"And we'll have no more of that in this house," he said shortly, emphasizing the angry remark with a reproachful slap to her bottom, nodding as she gasped in outrage. "You've been working in that garage for too long already, if that's any example of what you're being taught."

"I'm not a child!" she retorted. "I'm an adult!"

"No, you aren't," he replied, jerking her against him with a mocking smile. "But maybe I can help you grow up a little."

He bent his head and found her lips with a single smooth motion, pressing her neck back against his muscular shoulder with the fierce possessiveness of his hard mouth.

Mari thought that in all her life nothing so unexpected had ever happened to her. His lips were warm and hard and insistent, forcing hers open so that he could put the tip of his tongue just under them, his breath tasting of coffee and mint, the strength of his big body overwhelming her with its hard warmth.

For an instant she tried to struggle, only to find herself enveloped in his arms, wrapped up against him so tightly that she could hardly breathe. And everywhere her face turned, his was there, his mouth provocative, sensuous, biting at hers, doing the most intimate things to it.

Her legs felt funny. They began to tremble as they came

into sudden and shocking contact with his. Her heart raced. Her body began to ache with heat and odd longings. Her breath caught somewhere in her chest, and her breasts felt swollen. He held her tighter, not brutally but firmly, and went on kissing her.

His fingers were in her hair, tugging gently, strong and warm at her nape as they turned her face where he wanted it. His mouth pressed roughly against hers and opened softly, teaching hers. Eventually the drugging sweetness of it took the fight out of her. With a tiny sigh she began to relax.

"Open your mouth, Mari," he murmured in a deep, rough whisper, punctuating the command with a sensual brushing of his open lips against hers.

She obeyed him without hearing him, her body with a new heat, her hands searching over his arms to find hard muscle and warm strength through the fabric. She wanted to touch his skin, to experience every hard line of him. She wanted to open his shirt and touch his chest and see if the wiry softness she could feel through it was thick hair....

Her abandon shocked her back to reality. Her eyes opened and she tugged at his arms, only vaguely aware of the sudden, fierce hunger in his mouth just before he felt her resistance. He lifted his head, taking quick, short breaths, and by the time her eyes opened, he was back in control.

He was watching her, half amused, half mocking. He lifted his mouth, breathing through his nose, and let her move away.

"You little virgin," he accused in a tone that she didn't recognize. "You don't even know how to make love."

Her swollen lips could barely form words. She had to

swallow and try twice to make herself heard. "That wasn't fair," she said finally.

"Why not?" he asked. "You tried to kick me, didn't you?"

"That isn't the way…a gentleman gets even," she said, still panting.

"I'm no gentleman," he assured her, smiling even with those cold green eyes. The smile grew colder as he realized how close he'd come to letting her knock him off balance physically. She was dangerous. Part of him wanted her off the property. But another part was hungry for more of that innocently ardent response he'd won from her. His own emotions confused him. "Haven't you realized yet why you're here, Georgia peach?" he asked mockingly. And when she shook her head, he continued, half amused. "Aunt Lillian is matchmaking. She wants you to marry me."

Mari's pupils dilated. "Marry you!"

His back stiffened. She didn't have to make it sound like the rack, did she? He glared down at her. "Well, plenty have wanted to, let me tell you," he muttered.

"Masochists," she shot back, humiliated by her aunt, his attitude and that unexpectedly ardent attack just minutes before. "Anyway," she said salvaging her pride, "Aunt Lillian would never—"

"She did." He studied her with a cold smile. "But I'm too old for you and too jaded. And I don't want to risk my heart again. So go home. Fast."

"It can't be fast enough to suit me. Honest," she told him huskily as she tried to catch her breath. "I don't want to wake up shackled to a man like you."

"How flattering of you."

"I want a partner, not a possessor," she said shakily. "I

thought I knew something about men until just now. I don't know anything at all. And I'll be delighted to go back home and join a convent!"

"Was it that bad?" he taunted.

"You scare me, big man," she said and meant it. She backed away from him. "I'll stick to my own age group from now on, thanks. I'll bet you've forgotten more about making love than I'll ever learn."

He smiled slowly, surprised by her frankness. "I probably have. But you're pretty sweet all the same."

"Years too young for a renegade like you."

"I could be tempted," he murmured thoughtfully.

"I couldn't. You'd seduce me and leave me pregnant, and Aunt Lillian would quit, and I'd have to go away and invent a husband I didn't have, and our child would grow up never knowing his father..." she burst out.

His eyes widened. He actually chuckled. "My God, what an imagination."

"I told you I wanted to be a writer," she reminded him. "And now, since you're not dying, would you mind leaving me to pack? I think I can be out of here in ten minutes."

"She'll be heartbroken," he said unexpectedly.

"That's not my problem."

"She's your aunt. Of course it's your problem," he returned. "You can't possibly leave now. She'd—"

"Oh!"

The cry came from downstairs. They looked at each other and both dived for the door, opening it just in time to find Lillian on her back on the bottom step, groaning, one leg in an unnatural position.

Mari rushed down the stairs just behind Ward. "Oh,

Aunt Lillian!" she wailed, staring at the strained old face
with its pasty complexion. "How could you do this to me?"

"To you?" Lillian bit off, groaning again. "Child, it's
my leg!"

"I was going to leave—" Mari began.

"Leave the dishes for you, no doubt." Ward jumped in
with a warning glance in Mari's direction. "Isn't that right,
Miss Raymond?" Fate was working for him as usual, he
mused. Now he'd have a little time to find out just why this
woman disturbed him so much. And to get her well out of
his system, one way or another, before she left. He had to
prove to himself that Mari wasn't capable of doing to him
what Caroline had done. It was a matter of male pride.

Mari swallowed, wondering whether to go along with
Ward. He did look pretty threatening. And huge. "Uh, that's
right. The dishes. But I can do them!" she added brightly.

"It looks like…you may be doing them…for quite a
while, if you…don't mind," Lillian panted between groans
while Wade rushed to the telephone and dialed the emergency service number.

"You poor darling." Mari sighed, holding Lillian's wrin-
kled hand. "What happened?"

"I missed Ward and wondered if he might be…if you
might be…" She cleared her throat and stared at Mari
through layers of pain. "You didn't say anything to him?"
she asked quickly. "About his…condition?"

Mari bit her tongue. *Forgive me for lying, Lord,* she
thought. She crossed her fingers behind her. "Of course
not," she assured her aunt with a blank smile. "He was just
telling me about the ranch."

"Thank God." Lillian sank back. "My leg's broken, you
know," she bit off. She glanced up as Ward rejoined them,

scowling down at her. She forced a pitiful smile. "Well, boss, I guess you'll have to send for your grandmother," she said slyly.

He glared at her. "Like hell! I just got her off the place! Anyway, why should I?" he continued, bending to hold her other hand. "Your niece won't mind a little cooking, will she?" he added with a pointed glance at Mari.

Mari shifted restlessly. "Well, actually—"

"Of course she won't." Lillian grinned and then grimaced. "Will you, darling? You need to... recuperate." She chose her words carefully. "From your bad experience," she added, jerking her head toward Ward, her eyes pleading with her niece. "You know, at the shopping center?"

"Oh. That bad experience." Mari nodded, glancing at Ward and touching her lower lip where it was slightly swollen.

A corner of his mouth curved up and his eyes twinkled. "It wasn't that bad, was it?" he murmured.

"It was terrible!" Lillian broke in.

"You said it," Mari agreed blithely, her blue eyes accusing. "Besides, I thought you couldn't wait to push me out the door."

"You want her to leave?" Lillian wailed.

"No, I don't want her to leave," Ward said with suffering patience. He lifted his chin and stared down his straight nose at Mari, then smiled. "I've got plans for her," he added in a tone that was a threat in itself.

That was what bothered Mari. Now she was trapped by Lillian's lies and Ward's allegiance to his housekeeper. She wondered what on earth she was going to do, caught between the two of them, and she wondered why Ward Jessup wanted her to stay. He hated women most of the time, from what Lillian had divulged about him. He wasn't a marrying man, and he was a notorious womanizer. Surely he wouldn't try to seduce her. Would he?

She stared at him over Lillian's supine form with troubled eyes. He had an unscrupulous reputation. She wasn't so innocent that she hadn't recognized that evident hunger in his hard mouth just before she'd started fighting him.

But his green eyes mocked her, dared her, challenged her. She'd stay, he told himself. He'd coax her into it. Then he could find some way to make her show her true colors. He was betting there was a little of Caroline's makeup in her, too. She was just another female despite her innocence. She was a woman, and all women were unscrupulous and calculating. If he could make her drop the disguise, if he could prove she was just like all the other she-cats, he could rid himself of his unexpected lust. Lust, of course, was all it was. He forgave Lillian for her fall. It was going to work right in with his plans. Yes, it was.

CHAPTER FOUR

LILLIAN WAS COMFORTABLY settled in a room in the small Ravine hospital. The doctor had ordered a series of tests—not because of her broken leg but because of her blood pressure reading taken in the emergency room.

"Will she be all right, do you think?" Mari asked Ward as they waited for the doctor to speak to them. For most of the evening they'd been sitting in this waiting room. Ward paced and drank black coffee while Mari just stared into space worriedly. Lillian was her last living relative. Without the older woman she'd be all alone.

"She's tough," Ward said noncommittally. He glared at his watch. "My God, I hate waiting! I almost wish I smoked so that I'd have something to help kill the time."

"You don't smoke?" Mari said with surprise.

"Never could stand the things," he muttered. "Clogging up my lungs with smoke never seemed sensible."

Her eyebrows lifted. "But you drink."

"Not to excess," he returned, glancing down at her. "I like whiskey and water once in a blue moon, and I'll take a drink of white wine. But I won't do it and drive." He grinned. "All those commercials got to me. Those crashing beer glasses stick in my mind."

She smiled back a little shyly. "I don't drink at all."

"I guess not, tenderfoot," he murmured. "You aren't old enough to need to."

"My dad used to say that it isn't the age, it's the mileage."

His eyebrows arched. "How much mileage do you have, lady?" he taunted. "You look and feel pretty green to me."

Her face colored furiously, and she hated that knowing look on his dark face. "Listen here, Mr. Jessup—"

"Mr. Jessup." His name was echoed by a young resident physician, who came walking up in a white coat holding a clipboard. He shook hands with Ward and nodded as he was introduced tersely to Mari.

"She'll be all right," he told the two brusquely. "But I'd like to keep her one more day and run some more tests. She's furious, but I think it's for the best. Her blood pressure was abnormally high when we admitted her and it still is. I think that she might have had a slight stroke and that it caused her fall."

Mari had sudden horrible visions and went pale. "Oh, no," she whispered.

"I said, I think," the young doctor emphasized and then smiled. "She might have lost her balance for a number of reasons. That's why I want to run the tests. Even a minor ear infection or sinusitis could have caused it. I want to know for sure. But one thing's certain, and that's her attitude toward the high blood pressure medication she hasn't been taking."

Ward and Mari exchanged puzzled glances. "I wasn't aware that she had high blood pressure medication," Ward said.

"I guessed that," the young doctor said ruefully. "She was diagnosed a few weeks ago by Dr. Bradley. She didn't even get the prescription filled." He sighed. "She seems to look upon it as a death sentence, which is absurd. It's not, if she just takes care of herself."

"She will from now on," Mari promised. "If I have to roll the pills up in steak and trick them into her."

The young resident grinned from ear to ear. "You have pets?"

"I used to have a cat," Mari confided. "And the only way I could get medicine into him was by tricking him. Short of rolling him up in a towel."

Ward glared at her. "That's no way to treat a sick animal."

She lifted her thin eyebrows. "And how would you do it?"

"Force his mouth open and shove the pills down his throat, of course," he said matter-of-factly. "Before you say it," he added when her mouth opened, "try rolling a half-ton bull in a towel!"

The young doctor covered his mouth while Mari glared up at the taciturn oilman.

"I'll get the pills into her, regardless," Mari assured the doctor. She glanced at Ward Jessup. "And it won't be by having them forced down her throat like a half-ton bull!"

"When will you know something?" Ward asked.

"I'll have the tests by early afternoon, and I'll confer with Dr. Bradley. If you can be here about four o'clock, I'll have something to tell you," the young man said.

"Thank you, Doctor...?"

"Jackson," he replied, smiling. "And don't worry too much," he told Mari. "She's a strong-willed woman. I'd bet on her."

They stopped by Lillian's room and found her half sedated, fuming and glaring as she sat propped up in bed.

"Outrageous!" Lillian burst out the minute they entered the room. "They won't give back my clothes. They're making me spend the night in this icebox, and they won't feed me or give me a blanket!"

"Now, now." Mari laughed gently and bent to kiss the thin face. "You're going to be fine. They said so. They just want to run a few more tests. You'll be out of here in no time."

That reassured the older woman a little, but her beady black eyes went to Ward for reassurance. He wouldn't lie to her. Not him. "Am I all right?" she asked.

"You might have had a stroke," he said honestly, ignoring Mari's shocked glare. "They want to find out."

Lillian sighed. "I figured that. I sure did. Well," she said, brightening, "you two will have to get along without me for a day or so." That seemed to cheer her up, too. Her eyes twinkled at the thought of them alone together in the house.

Ward could read her mind. He wanted to wring her neck, too, but he couldn't hurt a sick lady. First he had to get her well.

"I'll take good care of baby sister, here," he said, nodding toward Mari, and grinned.

Lillian's face fell comically. "She's not that young," she faltered.

"Aunt Lillian!" Mari said, outraged. "Remember my horrible experience!"

"Oh, that." Lillian nibbled her lip. "Oh. That!" She cleared her throat, her eyes widened. "Well…"

"I'll help her get over it," Ward promised. He glanced down at Mari. "She's offered to help me get some of my adventures in the oil business down on paper. Wasn't that nice? And on her vacation, too," he added.

Lillian brightened. *Good.* They weren't talking about his "fatal illness" or her "brutal attack." With any luck they wouldn't stumble onto the truth until they were hooked on each other! She actually smiled. "Yes, how sweet of you, Mari!"

Although Mari felt like screaming, she smiled at her aunt. "Yes. Well, I thought it would give me something interesting to do. In between cooking and cleaning and such."

Lillian frowned. "I'm really sorry about this," she said, indicating her leg.

"Get well," Ward said shortly. "Don't be sorry. And one more thing. Whether or not this fall was caused by your blood pressure, you're taking those damned pills from now on. I'm going to ride herd on you like a fanatical ramrod on a trail drive. Got that?"

"Yes, sir, boss," Lillian said, pleased by his concern. She hadn't realized she mattered so much to anyone. Even Mari seemed worried. "I'll be fine. And I'll do what they tell me."

"Good for you," Ward replied. He cocked his head. "They said it could have been an ear infection or sinusitis, too. So don't go crazy worrying about a stroke. Did you black out before you went down?" he persisted.

Lillian sighed. "Not completely. I just got real dizzy."

He smiled "That's reassuring."

"I hope so. Now, you two go home," Lillian muttered. "Let me sleep. Whatever they gave me is beginning to work with a vengeance." She closed her eyes as they said their goodbyes, only to open them as they started to leave. "Mari, he likes his eggs scrambled with a little milk in them," she said. "And don't make the coffee too weak."

"I'll manage," Mari promised. "Just get well. You're all I have."

"I know." Lillian sighed as they closed the door behind them. "That's what worries me so."

But they didn't hear that troubled comment. Mari was fuming all the way to the car.

"You shouldn't have told her what the doctor said." She glowered at him as they drove out of the parking lot.

"You don't know her very well," he returned. He pulled into the traffic without blinking. Ravine had grown in the past few years, and the traffic was growing with it, but speeding cars didn't seem to bother him.

"She's my aunt. Of course I know her!"

"She isn't the kind of woman you nurse along," he shot back. "Any more than I'm that kind. I like the truth, even if it hurts, and so does she. You don't do people any favors by hiding it. You only make the impact worse when it comes out. God, I hate lies. There's nothing on earth I hate more."

He probably had a good reason for that attitude, but Mari wasn't going to pry into his privacy by asking.

At least now she understood Aunt Lillian's matchmaking frenzy. If the older woman had expected to die, she might also have worried about Mari's future. But to try to give Mari to a man like the one beside her was almost criminal! The very thought of being tied to that ex-drill rigger made her blanche. He frightened her in a way no other man ever had. It wasn't fear of brutality or even of rough behavior. It was fear of involvement, of being led on and dumped, the way Johnny Greenwood had teased her and taken her places, and then when she was drunk on loving him, he'd announced his engagement to someone else.

Ward Jessup wasn't the man for marriage, but he wouldn't mind amusing himself with a woman and then dropping her. He seemed to hate women, to be spoiling for revenge on the entire sex. She remembered him saying that he could only tolerate his grandmother and Lillian under his roof, and that said it all. She'd have to be very careful not to fall under his spell. Because he was just playing, and she didn't even know the first thing about his game.

She went to her room as soon as they were back at Three Forks, and although she hated her vulnerability, she actually locked her bedroom door. Not that he'd try anything, she assured herself. But, just in case, a little precaution wouldn't hurt.

The next morning she was awake at dawn. Rather than lie in bed and worry about Aunt Lillian, she got up, dressed in jeans and a yellow pullover and went to cook the beast's breakfast.

She did love this house, indoor waterway and all. It seemed to catch and scatter light so that the darkest corner was bright and cheery. The kitchen reflected the rest of the house. It was spacious and cheerful and contained every modern appliance known to man.

She started the coffee maker and fried bacon. By the time the aroma of coffee was filling the kitchen, she had biscuits in the oven and was setting the big, elegant dining room table.

"What the hell are you doing that for?" Ward Jessup asked from the doorway. "I don't mind eating in the kitchen."

She jumped, turning in time to see him shrug into a chambray shirt. His chest was…incredible. She couldn't help but stare. Despite her age and her exposure to men at the garage where she worked, she'd never in her life seen anything like Ward Jessup without his shirt. Talk about masculine perfection! His chest was as tanned as his face. Broad, rippling with muscle, tapering to his belt, it had a perfect wedge of dark, thick hair that made Mari's jaw drop.

"Close your mouth, honey, you'll catch flies that way," he said, then chuckled, torn between exasperation and honest flattery at her rapt and explicit stare.

She turned back to her table setting with trembling fingers, hating her youth and inexperience, hating the big man who was making fun ot it. "Excuse me. I'm not used to men…half dressed like that."

"Then you should have seen me ten minutes ago, sprout, before I got up. I sleep in the raw."

Now Mari was sure she was blushing. She pursed her lips as she put silverware at their places.

He came up behind her so that she could feel the heat of his big body and took her gently by the shoulders. "That wasn't fair, was it?" he murmured.

"No," she agreed, "considering what a beautiful breakfast I just fixed you."

His lips tugged into a smile. "Do I smell bacon?"

"And biscuits and an omelette and hash brown potatoes and hot coffee," she continued, glancing up at him.

"Then what are you standing here for?" he asked. "Feed me!"

She was rapidly becoming convinced that his appetite was the great love of his life. Food could stop his temper dead, keep him from teasing and prevent homicide, as that apple pie had done after she'd knocked him into the water. It was useful to have such a weapon, when dealing with such a formidable enemy, she thought as she went to put the platters on the table.

He ate without talking, and he didn't sit and read a newspaper, as her father always had done in her youth. She watched him curiously.

His eyebrows shot up. "Something bothering you?"

"Not really." She laughed self-consciously. "It's just that the only man I've ever had breakfast with was my father, and he read his paper all through it."

"I don't read at the table," he said. He finished his last mouthful of biscuit, washed it down with coffee and poured himself a second cup from the carafe. Then he sat back in his chair and stared straight into Mari's eyes. "Why does my chest disturb you?"

She tingled from her head to her toes at the unexpected question and felt a wave of heat wash over her. Some old lines about fighting fire with fire shot into her mind. "Because it's beautiful, in a purely masculine way," she blurted out.

He pondered that for a minute before he smiled into his coffee. "You don't lie well, do you?"

"I think it's a waste of time," she replied. She got to her feet. "If you're through, I'll clear the table."

She started to pick up his plate. His big hand, and it was enormously big, caught her wrist and swallowed it, staying her beside him.

"Have you ever touched a man, except to shake hands?" he asked quietly.

"I'm not a shrinking violet," she said, flustered. "I'm almost twenty-two years old, and I have been kissed a few times!"

"Not enough, and not by anyone who knew how." He pulled her closer, feeling her resistance, but he stopped short of dragging her down onto his lap. "Why are you afraid of me?"

"I am not!" she retorted.

His fingers on her wrist were softly caressing. She reacted to him in a way that shocked him. In all the years, with all the women, he'd never felt such response. She was innocent, despite her denials. He'd have bet an oil well on it.

"Calm down," he said softly, feeling so masculine that he could have swallowed a live rattler. He even smiled. "I won't hurt you."

She flushed even more and jerked away from him, but he was much too strong. "Please," she bit off. "Let me go. I don't know how to play this kind of game."

His thumb found her moist palm and rubbed it in a new and exciting way, tracing it softly, causing sensations that went far beyond her hand. "I stopped playing games a long time ago, and I never played them with virgins," he said quietly. "What are you afraid of, Mari?" He spoke her name softly, and she tingled like a schoolgirl.

"You hate women," she said in a voice barely above a whisper. She met his green eyes levelly. "I don't think there's any real feeling in you, any deep emotion. Sometimes you look at me as if you hate me."

He hadn't realized that. He stared down at their hands, hers so pale against his deeply tanned one. "I got burned once, didn't your aunt tell you?"

"I got burned once, too," she replied, "and I don't want to—"

"Again," he finished for her, looking up unexpectedly. "Neither do I."

"Then why don't you let go of my hand?" she asked breathlessly.

He drew it relentlessly to his hard mouth and brushed at it with soft, moist strokes that made her go hot all over. "Why don't you stop me?" he countered. He pried open her palm and touched his tongue to it, and she caught her breath and gasped.

He looked up, his eyes suddenly hotly green and acquisitive, and she felt the first tug of that steely hand on hers with a sense of fantasy. Her eyes were locked into his possessive gaze, her body throbbed with new longings, new curiosities.

"I'm going to teach you a few things you haven't learned," he said, his voice like velvet as he drew her relentlessly down toward him. "And I think it's going to be an explosive lesson for both of us. I feel like a volcano when I touch you..."

Her lips parted as her eyes dropped to his hard, hungry mouth. She could almost see it, feel it, the explosive desire that was going to go up like fireworks when he put his hard mouth on hers and began to touch her.

She almost cried out, the hunger was so formidable. Silence closed in on them. She could hear his breathing, she could feel her heartbeat shaking her. In slow motion she felt his hard thighs ripple as she was tugged down onto them, she felt the power and strength of his hands, smelled the rich fragrance of his cologne, stared into eyes that wanted her.

She parted her lips in breathless anticipation, aching for him. Just as his hand went to her shoulder, to draw her head down, the front door opened with a loud bang.

CHAPTER FIVE

"Good morning," a pleasant auburn-haired young man was saying before Mari was completely composed again. He seemed to notice nothing, equally oblivious to Mari's flushed face and Ward's uneven breathing.

"Good morning, David," Ward said in what he hoped was a normal voice. From the neck down he had an ache that made speech difficult. "Have some coffee before we start to work."

"No, thank you, sir," the young man said politely. "Actually, I came to ask for a little time off," he added with a sheepish grin. "You see... I've gotten married."

Ward gaped at him. His young secretary had always seemed such a levelheaded boy, with a head full of figures. As it turned out, the figures weren't always the numerical kind.

"Married?" Ward croaked.

"Well, sir, it was kind of a hurried-up thing," David said with a grin. "We eloped. She's such a sweet girl. I was afraid somebody else would snap her up. And I wondered, well, if I could just have a couple of weeks. If you could do without me? If you have to replace me, I'll understand," he added hesitantly.

"Go ahead," Ward muttered. "I'll manage." He shifted in the chair. "What would you like for a wedding present?"

David brightened immediately. "Two weeks off," came the amused reply.

"All right, you've got it. I'll hold your job for the time being. Now get out of here. You know weddings give me indigestion," he added for good measure and then spoiled the whole thing by smiling.

David shook his hand with almost pathetic eagerness. "Thank you, sir!"

"My pleasure. See you in two weeks."

"Yes, sir!" David grinned at Mari, to whom he hadn't even been introduced, and beat a path out the door before he could be called back. He knew his boss pretty well.

"That tears it," Ward grumbled. "What in hell will I do about the mail?"

She stared at him, stunned by his lack of feeling. "He just got married."

"So what?" he demanded. "Surely the only time he really needs to be with her is after dark."

"You male chauvinist!"

"What are you so keyed up about, honey?" he taunted irritably. "Frustrated because I couldn't finish what I started before he walked in on us?"

What good would it do to argue? she asked herself as she noisily loaded up the dirty plates and utensils and took them out to the kitchen without a single word.

He followed her a few minutes later, looking half out of humor and a little guilty.

Standing in the doorway he filled it with his big, tall frame. His hair looked rakish, falling over his broad forehead, and he was so handsome that she had to fight to keep from staring at him all over again.

"I've got to ride over and see about my rig on Tyson Wade's place," he said quietly. "Can you handle the phone?"

"Sure," she told him, walking over to the wall phone. "This is the receiver," she began, pointing to it, speaking in a monotone. "When it rings, you pick it up and talk right in here—"

"Oh, for God's sake," he burst out. "What I meant was that it rings all day long, with everything from stock options to social invitations to notices of board meetings!"

She pushed back her bangs. "I've worked in offices since I was eighteen," she told him.

He cocked his head. "Can you type?"

"How ever do you think I'll manage all the housekeeping and cooking as well as looking after your appointments and answering mail and waiting on Aunt Lillian all at once?" she demanded.

His eyebrows arched. "Well, if you aren't capable of it, I'll hire a cook and a maid and a nurse and a secretary…"

Mari could only imagine how her aunt would react to that. She glared at him. "And break Aunt Lillian's old heart by importing a lot of strangers to keep us apart?"

He laughed in spite of himself. "I guess it would," he confessed. His green eyes narrowed, and there was a light in them that disturbed her as he ran his gaze slowly over her slender body. "God forbid anything should keep us apart."

"Don't you have an oil well to check on?"

"Several, in fact," he agreed. He folded his arms. "But at the moment I'd rather look at you."

"And I'd rather you didn't," she said curtly, averting her eyes to the dishwater.

"I like the way you react to me, Mari," he said softly. "I like the way your body starts to tremble when I come close. If I'd started kissing you a few minute ago, we'd still be doing it. And that being the case," he added, leveling with her, "I think you'd better practice ways to discourage me. Lillian won't be around much when she comes back until her leg heals. So you and I are going to get a bit of each other's company. I'd just as soon manage your little visit without showing you how good I am in bed."

His blatant speech shocked her. She turned, soapy hands poised over the sink, and stared at him. "Are you?" she asked without thinking.

He nodded slowly, holding her gaze, his face dead serious. "A man doesn't have to be emotionally involved to make love well. I've had years of practice. But it's never meant much, except physically. It never will. So you keep that in mind, sprout, okay?"

"Okay," she replied, all eyes.

His eyes narrowed at her expression. "Haven't you ever discussed these things with a man?"

"My parents didn't discuss things like that," she replied. "Most of the girls I've known had a distorted view of it because they did it with so many people. I...find the thought of it distasteful, somehow. Sleeping with someone, well, it's intimate, isn't it? Like us-ing someone's toothbrush, only more so. I couldn't...just do that, without loving."

She sounded so hopelessly naive. He searched her face and realized with a start that he'd never made love to a virgin. Not one. Not ever. And the thought of touching her in all the ways that he'd touched other women produced a shocking reaction from his body—one he was grateful that she wouldn't recognize.

"What an unusual attitude," he said involuntarily.

"That isn't the word most people use," she replied, her eyes dull and lackluster. "Men avoid me like the plague, except to do typing and answer phones. I'm what's known as an oddball."

"Because you don't sleep around?" he asked, stunned.

"Exactly. Didn't you know that the pill has liberated women?" she explained. "They're allowed the same freedom as men. They can sleep around every night without any consequences. Of course, they sacrifice a few things along the way that the liberals don't mention. Things like that deep-seated guilt that all the permissive ideals in the world won't change."

He stared at her. "My God, you are a fanatic, aren't you?" he mused.

She smiled slowly. "How would you like marrying a woman and hearing all about her old lovers? Meeting them occasionally and wondering if you measured up? How would you like to have a pregnant wife and wonder if the baby was really yours? I mean, if she sleeps around before marriage, what's to keep her from doing it afterward? If promiscuity is okay, isn't adultery okay as well?"

Everything she was saying disturbed him. Caroline had slept around. Not only with him, but, as he'd later found out, with at least two of his business acquaintances. He frowned at the thought. Yes, he'd have wondered. And he'd only just realized it.

"But I'm just a prude," she announced dryly. "So don't mind me. I'll grow into happy spinsterhood and die with the reputation that Elizabeth I had."

"Unless you marry," he said involuntarily.

She laughed ruefully. "Men don't marry women they haven't slept with. Not these days." She turned back to the dishes, oblivious to the brief flash of pain that crossed the face of the man behind her. "I'm not into self-pity, but I do face facts," she continued calmly. "I'm not pretty, I'm just passable. I'm too thin, and I don't know how to flirt. And, as you yourself said, I'm a greenhorn when it comes to intimacy. All that adds up to happy spinsterhood." She gazed thoughtfully out the window over the sink. "I'll grow prize roses," she mused aloud. "Yes, that's what I'll do. And zinnias and crape myrtle and petunias and lantana and hibiscus."

He wasn't listening anymore. He was staring at the back of her head. Her hair was very dark and sleek, and he wished she'd left it long, the way it was in the photograph he'd seen. She wasn't a beauty, that was true. But she had a pretty good sense of humor, and she didn't take herself or anyone else too seriously. She had guts and she told the truth. Damn her.

He didn't like his attraction to her. He didn't like how she could make him tremble all over like a boy when he started to kiss her. He didn't want her knowing it, either. The whole point of this exercise was to *exorcise*. He had to get rid of this lunatic obsession he felt.

"I'm going," he said shortly, shouldering himself away from the doorjamb. "I'll be back by three-thirty to go to the hospital with you."

"I'll phone meanwhile," she said.

"Do what you please." He stormed off, leaving her curious and speechless. What an odd man. What a dangerous man.

She spent the rest of the day working herself into exhaustion so that she wouldn't dwell on what had happened at breakfast.

WHEN THEY GOT to the hospital, Lillian was sitting on the side of her bed, dressed.

"It's about time," she began hotly. "Get me out of here!

They've put on a cast and decided it was infected sinuses that made me fall. They've given me some tablets they say will lower my blood pressure, and if you don't spring me, I'll jump out a window!"

"With that?" Ward asked, nodding toward the heavy plaster walking cast on one of her legs.

"With that," she assured him. "Tell him I'm serious about this, Mari," she added.

Mari was trying not to laugh. "You look pretty serious."

"I can see that. Where's the doctor?"

"He'll be here any minute," Lillian began.

"I'll go find him," Ward returned, walking quickly out into the hall, moving lightly for a man his size.

"How's it going?" Lillian asked, all eyes.

"How's what going?" Mari asked with assumed innocence.

"You were alone all last night!" she hissed. "Did he try anything?"

Mari lifted her eyebrows and pursed her lips. "Well, he did try to call somebody on the phone, but he couldn't get them."

Lillian looked pained. "I mean, did he make a pass at you?"

"No," Mari lied. It was only a white lie, just enough to throw the bloodhound off the scent.

The older woman looked miserable. It didn't bode well that Ward was so irritable, either. Maybe her matched pair had been arguing. Lillian had to get out of here and do a little stage-managing before it was too late and her whole plan went down the tube!

Ward was back minutes later, looking as unapproachable

as he had since he'd driven up to the house at three-thirty with a face like a thunderhead.

"I found him. He says you're okay, no stroke," he told Lillian. "You can leave. I've signed you out. Let's go."

"But we need a wheelchair…" Mari began.

He handed her Lillian's purse, lifted the elderly woman easily in his arms and carried her out the door, his set features daring anyone to question or stop him.

Back at Three Forks Lillian's room was on the ground floor, and despite all the protests she immediately returned to the kitchen and started supper.

"Do you want to go back to the hospital?" Ward demanded, hands on hips, glaring. "Get into bed!"

"I can cook with a broken leg," she returned hotly. "It isn't my hands that don't work, and I've never yet used my toes!"

He sighed angrily. "Mari can do that."

"Mari's answering your letters," he was pointedly reminded. "She can't do everything. And with David gone…"

"Damn David," he muttered darkly. "What a hell of a time to get married!"

Lillian glared at him until he muttered something rough under his breath and strode off toward his den.

Mari was inside the paneled room, working away at the computer. She was trying to erase a mistake and was going crazy deciphering the language of the computer he'd shown her. The word processing program was one of the most expensive and the most complicated. She couldn't even get it to backspace.

"I can't do anything with your aunt," he grumbled, slamming the door. "She's sitting on a stool making a pie."

"No wonder you can't do anything with her," she commented innocently. "Your stomach won't let you."

He glared at her. "How's it going?"

She sighed. "Don't you have a typewriter?"

"What year do you think this is?" he demanded. "What kind of equipment have you got at that garage where you work?"

"A manual typewriter," she said.

His head bent forward. "A what?"

"A manual type—"

"That's what I thought you said. My God!"

"Well, until they hired me, one of the men was doing all the office work. They thought the manual typewriter was the latest thing. It did beat handwriting all the work orders," she added sweetly.

"I work with modern equipment," he told her, gesturing toward the computer. "That's faster than even an electronic typewriter, and you can save what you do. I thought you knew how to use it."

"I know how to turn it on," she agreed brightly.

He moved behind her and peered over her shoulder. "Is that all you've done so far?"

"I've only been in here an hour," she reminded him. "It took me that long to discover what to stuff into the big slots."

"Diskettes," he said. "Program diskettes."

"Whatever. Anyway, this manual explains how to build a nuclear device, not how to use the word processing program," she said, pushing the booklet away. "Or it might as well. I don't understand a word of it. Could you show me how it works?" She looked up at him with eyes the color of a robin's egg.

He actually forgot what he was saying. She had a way of looking at him that made his blood thaw, like the sun beating down on an icy pond. He could imagine how a colt felt on a spring morning with the breeze stirring and juicy grass to eat and a big pasture to run in.

"Could you?" she prompted, lost in his green eyes.

His big hand touched the side of her face tentatively, his thumb moving over her mouth, exploring its soft texture, mussing her lipstick, sensitizing her lips until they parted on a caught breath.

"Could I what, Mari?" he asked in a tone that curled her toes inside her shoes.

Her head was much too far back. It gave him access to her mouth. She saw the intent in his narrowing eyes, in his taut stance. Her body ached for his touch. She looked up at him helplessly, his willing victim, wanting his mouth on hers with a passion that overwhelmed her.

He bent slowly, letting his gaze fall to her parted lips. She could smell the heady fragrance of his cologne now because he was so close. There was mint and coffee on his breath, and he had strong white teeth; she could see them where his chiseled lips parted in anticipation of possession. Her breasts throbbed, and she noticed a tingling, yearning sensation there.

"Your skin is hot," he whispered, tracing her cheek with his fingers as he tilted his face across hers and moved even closer. "I can feel it burning."

Her hands were on his arms now. She could feel the powerful muscles through the white shirt that he'd worn with a tie and jacket when they went to pick up Lillian. But the jacket and tie were gone, and the shirt was partially unbuttoned, and now the overwhelming sight of him filled

Mari's world. Her short nails pressed into his skin, bending against those hard muscles as his lips brushed over hers.

"Bite me," he whispered huskily and then incited her to do it, teasing her mouth, teaching her.

She knew nothing, but she wanted so desperately to please him so that he wouldn't stop. This was magic, and she wanted more.

Her mouth opened and she nipped at his firm lower lip, nibbling it, feeling its softness. He laughed softly deep in his throat, and she felt his hand move from her cheek to her shoulder, down her arm to her waist. While he played with her mouth, his fingers splayed out and then moved up, and the thin fabric of her flowery shirtwaist dress was no barrier at all as he found her rib cage and began to tease it.

This was explosive. Mari trembled a little because she was catching fire. He hadn't been kidding when he told her he was a good lover. She hadn't dreamed of the kind of sensations that he was showing her. She hadn't realized how vulnerable she was. Her mind was telling her that it was a game, that he didn't mean it. He'd said so. But her body was enthralled by new feelings, new pleasures, and it wouldn't let her stop.

"Oh," she whispered unsteadily when his tongue began to taste the soft inner surface of her lips.

"Open my shirt," he whispered against her warm mouth. He drew her hands to the remaining buttons and coaxed them until they had the fabric away from him.

She put her hands against hard muscle and thick hair and gasped at the contact. She'd never touched a man this way, and he knew it and was excited by it.

He bit her lower lip with a slow, ardent pressure that was

arousing. "Draw your nails down to my belt," he murmured against her parted mouth.

She did, amazed at the shudder of his big body, at the soft groan her caress produced. She drew away slightly so that she could see his face, could see the lazy, smoldering desire in his green eyes.

"I like it," he told her with a husky laugh.

She did it again, lowering her eyes this time to watch his muscles ripple with pleasure as she stroked them, to watch his flat stomach draw in even more with a caught breath. It was exciting to arouse him. It gave her a sense of her femininity that she'd never experienced.

Meanwhile, his hand was moving again, this time up her rib cage. Not blatant but subtle in its caress, teasing lightly, provocative. It reached the outer edges of her breast even as her nails were tenderly scoring him, and his fingers lifted to touch around her nipple.

She shuddered, looking up at him with the residue of virginal fear in her wide blue eyes. Her hand went to his hairy wrist and poised there while she tried to choose between pleasure and guilt.

"Have you ever done this before?" he asked, his lips against hers.

"No," she confessed.

Odd, how protective that made him feel. And how much a man. He brushed his lips gently over hers. "Lillian isn't fifty feet away," he whispered. "And we won't do anything horribly indiscreet. But I'm as excited by this as you are, and I don't want to stop just yet. I want to touch you and feel your reaction and let you feel mine. Mari," he murmured, tracing a path up her soft breast, "I've never been the first.

Not in any way, even this. Let me teach you. I promise you, there's not the slightest danger. Not right now."

"Oh, but I shouldn't..." She was weakening and her voice betrayed her.

"Don't feel guilty," he whispered over her mouth. "This is love play. Women and men have indulged themselves this way since the beginning of time. I'm human. So are you. There's no shame in being hungry."

He made it sound natural. It was the seducer's basic weapon, but Mari was too outmatched to care. She arched toward his fingers because she couldn't help herself. That maddening tracing of his fingers was driving her to her limits. She wanted his hand to flatten on her body. She wanted him to touch her...there!

His teeth nibbled at her lower lip, catching it in a soft tug just as his fingers closed on an erect nipple and tightened gently.

She cried out. The sound would have penetrated the walls and door, but he caught it in his mouth and muffled it, half mad with unexpected arousal. Her cries and her trembling were driving him over the edge.

Somehow he had her on the sofa, flat on her back with his heavy body half covering her. Her dress was coming undone, she could feel the air on her bare skin, and her bra was all too loose, and his hand was...there.

She shuddered and her eyes opened, hazy with passion. Her mouth was swollen, her cheeks red, her upward gaze full of rapt wonder.

His big hand flattened over her soft breast, feeling the tip rub abrasively on his palm as he caressed her. His thumb circled it roughly, and she shuddered all over, her breath sighing out unsteadily like his own.

She wanted him to kiss her some more, but his eyes were on her dress now. He peeled it slowly away from the breast he was touching, moving her bra up so that he could see the pink and mauve contrast and that taut little nub. It was as if he'd never looked at a woman before. She was beautiful. Sweetly curving and high, and not too big or too little. Just right.

She felt as if she were watching from a distance. Her eyes wandered over his absorbed expression, seeing the veiled pleasure there, the wonder. If she was awed by him, so was he awed by her. He was touching her like some priceless treasure, taking his time, lovingly tracing every texture.

He took the nipple between his thumb and forefinger and felt its hardness. He looked up into her fascinated eyes. "If I put my mouth on you, you'll cry out again," he whispered softly. "And Lillian might mistake the sound and come hopping."

She was trembling. She wanted it. Her body arched sinuously. She reached up, shyly, and cupped his face, gently tugging at it.

"I won't...cry out," she whispered, biting her lower lip to make sure.

"Say 'taste me,'" he whispered back, searching her eyes.

She blushed feverishly and turned her face into his throat to hide her embarrassment.

"Virgin," he breathed, trembling himself with the newness of it. "Oh, God, I want to have you so much!"

She thought she knew what he meant, but just then he took her breast into his warm mouth, and she had to chew her lip almost through to keep from screaming at the incredible sensation.

Her hands released his face, and she clenched them over her head. Writhing helplessly, she was caught up in the throes of something so powerful that it stopped her breath in her throat. She twisted up toward him, her body shuddering, her breast on fire with the feel of his mouth.

With a rough groan he suddenly rolled away from her and sat up with his face in his hands, shuddering, bent over as if in agony.

She lay there without moving, shaking all over with reaction and frustration, too weak from desire to even cover herself.

After a minute he took a deep, steadying breath and looked down at her. If she expected mockery or amusement, she was surprised. Because he wasn't smiling.

His dark green eyes ran over her like hands, lingering on all the places where his mouth had been, devouring her. He drew the bra slowly back down and reached around her for the hooks, fastening them. Then he pulled the edges of her dress together and buttoned them. He didn't speak until he was through.

"Do you understand why I stopped?" he asked gently. Yes, there was that. There was tenderness in every line of his face, in his voice, in the fingers that brushed her cheek.

"Yes," she returned slowly. "I think so."

"I didn't frighten you?"

That seemed to matter very much. She felt suddenly old and venerable and deeply possessive. "No," she said.

He tugged gently on a strand of damp hair. "Did I please you?" he persisted and this time he smiled but without mockery.

"As if you couldn't tell," she murmured, lowering her face so that he couldn't see it.

"If we ever make love completely, it will have to be in a soundproof room," he said at her ear. "You'd scream the house down."

"Ward!" she groaned and buried her face in his chest.

"No." He shuddered, moving her away, and he looked pale all of a sudden.

Her eyes questioned his. All these feeling were very new to her.

He drew in a harsh breath, holding her hands in his. "Men are very easy to arouse," he told her without embarrassment. "When they get to fever pitch, it takes very little to fan the fire. Right now I'm beyond fever pitch," he mused with a faint laugh, "and if you touch me that way again, we're both going to be in a lot of trouble."

"Oh," she returned, searching his eyes. "Does it hurt?" she whispered softly.

"A little," he replied. He brushed back her hair. "How about you?"

"Wow." She laughed shakily. "I never dreamed that could happen to me."

He felt incredible. New. Reborn. He touched her face lightly as if he were dreaming. Bending over her, he took her mouth softly under his and kissed her. It was different from any other kiss in his life. When he let her go, he had to stand up or lay her down.

"You'd better get back to work," he said and gestured toward the computer. "And, no, I'm not going to try to teach you. My body won't let me that close without making impossible demands on both of us so you'll have to muddle through alone." He laughed angrily. "Damn it, are you a witch?"

She stood up, smoothing her dress and hair. "Actually, until about five minutes ago, I thought I was Lady Dracula."

"Now you know better, don't you?" He stood watching her, his mouth slightly swollen, his shirt open, his hands on his narrow hips. The sight of him still took her breath away.

She went quickly back to the computer and sat down, keeping her eyes on the screen. "I'll get these finished before supper, if I can," she promised.

He smiled to himself. It took him a minute to leave her, his mind grappling furiously with the conflict between his desire and his calculating mind that insisted she was only interested in what he had—his ranch, his oil, his money.

Women had never wanted him for himself; why should Mari be different? But why had she reacted with such sweet ardor unless she'd wanted him as desperately as he'd wanted her? That kind of fever was hard to fake. No, he thought. No, she'd wanted him. But was she really that unmaterialistic? The only women he'd let himself get close to were his mother and Caroline, both of whom had been self-centered opportunists. How could he trust this one? She bothered him terribly. He no longer felt any confidence in his own judgment. He left the room scowling.

CHAPTER SIX

MARI WAS SO shaken by what had happened with Ward that she had eventually needed to escape from the den. She was afraid everything they'd done would show on her face, and Lillian had sharp eyes. She also wondered if Ward would tease her. That would be the last straw, to have a worldly man like that make fun of her for a physical reaction she couldn't help.

She needn't have worried. Ward was nowhere in sight, and Lillian was muttering furiously as she hobbled around the kitchen with a crutch under one arm.

"I wish you'd let me do that," Mari scolded. She picked up the plate of ham that Lillian was trying to take to the table and carried it in for her. "You shouldn't be trying to lift things, Aunt Lillian. You know what the doctor said."

"Yes, but it's pretty hard asking people for help," the older woman said irritably. She glanced at Mari. "He's gone."

Mari tried to look innocent. "He?"

"The boss. He decided to fly down to South America. Just like that." She snapped her fingers while Mari tried not to let her eyes reflect the shock she felt.

"He left tonight?" Mari asked blankly. It didn't seem possible. She'd been talking with him—among other things—less than two hours ago.

"Yep. He sure did. Bag and baggage. Imagine, getting

a flight out of here that quickly. He'll go on a commercial flight from San Antonio, you see." She added, "Flew himself over to the airport, he did."

Mari cleared her throat. "You said a few days ago that he'd have to go to South America."

"Yes. But I didn't expect him to leave in the middle of my first night back home," Lillian said hotly.

"He knows I'm here," she returned and impulsively hugged the older woman. "I'll take care of you."

Lillian sighed miserably. "Nothing is working the way it was meant to," she grumbled. "Nothing!"

Now was her chance to perfect her acting ability. "Whatever do you mean, Aunt Lillian?" she asked with a smile.

Lillian actually flushed. "Nothing. Not a thing. Here, set the table and help me get the food in here. There'll be a lot for just the two of us, seeing the boss and his appetite are missing, but we can freeze the rest, I suppose."

"Did you take your pill?" Mari asked.

Lillian glowered at her. Then she grinned. "Yep."

"Good for you," Mari returned. "Now I'll get to keep you for a lot longer."

Lillian started to speak, and then she just laughed. But her eyes were troubled when she hobbled back out to the kitchen.

MARI WANDERED AROUND by herself during the next few days, when she wasn't helping Lillian, enjoying the spaciousness of the ranch and the feeling of being self-sufficient. It must have been very much like this a hundred years before, she thought as she gazed out at the level horizon, when bad men and cattlemen and refugees from the Confederacy had come through on the long trails that led north and south and west.

It was so quiet. Nothing like the noisy bustle of Atlanta. Mari felt at peace here, she felt safe. But she missed Ward in ways that she never would have expected. She'd only really known him for a matter of days, but even that made no difference to her confused emotions. She could close her eyes and feel his hard mouth, his hands holding her, touching her. It had been the most exquisite thing that she'd ever experienced, being in his arms that day. She wanted it again, so much.

But even wanting it, she realized how dangerous it was to let him that close a second time. He only wanted her, he'd admitted that. He didn't believe in marriage. Apparently, he'd had a rough time with a woman at some point in his life, and he'd been soured. Aunt Lillian had mentioned that his mother ran away with another man, leaving Ward and Belinda to be raised by their grandmother. So she couldn't really blame him for his attitude. But that didn't make her own emotions any easier to handle.

She found herself watching the driveway and looking out the window, waiting. When the phone rang, and it did constantly, she ran to answer it, sure that it would be him. But it never was. Five days passed, and despite the fact that she enjoyed Aunt Lillian's company, she was restless. It was almost the end of her vacation. She'd have to leave. What if she never saw him again before she had to go?

"Missing the boss?" Lillian asked one evening, eyeing her niece calculatingly over the chicken and stuffing the younger woman wasn't touching.

Mari actually jumped. "No. Of course not."

"Not even a little?"

Mari sighed as she toyed with a fresh roll. "Maybe a little."

Lillian smiled. "That's nice. Because he's just coming up the driveway."

Mari couldn't stop herself. She leaped up from the table and ran to the front door, threw it open and darted out onto the porch. She caught herself just before she dashed down the steps toward him. She hadn't realized until that moment just how deeply involved she already was. Boys had never paid her much attention. Surely it was just the newness of being touched and kissed. Wasn't it?

She held on to the porch railing, forcing herself not to take one more step.

He got out of the Chrysler, looking as out of humor as when he'd left, a flight bag slung over one shoulder. Striking in a deep-tan vested suit and creamy Stetson, he closed the door with a hard slam, turned and started for the steps. Then he spotted Mari and stood quite still, just looking.

She was wearing a gauzy sea-green blouse with beige slacks, and she looked young and very pretty and a little lonely. His heart shot up into his throat, and all the bad temper seeped out.

"Well, hello, little lady," he said, moving up the steps, and he was actually smiling.

"Hello." She forced herself to look calm. "Did you have a good trip?"

"I guess so."

He stopped just in front of her, and she could see new lines in his face, dark circles under his eyes. Had he been with some woman? Her eyes narrowed curiously.

"Do I look that bad?" he taunted.

"You look tired," she murmured.

"I am. I did two weeks' business in five days." He searched her big, soft blue eyes quietly. "Miss me?"

"I had lots to do," she hedged. "And the phone hasn't stopped."

"That's not surprising." He let the bag fall to the porch and took her face in his big hands, tilting it up to his curious green eyes. "Dark circles," he murmured, running his thumbs gently under her eyes. "You haven't slept, have you?"

"You look like you haven't, either," she returned. There was a note in her voice that surprised and secretly delighted him.

"I never mix business with women," he whispered lazily. "It's bad policy. I haven't been sleeping around with any of those gorgeous, dark-eyed Latinas."

"Oh." She felt embarrassed and lowered her shocked eyes to his chest. "That's none of my business, after all," she began.

"Wouldn't you like it to be?" he asked softly. He leaned toward her, nuzzling her face so that she lifted it helplessly and met his quiet, steady gaze. "Or would you rather pretend that what we did the night I left meant nothing at all to you?"

"It meant nothing at all to you," she countered. "You even said so, that you…"

He stopped the soft tirade with his mouth. His arm reached across her back, pillowing her head, and his free hand spread on her throat, smoothing its silky softness as he ravished the warm sweetness of her parted lips. He was hungry, and he didn't lift his head for a long time, not until he felt her begin to tremble, not until he heard the soft gasp and felt the eager ardor of her young mouth.

He was breathing through his nose, heavily, and his eyes frightened her a little. "You haunted me, damn you," he said roughly, spearing his fingers into her thick dark hair. "In my sleep I heard you cry out..."

"Don't hurt me," she whispered shakily, her eyes pleading with him. "I'm not experienced enough, I'm not...old enough...to play adult games with men."

That stopped him, softened him. The harsh light went out of his eyes, and he searched her delicate features with growing protectiveness.

"I'll never hurt you," he whispered and meant it. He kissed her eyes closed. "Not that way or in bed. Oh, God, Mari, you make me ache like a teenager!"

Her nails bit into his arms as he started to lean toward her again, and just as his lips touched hers in the prelude to what would have become a violently passionate exchange, they heard the soft, heavy thud of Lillian's cast as she headed toward them.

"Cupid approaches," he muttered, a subtle tremor in the hands that gently put her away from him. "She'd die if she knew what she just interrupted."

Mari stared at him, a little frightened by her lack of resistance, by the blatant hunger that she'd felt.

"Passion shouldn't be frightening to you," he said gently as the thuds grew closer. "It's as natural as breathing."

She shifted, watching him lift his bag without moving his eyes from her. "It's very new," she whispered.

"Then it's new for both of us," he said just before Lillian opened the door. "Because I've never felt this with another woman. And if that shocks you, it should. It damned well shocks me. I thought I'd done it all."

"Welcome home, boss." Lillian beamed, holding the door back. "You look good. Doesn't he, Mari?" Flushed face on the girl, and the boss looked a little flustered. Good. Good. Things were progressing. Absence worked, after all.

"I feel pretty good, too," he returned, putting an affectionate arm around Lillian. "Been behaving?"

"Yes, sir. Pills and all." Lillian glared at her niece. "It's pretty hard not to take pills when you're threatened with being rolled in a towel."

He laughed warmly, glancing over at Mari. "Good girl."

"I should get medals for this," Mari returned, her eyes searching his, searching his face, quiet and curious and puzzled.

He hugged Lillian. "No doubt. What's for dinner? I'm starved."

"Finally," Lillian said with a grin. "Things are back to normal. You should see all the food I've saved up."

"Don't just stand there, both of you, go fetch it," he said, looking starved. "I'll die if I don't eat soon!"

Lillian responded to his order, producing an abundance of hearty food. While Ward dug in, Mari watched him with pure admiration. She'd never seen a human being put it away with such pleasure. He didn't seem to gain an ounce, for all his appetite. But then he was on the run most of his life, which probably explained his trim but masculine build.

He finished the last of the dressing and sat back with a heavy sigh to sip his second cup of coffee while Lillian, despite offers of help and threats, pushed a trolley of dirty dishes out to the kitchen and dishwasher.

"She won't slow down," Mari said. "I've tried, but she won't let me take over. I called the doctor, but he said as long as she was taking her medicine and didn't overdo standing on that cast, she'd be okay. I do at least get her to sit down, and I help when she lets me."

"Good thing her room's on the ground floor," he remarked.

"Yes."

He studied her over the rim of his coffee cup, his eyes narrow and quiet and full of green flames. There was no amusement in them now, no mockery. Just frank, blatant desire.

She looked back because it was beyond her powers of resistance not to. He held her in thrall, his darkening eyes full of promised pleasure, exquisite physical delight. Her body recognized that look, even if her brain didn't, and began to respond in frightening ways.

"I should bring in the dessert," she said as she rose, panicked.

"I don't want dessert," he said deeply.

She thought she knew what he did want, and she almost said so, but she dropped back down into her chair and put more sugar in her already oversweet coffee.

"Keep that up, and you can take rust off with it." He nodded toward her efforts with the sugar bowl.

She flushed. "I like it sweet."

"Do you?" He reached over and stilled her hand, his fingers lightly caressing it. While he held her eyes, he took the spoon away from her and linked his fingers slowly with hers in a light, caressing pressure that made her want to scream with frustrated hunger.

She couldn't help it. Her fingers contracted, too, convulsively, and she looked at him with aching desire.

His face went hard. "Suppose we go over those phone messages?" he asked.

"All right."

They both knew it was only an excuse, a reason to be

alone together in the den to make love. Because that was surely what was going to happen. Being apart and then experiencing this explosive togetherness had taken its toll on them. He stood up and drew her along with him, and she could feel the throbbing silence that grew as they walked down the hall.

"Don't you want dessert?" Lillian called after them but not very heartily. She was grinning too much.

"Not right now," Ward replied. He looked down at Mari as he opened the door to the den, and there were blazing fires in his steady, possessive eyes.

Mari felt her lips part as she looked up at him. She started past him, feeling the warmth of his big body, the strength and power of it, and smelling his spicy cologne. She could hardly wait to be alone with him.

Just as he started to follow her into the room, into the secret silence of it, the heady atmosphere was shattered by a loud knock at the front door.

He cursed under his breath, whirling with such unexpected violence that Mari felt sorry for whoever was out there.

He opened the door and glared out. "Well?" he demanded.

"Well, you invited me, didn't you?" came an equally curt reply in a voice as deep and authoritative as Ward's. "You called me from the airport and said come over and we'd work out that second lease. So here I am. Or did you forget?"

"No."

"Do you want to serve my coffee on the damned porch?"

Ward tried not to grin, but he couldn't help it. Honest to God, Ty Wade was just like him.

"Oh, hell, come in," he muttered, holding the door open.

A tall, whipcord-lean man entered the house, Stetson in hand. He was as homely as leftover bacon, and he had eyes so piercing and coldly gray that Mari almost backed away. And then he saw her and smiled, and his face changed.

"Marianne, this is my neighbor, Tyson Wade," Ward told her curtly.

Ty nodded without speaking, glancing past Mari to where Lillian was standing in her cast. "What did you do, kick him?" he asked Lillian, nodding toward Ward.

Lillian laughed. "Not quite. How are Erin and the twins?"

"Just beautiful, thanks," Ty said with a quiet smile.

"Give them my best," Lillian said. "Coffee?"

"Just make it, I'll come and get the tray," Ward said firmly.

Lillian grumbled off toward the kitchen while Mari searched for words.

"I think I'll turn in," she said to Ward. "If you still want me to help with the office work, I need to get some sleep so that I can start early."

Ward looked harder than usual. Mari couldn't know that seeing Ty and the change marriage had made in him had knocked every amorous thought right out of his head. Ty spelled commitment, and Ward wanted none of it. So why in hell, he was asking himself, had he been coming on to a virgin?

"Sure," he told Mari. "You do that. If you don't mind, try to get your aunt into bed, too, could you? She's going to make a basket case of me if she doesn't start resting. Tell her that, too. Play on her conscience, girl."

Mari forced a smile. "I'll try. Nice to meet you, Mr. Wade," she told Ty and went after Lillian.

"Imagine, Tyson Wade in this very house," Lillian said with a sigh as she fixed a tray. "It's been a shock, seeing those two actually talk. They've been feuding as long as I've worked here. Then Mr. Wade got married and just look at him."

"He seems very much a family man," Mari commented.

"You should have seen him before." Lillian grinned. "He made the boss look like a pussycat."

"That bad?"

"That bad. Bad enough, in fact, to make the boss get rid of a half-wolf, half-shepherd dog he loved to death. It brought down some of Ty's cattle, and he came over here to 'discuss it' with the boss." She turned, grinning at her niece. "The very next day that dog was adopted into a good home. And the boss had to see his dentist. Tyson Wade was a mean man before Miss Erin came along. Ah, the wonder of true love." She gave Mari a sizing-up look and grinned even more when the younger woman blushed. "Well, let's get to the dishes, if you're determined to get in my way."

Mari was and she did, quickly shooing Lillian out. Then she disappeared herself before Ward came for the coffee tray. She'd had enough for one night.

BREAKFAST WAS AN ORDEAL, Ward was cold all of a sudden, not the amorous, very interested man of the day before. Mari felt cold and empty and wondered what she'd done to make him look at her with those indifferent eyes. She was beginning to be glad that her vacation was almost over.

He followed her into the office and started opening mail.

It had piled up in his absence, and he frowned over the amount waiting for him.

"Can you take dictation?" he asked Mari without looking up.

"Yes."

"Okay. Get a pad and pen out of the desk drawer and let's get started."

He began to dictate. The first letter was in response to a man who owed Ward money. The man had written Ward to explain that he'd had a bad month and would catch up on his payments as soon as he could. Instead of an understanding reply, Ward dictated a scorching demand for full payment that ended in a threatened lawsuit.

Mari started to speak, but the look he gave her was an ultimatum. She forced back the words and kept her silence.

Each letter was terse, precise and without the least bit of compassion. She began to get a picture of him that was disappointing and disillusioning. If there was any warmth in him, she couldn't find it in business. Perhaps that was why he was so wealthy. He put his own success above the problems of his creditors. So he had money. And apparently not much conscience. But Mari had one, and the side of him that she was seeing disturbed her greatly.

Finally Ward was finished dictating the letters, but just as she started to type them, the phone rang. Ward answered it, his face growing darker with every instant.

It was a competitor on the phone, accusing him of using underhanded methods to get the best of a business deal. He responded with language that should have caused the telephone company to remove his phone and burn it. Mari was the color of a boiled lobster when he finished and hung up.

"Something bothering you, honey?" he chided.

"You're ruthless," she said quietly.

"Hell, yes, I am," he returned without embarrassment. "I grew up the butt of every cruel tongue in town. I was that Jessup boy, the one whose mother was the easiest woman around and ran off with Mrs. Hurdy's husband. I was that poor kid down the road that never had a decent family except for his battle-ax of a grandmother." His green eyes glowed, and she wondered if he'd ever said these things to anyone else. "Success is a great equalizer, didn't you know? The same people who used to look down their noses at me now take off their hats and nod these days. I'm on everybody's guest list. I get recognized by local civic groups. I'm always being mentioned in the newspapers. Oh, I'm a big man these days, sprout." His face hardened. "But I wasn't always. Not until I had money. And how I get it doesn't bother me. Why should I be a good old boy in business? Nobody else is."

"Isn't Mr. Wade?" she fished.

"Mr. Wade," he informed her, "is now a family man, and he's missing his guts. His wife removed them, along with his manhood and his pride."

She stood. "What a terrible thing to say," she burst out. "How can you be so coldhearted? Don't you realize what you're doing to yourself? You're shriveling up into an old Scrooge, and you don't seem to realize it."

"I give to charity," he said arrogantly.

"For appearances and to get ahead," she replied hotly. "Not because you care. You don't, do you? You don't really care about one living soul."

His chin lifted and his eyes sparkled dangerously. "I care about my grandmother and my sister. And maybe Lillian."

"And nobody else," she said, hurt a bit by his admission that he didn't feel a thing for her.

"That's right," he said coldly. "Nobody else."

She stood there with her hands clenched at her sides, hurting in ways that she'd never expected she could. "You're a real prince, aren't you?" she asked.

"I'm a rich one, too," he returned, smiling slowly. "But if you had any ideas about taking advantage of that fact, you can forget them. I like my money's worth. And I'm not suited to wedding cake and rice."

When what he had said finally broke through the fog and she realized what he was accusing her of, she had to bite her tongue to keep from crying. So that was what he thought—that she was nothing but a gold digger, out to set herself up for life on his fortune.

"I know," she said with an icy look. "And that's good because most women who are looking for a husband want one who doesn't have to be plugged into a wall socket to warm up!"

"Get out of my office," he said shortly. "Since you're here to visit your aunt, go do it and keep the hell out of my way! When I want a sermon, I'll get it in church!"

"Any minister who got you into church would be canonized!" she told him bluntly and ran out of the room.

She didn't tell Lillian what had happened. Shortly thereafter Ward stormed out, slamming the door behind him. He didn't come back until well after bedtime. Mari hadn't gone back into the den, and by the time she crawled into bed, she was already planning how to tell Aunt Lillian that she'd have to return to Georgia.

It wouldn't be easy to leave. But now that she'd had a glimpse of the real man, the character under the veneer, she was sure that she was doing the right thing. Ward Jessup might be a rich man with a fat wallet. But he was ice-cold. If she had any sanity left, she'd get away from him before her addiction got so bad that she'd find excuses to stay just to look at him.

That remark about not caring for anyone except family had hurt terribly. She did understand why he was the way he was, but it didn't help her broken heart. She'd been learning to love him. And now she found that he had nothing at all to give. Not even warmth. It was the worst blow of all. Yes, she'd have to go home now. Aunt Lillian was coping beautifully, taking her medicine and even resting properly. At least Ward would take care of the older woman. He cared about *her*. He'd never care about Mari, and it was high time she faced facts.

CHAPTER SEVEN

MARI HAD A miserable day. She kept out of Ward's way, and she didn't go back into the den. Let him get a temporary secretary, she thought furiously, if he couldn't manage his dirty work alone. She wasn't going to do it for him.

"Talk about unarmed conflict," Lillian muttered as Mari went out the back door in a lightweight jacket and jeans.

"He started it," Mari said irritably. "Or didn't you know how he did business?"

Lillian's expression said that she did. "He's a hard man to understand sometimes," she said, her voice gentle, coaxing. "But you can't imagine the life he's had, Mari. People aren't cold without reason. Very often it's just a disguise."

"His is flawless."

"So is yours," Lillian said with a warm smile. "Almost. But don't give up on him yet. He might surprise you."

"He won't have time. Have you forgotten that I have to go home in two more days?"

The older woman looked worried. "Yes, I know. I had hoped you might stay a little longer."

"You're feeling better," she returned. "And he doesn't want me here. Not anymore. I'm not even sure I'd stay if I was asked." She opened the door. "I'm going to look at the horses."

She walked out without another word, crestfallen and miserable. She stuck her hands in the pockets of her jacket and walked aimlessly along the fence until she came in sight of the barn.

There he was, sitting astride a huge chestnut-colored horse, his working clothes making him look even bigger than usual, his Stetson cocked over one eye. Watching her.

She stopped in her tracks, glaring at him. He urged the horse into a slow trot and reined in beside her, resting his crossed hands on the pommel. The leather creaked as he shifted in the saddle and pushed back his hat.

"Are we still speaking?" he asked, his tone half amused.

"Can someone run me to the bus station in the morning?" she asked, ignoring the question. "My vacation is up the day after tomorrow. I have to get back to Atlanta."

He stared at her for a long moment before he spoke. "How are you going to explain that decision to Lillian?" he asked, carefully choosing his words. "You're supposed to think I'm dying, aren't you? You're supposed to be helping me write my memoirs."

"I don't think my stomach is strong enough," she replied.

His green eyes glittered at her. "Stop that. I'm trying to make friends with you."

"I tried to make friends with a gerbil once," she commented. "I stuck my hand down into its cage to let it have a nice sniff, and it tried to eat my little finger."

"You're making this difficult," he grumbled, tilting his hat back over his eyes.

"No, you are," she corrected. "I'm doing my best to relieve you of my gold-digging, sermonizing presence."

He sighed heavily, searching her eyes. "I've never had to justify myself to anyone," he told her. "I've never wanted to." He studied the pommel as if he hadn't seen one before, examining it as he spoke. "I don't want you to go, Mari."

Her heart ran away. "Why not?"

He shrugged and smiled faintly. "Maybe I've gotten used to you." He looked up. "Besides, your aunt will never get over it if you leave right now. All her plans for us will be ruined."

"That's a foregone conclusion as far as I'm concerned," she said, her voice curt. She clenched her hands in her pockets. "I wouldn't have you on a stick, roasted."

He had to work to keep from grinning. "Wouldn't you?"

"I'm going home," she repeated.

He tilted his hat back again. "You don't have a job."

"I do so. I work at a garage!"

"Not anymore." He did grin this time. "I called them last week and told them that you had to quit to take care of your sick aunt and her 'dying' employer."

"You what!"

"It seemed like the thing to do at the time," he said conversationally. "They said they were real sorry, and it sure was lucky they'd just had a girl apply for a job that morning. I'll bet they hired her that very day."

She could hardly breathe through her fury. She felt as if her lungs were on fire. "You...you...!" She searched for some names she'd heard at the garage and began slinging them at him.

"Now, shame on you," he scolded, bending unexpectedly to drag her up to sit in the saddle in front of him. "Sit still!" he said roughly, controlling the excited horse with one hand on the reins while the other was on Mari.

"I hate you," she snapped.

He got the gelding under control and wheeled it, careful not to jerk the reins and unseat them both. The high-strung animal took gentle handling. "Care to prove that?" he asked.

She didn't ask what he meant. There was no time. She was too busy trying to hold on to the pommel. She hadn't realized how far off the ground that saddle was until she was sitting in it. Behind her, she felt the warm strength of his powerful body, and if she hadn't been so nervous, she might have felt the tense set of it in the saddle.

He rode into a small grove of oak and mesquite trees and dismounted. Before she knew it, she was out of the saddle and flat on her back in the lush spring grass with Ward's hard face above her.

"Now," he said gently, "suppose you show me how much you hate me?"

His dark head bent, and she reached up, unthinking, to catch his thick hair and push him away. But it only gave him an unexpected opening, and she caught her breath as his full weight came down over her body, crushing her into the leaves and grass.

"Better give in, honey, or you could sink down all the way to China," he commented wickedly. His hands were resting beside her head, and somehow he'd caught hers in them. He had her effectively pinned, without any effort at all, and was just short of gloating about it. He wasn't trying to spare her his formidable weight, either, and she could just barely breathe.

She panted, struggling, until she felt what her struggles were accomplishing and reluctantly subsided. She contented herself with glaring up at him from a face the color of pickled beets.

"Coward," he chided.

She was very still, barely breathing. His hands were

squeezing hers, but with a caressing pressure not a brutal one. The look in his eyes was slowly changing from faint amusement to dark passion. If she hadn't recognized the look, his body would have told her as he began to move subtly over hers, sensually, with a practiced expertness that even her innocence recognized.

"Yes, that makes you tremble, doesn't it?" he breathed, watching her as his hips caressed hers.

"Of course…it does," she bit off. "I've never…felt this way with anyone else."

"Neither have I," he whispered, bending to brush his hard mouth over her soft one. "I told you that when I got home, and I meant it. Never like this, not with anyone…" His eyes closed, his heavy brows drawing together as he slowly fitted his mouth to hers.

She wanted to protest, but she couldn't move, let alone speak, and his mouth was making the most exquisite sensations in places far removed from her lips. With a shaky little sigh she opened her mouth a little to taste his and felt him stiffen. She felt that same tautness in her legs, her arms, even in her stomach, sensations that she'd never experienced.

His hard fingers flexed, linking with hers caressingly, teasing as he explored her mouth first with his lips and then with the slightest probing of his tongue.

She hadn't been kissed that way before, and her eyes opened, puzzled.

He lifted his head a little, searching her face with green eyes that were dark and mysterious and as full of answers as her blue ones were full of questions.

"You can trust me this once," he whispered, sensing her apprehension in the smooth as silk young body that

wouldn't give an inch to the dominance of his. "Even if I
went half mad with wanting, I wouldn't risk trying to make
love to you within sight of the barn."

He couldn't have been less convincing, but she did trust
him. She searched his eyes, feeling the warm weight of him,
smelling the leathery scent that clung to him, and she began
to relax despite the unknown intimacy of the embrace.

"You've never felt a man this way, have you?" he asked
quietly. "It's all right. You're old enough to leave chaste
kisses and daydreams behind. This is the reality, little
Mari," he whispered, shifting his hips as he looked down
into her wide, awed eyes. "This is what it's really like when
a man and a woman come together in passion. It isn't neat
and quiet and uncomplicated. It's hot and wild and com-
plex."

"Is it part of the rules to warn the victim?" she asked in
a husky whisper.

"It is when the victim is as innocent as you," he returned.
"I don't want a virgin sacrifice, you see," he added, bending again to her mouth. "I want a full-blooded woman. A
woman to match me."

At that moment she almost felt that she could. Her body
was throbbing, blazing with fire and fever, and instead of
shrinking from the proof of his desire for her, she lifted
her body up to his, gave him her mouth and her soft sighs.

Ward felt the hunger in her slender body, and it fostered
an oddly protective impulse in him. He, who was used to
taking what he wanted without regret or shame, hesitated.

His mouth gentled, slowed and became patiently caressing. He found that she followed where he led, quickly
learning the tender lessons that he gave her without words.
He let go of her hands and felt them go instinctively to his

shirt, pressing over the hard, warm muscles, searching. His heart pounded furiously against breasts whose softness he could feel under him. He wanted to strip off his shirt and give himself to her young hands, he wanted to strip off her own shirt and put his mouth on those tender breasts and look at them and watch her blush. It was then that he realized just how urgent the situation was becoming.

His body was taking over. He could feel himself grinding down against her, bringing her hips into intimate contact with his, he could feel his own taut movements. His mouth felt hot. Hers felt like velvet, feverish and swollen from the hungry probing of his own.

He lifted his head, surprised to find himself breathing in gasps, his arms trembling slightly as they held him poised over her. Her eyes were misty, half closed, her lips parted and moist, her body submissive. His.

She drew in a slow, lazy breath, looking up at him musingly, so hungry for him that she hadn't the strength to refuse him anything he wanted. From the neck down she was throbbing with sweet pulses, experiencing a pleasure that she'd never known before.

"No," he whispered roughly. "No. Not like this."

He rolled away from her, shuddering a little before he sat up and breathed roughly. He brushed back his hair with fingers that were almost steady but held a fine tremor.

Mari was just realizing what had happened, and she stared at him with slowly dawning comprehension. So that was what happened. That was why women didn't fight or protest. It wasn't out of fear of being overpowered. It was because of the sweet, tender pleasure that came from being held intimately, kissed and kissed until her mind got lost in her body's pleasure. He could have had her. But he stopped.

"Surprised?" He turned his head, staring down at her with dark green eyes that still held blatant traces of passion. "I told you I wouldn't take advantage, didn't I?"

"Yes. But I forgot."

"Fortunately for you I didn't." He got to his feet and stretched lazily, feeling as if he'd been beaten, but he wasn't letting her see that. He grinned down at her. "Men get good at pulling back. It comes from years of practice dating virgins," he added in a wicked whisper as he extended a hand to her.

She sat up, flushed, ignoring his outstretched hand as she scrambled to her feet. "I can't imagine that many of them were still virgins afterward," she muttered with a shy glance.

"Oh, some of them had great powers of resistance," he admitted. "Like you."

"Sure," she said shakily, pushing back her damp hair. "Some great resistance. If you hadn't stopped…"

"But I did," he interrupted. He picked up his hat from where he'd tossed it and studied the crown before he put it back on his head. "And for the time being you can forget going back to Georgia," he added with a level gaze. "Lillian needs you. Maybe I need you, too. You've given me a new perspective on things."

"I've butted in and made a spectacle of myself, you mean," she said, her eyes quietly curious on his hard, dark face.

"If I'd meant that, I'd have said it," he returned. "You're a breath of fresh air in my life, Mari. I was getting set in my wicked ways until you came along. Maybe you were right about my attitude toward money. So why don't you stay and reform me?"

"I can't imagine anyone brave enough to try," she said. She lifted her face. "And besides all that, how dare you cost me my job!"

"You can't work in a garage full of men anymore," he said blandly. "Remember your horrible nightmares about the assault?" he added. "Men make you nervous. Lillian said so."

"Those men wouldn't make anyone nervous. All they did was work on cars and go home to their wives," she informed him. "Not one of them was single."

"How sad for you. What wonderful luck that Lillian found me dying and sent for you." He grinned. "It isn't every girl who gets handed a single, handsome, rich bachelor on a platter."

"I am not a gold digger," she shot at him.

"Oh, hell, I know that," he said after a minute, studying her through narrowed eyes. "But I had to have some kind of defense, didn't I? You're a potent little package, honey. A fish on the hook does fight to the bitter end."

His words didn't make much sense to her, but Mari was a little dazed by everything that had happened. She just stared at him, puzzled.

"Never mind," he said, taking her hand. "Let's go back. I've got a few odds and ends to take care of before lunch. Do you like to ride?"

"I think so," she admitted.

"You can have your own horse next time," he promised. "But for now I think we'll walk back. I'm just about out of self-control, if you want the truth. I can't handle you at a close proximity right now."

That was embarrassing and flattering, and she hid a smile. But he saw it and gathered her close to his side, lead-ing the horse by the reins with one hand and holding her with the other. The conversation on the way back was general, but the feel of Ward's strong arm had Mari enthralled every step of the way.

He went off to make some business calls. Lillian took one look at Mari's face and began humming love songs. Mari, meanwhile, went up to her room to freshen up and took time to borrow one of the outside lines to call Atlanta. Her boss at the garage was delighted to hear from her and immediately burst into praise of her unselfishness to help that "poor dying man in Texas." How fortunate, he added brightly, that a young woman about Mari's age had just applied for a job the morning poor Mr. Jessup had called him. Everything had worked out just fine, hadn't it, and how did she like Texas?

She mumbled something about the weather being great for that time of year, thanked him and hung up. Poor Mr. Jessup, indeed!

Ward had to go out on business later in the day, and he wasn't back by supper time. Lillian and Mari ate alone, and after Mari had finished helping in the kitchen, she kissed her aunt good night and went upstairs. She was torn between disappointment and relief that Ward hadn't been home since that feverish interlude. It had been so sweet that she'd wanted it again and that could be dangerous. Each time it got harder to stop. Today she hadn't been able to do anything except follow where he led, and it was like some heady alcoholic beverage—she just couldn't get enough of him. She didn't really know what to do anymore. Her life seemed to be tangled up in complications.

She laid out a soft pink gown on the bed—a warm but revealing one with a low neckline—and fingered it lovingly. It had been an impulse purchase, something to cheer her up on a depressing Saturday when she had been alone. It was made of flannelette, but it was lacy and expensive, and she loved the way it felt and clung to the slender lines of her body.

She ran a bath in the big Jacuzzi and turned on the jets after filling the tub with fragrant soap that was provided, along with anything else a feminine guest might need, in the pretty blue-tiled bathroom. To Mari, who lived in a small efficiency apartment in Atlanta, it was really plush. She frowned as she stripped off her clothing and climbed into the smooth tub with its relaxing jets of water surging around her. The apartment rent was due in a week or so, and she hadn't paid it yet. She'd have to send a check. She also wished that she'd brought more clothes with her. She hadn't counted on being here for life, but it looked as if Ward wasn't in any hurry to let her go.

Too, there was Lillian, who was behaving herself only as long as her niece was around to make her. If Mari left, what would happen to the older woman? With Ward away on business so often, it was dangerous for Lillian to be left alone now. Perhaps Ward had considered that, and it was why he wanted Mari to stay. The real reason, anyway. He didn't seem to be dying of love for her, although his desire was apparent. He wanted her.

With all her turbulent thoughts and the humming sound of the Jacuzzi, she didn't hear the door to her room open or hear it close again. She didn't hear the soft footfalls on the carpet, or the soft sound that came from a particularly male voice as Ward saw her sitting up in the tub with her pretty pink breasts bare and glistening with soap and water.

She happened to glance up then and saw him. She

couldn't move. His green eyes were steady and loving on the soft curves of her body, and with horror she felt the tips of her breasts harden under his intent scrutiny.

He shook his head when she started to lift her hands to them. "No," he said gently, moving toward her. "No, don't cover them, Mari."

She could hardly get her breath. Although she'd never let anyone see her like this in all her life, she couldn't stop him. Mari couldn't seem to move at all. He towered over her, still and somber, and as she watched, he began to roll up the sleeves of the white shirt that was open halfway down his chest. He'd long ago shed his jacket and tie, although he was still wearing dress boots and suit trousers. He looked expensive and very masculine and disturbing, and as he bent beside the tub, she caught the scent of luxurious cologne.

"You mustn't!" she began frantically.

But he picked up the big fluffy sponge she'd soaped and shook his head, smiling faintly. "Think of it as a service for a special, tired guest," he whispered amusedly, although his eyes were frankly possessive. "Lie back and enjoy it."

She started to protest again, but he didn't pay the least attention. One lean hand moved behind her neck to support her in the bubbling water while the other slowly, painstakingly, drew the sponge over every soft line and curve of her body.

She hadn't realized how many nerve endings she had, but he found every single one. In a silence that throbbed with new sensation, he bathed her, pausing now and again to put the sponge down and touch her, experience the softness of her skin with the added silkiness of soap and water making it vibrantly alive.

Her eyes were half closed, languorous, as his fingers brushed lightly over her small, high breasts and found every curve and hardness, every sensual contrast, every texture, as if she fascinated him.

She trembled a little when he turned off the Jacuzzi and let the water out of the tub, especially when he began to sponge away the last traces of soap, and her body was completely revealed to him.

He lifted his dark, quiet eyes to hers and searched them, finding apprehension, fear, awe and delight in their blue depths. "I've never bathed a woman before," he said softly. "Or bathed with one. In some ways I suppose I'm pretty old-fashioned."

She was breathing unsteadily. "I've never let anyone look at me before," she said in a hesitant tone.

"Yes. I know." He helped her out of the tub and removed a warmed towel from the rail. It was fluffy and pink, and warm against her skin as he slowly dried her from head to toe. This time she could feel his hands in a new way, and she clutched at his broad shoulders when he reached her hips and began to touch her flat stomach. She felt a rush of sensation that was new and shocking.

"Ward?" she whispered.

He knelt in front of her, discarding the towel and all pretense as he held her hips and pressed his mouth warmly against her stomach.

She cried out. It was a high-pitched, helpless cry, and it made his blood surge like a flood through his veins. His fingers flexed and his mouth drew over her stomach with agonizing slowness, moving up with relentless hunger to her soft, smooth breasts.

She held him there, held his hard, moist mouth over the

tip of one, felt him take her inside, warming her. He touched her then in a way she'd never expected, and her breath drew in harshly and she shivered.

"Shhhh," he whispered at her breast. "It's all right. Don't fight me."

She couldn't have. She shuddered and trembled, crying as he made the most exquisite sensations felt in the nether reaches of her slender body. Her nails dug into him and she couldn't help it.

"Marianne," he whispered, shifting his mouth over hers. He stopped his delicate probing and lifted her in his arms. She felt the soft shock of his footsteps as he carried her to the bed, felt the mattress sink under their combined weights.

His mouth moved slowly back down her to her stomach, her thighs, and then she did fight him, fought the newness and the strangeness and the frank intimacy.

He lifted his head and slid back up to look at her shocked face. "All right," he said gently. "If you don't want it, I would never force you."

Her face was creamy pink now, fascinated. He looked down at her body, smoothing over it with a lean, very dark hand, savoring its soft vulnerability.

"This is so new," he whispered. "I never realized how soft a woman's body really was, how exquisitely formed. I could get drunk just on the sight of you."

She was trembling all over but not from the soft chill of the room. She felt reckless under his intense gaze.

He looked up into her eyes. "You aren't protected, are you?" he asked softly.

It took a minute for her to realize what he was asking, and it made the situation take on alarming, very adult implications. To him this was familiar territory. But Mari was a pioneer.

"No," she whispered unsteadily. "I'm not."

"It's just as well," he murmured, bending to her mouth. "I think…it might spoil things right now to force that kind of total intimacy on you." His hand smoothed tenderly over her breast as he probed at her trembling lips. "Don't you want to touch me like this?"

She did, but she couldn't say it. Her hands went slowly to his shirt and slid under it, finding the exciting abrasion of thick chest hair over warm muscle a heady combination. His mouth moved hungrily against hers at the first tentative touch, and one hand went between them to rip the fabric completely out of the way and give her total access.

His harsh breathing disturbed her, but she was intoxicated by the intimacy they were sharing. Impulsively she moved her hands and arched upward letting her breasts tease his chest, feeling the sudden acceleration of his heartbeat with wonder.

He poised over her, lifting his head. His eyes were dark with passion, his chest shuddering with it. "Do that again," he said roughly.

She did, on fire with hunger, wanting something more than the teasing, wanting him. She felt his chest tremble, and she looked down at his darkness against her paler flesh with a sense of wonder.

"Yes, look at it," he whispered, his voice harsh, shaken as he stared, too. "Look at the differences. Dark against light, muscle against softness. Your breasts are like bread and honey."

As he spoke, he eased down. His heavy body surged against hers as he fitted it over her bareness, and her pupils dilated helplessly at the warm ecstasy of his full weight over her.

"Give me your mouth now," he whispered, bending. "Let me feel you completely."

It was a kiss like nothing she'd ever imagined in her life. She held him tenderly, her hands smoothing his thick, dark hair, her body throbbing its whole length where she could feel the powerful muscles of his body taut and smooth.

He tasted of coffee, and there was a new tenderness in him, in the lips that delicately pushed at hers so that his tongue could enter the soft, sweet darkness of her mouth. She felt it touch hers, tangle with it, and she gave herself up to a sensation that was all mystery and delight.

His hands smoothed down her sides, her back, savoring the smooth suppleness of her skin. He ached like hell, and he could have cursed himself for causing this, for forgetting how naive she was. She wanted him and, God, he wanted her! But he could make her pregnant. And part of her would hate him forever if he forced this on her. It wasn't going to be good for her. She was so much a virgin...

His cheek slid against hers, and he rolled onto his side, holding her protectively to him, feeling her breasts crush softly against his chest.

"Hold me," he whispered. "Just hold me until we stop trembling."

"I want you," she whimpered, beyond thought, beyond pride. She bit his shoulder. "I want you."

"I know. But we can't." His cheek nuzzled hers, and his lips touched her tear-streaked face tenderly. He hadn't realized she was crying until then. He drew a breath. "Are you all right?" he asked softly.

"I ache," she sobbed.

"I could satisfy you," he whispered. "Without going all the way."

She sensed that. Her eyes searched his in wonder. "No," she said after a minute. "I won't do that to you." She touched his face, fascinated by the look the words produced. "I'm sorry. I should have said something a long time ago. I should have asked you to stop."

"But it was too sweet, wasn't it?" he asked, his voice quiet and deep as he touched her face with fingers that were possessive and gentle. "So sweet, like making love with every part of us. I've never in my life experienced anything like it. Not even sex was ever this good."

That shocked her, and her eyes mirrored it. "Not... even sex?"

He shook his head. "With you I think it would be love-making, not sex. I don't think you and I could accept something as coldly clinical as that."

She was so tempted. She wanted him desperately. Everybody did it these days, didn't they? Maybe she wouldn't get pregnant. She loved him. Loved him!

But he saw the uncertainty in her eyes and mistook it for fear. For God's sake, where was his brain, anyway? She was a virgin. Lillian was right downstairs. Was he crazy? He ignored the feverish hunger of his body and managed to smile reassuringly as he slowly drew away from her to sit up with a hard sigh.

"No more, honey," he said heavily and managed to laugh. "I'm too old for this kind of playing."

Playing? She stared at him helplessly as he forced his staggered brain to function and found her gown. He put her into it with a minimum of fuss and then lifted her long enough to turn down the covers. He put her under them, smoothing them over her breasts.

He couldn't tell her that his own vulnerability and weakness had shocked him. He hadn't planned this, he hadn't expected to be drawn into such a long, intimate loving. It had been loving, of a kind. He scowled, watching her, fascinated by her innocence, her helpless reaction to his touch. He'd come to her room, in fact, to tell her that he wanted to get on a friendly footing with her, to stop the intimacy that could all too easily overwhelm both of them. But the sight of her in that tub had wiped every sane thought right out of his mind. Now he looked at her and saw commitment and the loss of his precious freedom. He saw all the old wounds, the helplessness of his attraction to that tramp who'd taken him in.

With a rough curse he got to his feet, running an angry hand through his hair.

"You needn't look at me that way," she bit off, close to tears again but for a totally different reason. "As if I were a fallen woman. I didn't walk into your bathroom and start staring at you."

"I didn't mean for that to happen," he said curtly.

She softened a little at the confession. He looked as shaken as she felt. "It's all right," she replied, fumbling with the coverlet. "I didn't, either."

"I'm old enough to know better, though," he murmured, feeling venerable and protective as he stared down at her. He put his hands in his pockets with a long sigh. "I came up here to see if we might get on a different footing. A friendly footing, without all these physical complications." He laughed softly. "I suppose you noticed how well I succeeded."

"Yes," she murmured tongue in cheek. She recalled everything she'd let him do and went scarlet, dropping her embarrassed eyes.

"None of that," he chided. "You're a woman now, not a little girl. Nothing we did would make you pregnant."

"I know that!" she burst out, feverishly avoiding his mocking gaze.

"I just wanted to reassure you." He stretched lazily, very masculine with his shirt unbuttoned and his hair mussed. Very disturbing, watching her that way. "No one will ever know what we did in here," he added. "Just you and me. That makes it a very private thing, Mari."

"Yes." She glanced up and then down again. "I hope you don't think I do that with just anyone."

"I don't think that at all." He bent and brushed his lips gently over her forehead. "It's very exciting being the first," he whispered. "Even in this way."

Her face felt hot as she looked up into lazy, warm eyes. "I'm glad it was with you."

"Yes. So am I." He searched her eyes gently and started to lean toward her, but his survival instincts warned him against it. Instead, he stood up with a smile and went to the door. "Good night, honey. Sleep well."

"You, too."

He closed the door without looking back, and Mari stared at it for a long time before she drew a shuddering sigh and turned out the light.

CHAPTER EIGHT

MARI HARDLY SLEPT. She felt his hands all through the night, along with a new and curious kind of frustration that wouldn't subside. Every time she thought about Ward, her body began to throb. These new feelings frightened her because they were so unexpected. She didn't know what to do. The urge to cut and run was very strong.

Lillian was hobbling around putting platters on the table for breakfast. She looked up, smiling, as Mari came into the room dressed in jeans and a pullover burgundy knit blouse.

"Good morning, glory," Lillian said brightly. "Isn't it a beautiful day?"

It was, in fact, but Lillian seemed to be overjoyed at something besides the great outdoors. "Yes," Mari returned. She glanced at the empty chair at the head of the table.

"He'll be back in a minute," the older woman said knowingly. "Looks like a storm cloud this morning, he does. All ruffled and absentminded. Been staring up that staircase ever since he came downstairs, too," she added wickedly.

Mari darted into the kitchen. "I'll help you get breakfast on the table," she said quickly, avoiding that amused gaze. At least Lillian was enjoying herself. Mari wasn't. She was afraid.

She and Lillian had started eating before Ward came back. He looked tired, but his face brightened when he spotted Mari. He smiled without really wanting to and tossed his hat onto a side table before he sprawled into a chair. His jeans were dusty and his blue checked shirt was a little disheveled.

"I've washed up," he told Lillian before she could open her mouth. "I had to help get a bull out of a ditch."

"How did he get into the ditch?" Mari asked curiously.

Ward grinned. "Trying to jump a fence to get to one of my young heifers. Amazing how love affects the mind, isn't it?"

Mari flushed. Lillian giggled. Ward leaned back in his chair, enjoying the view, watching Mari try to eat scrambled eggs with forced enjoyment.

"Don't you want something to eat, boss?" Lillian asked.

"I'm not really hungry," he said without realizing what he was giving away to the old woman, who beamed at him. "But I'll have some toast and coffee, I guess. Sleep well, Mari?" he asked as Lillian handed him the carafe.

Mari lifted her eyes. "Of course," she said, bluffing. "Did you?"

He shook his head, smiling faintly. "Not a wink."

She got lost in his green gaze and felt the force of it all the way to her toes. It took several seconds to drag her eyes down to her plate, and even then her heart ran wild.

Ward watched her with evident enjoyment, caught up in the newness of having a woman react that way to his teasing. Everything was new with Marianne. Just ordinary things, like sharing breakfast, took on new dimensions. He found that he liked looking at her. Especially now since he knew exactly what she looked like under her clothes. His eyes darkened in memory. God, how exquisite she was!

Mari felt his intent stare all through her body. She could have made a meal of him, too, with her eyes. He looked so good. For all his huge size he was lithe and graceful, and she loved the way he moved. He was as sensuous a man as she'd ever known, a very masculine presence with a disturbing effect on her senses. She didn't think her feet would ever touch the ground again. Just being near him set her on fire. She wanted to get up and touch him, put her mouth on his, feel his arms crushing her to every inch of that long, elegant body. Her fingers trembled on her fork, and she flushed with embarrassment when he noticed her nervousness.

"Come for a ride with me," Ward said suddenly.

She looked up at him. "Now?"

He shrugged. "Lillian can answer the phone. There's nothing pressing for today. Why not?"

"No reason at all," Lillian agreed quickly. "Go ahead. I'll handle the home front."

Mari submitted before she could begin to protest. Why pretend? She wanted to be alone with him, and he knew it. Her blue eyes searched his green ones longingly, everything plain and undisguised in her oval face. He felt explosive. Young. A boy again with a special girl.

He threw down his napkin and got to his feet, hoping his helpless urgency didn't show too much. "Let's go," he bit off.

Mari followed him. She barely heard Lillian's voice behind her saying something about having fun. Her eyes were on Ward's strong back, her body moving as if she were a sleepwalker. She was on fire for him. Whatever happened now happened. She loved him. If he wanted her, she wasn't going to stop him. He had to feel something for her, too. He had to care just a little!

He saddled two horses in stark silence, his hands deft and firm as he pulled cinches tight and checked bridles.

When he helped her into the saddle, his eyes were dark and possessive, his hand lingering when she was seated. "You look good on a horse, honey," he said quietly.

She looked down at him and smiled, feeling the warmth of his chest against her leg. "Do I?" she asked gently, her voice soft with longing.

"I want you, Marianne," he said half under his breath. "I've thought about nothing else all night. So go slow, will you? I want to talk today. Just talk. I want to get to know you."

That was flattering and a little surprising. Maybe even disappointing. But she had to keep it from showing so she kept smiling. "I'd like that," she said.

He didn't answer her. He felt the same hunger she did, but he was more adept at hiding his yearnings. He didn't want to frighten her off, not before he made a stab at establishing a relationship with her. He didn't know how she was going to react to what he had in mind, but he knew they couldn't go on like this. Things had to be settled— today. Business was going to suffer if he kept on mooning over that perfect young body. Physical attraction was a damnable inconvenience, he thought angrily. He'd thought he was too old to be this susceptible. Apparently he was more vulnerable than he'd ever realized.

He swung into the saddle and led the way down the long trail that ran around the ranch. His men were out working with the cattle, getting them moved to summer pasture, doing all the little things around the ranch that contributed to the huge cow-calf operation. Fixing machines. Planting feed. Cleaning out stalls. Checking supplies. Making lists of chores. It was a big task, running a ranch even this size, but Ty Wade's, which adjoined it, was huge by comparison. The oil business was Ward's main concern, but he did like the idea of running cattle, as his grandfather had done so many years before. Perhaps it got into a man's blood. Not that he minded sinking wells under his cattle. He had one or two on his own property, and Tyson Wade's spread was proving to be rich in the black gold. His instincts hadn't failed him there, and he was glad. Ty would never have let him live it down if he'd been wrong and the oil hadn't been there. As it was, the discovery on that leased land had saved Ty from some hard financial times. It had worked out well all the way around.

Mari glanced at him, curious about that satisfied look on his hard, dark face. She wondered what thoughts were giving him such pleasure.

He laughed out loud, staring ahead. "Those old instincts never seem to let me down," he murmured. "I think I could find oil with my nose."

"What?"

He looked over at her. "I was thinking about that oil I found on Ty Wade's place. It was a hell of a gamble, but it sure paid off."

So. It was business that made him feel so good, not her company. "Is business the only pleasure in your life?" she asked gently.

He shrugged. "The only lasting one, I guess." He stared toward the horizon. "There were some pretty hard times around here when I was a kid. Oh, we always had plenty of food, you know—that's one of the advantages of living on a ranch. But we didn't have much in the way of material things. Clothes were all secondhand, and I wore boots with holes in the soles for most of my childhood. That wasn't so bad, but I got ragged a lot about my mother."

She could imagine that he had. "I guess I was pretty lucky," she said. "My parents were good to me. We always got by."

He studied her quietly. "I'll bet you were a tomboy."

She laughed, delighted. "I was. I played sandlot baseball and climbed trees and played war. There was only one other girl on my street, and she and I had to be tough to survive with all the boys. They didn't pull their punches just because we were girls. We had a good time growing up all the same."

He fingered the reins as they rode along to the musical squeak of saddle leather. "I spent a lot of time working rigs when I was younger," he recalled. "Had my own horse."

She'd noticed how tan his skin was when he'd stripped off his shirt the night before and let her touch him. Her eyes went involuntarily to the hard muscles of his torso and lingered there.

"You don't do much sunbathing, do you?" he asked unexpectedly, and his eyes told her that he was remembering how pale she was.

Her face colored. "No. There's no beach nearby, and I live upstairs in an apartment building. I don't have any place to sunbathe."

"It isn't good for the skin. Mine's like leather," he commented. "Yours is silky soft...."

She urged her mount ahead, embarrassed because she knew what he was seeing in his mind.

His mount fell into easy step beside her. "Don't be shy with me," he said gently. "There's nothing to be ashamed of."

"I guess I seem grass green to you," she commented.

"Sure you do," he replied and smiled. "I like it."

Her eyes went to the flat horizon beyond, to the scant trees and the long fence lines and the red coats of the cattle. "I never had many boyfriends," she told him, remembering. "My dad was very strict."

"What was he like?"

"Oh, very tall and stubborn. And terrific," she added. "I had great parents. I loved them both. Losing Mama was hard, but having both of them gone is really rough. I never missed having brothers or sisters until now."

"I suppose it makes you feel alone."

"I've felt that way for a long time," she said. "My father wasn't really an affectionate man, and he didn't like close ties. He thought it was important that I stand alone. Perhaps he was right. I got used to being by myself after Mama died."

He studied her averted features. "At least I had Grandmother and Belinda," he said. "Although with Grandmother it's been a fight all the way. She's too much like me."

She remembered him saying that the only women he cared about where those two. "What is your sister like?" she asked.

He grinned. "Like Grandmother and me. She's another hardheaded Jessup."

"Does she look like you?" she asked curiously.

"Not a lot. Same green eyes, but she's prettier, and we're built differently."

She glared at him. "I do realize that."

"No. She's small. Petite," he clarified. "I suppose I take after my father. He was a big man."

"An oilman?"

He nodded. "Always looking for that big strike." His eyes suddenly had a faraway look. "Right out there is where we found him, in that grove of trees." He gestured to the horizon. "Hell of a shock. There was hardly a mark on him. He looked like he was asleep."

"I'm sorry."

"It was a long time ago." He turned his horse, leaving her to follow where the trail led down to the river and a grove of trees. He dismounted, tying his horse to a small tree growing on a grassy knoll. He helped Mari down and tied hers nearby.

"Funny, I never thought of Texas being like this," she mused as she watched the shallow river run over the rocks and listened to its serene bubbling. "It's so bare except for occasional stands of timber. Along the streams, of course, there are more trees. But it's not at all what I expected. It's so…big."

"Georgia doesn't look like this?" he asked.

She watched him stretch out on the leaves under a big live oak tree, his body relaxed as he studied her. "Not a lot, no. We don't have mesquite trees," she said. "Although around Savannah we do have huge live oaks like these. Near Atlanta we have lots of dogwoods and maples and pines, but there's not so much open land. There are always trees on the horizon, except in south Georgia. I guess southwest Georgia is a lot like here. I've even seen prickly pear cactus growing there, and there are diamondback rattlers in that part of the state. I had a great aunt there when I was a child. I still remember visiting her."

He drew up a knee and crossed his arms, leaning back against the tree. "Homesick yet?"

"Not really," she confessed shyly. "I always wanted to

visit a real ranch. I guess I got my wish." She turned. "Do you think Aunt Lillian will be all right now?"

"Yes, I do." He laughed. "She's having a hell of a good time with us. You haven't told her that we know the truth about each other?"

"No," she said. "I didn't want to disappoint her. But we really ought to tell her."

"Not yet." He let his darkening eyes run down her body, and his blood began to run hot. "Come here."

She gnawed her lower lip. "I don't think that's a good idea," she began half convincingly.

"Like hell you don't," he returned. "You didn't sleep last night any more than I did, and I'll bet your heart is doing the same tango mine is."

It was, but she was apprehensive. Last night it had been so difficult to stop.

"You want me, Marianne," he said under his breath. "And God knows, I want you. We're alone. No prying eyes. No one to see or hear what we do together. Make love with me."

Her mind kept saying no. So why did her legs carry her to him? She couldn't hear reason through the wild slamming of her heart at her throat. She needed him like water in the desert, like warmth in the cold.

He opened his arms, and she went down into them. Coming home. Feeling his big body warm and close to hers, his arms protecting, his eyes possessive.

He rolled over, taking her with him until she was lying on her back under the shade of the big tree with its soft green leaves blowing in the warm breeze.

As she watched, his hand went to his shirt. He flicked open the buttons until his chest was bare, and then his hand went to the hem of her blouse. She caught his wrist, but it didn't even slow him down. He slid his hand under it and around to the back, easily undoing the catch of her bra.

"Why bother with that thing?" he whispered, sliding his hand around to tease the side of her breast. "It just gets in my way."

Her body trembled at the lazy brushing of his fingers. "Why can't I fight you?" she whispered huskily.

"Because what we give each other defies reason," he whispered. He looked down at her mouth as his fingers brushed closer and closer to the hard, aching tip of her breast. "Little virgin, you excite me beyond bearing, do you know that? I can feel what this does to you. Here…"

His forefinger touched the hard tip and she gasped, shuddering under him, her eyes huge and frightened.

"My God, you can't imagine what it does to me," he said curtly. "Feeling that and knowing that I'm causing it. Knowing how hungry you are for me. If I took you right now, you'd scream, Marianne. You'd writhe and cry out, and I wouldn't be able to hold back a damned thing because you've already got me so aroused I don't know where I am."

As he spoke, he moved, letting her feel the proof of the statement as his weight settled against her. His big hand smoothed up, cupping her warm breast, and his mouth opened, taking her lips with it in a silence that shattered her resistance.

Her body lifted toward him as he slid both hands under it, taking her breasts, savoring them with his warm, callused hands. His mouth was taking a wild toll of hers, crushing against her parted lips, tasting the sweetness of them in a blazing hunger.

Her hips shifted and he groaned huskily. Her eyes opened, looking curiously up into his.

"What you feel is getting worse by the minute," he whispered huskily. "If you start moving your hips, I'm going to lose it. Are you willing to take that risk?"

She almost was. Her body was crying out for fulfillment. She wanted his hands on all of her. She wanted his clothes out of the way so that she could touch his skin. She wanted to smooth her fingers down the hard muscles of his back and thighs and feel him in the most intimate embrace of all.

He groaned at the look in her eyes. His hand found hers, pulling it to his body, pressing it flat against him, letting her experience him.

She trembled and jerked away from that intimacy, and it brought him to his senses. He rolled over, bringing up his legs, covering his eyes with his forearms. He stiffened, groaning harshly.

"I'm sorry," she whispered, biting her lip. "Ward, I'm sorry!"

"Not your fault," he managed roughly. His teeth clenched. "God, it hurts!"

She sat up, helpless. She didn't know what to do, what to say. It must be horrible for him, and it was her fault, and she didn't know how to ease that obvious pain.

He jackknifed to a sitting position, bent over his drawn-up legs, breathing unsteadily. His hands were clenched together, and the knuckles went white. He shuddered and let out an uneven breath.

"I never realized…it hurt men like that," she faltered. "I'm so sorry!"

"I told you it's not your fault," he said curtly. He didn't look at her. He couldn't yet. His body was still in torment, but it was easing just a little. He sat quietly, waiting for the ache to go away. She was potent. He wondered if he was ever going to be able to stand up again. Damn his principles and damn hers!

"If I were modern and sophisticated…" she began angrily.

"That's what we're going to talk about in a minute," he said.

She stared at his downbent head, absently fumbling to close her bra and pull down her blouse. Together they were an explosive pair. She loved him beyond bearing. Did he, could he, feel the same way? Her heart flew up into the sun. Was he going to ask her to marry him?

She scrambled to her feet, feeling nervous and shy and on the edge of some monumental discovery. "What are we going to talk about?" she asked, her eyes bright, her smile shy and soft.

He looked up, catching his breath at the beauty in her face. "I want you."

"Yes, I know."

He smiled slowly. "I guess you do, honey," he said, reminding her of that forbidden touch that made her blush.

She lowered her eyes to the ground, watching an ant make its way across a twig. "Well?"

"We can't go on like this," he said, getting slowly to his feet. He stopped just in front of her, near the edge of the river. "You realize that, don't you?"

"Yes," she said miserably.

"And one of these days I'm going to go off my head. It could have happened just now. Men aren't too reliable when their bodies start getting that involved," he added quietly. "I'm just like any other man in passion. I want fulfillment."

She swallowed. This was it. She looked up. "So. What do you want to do about it?" she asked gently.

He stuck his hands into his pockets and searched her eyes with a weary sigh. "I'll set you up in an apartment for a start," he said, his voice reluctant but firm. "I'll open an expense account for you, give you whatever you need. Lillian can be told that you've got a job in the city. Not Ravine, obviously. Maybe in Victoria. That's not too far away for me to drive, and it's big enough that people won't be too curious."

She stared at him. "But it's so far from the ranch…" she began, wondering how they were going to stay married with that kind of arrangement.

"Far enough to keep people from making remarks," he said. "I don't want to expose you to gossip."

"Gossip?" She blinked. Wasn't he proposing?

"You know how I feel about my freedom," he said curtly. "I can't give that up. But you'll have a part of my life that I've never shared with anyone else. You'll never want for anything. And there won't be another woman. Not ever. Just you. I'll manage enough time to keep us both happy when we're together."

It was all becoming clear now. His hard face and his determined eyes gave her all the information she needed.

"You're asking me to be your mistress." She almost choked on the word, but she had to be sure.

He nodded, confirming her worst fears. "That's all I can give you, Marianne. That's all I have to give. Marriage isn't something I want. I've had a taste of commitment that left me half demented. I'll never risk it again."

"And you think that I can be satisfied with this kind of arrangement?" she asked in a ghost of her normal voice.

"You'll be satisfied, all right," he said, his voice sensual and low. "I'll satisfy you to the roots of your hair, little virgin."

"And... Aunt Lillian?"

He shifted uncomfortably. Somehow this was all leaving a bad taste in his mouth. It had seemed the right thing, the only thing, to do when he'd worked it out last night. But now it sounded and felt cheap.

"Lillian will never have to know," he said shortly.

"And what if I get pregnant?" she asked blatantly. "Nothing is foolproof."

He drew in a slow breath. Children. He hadn't realized that children might come of such a liaison. He studied her, wondering absently if they might have a son together. His body surged in a new and unexpected way. His reaction shocked him.

"Pregnant." He said the word aloud, savoring it.

"It does happen," she reminded him, going colder by the second. "Or hasn't the problem ever arisen before?" she added, wondering how many women had come and gone in his life.

"I've never been desperate enough to compromise a virgin before," he said quietly, searching her eyes. "I've never wanted anything the way I want you."

She pulled herself erect. "I'm sorry," she said stiffly. "Sorry that you think so little of me that you could make a proposition like that. I guess I've given you every reason to think I'd accept, and I'm sorry for that, too. I never realized how...how easy it would make me seem to you."

His face fell. He could feel his heart sinking. "Easy?" he asked softly. "Marianne, that's the last thing I think of you!"

"Do tell?" She laughed through building tears. "I'll

bet you've made that little speech until it's second nature to you! I'll bet you've even forgotten the names of the women you've had in your bed!"

His lips parted on a caught breath. This wasn't working out the way he'd envisioned. Nothing was going right. There were tears in her eyes, for God's sake.

"Marianne, don't..." he began, reaching for her.

"Don't you touch me, Ward Jessup," she sobbed, sidestepping. "I've made an awful fool of myself, and I guess you had every reason to ask me what you did, but I don't want to be any rich man's kept woman, thanks."

"Look here—" He started toward her again.

Instinctively her hands went out, and she pushed jerkily at his chest. Ordinarily it wouldn't have moved him. But the riverbank was slick, and his boots went out from under him. He went over backward with a horrible splash.

Mari didn't stay around to see how wet he was. She ran for her horse, fumbled for the reins from around the trunk of the tree and struggled into the saddle through a blur of tears.

Ward stood up, dripping wet, watching her ride away. He didn't think he'd ever in his life felt so miserable or so stupid. It had seemed like a good idea, that proposition. He didn't want marriage, he didn't. For God's sake, why did women have to have so much permanence? Why couldn't they just enjoy themselves like men did? Then he thought about Mari "enjoying" herself with another man, and his face went ruddy with bad temper. He didn't understand himself lately. But the sight of her riding away, almost certainly to a speedy departure from the ranch, made him feel hollow inside.

Mari rode home feeling just as hollow herself. She

should have been flattered, she supposed, at such a generous offer. But she only felt cheap. Stupid, she told herself. You let him do whatever he wants and then get angry at him for making the obvious assumption. She hated herself for giving in, for giving him license to such intimacy. Her body had betrayed her, hungry for pleasure, and she'd lost her reason somewhere along the way. Now she was going to have to leave here. All because she hadn't been sensible. All because she loved him too much to deny herself the ecstasy of his lovemaking.

"You've got a lot to answer for," she told her body angrily. She could have died of shame. Now he'd be sure that she was an idiot.

What was she going to tell Lillian? Her heart sank. The older woman would be heartbroken. Mari closed her eyes, feeling the tears burn them. Why had she ever come here? It had begun so sweetly, only to end in such tragedy. Well, she'd made her bed. Now she'd have to try to lie in it. That wouldn't be much comfort in the lonely years ahead. Leaving Ward Jessup behind would hurt more than anything else ever had. She'd loved him too much, and now she was going to lose him because of it. Because he didn't want commitment and she did.

Perhaps she should have said yes, she thought miserably. Then she thought about how she'd feel, being kept, being used and then abandoned. No. It was better to never know him that way than to have a taste of him and lose him. It would only make things worse, and she'd never respect herself again. Oddly enough, she had a feeling that he wouldn't have respected her, either. Pride would get her through, she promised herself. Yes. She still had that, even if her heart was shattered. She lifted her face and dried the tears on her sleeve. She had to think up some good excuse to go back to Georgia. Something that would give Lillian a reason to think she'd be back, which would keep her on the mend. Her eyes narrowed in deep thought as she approached the ranch house.

CHAPTER NINE

MARI THOUGHT SHE had it down pat when she left her horse with one of the men at the stable and went into the house to tell Lillian she was leaving.

The older woman was sitting down in the living room, looking smug while she thumbed through a magazine.

Mari paused in the hall, took a deep breath and went into the room determinedly. "Well," she said brightly, "I've got a terrific assignment!"

"You've what?" Lillian asked, staring at her niece.

"Mr. Jessup is sending me to Atlanta to get some information on a distant relative of his," she continued, pretending for all she was worth. "You know, to go into his memoirs. It will give me a chance to see about my rent at the apartment and get some more clothes, too."

Lillian had stiffened, but she relaxed all at once with a smile. "Just for a few days, I guess?" she probed.

"That's right." Mari sighed, laying it on thick. "Isn't he just the nicest man? What a pity he's got so little time." She peeked at Lillian out of the corner of one eye. "There's not much sense in getting attached to a dying man, you know."

Lillian hadn't considered that. She gnawed her lip thoughtfully. "He's not a goner yet," she said. "He could get well." She warmed to her topic. "That's right. They could find a treatment that would work and save him!"

"That would be lovely. He's so macho, you know," Mari said with a forced smile.

"Isn't he, though? You two seem to be spending quite a lot of time together these days, too," she added. "Exchanging some very interesting looks as well."

Mari lowered her eyes demurely. "He's very handsome."

"You're very pretty." Lillian put the magazine aside. "When are you going to Atlanta?"

"This very afternoon!" Mari enthused. "I want to hurry and get back," she added.

Lillian fell for it, hook, line and sinker. "Is he going to let you fly there?" she asked.

"No, I'm, uh, taking the bus. Hate flying, you know. Just do it when I have to." Actually, she didn't have the price of a ticket, thanks to her lost job and small savings account. It would take all she had to pay her rent, and then she'd have to pray that she could find another job. Damn Ward Jessup!

"Bus?" Lillian began, giving her suspicious looks.

"He'll come after me, of course," she said. "We might drive back…."

The older woman brightened. Lots of opportunities if they had to stop overnight. Of course, they wouldn't do anything reckless. She knew Mari wouldn't.

"Do you need some help packing?" she asked Mari.

"No, thanks, dear, I can do it. And I'd better get busy!" She blew Aunt Lillian a kiss. "You'll be all right until I get back?" she added, hesitating.

"Of course," Lillian huffed. "I just have a broken leg. I'm taking those stupid pills."

"Good." Mari went upstairs and quickly threw things into her bag. She called the bus station to ask about an outgoing bus and was delighted to find that she had an hour to get to the station. She grabbed her bag and rushed back down the staircase just in time to watch a wet, angry, coldly polite Ward Jessup come in the front door.

"I told Aunt Lillian about the job, Mr. Jessup," she said, loud enough for Lillian to hear. "My goodness, what happened to you? You're all wet!"

Ward glared at her. "So I am, Miss Raymond," he returned. His gaze went to the bag in her hand. Well, he'd expected it, hadn't he? What did she think he'd do, propose marriage?

Mari went the rest of the way down the staircase, keeping her features calm when she felt like throwing herself at his wet boots and begging him to let her stay. She did have a little pride left. Anyway, he was the one who should be ashamed of himself, going around propositioning good girls.

"Boss, you'd better get into some dry clothes," Lillian fussed.

"I will in a minute." He glared at Mari. "When do you leave?"

"In an hour. Can you get somebody to run me to the bus station? After all, the research trip," she raised her voice, "was your idea."

"Tell Billy I said to drive you," he said curtly, and his eyes cut into hers.

"I'll do that," she replied, struggling to maintain her tattered pride. Her hands clutched the bag. "See you."

He didn't reply. Lillian was getting suspicious.

"Aren't you going to drive her?" Lillian asked him.

"He's soaking wet, poor thing," Mari reminded her. "You wouldn't want him to get worse."

"No, of course not!" Lillian said quickly. "But should you go alone, Mari, with your bad experience."

"She's tough," Ward told his housekeeper, and his eyes were making furious statements in the privacy of the hallway. "She'll get by."

"You bet I will, big man," she assured him. "Better luck next time," she added under her breath. "Sorry I wasn't more…cooperative."

"Don't miss your bus, honey," he said in a tone as cold as snow.

She smiled prettily and went past him to kiss Lillian goodbye.

Lillian frowned as she returned the hug. "Are you sure nothing's wrong?"

"Not a thing," Mari said and smiled convincingly. "He's just trying not to show how hurt he is that I'm leaving," she added in a whisper.

"Oh," Lillian said, although she was feeling undercurrents.

"See you soon," Mari promised. She walked straight past Ward, who was quietly dripping on the hall carpet, his fists clenched by his side. "So long, boss," she drawled. "Don't catch cold, now."

"If I die of pneumonia, I hope your conscience hurts you," he muttered.

She turned at the doorway. "It's more likely that pneumonia would catch you and die. You're dripping on the carpet."

"It's my damned carpet. I'll drip on it if I please."

She searched his hard eyes, seeing nothing welcoming or tender there now. The lover of an hour ago might never have been. "I'll give Georgia your regards."

"Have you got enough money for a bus ticket?" he asked.

She glared at him. "If I didn't have it," she said under her breath, "I'd wait tables to get it! I don't want your money!"

He was learning that the hard way. As he tried to find the right words to smooth over the hurt, to stop her until he could sort out his puzzling, disturbing new feelings, she whirled and went out the door.

"She sure is in a temper." Lillian sighed as she hobbled out of the living room and down the hall. "Sure is going to be lonesome around here without her." She stopped and turned, her eyes full of regret and resignation. "I guess you know what I told her."

"I know," he said curtly. "Everything."

She shrugged. "I was getting older. She was alone. I just wanted her to have somebody to care about her. I'm sorry. I hope both of you can forgive me. I'll write Mari and try to explain. No sense trying to talk to her right now." She knew something had gone badly wrong between them, and the boss didn't look any more eager to discuss it than Mari had. "I hope you'll forgive me."

"I already have."

She looked up with a wan smile. "She's not a bad girl. You...will let her come back if I straighten things out and stop trying to play cupid?"

He studied her quietly. "You heard what was said out here, didn't you?"

She stared at the floor. "I got ears that hear pins falling. I was all excited about it, I thought you two were... Well, it's not my business to arrange people's lives, and I've only just realized it. I'll mind my own business from now on." She looked up. "She'll be all right, won't she? Thanks to us, she doesn't even have a job now."

He was dying inside, and that thought didn't help one bit. He didn't want her to go, but he was going to have to let her.

"She'll be all right," he said, for his own benefit as well as Lillian's. Of course she'd be all right. She was tough. And it was for the best. He didn't want to get married.

What if she went back and married someone else? His heart skipped a beat and he scowled.

"Can she come back, at least to visit?" Lillian asked sadly.

"Of course she can!" he grumbled. "She's your niece."

Lillian managed a smile. "Thanks for letting her come. You could have fired me."

"Not on your life—I'd starve to death." He smiled half-heartedly. "I'd better change."

A truck started up, and they both looked toward the window as Mari went past sitting beside Billy in the ranch truck.

Ward's face hardened. He turned on his heel without a word and went up the staircase. Lillian sighed, watching him. Well, the jig was up and no harm done. Or was there? He did look frustrated. She turned and went toward the kitchen. Maybe things might work out better than she had expected. She hummed a little, remembering the explosive force of that argument she'd overheard. And then she smiled. Where there was smoke, there was fire, her daddy used to say.

A WEEK LATER, back in Atlanta, Mari was just getting over bouts of crying. Her small savings account was enough to pay the rent for the next month, thank goodness. She had bought groceries and cleaned her apartment and done her best not to think about what had happened in Texas.

Getting a job was the big problem, and she haunted the unemployment office for secretarial positions. There just weren't any available, but when there was an opening for a beginning bank clerk, she jumped at it. She hated figures and adding numbers, but it wasn't a good time to be choosy. She reported for work at a big bank in downtown Atlanta, and began the tedious process of learning to use computers and balance accounts.

After Mari was settled in Aunt Lillian called to make sure she'd made it home all right.

"I'm sorry, girl," the older woman said gruffly. "I never meant to cause you any hurt. I just wanted someone to look after you when I was gone. Now that I know I'm going to live, of course, I can do it by myself."

Mari was touched by her aunt's concern, even though she felt as if part of her had died. "I'll be okay," Mari promised brightly. "I'm sorry I had to leave so suddenly. I guess you figured out that we'd had a big argument."

"Hard to miss, the way you were going at each other before you left," Lillian said. "I knew the jig was up when he asked if you had the bus fare. He said you both knew I'd been spinning tales."

"We knew almost from the beginning," Mari said with a sigh. "We played along because we both think so much of you. But no more cupid, all right? You're much too tall to pass for the little guy, and you'd look pretty funny in a diaper carrying a bow and arrow."

Lillian actually laughed. "Guess I would, at that." She paused. "The boss left an hour ago for Hawaii. He said it was business, but he wasn't carrying any briefcase. He looked pretty torn up."

That would have been encouraging if Mari hadn't known

him so well, but she didn't allow herself to feel hopeful. She wanted to tell Lillian just what the scalawag had offered to do, but she didn't want to crush all her aunt's illusions. He had been pretty good to Lillian, after all. He could afford to be. It was only eligible women he seemed to have it in for.

"He'll be back in form in no time," Mari told her aunt. "He'll proabably find some new woman to make passes at in Hawaii."

"He made a pass?" Lillian sounded almost girlish with glee.

Mari groaned, realizing what she'd given away. "Well, that was what you wanted, wasn't it?" she asked miserably. "You got your wish, but it wasn't commitment he had in mind."

"No man in his right mind ever wants to make a commitment," the other woman assured her. "They have to be led into it."

"I don't want to lead your boss anywhere except maybe into quicksand," Mari said darkly.

"You will come and see me again, won't you?" Lillian probed gently. "When you get over being mad at him?"

"Someday maybe."

"How about a job? Do you have any prospects yet?"

"Finally," Mari sighed. "I started working in the accounts department of a bank this morning."

"Good girl. I knew you'd bounce back quickly. I love you, Marianne."

Mari smiled in spite of herself. "I love you, too, Aunt Lillian. Take care of yourself. Please take your pills."

"I will, I promise. Good night."

Mari hung up and stared at the receiver. So the boss had gone to Hawaii. How nice for him. Balmy breezes, blooming flowers, beautiful women doing the hula. Well, he wouldn't be depressed for long or even missing the one that got away. Thank goodness she'd had sense enough to refuse his proposition. At least she still had her pride and her self-respect.

"And they'll keep you very warm on winter nights, too," Mari muttered to herself before she went to bed.

The bank job was interesting, at least, and she met some nice people. She liked Lindy and Marge, with whom she worked, and there was even a nice young assistant vice president named Larry, who was single and redheaded and just plain nice. She began to have coffee and sweet rolls with him in the mornings the second week she was at the bank. Little by little she was learning to live without the shadow of Ward Jessup.

Or she told herself she was. But the memory of him haunted her. She could close her eyes and feel the warm, hard crush of his mouth, the tantalizing seduction of his big hands. It had been so beautiful between them, so special. At no time in her life had she felt more secure or safe than she had with him. Despite his faults he was more man than she'd ever known. She found that love forgave a lot. She missed him terribly. Sometimes just seeing the back of a dark-headed tall man would be enough to make her heart jump. Or if she heard a deep masculine voice. Or if she saw Texas license plates on a car. She began to wonder if she was going to survive being away from him.

She called Lillian the third week, just to see how her aunt was getting along, she told herself. But it wasn't Lillian who answered the phone.

When she heard Ward's deep voice, her heart ran away.

She hadn't realized how shattering it was going to be to talk to him. She'd assumed Lillian would answer.

"Hello?" he repeated impatiently.

Mari took a calming breath. "Is Aunt Lillian there, please?" she asked formally.

There was a long pause. She couldn't know that hearing her voice had made a similar impact on him.

"Hello, Mari," he said quietly. "Are you all right?"

"I'm very well, thank you. How is Aunt Lillian?"

"She's fine. It's her church social night. Billy ran her over there in the pickup. She'll be home around nine, I guess. Have you got a job?"

That was no business of his, especially seeing as how he'd caused her to lose the one she had in the first place. But hearing his voice had done something to her pride.

"Yes, I'm working at a bank," she told him, mentioning its name. "It's big and convenient to where I live. I work with nice people, and I'm making a better salary there than at the garage. You needn't worry about me."

"But I do," he said quietly. "I worry about you a lot. And I miss you," he added curtly, the words so harsh that they sounded quite involuntary.

She closed her eyes, gripping the receiver. "Do you?" she asked unsteadily, trying to laugh. "I can't imagine that."

"Someday soon I may work on making you imagine it," he said, his voice deep and slow and sensuous.

"I thought I'd told you already that I am not in the market for a big bank account and my own luxury apartment in Victoria, Texas," she returned, hating the unsteadiness that would tell him how much that hateful proposition had hurt her.

He said something rough under his breath. "Yes, I know

that," he said gruffly. "I wish you were here. I wish we could talk. I made the biggest mistake of my life with you, Marianne. But I think it might help if you understood why."

Mistake. So now that was all he felt about those magical times they'd had. It had all been just a mistake. And he was sorry.

Tears burned her eyes, but she kept her voice steady. "There's no need to explain," she said gently. "I understand already. You told me how much you loved your freedom."

"It wasn't altogether just that," he returned. "You said Lillian had told you about what happened to me, about the woman I planned to marry."

"Yes."

He sighed heavily. "I suppose she and my mother colored my opinion of women more than I'd realized. I've seen women as nothing more than gold-digging opportunists for most of my adult life. I've used them that way. Anything physical came under the heading of permissible pleasure with me, and I paid for it like I paid for business deals. But until you came along, I never had a conscience. You got under my skin, honey. You're still there."

She imagined that he hadn't told anyone what he was telling her. And while it was flattering, it was disturbing, too. He was explaining why he'd made that "mistake" and was trying to get them back on a friendly footing. She remembered him saying the night he'd come to her room that he'd had that intention even then. It was like lighting a match to the paper of her hopes. An ending.

"Don't let me wear on your conscience, Ward," she said quietly. "You can't help the way you are. I'm a puritan. An old-fashioned prude. I won't change, either, even if the whole world does. So I guess I'll be like Aunt Lillian when

I'm her age. Going to church socials and playing cupid for other women…" Her voice broke. "Listen, I have to go."

"No," he ground out. "Marianne, listen to me!"

"Goodbye, Ward."

She hung up before he could hear the tears that were falling hotly down her cheeks, before the break in her voice got worse. She went to bed without calling back. He'd tell Lillian she'd called, she knew, but she couldn't bear the risk that he might answer the phone again. Her heart was in tatters.

She went to work the next morning with her face still pale and her eyes bloodshot from the night before. She sat at her desk mechanically, answering the phone, going over new accounts, smiling at customers. Doing all the right things. But her mind was still on Ward and the sound of his voice and the memory of him that was eating her alive.

It would get better, wouldn't it? It had to! She couldn't go on like this, being haunted by a living ghost, so much in love that she could barely function as a human being. She'd never understood the idea of a couple being halves of the same whole until she met Ward. Now it made perfect sense because she felt as if part of her was missing.

When a long shadow fell across her desk just before lunchtime, she didn't even look up.

"I'll be with you in just a minute," she said with a forced smile as she finished listing a new account. And then she looked up and her body froze.

Ward stared down at her like a blind artist who could suddenly see again. His green eyes found every shadow, every line, every curve of her face in the stark, helpless silence that followed. Around them was the buzz of distant voices, the tap of fingers on keyboards, the ringing of telephones. And closer there was the rasp of Mari's hurried breathing, the thump of her heart shaking the silky pink blouse she was wearing with her gray skirt.

Ward was wearing a suit—a very elegant three-piece beige one that made him look even taller than he actually was. He had a creamy dress Stetson in one big hand, and his face looked thinner and drawn. His green eyes were as bloodshot as hers, as if he hadn't slept well. She thought as she studied him that he was the handsomest man she'd ever seen. If only he wasn't such a cold-blooded snake.

She stiffened defensively, remembering their last meeting. "Yes, sir?" she said with cold politeness. "May I help you?"

"Cut that out," he muttered. "I've had a long flight and no breakfast, and I feel like hell."

"I would like to point out that I work here," she informed him. "I have no time to socialize with old acquaintances. If you want to open an account, I'll be delighted to assist you. That's what I do here. I open accounts."

"I don't want to open an account," he said through his teeth.

"Then what do you want?" she asked.

"I came to take you home—where you belong." He searched her puzzled eyes. "Your boss will be sorry you have to leave, but he'll understand. You can come with me right now."

She blinked. Somewhere along the line she was sure that she'd missed something.

"I can what?" she asked.

"Come with me right now," he repeated. He turned the Stetson in his hands. "Don't you remember my condition? I'm dying, remember. I have something vaguely terminal, although medical science will triumph in plenty of time to save me."

"Huh?" she said blankly. None of this was getting through to her. She just stared at him.

"You're going to help me write my memoirs, remember?" he persisted.

"You aren't dying!" she burst out, coming to her senses at last.

"Shhhhh!" he said curtly, glancing stealthily around. "Somebody might hear you!"

"I can't quit! I just started working here the week before last!"

"You have to quit," he insisted. "If I go home without you, Lillian is going to starve me to death. She's getting her revenge in the kitchen. Small portions. Desserts without sugar. Diet foods." He shuddered. "I'm a shadow of my former self."

She glared at him. "Poor old thing," she said with poisonous sweetness.

He glared back. "I am not old. I'm just hitting my prime."

"That's nothing to do with me," she assured him. "I hope you didn't come all the way to Atlanta just to make this little scene!"

"I came to take you back with me," he replied. His eyes took on a determined hardness. "And, by God, I'm taking you back. If I have to pick you up bodily and carry you out of here in a fireman's lift."

Her heart jumped, but she didn't let him see how he was disturbing her. "I'll scream my head off," she said shortly.

"Good. Then everyone will think you're in pain, and I'll tell them I'm taking you to the hospital for emergency treatment." He glared at her. "Well?"

He had a stubborn streak that even outmatched her own. She weighed the possibilities. If he carried her out by force, she'd lose all credibility with her colleagues. If she fought him in front of everyone, Ward would get all the sympathy, and Mari would look like a heartless shrew. He had her over a barrel.

"Why?" she asked, her voice quiet and defeated. "Why not just let me stay here?"

He searched her eyes. "Your aunt misses you," he said gruffly.

"She could call me collect and talk to me," she replied. "There's no reason at all for me to go back to Texas and complicate my life and yours."

"My life is pretty boring right now, if you want to know the truth." He sighed, watching her. "I don't even enjoy foreclosing on people anymore. Besides all that, my cousin Bud's come to stay, and he's driving me out of my mind."

Cousin Bud was a familiar name. He was the one Ward's fiancée had wound up marrying for a brief time. She couldn't imagine Ward actually welcoming the man as a guest.

"I'm surprised that you let him," she confessed.

He stared at her. "So you know all about that, too?"

She flushed, dropping her eyes to the desk. "Aunt Lillian mentioned it."

He sighed heavily. "Well, he's family. My grandmother worships him. I couldn't say no without having her jump all over me—and maybe even rush home to defend him. She's having a good time at Belinda's. No reason to disturb her."

She knew about old Mrs. Jessup as well, and she almost smiled at his lack of enthusiasm for his grandmother's company.

"If you've already got one houseguest, you surely don't need another one."

He shrugged. "There's plenty of room. My secretary quit," he added, studying his hat. "I sure could use some help in the office. You could almost name your own salary."

"You forced me to leave Texas in the first place," she shot back, glaring up at him. "You did everything but put me on the bus! You propositioned me!"

His cheeks had a sudden flush, and he looked away. "You can't actually like this job," he said shortly. "You said you hated working with numbers."

"I like eating," she replied. "It's hard to eat when you aren't making money."

"You could come home with me and make money," he said. "You could live with your aunt and help me keep Cousin Bud from selling off cattle under my nose."

"Selling off cattle?"

His powerful shoulders rose and fell. "He owns ten percent of the ranch. I had a weak moment when he was eighteen and made him a graduation present of it. The thing is, I never know which ten percent he happens to be claiming at the moment. It seems to change quarterly." He brushed at a speck of dust on his hat. "Right now, he's sneaking around getting statistics on my purebred Santa Gertrudis bull."

"What could I do about Cousin Bud—*if* I went with you?" she asked reasonably.

"You could help me distract him," he said. "With you in the office, he couldn't very well get to any statistics. He couldn't find out where I keep that bull unless he found it on the computer. And you'd be watching the computer."

It was just an excuse, and she knew it. For reasons of his own it suited him to have her at the ranch. She didn't flatter herself that it was out of any abiding love. He probably did still want her, but perhaps it was more a case of wanting to appease Lillian. She frowned, thinking.

"Is my aunt all right?" she asked.

He nodded. "She's fine. I wouldn't lie to you about that. But she's lonesome. She hasn't been the same since you left." Neither had he, he thought, but he couldn't tell her. Not yet. She didn't trust him at all, and he couldn't really blame her.

She fiddled with a pencil, considering Ward's offer. She could tell him to go away and he would. And she'd never see him again. She could go on alone and take up the threads of her life. What a life it would be. What a long, lonely life.

"Come with me, Mari," he said softly. "This is no place for you."

She didn't look up. "I meant what I said before I left. If I come back, I don't… I don't want you to… to…"

He sighed gently. "I know, I know. You don't have to worry," he told her. "I won't proposition you. You have my word on that."

She shifted. "Then I'll go."

He forced back a smile. "Come on, then. I've got the tickets already."

She lifted her eyebrows. "Were you that confident?"

"Not confident at all," he replied. "But I figured I could always put my Stetson in one of the seats if you refused."

She did smile faintly at that. "I always heard that a real Texan puts his hat on the floor and his boots on the hat rack."

He lifted a tooled leather boot and studied it. "Yep," he said. "I guess I'd put my boots in the extra seat, at that. But I'd rather have you in it."

She got to her feet and put her work aside. "I need to see Mr. Blake, my boss."

"I'll wait." He wasn't budging.

After Mari had apologetically informed her boss of her departure, she picked up her purse, waved at her new friends and went quietly out the door with Ward. It felt odd, and she knew it was foolhardy. But she was too vulnerable still to refuse him. She only hoped that she could keep him from knowing just how vulnerable she was.

He drove her back to her apartment and then wandered around the living room while she packed.

His fingers brushed the spines of the thick volumes in her small bookcase. *"The Tudors of England,"* he murmured, "ancient Greece, Herodotus, Thucydides—quite a collection of history."

"I like history," she commented. "It's interesting reading about how other people lived in other times."

"Yes, I think so, too," he agreed. "I prefer Western history myself. I have a good collection of information on the Comanche and the cowboy period in south Texas, from the Civil War up to the 1880s."

She took her bag into the living room, watching the way he filled the room. He was so big. So masculine. He seemed to dwarf everything.

"We don't really know a lot about each other, do we?" he asked as she joined him. He turned, hands in his pockets, spreading the fabric of his trousers close against the powerful muscles of his legs.

"Getting to know women isn't one of your particular interests, from what I've heard," she returned quietly. "At least, not in any intellectual way."

"I explained why," he reminded her, and his green eyes

searched her blue ones. "It isn't easy learning to trust people."

She nodded. "I suppose not." She wanted to ask him
why he seemed to be so interested in where she lived, but
she was too shy. "I'm packed."

He glanced toward her suitcase. "Enough for a little
while?"

"Enough for a week or so," she said. "You didn't say
how long I was to stay."

He sighed heavily. "That's something we'll leave for
later. Right now I just want to go home." He looked around
him. "It's like you," he said finally. "Bright. Cheerful, Very
homey."

She hadn't felt bright and cheerful and homey in recent
weeks. She'd felt depressed and miserable. But it fascinated
her that her apartment told him so much.

"It doesn't have an indoor stream," she commented.

He smiled slowly. "No, it doesn't. Good thing. With my
batting average so far, I guess I'd be in it by now, wouldn't
I?"

She cleared her throat, feeling embarrassed. "I didn't
mean to push you in the river."

"Didn't you? It seemed like it at the time." He searched
her eyes quietly. "I meant what I said, Marianne. I won't
make any more insulting propositions."

"I appreciate that. I'm just sorry that I gave you such a
poor opinion of me," she added, admitting her own guilt.
"I shouldn't have let things go on the way they did."

He moved closer, lifting his hands to her shoulders,
lightly holding her in front of him. "What we did together
was pretty special," he said hesitantly. "I couldn't have

stopped it any more than you could. Let's try not to look back. That part of our relationship is over."

He sounded final, and she felt oddly hurt. She stared at his vest, watching the slow rise and fall of his chest.

"Yes," she murmured.

He looked down at her silky dark hair, smelled the soft floral scent that clung to her, and his heart began to throb. It had been so long since he'd held her, kissed her. He wanted to, desperately, but he'd just tied his own hands by promising not to start anything.

"Do you like kittens?" he asked unexpectedly.

Her eyes came up, brightly blue and interested. "Yes. Why?"

"We've got some," he said with a grin. "Lillian found an old mama cat squalling at the back door in a driving rain and couldn't help herself. The very next morning we had four little white kittens with eyes as blue as—" he searched hers with a disturbing intensity "—as yours."

"You let her keep the kittens?" she asked softly.

He shifted restlessly. "Well, it was raining," he muttered. "The poor little things would have drowned if I'd put them outside."

She wasn't buying that. Odd, how well she'd come to know him in the little time she'd spent on his ranch. "And...?" she prodded with raised eyebrows.

He almost smiled at the knowing look on her face. She knew him, warts and all, all right. "Cousin Bud's got one hell of an allergy to little kitties."

He was incorrigible. She burst out laughing. "Oh, you black-hearted fiend, you!" she groaned.

"I like little kitties," he said with mock indignation. "If

he doesn't, he can leave, can't he? I mean, I don't lock him in at night or anything."

If love was knowing all about someone—the good things and the bad—and loving them just the same, then it sure did apply here, she mused silently. "Ward Jessup," she said, sighing, "you just won't leave Bud alone, will you?"

"Sure I will, if he'll go home and leave my bull alone," he returned. "My God, you don't know how hard I fought to get that critter into my breeding program. I outbid two of the richest Texans in cattle to get him!"

"And now Cousin Bud wants him. What for?" she asked.

"Beats me." He sighed. "Probably for his advertising agency."

She sat down on the sofa. "He wants your bull for an ad agency?" she asked dubiously.

His eyebrows rose while his brain began to grasp what she was thinking. "Ad agency...oh, no, hell, no, he isn't going to use the bull to pose for male underwear commercials! He wants to sell it to finance expanding his advertising agency!"

"Well, don't glare at me, it sounded like he wanted to make a male model out of it," she defended herself.

He sighed heavily. "Woman, you're going to be my undoing," he said. And probably she would if he let himself think too hard about just why he'd come all this way after her. But missing her was just part of the torturous process. Now he had to prove to himself that he could have her around and not go off his head anymore. He still wanted her for certain, but marriage wouldn't suit him any more than being his mistress would suit her. So they'd be...friends. Sure. Friends. Lillian would stop starving him. There. He had noble motives. He just had to get them cemented in his mind, that was all.

"Can't you just tell Cousin Bud to go home?" she asked curiously.

"I have!" he grumbled. "Lillian has, too. But every time we get him to the front door, he calls up my grandmother and she raises hell with Lillian and me for not offering him our hospitality."

"She must like him a lot," she mused.

"More than she likes me, I'm afraid," he returned. He whirled his Stetson in his hands. "I'll give you one of the kittens if you want it."

"Bribery," she said in a stage whisper and actually grinned.

He grinned back. She was pretty that way. "Sure it is," he said shamelessly. He glanced around her small apartment. "Will they let you keep a cat here?"

"I guess so. I haven't ever asked." So he was already planning for her to come back here, she thought miserably.

He shrugged. "You might not want to come back here, though," he said unexpectedly. He smiled slowly. "You might like working for me. I'm a good boss. You can have every Sunday off, and I'll only keep you at the computer until nine every night."

"You old work horse!"

He didn't laugh as she'd expected him to. He just stared at her. "Am I old to you?" he asked softly as if it really mattered.

Watch it, girl, she warned herself. Take it easy, don't let the old devil fox you. "No," she said finally. "I don't think you're that old."

"To a kid like you I guess I seem that way," he persisted, searching her blue eyes with his darkening green ones.

She didn't like remembering how much older she felt because of his searching ardor. She dropped her eyes to the floor. "You said the past was over. That we'd forget it."

He shifted his booted feet. "I guess I did, honey," he agreed quietly. "Okay. If that's how you want it."

She looked up unexpectedly and found a strange, haunting look on his dark face. "It's an impasse, don't you think?" she asked him. "You don't want a wife, and I don't want an unattached temporary lover. So all that's really left is friendship."

He clutched the hat tighter. "You're making it sound cheap," he said in a faintly dangerous tone. He didn't like what she was saying.

"Isn't it?" she persisted, rising to her feet. He still towered over her, but it gave her a bit of an advantage. "You'd get all the benefits of married life with none of the responsibility. And what would I get, Ward? A little notoriety as the boss's mistress, and after you got tired of me, I'd be handed some expensive parting gift and left alone with my memories. No respectability, no self-respect, tons of guilt and loneliness. I think that's a pretty poor bargain."

"You little prude," he said curtly. "What do you know about grown-up problems, you with your spotless conscience? It's so easy, isn't it, all black and white. You tease a man with your body until he's crazy for it, you try to trap him into a marriage he doesn't want, you take whatever you can get and walk out the door. What does the man have out of all that?"

His attitude shocked her. She hadn't realized just how

poisoned he was against the female sex until he made that bitter statement.

"Is that what she did to you?" she asked gently. "Did she tease you beyond endurance and then marry someone else because what you gave her wasn't enough?"

His face grew harder than she'd ever seen it. He'd never talked about it, but she was forcing his hand.

"Yes," he said curtly. "That's precisely what she did. And if I'd been fool enough to marry her, she'd have cut my throat emotionally and financially, and she wouldn't even have looked back to see if I was bleeding to death on her way to the bank!"

She moved closer to him, hating that hurt in his eyes, that disillusionment that had drawn his face muscles taut. "Shall I tell you what most women really want from marriage? They want the closeness of caring for one man all their lives. Looking after him, caring about him, doing little things for him, loving him…sharing good times and bad. A good marriage doesn't have a lot to do with money, from what I've seen. But mutual trust and caring about each other makes all the difference. Money can't buy those."

He felt himself weakening and hated it. She was under his skin, all right, and it was getting worse all the time. He wanted her until he ached, and it didn't stop with his body. She stirred him inside, in ways no other woman ever had. Except Caroline. Caroline. Would he ever forget?

"Pretty words," he said bitterly, searching her eyes.

"Pretty ideals," she corrected. "I still believe in those old virtues. And someday I'll find a man who believes in them, too."

"In some graveyard, maybe."

"You are so cynical!" she accused, exasperated.

"I had good teachers," he retorted, slamming his Stetson down on his head to cock it arrogantly over one eye. "Are you ready?"

"I'm ready," she muttered, sounding every bit as bad-tempered as he did.

He took her bag in one hand and opened the apartment door with the other. She followed him out, locked the door with a sigh and put the key in her purse. Her life was so unpredictable these days. Just like the man beside her.

The commercial flight seemed longer than it actually was. Mari had found a few magazines to read at the huge Atlanta Hartsfield International Airport, and it was a good thing that she had because Ward pulled his hat over his eyes and folded his arms and he hadn't said one word to her yet. The flight attendants were already serving their lunch, but Ward only glanced up, refusing food. Mari knew, as she nibbled at ham and cheese on a bun, that he had to be furious or sick. He never refused food for any other reason.

Mari was sorry that they'd quarreled. She shouldn't have been because, if he was angry, at least he wouldn't be making passes at her. But if he stayed angry, it was going to make working for him all that much harder, and she'd promised, God knew why, to do his secretarial work. Now she couldn't imagine what had possessed her to agree. At the time it had seemed a wonderful idea. Of course, she'd had some crazy idea that he'd cared a little in order to come all that way to get her. Now it was beginning to seem as if he hated himself for the very thought. Mari was miserable. She should have said no. Then she remembered that she had, and that, ultimately, she had little choice in the matter.

She sighed over her food, glancing at him under the hat. "Aren't you hungry?" she offered.

"If I was hungry, I'd be eating, wouldn't I?" he muttered indistinctly.

She shrugged. "Then go right ahead and starve if you want to. I couldn't care less."

He lifted the brim of the hat and glared at her. "Like hell you couldn't," he retorted. "You and your pristine little conscience would sting for months."

"Not on your account," she assured him as she finished the ham. "After all, you're starving yourself. I haven't done anything."

"You've ruined my appetite," he said curtly.

Her eyebrows arched. "How did I do that, pray tell? By mentioning the word marriage? Some people don't mind getting married. I expect to do it myself one of these days. You see, I don't have your blighted outlook. I think you get out of a relationship what you put into it."

His green eyes narrowed, glittering. "And just what would you plan to put into one?"

"Love, laughter and a lot of pillow talk," she said without hesitation. "I expect to be everything my husband will ever want, in and out of bed. So you just go right ahead and have affairs, Mr. Jessup, until you're too old to be capable of it, and then you can live alone and count your money. I'll let my grandchildren come and visit you from time to time."

He seemed to swell all over with indignation. "I can get married any time I want to," he said shortly. "Women hound me to death to marry them!"

Her mouth made a soft whistle. "Do tell? And here you are pushing forty and still single..."

"I'm pushing thirty-six, not forty!"

"What's the difference?" she asked reasonably.

He opened his mouth to answer, glared fiercely at her

and then jerked his hat down over his eyes with a muttered curse. He didn't speak to her again until the plane landed in Texas.

"Are you going to ignore me the rest of the way?" Mari said finally when they were in the Chrysler just a few minutes outside of Ravine.

"I can't carry on a civilized conversation without having you blow up at me," he said gruffly.

"I thought it was the other way around." She picked a piece of lint off her sleeve. "You're the one doing all the growling, not me. I just said that I wanted to get married and have babies."

"Will you stop saying that?" He shifted angrily in the seat. "I'll get hives just thinking about it."

"I don't see why. They'll be my babies, not yours."

He was grinding his teeth together. He'd just realized something that he hadn't considered. Cousin Bud was young and personable and hungry to settle down. He'd take one look at this sweet innocent and be hanging by his heels, trying to marry her. Bud wasn't like Ward; he was carefree and his emotions were mostly on the surface. He didn't have scars from Caroline, and he wasn't afraid of love. In fact, he seemed to walk around in a perpetual state of it. And here was Ward, bringing him the perfect victim. The only woman Ward had ever wanted and hadn't got. Bud might be the one… Suddenly he slammed on the brakes.

"What!" Mari burst out, gasping as she grasped the dash. "What is it?"

"Just a rabbit," he muttered with a quick glance in her direction. "Sorry."

She stared at him. She hadn't seen any rabbit, and he sure was pale. What was wrong with him?

"Are you all right?" she asked cautiously, her voice soft with helpless concern.

It was the concern that got to him. He felt vulnerable with her. That evidence of her soft heart wound strands around him, binding him. He didn't want marriage or ties or babies! But when he looked at her, he felt such sweet longings, such exquisite pleasure. It had nothing to do with sex or carefree lust. It was…disturbing.

"Yes," he said quietly. "I'm all right."

A little farther down the road he suddenly pulled into a shallow farm road that was little more than ruts in the grass. It went beyond a closed fence, through a pasture, toward a distant grove of trees.

"My grandfather's place," he said as he turned off the engine. "My father was born out there, where you see those trees. It was a one-room shack in those days, and my grandmother once fought off a Comanche raiding party with an old Enfield rifle while my grandfather was up in Kansas on a trail drive."

He got out of the car and opened her door. "I know the owner," he said when she was standing beside him. "He doesn't mind if I come here. I like to see the old place sometimes."

He didn't ask if she wanted to. He just held out his big hand. Without hesitation she placed her slender one in it and felt tingly all over as his fingers closed warmly around it.

She felt small beside him as they walked. He opened and closed the gate, grinning at her curious stare.

"Any cattleman knows the value of a closed fence," he remarked as he grasped her hand once more and began to walk along the damp ruts. It had rained recently and there were still patches of mud. "In the old days a rancher might very well shoot a greenhorn who left a gate open and let his cattle get out."

"Were there really Indian raids around here?" she asked.

"Why, sure, honey," he said, smiling down at her. "Comanche, mostly, and there were Mexican bandidos who raided the area, too. Cattle rustling was big business back then. It still is in some areas. Except now they do it with big trucks, and in the old days they had to drive the herd out of the country or use a running iron."

She glanced up curiously. "What's a running iron?"

"A branding iron with a curved tip," he said. "It was used to alter brands so a man could claim another man's cattle. Here." He let go of her hand and found a stick and drew a couple of brands in the dirt, explaining how a running iron could be used to add an extra line or curve to an existing brand and change its shape entirely.

"That's fascinating!" she said.

"It's also illegal, but it happened quite a lot." He put the stick down and stuck his hands in his pockets, smiling as he looked around at feathery mesquite and live oak trees and open pasture. "God, it's pretty here," he said. "Peaceful, rustic… I never get tired of the land. I guess it's that damned Irish in my ancestry." He glanced down. "My grandmother, now, says it's British. But just between us, I don't think O'Mara is a British name, and that was my great-grandmother's maiden name."

"Maybe your grandmother doesn't like the Irish," she suggested.

"Probably not since she was jilted by a dashing Irishman in the war."

"Which war?" Mari asked cautiously.

"I'm afraid to ask," he said conspiratorially. "I'm not quite sure just how old she is. Nobody knows."

"How exciting," she said with a laugh.

He watched her with a faint smile, fascinated by the change in her when she was with him. That pale, quiet woman in the bank bore no resemblance to this bright, beautiful one. He scowled, watching her wander through the wooded area where the old ramshackle ranch house sagged under the weight of age and rotting timbers and rusting tin. She made everything new and exciting, and the way she seemed to light up when he was near puzzled him, excited him. He wondered if she might care about him. Love him...

She whirled suddenly, her face illuminated with surprised delight. "Ward, look!"

There were pink roses by the steps. A profusion of vines bore pink roses in tight little clusters, and their perfume was everywhere.

"Aren't they beautiful!" she enthused, bending to smell them. "What a heavenly aroma!"

"Legend has it that my father's grandmother, Mrs. O'Mara, brought those very roses from Calhoun County, Georgia, and nursed them like babies until they took hold here. She carried them across the frontier in a pot. In a Conestoga wagon, and saved them from fire, flood, swollen river crossings, robbers, Indians and curious little children. And they're still here. Like the land," he mused, staring around with eyes full of pride. "The land will be here longer than any of us and very little changed despite our meddling."

She smiled. "You sound just like a rancher."

He turned. "I am a rancher."

"Not an oilman?"

He shrugged. "I used to think oil was the most important thing in the world. Until I got plenty of it. Now I don't know what's the most important thing anymore. My whole life seems to be upside down lately." He stared straight at her. "I was a happy man until you came along."

"You were a vegetable until I came along," she replied matter-of-factly. "You thought robbing people was all right."

"Why, you little devil," he said in a husky undertone, and his eyes went a glittering green. "You little devil!"

She laughed because there was as much mischief as threat in that look. She started running across the meadow, a picture in her full gray skirt and pretty pink blouse, with her dark hair gleaming in the sun. He ran after her in time to catch the colorful glimmer of something moving just in front of her in the grass.

"Mari!" he called out, his voice deep and cutting and full of authority. "Stop!"

She did, with one foot in midair, because he sounded so final. She didn't look down. With her inborn terror of snakes, she knew instinctively what he was warning her about.

"Don't move, baby," he breathed, stopping himself just within reach of a fallen limb from one of the oaks. "Don't move, don't breathe. It's all right. Just stand perfectly still...."

He moved with lightning speed picking up a heavy branch and swinging his arm down, slamming. There was a feverish rattling, like bacon sizzling in a pan, and then only a bloody, writhing, coiling mass on the ground.

She was numb with unexpressed terror, her eyes huge at the thing on the ground that, only seconds ago, could have taken her life. She started to speak, to tell him how grateful she was, when he caught her up in his arms and brought his hard mouth down bruisingly on hers.

She couldn't breathe, couldn't move. He was hurting her, and she hardly noticed. His mouth was telling her things words couldn't. That he was afraid for her, that he was glad she was safe, that he'd take care of her. She let him tell her that way, glad of his strength. Her arms curled around his broad shoulders, and she sighed under his warm, hungry mouth, savoring its rough ardor.

"My God," he whispered unsteadily, his mouth poised over hers, his eyes dark in a face that was pale under its tan, his breath rough. "My God, one more step and it would have had you!"

"I'm all right, thanks to you." She managed to smile through the shaking relief, her fingers traced his rough cheek, his mouth. "Thank you."

He lifted her against his body, as rugged as any frontier man would have been, his face mirroring pride and masculinity. "Thank me, then," he whispered, opening his mouth as he bent to her lips. "Thank me..."

She did, so hungrily that he had to put her away from him or let her feel how easily she could arouse him. He held her by the waist, breathing unsteadily, watching her flushed face.

"We agreed that wouldn't happen again," he said.

She nodded, searching his eyes.

"But the circumstances were...unusual," he continued.

"Yes," she whispered, her eyes falling to his hard mouth with languorous remembered pleasure. "Unusual."

"Stop looking at me like that, or it won't end with

kisses," he threatened huskily. "You felt what you were doing to me."

She averted her eyes and moved away. Sometimes she forgot how experienced he was until he made a remark like that and emphasized it. She had to remember that she was just another woman. He felt responsible for her, that was why he'd reacted like that to the snake. It wasn't anything personal.

"Well, thanks for saving me," she said, folding her arms over her breasts as she walked back to the car, and carefully she avoided looking at the dead snake as she went.

"Watch where you put your feet, will you?" he asked from behind her. "One scare like that is enough."

Scare for which one of us? she wanted to ask. But she was too drained to say it. Her mouth ached for his. She could hardly bear to remember that she'd inflicted this torment on herself by letting him bring her out here. How was she going to bear days or weeks of it, of being near him and being vulnerable and having no hope at all for a future that included him?

CHAPTER TEN

WARD WAS QUIET the rest of the way to the ranch, but he kept watching Mari and the way he did it was exciting. Once he reached across the space between them and found her hand. He kept it close in his until traffic in Ravine forced him to let go, and Mari found her heart doing spins.

She didn't know how to handle this new approach. She couldn't quite trust him yet, and she wasn't altogether sure that he didn't have some ulterior motive for bringing her back. After all, he wasn't hampered by emotions as she was.

Lillian came quickly out to meet them, looking healthy and fit and with a healed leg.

"Look here," she called to Mari and danced a jig. "How's that for an improvement?" She laughed gaily.

"Terrific!" Mari agreed. She ran forward to embrace the older woman warmly. "It's good to see you again."

"He's been horrible," Lillian whispered while Ward was getting the bag out of the car. "Just horrible. He moped around for days after you left and wouldn't eat at all."

"He should have foreclosed on somebody, then," Mari said matter-of-factly. "That would have cheered him up."

Lillian literally cackled. "Shame on you," she said with a laugh.

"What's all the humor about?" Ward asked as he joined them, his expression tight and mocking.

"Your appetite," Mari volunteered tongue in cheek.

Lillian had turned to go back inside. Ward leaned down, holding Mari's eyes. "You know more about that than most women do, honey," he said in a seductive undertone. "And if you aren't careful, you may learn even more."

"Don't hold your breath," she told him, rushing away before she fell under the spell of his mocking ardor.

"Where's Bud?" Ward asked as they entered the hall.

"Did somebody call me?" came a laughing voice from the study.

The young man who came out to greet them was a total surprise for Mari. She'd been expecting Ward's cousin to be near his own age, but Bud was much younger. He was in his late twenties, at a guess, and lithe and lean and handsome. He had Ward's swarthy complexion, but his eyes were brown instead of green and his hair was lighter than his cousin's. He was a striking man, especially in the leather and denim he was wearing.

"Have you been sneaking around after my bull again?" Ward demanded.

"Now, Cousin," Bud said soothingly, "how would I find him in there?" He jerked his hand toward the study and shuddered. "It would take a team of secretaries a week just to find the desk!"

"Speaking of secretaries," Ward said, "this is my new one. Marianne Raymond, this is Bud Jessup. My cousin."

"Ah, the much-talked-about niece," Bud murmured, winking at Mari. "Hello, Georgia peach. You sure do your home state proud."

Ward didn't like Bud's flirting. His eyes told his cousin so, which only made Bud more determined than ever.

"Thank you," Mari was saying, all smiles. "It's nice to meet you at last."

"Same here," Bud said warmly, moving forward.

"Here, son," Ward said, tossing the bag at him. "You can put that in the guest room, if you don't mind. I'm sure Mari would like to see the study." Before anybody could say anything else, Ward had taken Mari by the arm and propelled her none too gently into the study.

He slammed the door behind them, bristling with masculine pride, and turned to glare at her. "He's not marrying material," he told her immediately, "so don't take him too seriously. He just likes to flirt."

"Maybe I do, too," she began hotly.

He shook his head, moving slowly toward her. "Not you, honey," he replied. "You aren't the flirting kind. You're no butterfly. You're a little house wren, all feathered indignation and quick eyes and nesting instinct."

"You think you know a lot about me, don't you?" She faltered on the last word because she was backing away from him and almost fell over a chair. He kept coming, looming over her with threatening eyes and sheer size.

"I know more than I ever expected to," he agreed, coming closer. "Stop running. We both know it's me you really want, not Bud."

She drew herself up, glaring at him. "You conceited…"

He moved quickly, scooping her up in his arms, holding her off the floor, his eyes wavering between amusement and ardor. "Go ahead, finish it," he taunted.

She could have if he hadn't been so close. His breath was minty and it brushed her lips when he breathed, warm and moist. He made her feel feminine and vulnerable, and when she looked at his hard mouth, she wanted to kiss it.

"Your office," she swallowed, "is a mess."

"So am I," he whispered huskily, searching her eyes. "So is my life. Oh, God, I missed you!"

That confession was her undoing. She looked up at him and couldn't look away, and her heart felt like a runaway engine. Her head fell back onto his shoulder, and she watched him lower his dark head.

"Open your mouth when I put mine over it," he breathed against her lips. "Taste me..."

Her breath caught. She was reaching up, she could already feel the first tentative brushing of his warm lips when a knock at the door made them both jump.

He lifted his head with a jerky motion. "What is it?" he growled.

Mari trembling in his arms, heard a male voice reply, "Lillian's got coffee and cake in the dining room, Cousin! Why don't you come and have some refreshment?"

"I'd like to have him, fricasseed," Ward muttered under his breath as Bud's laughing voice became dimmer along with his footsteps.

"I'd like some coffee," she said hesitantly even though she was still shaking with frustrated reaction and her voice wobbled.

He looked down into her eyes. "No, you wouldn't," he said huskily. "You'd like me. And I'd like you, right there on that long sofa where we almost made love the first time. And if it hadn't been for my meddling, jealous cousin, that's where we'd be right now!"

He put her down abruptly and moved away. "Come on, we'll have coffee." He stopped at the door with his hand on the knob. "For now," he added softly. "But one day, Marianne, we'll have each other. Because one day neither one of us is going to be able to stop."

She couldn't look at him. She couldn't even manage a defiant stare. It was the truth. She'd been crazy to come here, but there was no one to blame but herself.

From that first meeting, Cousin Bud seemed determined to drive Ward absolutely crazy. He didn't leave Mari alone with the older man for a second if he could help it. He found excuse after excuse to come into the office when she was typing things for Ward, and if she ever had to find Ward to ask a question, Bud would find them before they said two words to each other. Mari wondered if it might just be mischief on Bud's part, but Ward treated the situation as if he had a rival.

That in itself was amazing. Ward seemed possessive now, frankly covetous whenever Mari was near him. He shared things with her. Things about the ranch, about his plans for it, the hard work that had gone into its success. When he came home late in the evening, it was to Mari that he went, seeking her out wherever she might be, to ask for coffee or a sandwich or a slice of cake. Lillian took this new attitude with open delight, glad to have her former position usurped when she saw the way he was looking at her puzzled niece.

Bud usually managed to weasel in, of course, but there eventually came a night when he had business out of town. Ward came in about eight o'clock, covered in dust and half starved.

"I sure could use a couple of sandwiches, honey," he told Mari gently, pausing in the living room doorway. Lillian had gone to bed, and curled up on the sofa in her jeans and a yellow tank top, Mari was watching the credits roll after an entertainment special.

"Of course," she said eagerly and got up without bothering to look for her shoes.

He was even taller when she was barefoot, and he seemed amused by her lack of footwear.

"You look like a country girl," he remarked as she passed close by him, feeling the warmth of his big body.

"I feel like a country girl," she said with a pert smile. "Come on, big man, I'll feed you."

"How about some coffee to go with it?" he added as he followed her down the hall into the spacious kitchen.

"Easier done than said," she told him. She flicked the on switch of the small coffee machine, grinning at him when it started to perk. "I had it fixed and ready to start."

"Reading my mind already?" he teased. He pulled out a chair and sat down, sprawling with a huge stretch before he put his long legs out and rested his booted feet in another chair. "The days are getting longer, or I'm getting older," he said with a yawn. "I guess if I keep up this pace, before long you'll be pushing me around in a wheelchair."

"Not you," she said with loving amusement. "You're not the type to give up and get old before your time. You'll still be chasing women when you're eighty-five."

He sobered with amazing rapidity, his green eyes narrowing in his handsome face as he studied her graceful movements around the kitchen. "Suppose I told you that you're the only woman I'll want to chase when I'm eighty-five, Marianne?" he asked gently.

Her heart leaped, but she wasn't giving in to it that easily. He'd already come too close once and hurt her. She'd been deliberately keeping things light since she'd come back to the ranch, and she wasn't going to be trapped now.

She laughed. "Oh, I guess I'd be flattered."

"Only flattered?" he mused.

She finished making the sandwiches and put them down on the table. "By that time I expect to be a grandmother many times over," she informed him as she went back to pour the coffee. "And I think my husband might object."

He didn't like thinking about Marianne with a husband. His face darkened. He turned his attention to the sandwiches and began to eat.

"I have to go over to Ty Wade's place tomorrow," he murmured. "Want to come and meet Erin and the babies?"

She caught her breath. "Me? But won't I be in the way if you're going to talk business?"

He shook his head, holding her soft blue eyes. "You'll never be in my way, sweetheart," he said with something very much like tenderness in his deep voice. "Not ever."

She smiled at him. The way he was looking at her made her feel trembly all over. He was weaving subtle webs around her, but without the wild passion he'd shown her at the beginning of their turbulent relationship. This was new and different. While part of her was afraid to trust it, another part was hungry for it and for him.

"How about it?" he asked, forcing himself to go slow, not to rush her. He'd already had to face the fact that he wasn't going to be able to let her go. Now it was a question of making her see that he didn't have ulterior motives, and she was as hard to trust as he was.

"I'd like to meet Mrs. Wade," she said after a minute. "She sounds like quite a lady."

He laughed under his breath. "If you'd known Ty before she came along, you'd think she was quite a lady," he agreed with a grin. "It took one special woman to calm down that cougar. You'll see what I mean tomorrow."

THE NEXT AFTERNOON Mari climbed into the Chrysler beside Ward for the trip over to the Wades' place. Ward was wearing slacks with a striped, open-necked green shirt, and she had on a pretty green pantsuit with a gaily striped sleeveless blouse. He'd grinned when he noticed that their stripes matched.

Erin Wade opened the door, a picture in a gaily flowing lavender caftan. She looked as if she smiled a lot, and she was obviously a beauty when she was made up, with her long black hair and pretty green eyes. But she wasn't wearing makeup. She looked like a country girl, clean and fresh.

"Hello!" she said enthusiastically. "I'm glad you brought her, Ward. Hello, I'm Erin, and you have to be Marianne. Come in and see my boys!"

"I'm glad to meet you, too." Marianne grinned. "I've heard legends about you already."

"Have you, really?" Erin laughed. She was beautiful even without makeup, Marianne thought, the kind of beauty that comes from deep within and makes even homely women bright and lovely when it shows. "Well, Ty and I got off to a bad start, but we've come a long way in very little time. I don't think he has many regrets about getting married. Not even with twin boys."

"I can just see him now, changing a diaper." Ward chuckled.

Erin's green eyes widened. "But you can," she said. "Follow me."

Sure enough, there he was, changing a diaper. It looked so touching, the big, tough rancher Marianne had met before bending over that tiny, smiling, kicking baby on the changing table in a bedroom decorated with teddy bear wallpaper and mobiles.

"Oh, hello, Jessup," he murmured, glancing over his shoulder as he put the last piece of adhesive in place around the baby's fat middle. "Matthew was wet, I was just changing him," he told Erin. He glanced toward a playpen, where another baby was standing on unsteady little fat legs with both chubby hands on the rail, biting delightedly on the plastic edging. "Jason's hungry, I think. He's been trying to eat the playpen for the past five minutes."

"He's teething," Erin said, leaning over to pick him up and cuddle him while he cooed and patted her shoulder and chanted, "Da, Da, Da, Da."

Ty grinned mockingly at his frowning wife. "She hates that," he told the guests. "Most babies say Mama first. Both of them call me instead of her."

"Don't gloat." Erin stuck her tongue out at him. "You just remember who got up with them last night and let you sleep."

He winked at her, with torrents of love pouring on her from his light eyes. Marianne glanced up at Ward and found him watching her with the oddest look on his face. His green eyes went slowly down to her flat stomach and back up again, and she blushed because she knew what he was thinking. *Exactly* what he was thinking. She could read it in the sudden flare of his eyes, in the set of his face. She went hot all over with the unexpected passion that boiled up so suddenly and had to turn away to get herself under control again.

"How about some coffee?" Erin asked them, handing Jason to his dad. "Ward, if you'll bring the playpen, the boys can come with us."

Ward, to his credit, tried to figure out how the device

folded up, but he couldn't seem to fathom it. Ty chuckled. "Here, if Marianne will hold the boys, I'll do it."

"Surely!" She took them, cooing to them both, loving their little chubby smiling faces and the way they tried to feel every inch of her face and hair as she carried them into the living room.

"Oh, how sweet," she cooed, kissing fat cheeks and heads that had just a smattering of hair. The twins had light eyes like their father, but they were green.

"Thank God they both take after Erin and not me," Ty said with a sigh as he set up the playpen and took the boys from Marianne to put them back in.

"You're not that bad," Ward remarked, cocking his head. "I've seen uglier cactus plants, in fact."

Ty glared at him. "If you want that second damned lease, you'd better clean up your act, Jessup."

Ward grinned. "Can I help it if you go asking for insults?"

"Watch it," Ty muttered, turning back to help Erin with the coffee service.

The men talked business, and Marianne and Erin talked babies and clothes and fashion. It was the most enjoyable afternoon Marianne had spent in a long time and getting to cuddle the babies was a bonus. She was reluctant to leave.

"Ward, you'll have to bring her back to see me," Erin insisted. "I don't have much company, and I do love to talk clothes."

"I will," Ward promised. He shook hands with Ty, and they said their goodbyes. As they drove away, Ty had one lean arm around Erin, looking as if he were part of her.

"That marriage will outlast this ranch," she murmured, watching the landscape turn gray with a sudden shower. It seemed chilly in the car with that wetness beating on the hood and windshield. "They seem so happy."

"They are," he agreed. He glanced at her and slowly pulled the truck off onto one of the farm roads, pulling up under a huge live oak tree before cutting the engine. "Would you like to guess why I stopped?" he asked, his voice slow and tender as he looked at her. "Or do you know?"

CHAPTER ELEVEN

No, MARIANNE THOUGHT, she didn't really have to wonder why he'd parked the car. His face gave her the answer. So did the heavy, quick rise and fall of his chest under the green-striped shirt. He looked so handsome that she could hardly take her eyes off him, and the sheer arrogance in his narrowed eyes was intimidating.

But she wasn't sure she wanted a sweet interlude with him. Her defenses were weak enough already. Suppose he insisted? Could she resist him if she let herself fall in that heady trap?

"I don't think this is a good idea," she began as he unfastened his seat belt and then hers.

"Don't you?" he asked. "Even after the way you went scarlet when I stared at your waistline in the twins' room? You knew what I was thinking, Marianne," he whispered, reaching for her. "You knew."

He lifted her across him, finding her mouth even as he eased her down against his arm with her head at the window. Outside rain was streaming down the glass, making a quick tattoo on the hood and the roof, as driving as the passion that began to take over Mari's blood.

He bit at her soft lips, tender little nips that made her want him. His big hand smoothed over her blouse, under it, finding the softness of her breast in its silky casing.

"Lie still," he whispered when her body jerked under

that gentle probing. "It's been a long time since we've enjoyed each other like this. Too long."

He kissed her wide eyes shut and found the catch that bared her to his warm, hard fingers. She couldn't let this happen, she kept telling herself. It was just a game to him, he didn't mean it. Any minute now he was going to let that seat down and turn her in his arms....

With a wounded cry she pulled out of his arms so suddenly that he was startled into releasing her. She fumbled the door open, deaf to his sharp exclamation, and ran out into the rain.

The long grass beat against her slacks as she ran, not really sure why she was running or where she was trying to go. Seconds later it didn't matter because he'd caught her and dragged her down onto the ground in the wet grass with him.

"Never run from a hunter," he breathed roughly, turning her under him as he found her mouth with his. The rain beat down on them, drenching them, making their bodies as supple as silk-covered saplings, binding them as if there had been no fabric at all in the way.

It was new and exciting to lie like this, to kiss like this, feeling the warm, twisting motions of Ward's big body against hers, their clothes wet and their skin sensitive.

"We might as well have no clothes on at all," he breathed into her open, welcoming mouth, his voice husky with passion. "I can feel you. All of you."

His hands were sliding down her body now, exploring, experiencing her through the wet thinness of fabric, and it was like feeling his hands on her skin.

She moaned as she slid her own hands against his hard-muscled back, his chest, his hips. She didn't understand what was happening, how this passion had crept up on her. But she was lost now, helpless. He could do anything he liked, and she couldn't stop him. She was on fire despite the drenching rain, reaching up toward him, sliding her wet body against his in the silence of the meadow with the rain slicking their hair as it slicked their skin.

He eased his full weight onto her, devouring her mouth with his. His hands smoothed under her back, sensuously pressing her up against him.

Her body throbbed, burned, with the expertness of his movements. Yes, he knew what to do and how to do it. He knew...too much!

"Tell me to stop," he challenged under his breath, probing her lips with his tongue. "Tell me to let you go. I dare you."

"I can't," she whimpered, and her eyes stung with tears as she clung to his broad, wet shoulders. "I want you. Oh, I want you!"

His lips were all over her face. Tender, seeking, gentling, his breath catching in his throat at her devastating submission. He was trembling all over with the force of this new sensation. He wanted to protect her. Devour her. Warm her. Hold her until he died, just like this.

His big hands framed her face as he touched it softly with his lips. "I want to give you a baby," he whispered shakily. "That's what you saw in my face at Wade's, and it made you go red all over. You saw, didn't you?"

"Yes," she whispered back, her body trembling.

He searched her wide eyes, his own blazing with hunger. "I could take you, Marianne," he said very quietly. "Right here. Right now. I could have you, and no one would see us or hear us."

She swallowed, closing her eyes. Defeated. She knew that. She could feel how capable he was of it, and her body trembled under his fierce arousal. She wanted him, too. She loved him more than her honor.

"Yes," she whispered, so softly that he could barely hear.

He didn't move. He seemed to stop breathing. She opened her eyes and saw his face above her, filled with such frank exultation that she blinked incomprehensibly.

"Baby," he breathed softly, bending. He kissed her with such aching tenderness that her eyes stung, tasting her lips, smoothing his lips over her cheeks, her forehead, her nose, her eyes. "Baby, sweet, sweet baby. You taste of roses and gardenias, and I could lie here doing this for all my life."

That didn't sound like uncontrollable passion. It didn't even sound like lust. She reached up and touched his face, his chin.

He kissed the palm of her hand, smiling down at her through wildly exciting shudders. "Do you know how wet you are?" he said with a gentle smile, glancing down at her blouse, which was plastered against breasts that no longer had the shelter of a bra.

"So are you," she replied unsteadily and managed to smile back. What good was pride now when she'd offered herself to him?

He touched her taut nipples through the cloth. "No more embarrassment?" he asked quietly.

"You know what I look like," she whispered.

"Yes." He opened her blouse, no longer interested in the rain that had slowed to a sprinkle, and his eyes feasted on her soft skin before he bent and tasted it warmly with his mouth.

Mari lifted softly toward his lips, savoring their sweet

touch, so much a part of him that nothing seemed wrong anymore.

"You're so sweet," he whispered. He drew his cheek across her breasts, his eyes closed, savoring her. "For the rest of my life, I'll never touch another woman like this. I'll never lie with another woman, taste another woman, want another woman."

That was how she felt, too, about other men. She closed her eyes, smoothing his wet hair as he brushed his mouth over her pulsating, trembling body. She loved him so much. If this was all he could give her, it would be enough. Fidelity would do. She couldn't leave him again.

"I'll never want another man," she replied quietly.

He laid his cool cheek against her and sighed, holding her as she held him, with the wind blowing softly and the rain coming down like droplets of silk over them.

Then he moved away, gently rearranging her disheveled clothing. He brushed back her damp hair, kissed her tenderly one last time and carried her in his arms back to the car with her face pressed wetly into his warm throat.

"The car," she faltered. "We'll get the seats wet."

"Hush, baby," he whispered, brushing a kiss against her soft mouth as he put her into the passenger seat and fastened her seat belt. "It doesn't matter. Nothing matters now."

He got in beside her, found her warm hand and linked her fingers with his. He managed to start the car and drive it all the way home with one free hand.

Lillian took one look at them, and her eyebrows shot up.

"Not one word," Ward cautioned as he led Marianne inside. "Not one single word."

Lillian sighed. "Well, at least now you're getting wet together," she murmured with a smile as she wandered back toward the kitchen. "I guess that's better than mildewing alone."

Marianne smiled gently at Ward and went upstairs to change her clothing. He disappeared a few minutes later after an urgent telephone call and drove off by himself with only a wink and a smile for Mari. She walked around in a daze, dodging Lillian's hushed questions, waiting for him to come home. But when bedtime came, he still wasn't back.

Mari went up to her room and paced the floor, worrying, wondering what to do. She couldn't leave, not after this afternoon. He wanted her and she wanted him. Maybe he couldn't offer her marriage, but she'd just settle for what he could give her. He had to care a little. And she loved him enough for both of them.

Why hadn't he gone ahead, she wondered, when he had the chance this afternoon? Why had he stopped? Was he just giving her time to make up her mind, to be sure she could accept him this way? That had to be it. Well, it was now or never.

She put on her one seductive gown, a pretty white one with lots of lace and long elegant sleeves. She brushed out her dark hair until it was smooth and silky and dabbed on perfume. Then, looking in the mirror, she stared into her troubled blue eyes and assured herself that she was doing the right thing.

An hour later she heard Ward drive up. He came up the stairs, pausing at her door. Seconds later he started away, but Mari was already on her feet. She opened the door breathlessly and looked up at him.

He was wearing a dark pair of slacks with a patterned gray shirt open at the throat. His creamy dress Stetson was held in one hand. The other worried his hair. He stared at Mari with eyes that devoured her.

"Dangerous, baby, wearing something like that in front of me," he said softly and smiled.

She swallowed her pride. "I want you," she whispered shakily.

He smiled down at her. "I know. I want you, too."

She opened the door a little wider, her hands unsteady.

He cocked an eyebrow. "Is that an invitation to be seduced?"

She swallowed again. "I don't think I quite know how to seduce you. So I think you'll have to seduce me."

His smile widened. "What about precautions, little temptress?"

She blushed to her toes. She hadn't expected resistance. "Well," she began, peeking up at him, "can't you take care of that?"

His white teeth showed under his lips. "No."

Her blush deepened. "Oh."

He tossed his hat onto the hall table and went inside the room, gently closing the door behind him. "Now, come here." He drew her in front of him, holding her by both shoulders, his face gentle and almost loving. "What do you think I want, Marianne?"

"You've made what you want pretty obvious," she replied sadly.

"What you think I want," he corrected. His eyes went over her like hands, enjoying the exciting glimpses of her silky skin that he was getting through the gossamer-thin fabric of her gown. "And you're right about that. I could make a banquet of you in bed. But not tonight."

She turned her head a bit, looking up at him. "Are you too tired?" she asked innocently.

He grinned. "Nope."

None of this was getting through to her. "I don't understand," she said softly.

"Yes, I gathered that." He reached into his pocket and drew out a box. It was black and velvety and small. He opened it and handed it to her.

The ring was a diamond. A big, beautiful diamond in a setting with lots of little diamonds in rows encircling the large stone. Beside it was a smaller, thinner matching diamond band.

"It's an engagement ring," he explained. "It goes on the third finger of your left hand, and at the wedding I'll put the smaller one on your finger beside it."

She was hearing things. Surely she was! But the ring looked real. She couldn't stop staring at it.

"You don't want to get married," she told him patiently, her eyes big and soft. "You hate ties. You hate women. They're all deceitful and greedy."

He traced a slow, sensuous pattern down her silky cheek, smiling softly. "I want to get married," he said. "I want you to share your life with me."

It was the way he put it. She burst into tears. They rolled down her cheeks in a torrent, a sob broke from her throat. He became a big, handsome blur.

"Now, now," he murmured gently. He bent to kiss the tears away. "It's all right."

"You want to marry me?" she whispered unsteadily.

"Yes," he said, smiling.

"Really?"

"Really." He brushed back her hair, his green eyes possessive on her oval face. "I'd be a fool to let go of a woman who loves me as much as you do."

She froze in place. Was he fishing? Was he guessing? Did he know? If he did, how?

"You told me this afternoon," he said gently, pulling her to him. "You offered yourself to me with no strings. You'd never make an offer like that to a man you didn't love desperately. I knew it. And that's why I stopped. It would have been cheap, somehow, to have our first time on the ground without doing things properly."

"But…but…" she began, trying to find the right words.

"But how do I feel?" he probed softly, touching her lips with a faintly unsteady index finger. "Don't you know?"

His eyes were telling her. His whole face was telling her. But despite her rising excitement, she had to have it all. The words, too.

"Please tell me," she whispered.

He framed her face and lifted it to his darkening eyes, to his firm, hungry mouth. "I love you, Marianne," he breathed against her mouth as he took it. "And this is how much…"

It took him a long time to show her how much. When he was through, they were lying on the bed with her gown down to her waist, and he looked as if he were going to die trying to stop himself from going the whole way. Fortunately, or unfortunately, Lillian had guessed what was going on and was trying to knock the door down.

"It's bedtime, boss," she called loudly. "It's late. She's a growing girl. Needs her sleep!"

"Oh, no, that's not what I need at all," Marianne said with such tender frustration that Ward laughed through his own shuddering need.

"Okay, aunt-to-be," he called back. "Give me a minute to say good-night and I'll be right out."

"You're getting married?" Lillian shouted gleefully.

"That's about the size of it," he answered, smiling down at Mari. "Aren't you just overjoyed with your meddling now?"

"Overjoyed doesn't cover it," Lillian agreed. "Now, speaking as your future aunt-in-law, come out of there! Or wait until supper tomorrow night and see if you get fed! We're going to do this thing right!"

"I was just about to do this thing right," he whispered to Mari, his eyes softly mocking. "Wasn't I?"

"Yes." She laughed. "But we can't admit that."

"We can't?" He sighed. "I guess not."

He got up reluctantly, rebuttoning the shirt that her darting fingers had opened over a chest that was aching for her hands. "Pretty thing," he murmured, watching her pull the gown up again.

"You're pretty, too, so there," she teased.

"Are you coming out, or am I coming in?" Lillian was sounding militant.

Ward glowered at the door. "Can't I even have a minute to say good-night?"

"You've been saying good-night for thirty minutes already, and that's enough," she informed him. "I'm counting! One, two, three…"

She was counting loudly. Ward sighed at Mari. "Good night, baby," he said reluctantly.

She blew him a kiss. "Good night, my darling."

He took one last look and opened the door on "…Fourteen!"

Mari laid back against the pillows, listening to the

pleasant murmur of voices outside the door as she stared at her ring.

"Congratulations and good night, dear!" Aunt Lillian called.

"Good night and thank you!" Mari called back.

"Oh, you're very welcome!" Ward piped in.

"Get out of here," Lillian muttered, pushing him down the hall.

Alone in her room Mari was trying to convince herself that she wasn't dreaming. It was the hardest thing she'd ever done. He was hers. They were going to be married. They were going to live together and love each other and have children together. She closed her eyes reluctantly, tingling all over with the first stirrings of possession.

CHAPTER TWELVE

THE NEXT MORNING Mari was sure it had all been a beautiful dream until she looked at the ring on her finger. When she went down to breakfast, she found a new, different Ward waiting for her.

He went to her without hesitation, bending to brush a tender kiss against her smiling lips.

"It was real, after all," he murmured, his green eyes approving her cool blue knit sundress. "I thought I might have dreamed it."

"So did I," she confessed. Her hands smoothed hesitantly over the hard, warm muscles of his chest. It felt wonderful to be able to do that, to feel so much a part of him that it no longer was forbidden to touch him, to look at him too long. "Are you really mine now?" she murmured aloud.

"Until I die," he promised, bringing her close against him. He sighed into her hair, rocking her against the powerful muscles of his body. "I never thought this would happen. I didn't think I'd ever be able to love or trust a woman again after Caroline. And then you came along, pushing me into indoor streams, backing me into corners about my business sense, haunting me with your soft innocence. You got under my skin that first night. I've spent the rest of the time trying to convince myself that I was still free when I knew all along that I was hopelessly in love with you."

She burrowed closer, tingling all over at that sweet, possessive note in his deep voice. "I was so miserable in Atlanta," she confessed. "I missed you every single day. I tried to get used to being alone."

"I shouldn't have propositioned you," he said with a sigh, lifting his head to search her eyes with his. "But I still thought I could stop short of a commitment. God knows how I'd have coped with the conscience I didn't even have until you came along. Every time Ty Wade was mentioned, I got my back up, thinking how he'd changed." He touched her face with wonder in his whole look. "And now I know how and why, and I think he must have felt this way with his Erin when he realized what he felt for her."

She sighed softly, loving him with her eyes. "I know I felt like part of me was missing when I left here. It didn't get any better, either."

"Why do you think I came after you?" he murmured dryly. "I couldn't stand it here without you. Not that I admitted that to myself in any great rush. Not until that rattler almost got you, and I had to face it. If anything had happened to you, I wouldn't have wanted to live," he added on a deep, husky note that tugged at her heart.

"I feel that way, too," she whispered, searching his eyes. "Can we really get married?"

"Yes," he whispered back, bending his head down. "And live together and sleep together and raise a family together..."

Her lips opened for him, welcoming and warm, just for a few seconds before Lillian came in with breakfast and knowing grins. Ward glowered at her.

"All your fault," he told her. "I could have gone on for years living like a timber wolf but for you."

"No need to thank me," she said with a big smile. "You're welcome."

She vanished back into the kitchen, laughing, as Ward led Mari to the table, shaking his head with an exasperated chuckle.

THE WEDDING WAS a week later, and old Mrs. Jessup and Belinda had come home just for the occasion. They sat on either side of Lillian, who was beaming.

"Nice girl," Belinda whispered. "She'll make a new man of him."

"I think she has already." Old Mrs. Jessup grinned. "Spirited little thing. I like her, too."

"I always did," Lillian said smugly. "Good thing I saw the shape he was getting in and brought her out here. I knew they'd be good for each other."

"It isn't nice to gloat," Belinda reminded her.

"Amen," Mrs. Jessup harrumphed. "Don't I seem to remember that you introduced that Caroline creature to him in the first place?"

Lillian was horrified. "That wasn't me! That was Belinda!"

Mrs. Jessup's eyes widened as she glared past Lillian at the restless young woman on the other side. "Did you?"

"It was an accident," Belinda muttered. "I meant to introduce her to Bob Whitman, to get even for jilting me. Ward kind of got in the way. I never meant for her to go after my poor brother."

"It's all in the past now, anyway," Lillian said, making peace. "He's got the right girl, now. Everything will be fine."

"Yes." Old Mrs. Jessup sighed, glancing past Lillian again. "If only Belinda would settle down. She goes from boyfriend to boyfriend, but she never seems to get serious."

Lillian pursed her lips, following the older woman's gaze

to Belinda, who was sighing over Mari's wedding gown as she walked down the aisle accompanied by the organ music. She'd have to see what she could do....

The wedding ceremony was short and beautiful. Mari thought she'd never seen a man as handsome as her Ward, and when the minister pronounced them husband and wife, she cried softly until Ward kissed away the tears.

Lillian, not Belinda, caught the wedding bouquet and blushed like a schoolgirl when everyone giggled. The guests threw rice and waved them off, and Mari caught a glimpse of tall, slender Ty Wade with his Erin just on the fringe of the guests.

"Alone at last." Ward grinned, glancing at her.

"I thought they'd never leave," she agreed with a wistful sigh. "Where are we going? I didn't even ask."

"Tahiti," he said with a slow smile. "I booked tickets the day after you said yes. We're flying out of San Antonio early tomorrow morning."

"What about tonight?" she asked curiously and flushed at the look on his face.

"Let me worry about tonight," he murmured softly.

He held her hand as he drove, and an hour later he drove up to a huge, expensive hotel in the city.

He'd reserved the bridal suite, and it was the most incredible sight Mari had ever seen. The bed was huge, dominating the bedroom. She stood in the doorway just staring at it while Ward paid the bellhop and locked the door.

"It's huge," she whispered.

"And strategically placed, did you notice?" he murmured with a laugh, suddenly lifting her clear of the floor in her neat white linen traveling suit.

"Yes, I did notice," she said huskily, clinging to him. "You looked so handsome."

"You looked so lovely." He bent to her mouth and started walking. "I love you to distraction, did I tell you?"

"Several times."

"I hope you won't mind hearing it again frequently for the next hour or so," he murmured against her eager mouth and laid her gently down on the bed.

Mari had expected ardor and passion, and she had experienced a tiny measure of apprehension. But he made it so natural, so easy. She relaxed even as he began to undress her, his hands and mouth so deeply imprinted on her memory that she accepted them without the faintest protest.

"This is familiar territory for us, isn't it?" he breathed as he moved back beside her after stripping off his own clothing. "Up to this point, at least," he added at her rapt, faintly shocked visual exploration of him. "But you know how it feels to have my eyes and my hands and my mouth on you. You know that I won't hurt you. That there's nothing to be afraid of."

She looked back up into his eyes. "I couldn't be afraid of you."

"I won't lose control right away," he promised, bending slowly to her mouth. "Give yourself to me now, Mari. Remember how it was on the ground, with the rain soaking us, and give yourself to me the way you offered then."

She felt all over again the pelting rain, the sweetness of his hands, the wild fever of his mouth claiming hers in the silence of the meadow. She reached up to him, suddenly on fire with the unaccustomed removal of all barriers, physical and moral, and she gave herself with an abandon that frankly startled him.

"Shhh," she whispered when he tried to draw back at the last minute, to make it gentle, to keep from hurting her. But she reached up to his hips and softly drew them down again, lifting, and a tiny gasp was the only sound she made as she coaxed his mouth back to hers. "Now," she breathed into his devouring lips. "Now, now..."

"Mari," he groaned. His body surged against hers, his arms became painfully strong, his hands biting into her hips, his mouth trembling as his body trembled. He was part of her. She was part of him. Locking together, loving, linking...

"Mari!"

She went with him on a journey as exquisitely sweet as it was incredibly intimate, yielding to his strength, letting him guide her, letting him teach her. She used muscles she hadn't realized she possessed, she whispered things to him that would shock her later. She wound herself around him and lost all her inhibitions in a wild, fierce joining that ripped the veil of mystery from the sweetest expression of shared love. Even the first time it was still a kind of pleasure that she hadn't known existed.

She stretched lazily, contentedly, and snuggled close to him under the lightweight sheet, nuzzling against his matted chest with a face radiant with fulfillment.

"I love you," he said softly as if the words still awed him. He smoothed her hair tenderly. "I always will."

"I love you just as much." She smoothed her hand over his chest. "Cousin Bud wasn't at the wedding." She frowned. Her mind had been curiously absent for a week. She lifted up. "Ward, Bud hasn't been at the house!"

"Not for a week," he agreed complacently, grinning. "Not since that day I took you to see Ty and Erin."

"But this is horrible! I didn't notice!"

"That's all right, sweetheart, I don't mind," he said, drawing her back down.

"Where is he?"

"Oh, I sent him on a little trip," he murmured at her temple. "I told him that bull he wanted was out to stud at a cattle ranch in Montana, and he went up there looking."

"Looking?" She frowned.

"Well, honey, I didn't exactly tell him which ranch it was on. Just the state. There are a lot of ranches in Montana."

"You devil!" she accused, digging him in the ribs.

He pulled her over him, smiling from ear to ear. "All's fair, don't they say? Cousin Bud always did cramp my style." He coaxed her mouth down to his and kissed it softly. "I didn't want him on my case until I had you safely married to me."

"You couldn't have been jealous?"

"I've always been jealous," he confessed, tugging a strand of her hair playfully. "You were mine. I didn't want him trying to cut me out. Don't worry, he'll figure it out eventually."

"I shouldn't ask," she mumbled. "Figure what out?"

"That the bull is still on my ranch, just where I had him all along."

"What are you going to tell Cousin Bud?"

"That I misplaced him," he said easily. "Don't worry, he'll believe me. After all, he didn't think I was serious about you, either, and look how I fooled him!"

She would have said something else, but he was already rolling her over on the big bed and kissing the breath out of her. So she just closed her eyes and kissed him back. Outside it was raining softly, and Mari thought she'd never heard a sweeter sound.

* * * * *

RAGE OF PASSION

For my niece Helen, who sews a fine seam

CHAPTER ONE

THE TELEGRAM CRUMPLED in the slender hand, a scrap of badly used timber that would have served better as the tree it once was. Pale green eyes stared down at it, hated it.

"Is it bad news, Mama?"

Becky's soft young voice broke through the anguish, brought her back to the reality of the huge empty Victorian house and the plain, withdrawn child.

"What, darling?" Her voice sounded odd. She cleared her throat and helplessly twisted the crumpled telegram in her hand. "Bad news? Well…yes."

Becky sighed. She was so old for six, Maggie sometimes thought. Her life had been disordered from the very beginning. An exclusive boarding school hadn't made her an extrovert; it had only emphasized her painful shyness, made it more obvious.

"Is it Daddy again?" Becky asked quietly. She read the answer in her mother's worried eyes and shrugged. "Well, Auntie Janet is coming today," she said with childlike enthusiasm and smiled. "That should make you feel better."

Margaret Turner smiled back. Her daughter's rare smiles were magic. "So she is, although she isn't really your aunt. She's my godmother. She and your Grandmother Turner were best friends. What a nice surprise for us, meeting her last week. She didn't even know I had you, you lovely little surprise, you."

Becky giggled—one of those sweet sounds that Maggie had heard so seldom lately. The boarding school was taking its toll on Becky, but there'd been no choice about it once Maggie went to work. She had no one to keep Becky after school, and her job meant occasional long hours and Saturday work. That left the child vulnerable, and Dennis wasn't above taking her away and hiding her somewhere. He was capable of anything where money was involved. And this newest threat, this telegram, made it plain that he was going to sue for full custody of Rebecca. He wanted Maggie to know immediately that he'd just given his lawyer the green light to go back to court.

Maggie swept back a strand of her short dark hair, which was very straight, curving into her high cheekbones. She was slender and tall, a good silhouette for the clothes that were such a rage this season. Not that she was buying new clothes. Thanks to her ex-husband's incredible alimony suit against her—which he'd won—and the fact that her attorneys were still draining her financially, times were getting harder by the day.

About all that was left was this white elephant they lived in and a relatively new car—and Becky's trust. Maggie's own father had never approved of her marriage to Dennis, although—at the time—she hadn't understood why. He'd cut Maggie out of his will entirely, leaving everything in trust for Becky. Maggie hadn't known this until his death, and she'd never forget the outburst from Dennis at the reading of the will. Her heart already broken, his callous attitude had taken the last of her spirit. After that, she hadn't really felt alive at all. She'd kept going for Becky's sake, not her own.

Dennis had tried to break the will. It couldn't be broken, but there were loopholes that would allow the administrator of the trust to sell stocks and bonds and reinvest them. Maggie could imagine what Dennis would do with that kind of control; in no time he'd have reduced Becky to poverty, robbed her of her inheritance.

As it was, Maggie was working long hours in a bookstore to make ends meet. She loved books, and the job was nice. But being without her daughter wasn't. She prayed for the day when she could bring Becky home and not have to worry that Dennis might kidnap her if she was left with a sitter. It was a good thing that Maggie didn't have a social life. But even in the days when her family had been wealthy and she'd had every advantage, she'd never cared for socializing. She'd kept to herself and avoided the fast crowds. She'd been much like Becky as a child—shy and introverted. She still was.

"I won't have to live with Daddy, will I?" Becky asked suddenly, and the look in her big eyes was poignant.

"Oh, darling, of course you won't!" Maggie drew the spindly-legged child close to her, caressing the incredibly thick hair that trailed down her daughter's ramrod-stiff back. Becky was all she had in the world now, the most precious thing she had left; the only thing of worth to come from the six-year marriage that she'd finally garnered enough courage to end just months before. The instant the divorce had become final, she'd gone back to using her maiden name, Turner. She wanted nothing of Dennis in her life—not even his name.

"Never," Maggie added absently. "You won't have to live with him."

That might become a well-meant lie, she thought miserably as she cuddled her daughter, because Dennis was threatening to take Becky from her. They both knew that all he wanted was the mammoth trust Alvin Turner had set up for his grandchild before his death. Whoever had responsibility for Becky had access to that fortune. So far, Maggie had managed to keep the child out of her ex-husband's hands. He'd already announced his engagement to the woman he'd moved in with following the divorce, and Maggie's attorney was worried that Dennis might get the edge in a custody suit if he had a stable family life to offer little Rebecca.

Stability! If there was one thing Dennis Blaine didn't possess, it was stability. She should never have married him. She'd gone against her father's wishes, and against the advice of Aunt Janet. It had been a whirlwind courtship, and they'd made a handsome couple—the shy young debutante from San Antonio and the up-and-coming young salesman. Only after the wedding and her subsequent immediate pregnancy did Maggie learn that Dennis's main ambition was wealth, not a happy marriage. He liked women—and one wasn't enough. Barely three weeks after their wedding, he was having an affair with another woman, mostly as an act of vengeance against Maggie, who'd refused to stake him in a get-rich-quick scheme he'd concocted.

She sighed over her daughter's silky hair. Dennis, she'd discovered, had a vindictive nature, and it had grown worse as time passed. His affairs were legion. She'd tried to leave him, and he'd beaten her. It was the first and last time. She'd threatened to go to the police, with all the scandal that would have raised, and he'd promised in tears never to do it again. But there were other ways he'd been able to get back at her, especially after Becky came along. More than once he'd threatened to abduct the child and hide her if Maggie didn't go along with his demands for more money.

In the end, it had been because of Becky that she'd moved out and filed for divorce. Dennis had brought one of his ladyloves into the house and had been cavorting with her in bed when Becky had come home unexpectedly and found them. Dennis had threatened Becky, warning her not to tell what she'd seen. But Becky was spunky. She had told. And that very day, Maggie had moved with the child back to her old family home in San Antonio. Thank God her parents had held on to the house even after they'd moved to Austin.

Dennis, meanwhile, had cut his losses and stayed in Austin, where he and Maggie had lived together for the six years of their disastrous marriage. Once the divorce had become final, he'd initiated a grueling lawsuit—with Maggie's money, ironically enough—and had ultimately been granted visitation rights.

Well, she wasn't giving up her child to that money-grubbing opportunist. She said so, frequently. But Dennis's forthcoming remarriage could cause some devilish problems. She didn't quite know what to do, how to handle this new development.

"Couldn't we run away?" Becky asked as she drew back. "We could go live with Aunt Janet and her family, couldn't we? They own a real ranch, and Aunt Janet's so nice. She said after she visits us, we could visit her and ride horses—"

"I'm afraid we can't do that," Maggie said quickly, forcing down the image of Gabriel Coleman that swam with sickening intensity before her eyes. He frightened her, colored her dreams, even though it had been years since she'd seen him. Even now, she could close her eyes, and there he was. Big, lean, rawhide tough. All man. Dennis wouldn't dare threaten her around Gabe, but Maggie was too frightened of him to ask for sanctuary. It was a well-known fact that Janet and her son didn't get along. Maggie had enough problems already without adding Gabe's antagonism to them. He didn't care for her. He thought of her as a bored socialite; he always had. She was prejudged and predamned in his pale eyes. She'd never stood a chance with him, even in her younger days. He hadn't given her a second look. Once, she'd wanted him to. But after Dennis, she'd had too many scars for another relationship. Especially with a man like Gabriel, who was so much a man.

"But why can't we?" Becky persisted, all eyes—green eyes, like her mother's.

"Because I have a job," Maggie said absently, smoothing the long silky hair of the little girl. "Well, except for this month-long vacation I'm getting while Trudie is in Europe. She owns the shop, you see." Trudie had decided that Maggie needed some time off, too, and she'd closed up shop despite the loss of cash. It was one of many reasons that Maggie loved her friend so much.

"Then can't we go home with Aunt Janet? Oh, can't we?" Becky pleaded, all but jumping up and down in her enthusiasm.

"No, and you mustn't ask her, either," Maggie said shortly. "Anyway, you have one more week at school before vacation. You have to go back and finish out the semester."

"Yes, Mama," Becky sighed, giving in without a fight.

"Good girl. Suppose you dash out to the kitchen and remind Mary that we're to have an apple pie tonight in Aunt Janet's honor," she added with a smile.

"Yes, Mama," Becky agreed, brightening. She ran,

skirts flying, out of the immaculate living room with its wing chairs and Chippendale sofa—beautiful relics of a more graceful age—down the long hall toward the spacious kitchen.

The house had been in Maggie's family for eighty years or more. It was here that she and Dennis had spent an occasional weekend with her mother after her father's death from a heart attack, but she didn't mind the memories as much as she would have minded losing the home place. She touched the arm of the sofa lovingly. Her mother had sat here in happier days, doing embroidery, while her father had sprawled in the big armchair on his visits home—and they'd been few, those last years, because as an ambassador his duty had kept her away.

Maggie's mother had traveled with him until ill health had forced her to remain in Texas. She'd died within six months of her tragic loss, swiftly following the husband she'd adored. Maggie often thought that such love was a rare thing. Certainly she hadn't found it in her marriage. She wondered if she ever would find it. She was much too frightened to take the chance a second time; the risk, to Becky, was even greater than the risk to herself.

She studied her slender hands quietly, drinking in the subtle scent of lavender that clung like dust to the old furniture. A knock on the door disturbed her thoughts, then the knob twisted and Janet Coleman breezed in.

"Darling! Oh, it's so hot outside! Why I keep an apartment in San Antonio I don't know, when I could have one someplace cold."

Like a white-haired whirlwind, Janet embraced the younger, taller woman with a deep sigh.

"You must love the city. You've had that apartment ever

since I can remember." Maggie smiled, drawing back to stare down at the older woman in the chic gray suit.

"I've got my nerve, haven't I, inviting myself for dinner." Janet laughed. "But I couldn't resist it. It's been so many years, and to run into you out of the blue in that department store! Shocking, to think I didn't even know about Becky! And here you'd been married for six years, and getting a divorce…" She shook her head. "I miss your mother so much. I have no one to talk to these days, with the girls away from home and Gabe so business oriented. And," she added quietly, "I'm hardly ever at the ranch these days myself. I've been in Europe for the past seven months."

Maggie had gone to boarding school with the girls, Audrey and Robin—the same school, in fact, that Becky was in now.

"Audrey is living with a man in Chicago," Janet said, exasperated. She flushed a little at Maggie's pointed stare. "Yes, that's what I said. Isn't it outrageous? I know it's the in thing to do these days, but honestly, Maggie, I had to stop Gabriel from getting the next train up there. He was all for putting a bullet in the man. You know Gabe."

Maggie nodded. Yes, that was Gabe all right. His answer to most things was physical. She trembled a little with inner reaction to him—a reaction that had always been there, but one she'd never really understood.

"I talked him out of it, but he's still simmering." She shuddered delicately. "I just hope Audrey has the good sense to stay away until he cools down. He'd have them married at gunpoint."

"Yes, I don't doubt it. How's Robin?" she added with a smile, because she liked Janet's younger daughter.

"She's still trying to be an oil rigger." Janet shook her head. "She says it's what she wants to do."

"Times have changed, Janet." Maggie laughed. "Women are taking over the world."

"Please don't say that in front of Gabe," the older woman murmured dryly. "He doesn't like the modern world."

"Neither do I, at times." Maggie sighed. She stared at Janet. "Is he still ranching?"

"With a vengeance. It's roundup time, darling." Janet laughed. "He doesn't speak to anyone for days during roundup. He's hardly even home anymore. He has board meetings and buying trips and selling trips and seminars, and he sits on the boards of God knows how many corporations and colleges and banks… Even when I'm home, he never listens to me."

"Does he know about Becky and me?" she wondered aloud.

"I've mentioned your mother over the years," Janet said. "But no, I don't suppose I've had a lot to say about you. He's so touchy when I mention women, I've given up trying. I did find this lovely girl and I brought her out to the ranch to meet him." Janet flushed. "It was terrible." She shook her head. "Since then, I've decided that it's better if I let him lead his own life. So I don't mention anybody to him. Especially eligible women," she added with a pert laugh.

Maggie shook her head. "Well, he'd never have to worry about me. I'm off men for life!"

"I can understand why," Janet muttered. "I never liked that man. He smiled too much."

This from a woman whose son was a caveman…. But Maggie wasn't going to remark on that. She had no use at all for that kind of man. She'd had enough of being afraid and dominated and intimidated. No man was ever going to get the chance to do to her what Dennis had. Not ever again.

"If only Gabe would get married," Janet said. And there was such bitter remorse in her voice. "He never had the chance to do the things most young men do. I feel responsible for that, sometimes." The remorse in the tired old voice made Maggie feel sympathetic.

She knew about Janet's family, of course. Janet and her own mother had been best friends for years, and Maggie had learned things about the other family, especially the one son, that she wished she could forget. Janet's girls had been spoiled rotten by two doting parents, and that hadn't helped. After Jonathan Coleman's death, Audrey had run wild and Robin had gone off to college. Gabe was left at the head of the massive ranch holding—with no help at all from his family, none of whom knew anything about business.

Gabe had shouldered the burden, though, and that strong back had never bent in all the years since. Maggie had always admired his strength. He was unique. A pioneer with a rugged spirit and a savage determination to persevere.

"Here's my Becky," Janet gushed, opening her arms to the little girl, who darted into them with unabashed affection.

"Oh, Auntie Janet, I'm so glad you came," Becky enthused. Becky had taken instantly to the older woman during that chance meeting, and when she'd learned that Maggie was Janet's goddaughter, she'd "adopted" herself as Janet's niece. Maggie hadn't fussed, and Janet had been delighted. The poor child had no other living relatives, except her terror of a father.

Becky hugged the old lady tightly, her eyes closed. She drew back a long minute later. "My daddy is trying to make me come and live with him, and I told Mama we should run away, but she won't."

Janet darted a searching glance at Maggie, who was standing red-faced in the center of the kitchen while old Mary gaped briefly at the small group before ambling back to her tea cakes and silverware. Mary had been with the family since Maggie was a child. She didn't work for them full-time anymore but only came in when she needed a little extra money—and Maggie often worked overtime to provide that money, to help the woman who'd been so much a part of her childhood.

"So that's still going on, is it?" Janet asked haughtily. "Really, dear, you should let me ask Gabriel to speak to Dennis. He wouldn't mind."

Maggie could just imagine Gabriel doing anything for her. It was whimsical. She shrugged. "My attorneys are handling it, but thank you for the offer."

"I feel guilty. I've lost touch with you all since you moved to Austin," Janet said. "If it hadn't been for our chance meeting downtown, I wouldn't have invited myself to visit you."

"You know you're always welcome here," Maggie chided.

Janet searched her face quietly. "I've been away too long, haven't I, dear? I should have been keeping an auntly eye on you." She shook her head. "I lose track of things these days. Absentmindedness, I suppose. I remembered after I ran into you that I hadn't ever mentioned your marriage to the girls. That's how terrible I am."

"We haven't seen each other in a long time," Maggie reminded her with a smile. "But it's so nice to have you here." She led Janet into the dining room, where the older woman sat down at the cherrywood table, fanning herself with her hand.

"Darling, it's so hot, even for spring. How ever do you stand it?"

"I'll get you a fan," Becky volunteered, and opened the buffet drawer, pulling out a large wooden fan with a beautiful spring scene on one side and the name of a local funeral parlor in huge black letters on the other.

Janet smiled appreciatively at her and began to fan herself furiously. "If you only had air conditioning." She shook her head. "We had to put it in two years ago. The heat is getting more unbearable every year."

Becky seated herself primly in a chair beside Janet while Mary bustled around serving tea cakes and steaming cups of freshly brewed tea. Afterward, Becky was sent out to play and Mary went into the kitchen to finish dinner and watch the little girl out the back window.

"Now," Janet said firmly, transfixing Maggie with those piercing light eyes. "Let's hear it all."

Maggie knew she had no choice, so she told her godmother everything. It felt good to get it off her chest. It had been so long since she'd had anybody she could talk to.

Janet listened, only occasionally asking questions. When Maggie had finished, she stared into her teacup for a minute, then spoke. "Come home with me," she said, looking up. "You need a little time away, to think things through. The ranch is the perfect refuge—and the one place Dennis won't come looking for you."

That was true enough. Dennis, like Maggie, had heard plenty about Gabriel Coleman, and Dennis wasn't suicidal.

"But what about Becky?" Maggie asked. "I can't take her out of school now...."

"We'll come back for her week after next," Janet assured her. "She's in boarding school, darling. They won't let Dennis have her without a court order. She'll be safe."

Maggie fingered her cup with a sigh. It sounded like heaven—to get away from the city, to be able to think in placid surroundings. If only it weren't for Gabriel...

Memories of him had colored her young life for years. He was stamped permanently on her thoughts like an indelible ink. She knew so much about him. Like the time he'd forced some rustlers off the road into a ditch and held the three men with a shotgun until one of his hands got the sheriff there. Then there was the knock-down-drag-out fight with one of his men right in the street.

Maggie had actually witnessed that. Sometimes she wondered if it hadn't happened because of her. She'd been spending a couple of weeks with his sisters at the ranch when she was about sixteen. They'd gone into town with Janet to shop, driven by one of the hands, a new man with too-interested eyes and a way of talking to the young girls that amused Robin and Audrey but terrified Maggie. Gabe had been at the hardware store, right next door to the grocery store where Janet shopped. And when the girls had come out, the new man had put his hand on Maggie's waist and insolently let it drop to her hip in a blatant caress.

Gabe had moved over a rack of shovels with alarming speed, and his powerful fists had made a shuddering mess of the new cowhand. Gabe had fired him on the spot, oblivious to the fascinated stares of passersby, and in language that had colored Maggie's face a bright red.

Gabe had started to move toward her, and with visible apprehension she'd backed away from him, her green eyes wide and frightened. Whatever he'd meant to say never got said. He'd glared at the girls and demanded to know what they were staring at. Then he'd ordered them back to the car and stalked off, lighting a cigarette as calmly as if nothing had happened. The girls had said later that he'd explained the man had gotten in trouble for mistreating an animal. But Maggie had always wondered if it hadn't been because he'd insulted her. It was one of those unfinished episodes that haunted her.

Maybe it had all happened a long time ago, she conceded. Still... Memories were one thing, but living under his roof was quite another. And she definitely preferred to keep Gabe at a safe distance. Like the distance from San Antonio to the Coleman ranch.

But saying no to Janet Coleman was like talking to a wall. Within minutes, Maggie found herself agreeing to the visit.

CHAPTER TWO

IF MAGGIE HAD thought Janet would just go back home and leave Maggie to follow, she was dead wrong. Janet helped her pack and even drove them to the exclusive boarding school to drop Becky off and tell the office where Maggie could be reached if she was needed.

Mrs. Haynes, who ran the school, was a good friend of the family. It was comforting to Maggie to know that the woman was aware of the situation with Dennis and knew not to let him take the child. She still felt uneasy about leaving Becky, but she needed time to think and plan. If she was to keep her daughter, she had to act quickly.

"I hate leaving you here," Maggie told the child as she hugged her goodbye. "Becky, I promise you, as soon as school is out, we'll make some better arrangements, so that you can stay with me all the time."

"You mustn't worry, Mama," Becky said seriously, sounding for all the world like an adult. "I'll be just fine. And as soon as school is out, you come right back here and get me, all right?"

"All right, darling," Maggie promised, smothering an amused smile. "I will. Be a good girl."

Minutes later, Maggie and Janet were on their way to the massive ranch the Colemans owned, which was far to the north of San Antonio, up near Abilene. The nearest town was Junction, a modern little place with just enough stores to qualify for a post office. It even had an airport of sorts.

"I'm sorry I couldn't get Gabriel to fly me here," Janet apologized as they sped up the long highway in the sleek silver Lincoln Mark IV that was the older woman's pride and joy. "But he was busy with roundup and couldn't be bothered," she muttered darkly. "After all, I'm just his mother. Why should I come before the cattle? He couldn't even get a good price for me since I'm too old and tough!"

It was all Maggie could do to keep from laughing. Janet had a dry sense of humor and she was delightful as a companion. Yes, maybe this would turn out for the best after all. It was going to be a nice visit, and she'd be able to put Dennis and the horror of the past into perspective and plan her strategy to keep Becky out of her ex-husband's clutches. If only it weren't for Gabriel...

It was spring and already hot in this part of the world, and the ride was tiring despite the air conditioning and the car's luxurious interior. Janet had to stop frequently for gas and soft drinks and rest rooms. But eventually they passed through the edges of the beautiful hill country, nearing Abilene, and brush turned to lush, cultivated flatland.

"We have two airplanes, after all," Janet continued her chatter as they drove the final few miles. "Not to mention a helicopter." She glanced at Maggie. "You're worn out, aren't you, dear?" She sighed.

"No, not at all," Maggie said gently, and even managed to laugh. It had been a long time since she'd felt like laughing, but there was something very relaxing about Janet's company. "We've seen some beautiful country, and I'm really kind of glad we did it this way. You're tired, though, aren't you?" she probed gently.

"Me?" the older woman scoffed. "My dear, in my youth, I could break wild horses. I'm a Texan."

So was Maggie, and the girl she'd been would have gloried in the challenge of a wild horse. But so much of the spirit had been drained out of her in the past few years. If it hadn't been for Becky, she wasn't sure how long she could have kept her sanity under that kind of pressure.

"I hope you're going to enjoy the ranch," Janet was murmuring as she pulled off onto a graveled road with a huge sign near it that read, "Coleman Ranch, Purebred Santa Gertrudis Cattle."

"I know I will," Maggie promised. She smiled at the sight of the big red-coated cattle grazing behind rugged, rustic fences. "Santa Gertrudis is the only native American breed, isn't it?" she murmured knowledgeably. "Founded on the King Ranch and now famous all over the world. They're so beautiful. . . . Oh, what I wouldn't give for some of my own."

Janet drew in a deep breath, her gaze wistful. "Oh, my dear, if only I'd brought you here sooner..." She shook her head as she turned back to the road and eased the car forward. "It's so ironic. Gabriel is obsessed with cattle. You'd have made the perfect daughter-in-law."

"No matchmaking," Maggie cautioned, feeling herself go taut with apprehension. "With all due respect to your son, the last thing in the world I want is a domineering man in my life again. Okay?"

Janet smiled gently. "Okay. And I wouldn't do that to you, truly. But you are so special, my dear."

She smiled back. "You're pretty special yourself." She glanced toward the big white clapboard house with its graceful long porches and green shutters. It had a faintly colonial look about it, but without the huge columns. There were wicker chairs all over, a big porch swing, and flowers blooming in wild profusion everywhere. It was spectacular.

"It's about the same size as your own, isn't it?" Janet laughed. "My father built it with no particular style in mind. It often draws comment for that."

"It's lovely," Maggie sighed. She glanced toward the long wire fences, frowning. "I expected white fences," she murmured.

Her companion laughed. "Gabriel is tight with a dollar," she teased. "There are hundreds of acres of land here, and fencing is expensive. Especially electric fences, which are all he uses these days. He cuts costs wherever he can. Actually," she added, "it's a full-time job just keeping track of cattle and keeping rustlers out. We only keep purebreds here, and when a bull can bring as much as half a million dollars, you can understand why Gabriel is so careful about security. He has a man full-time to do nothing but maintain security here."

"Good heavens," Maggie exclaimed. "People still rustle cattle?"

"Yes, they do. They come in big trucks. It's been modernized along with cattle ranching, but rustling is still a problem."

"I wouldn't have guessed," Maggie said as Janet pulled up to the steps and stopped. She barely noticed Janet's sudden stiffening or the disturbed look in her eyes; she was too busy watching the man who was approaching the stopped car.

He was tall. Lithe and lean, he walked with an arrogance that immediately put Maggie's back up. He was dressed like a working cowboy, but he moved like no other man she'd ever seen. He was graceful, from the top of his wide-brimmed tan hat to the toes of his worn, warped boots. His dusty leather batwing chaps were flying with the sharp movements of long, powerfully muscled legs, and what she could see of his darkly tanned face under his hat wasn't at all welcoming.

He paused beside the car, and Janet rushed out with an exclamation of pleasure to hug him with the enthusiasm and warmth that seemed so much a part of her. But he drew back sharply.

"For God's sake, stop that!" he bit off, grimacing. He held his side and caught his breath with a hot curse. "I've been bitten by a rattlesnake. The arm's still swollen, and it'll be days before I can get back to work. I don't need it broken!"

Janet flushed, looking flustered and taken aback. "I'm sorry, dear…"

"I can't ride a horse, can't bounce around in the damned trucks, I can't even fly the plane!" He glared at Janet as if it were all her fault. "Landers is even having to drive me around. I've been sicker than an overfed dog."

"I… I'm sorry. You do look pale," Janet said uneasily. "It must be painful."

"I'll live." He looked past Janet to the younger woman, and his chin lifted, his eyes narrowing. He scowled thoughtfully as Maggie stepped from the car, and she saw his eyes under the shadowy brim of the hat.

She was tempted to turn around and run. It was that kind of look. There was nothing welcoming in his lean, sharp-featured countenance. He had a crook in the middle of his nose, as if somebody had broken it. His black eyebrows were as shaggy and thick as the hair on his head, and his protruding brow shadowed eyes as light as candles, as penetrating as only blue eyes could be. His high cheekbones ran down to a firm, hard-looking mouth over a stubborn chin. He wasn't a handsome man, although his face had character and his body was as sensuously powerful as that of a movie star. The fabric of her dreams—in the flesh. But it was no surprise to Maggie that he was thirty-eight and unmarried. It would take a strong woman, a fiery woman, for a man like that. She felt cold chills at the thought of what he might expect of a woman in intimacy.

The feeling must have been mutual, because the look he was giving her spoke volumes. She could imagine how citified she must seem to him, in her lacy white blouse and white slacks, with dainty strapped sandals. She should have worn jeans, she thought belatedly, as she'd planned to in the beginning. Why had she dressed up so? She needed this vacation so badly, and here she'd gone and antagonized him at first glance.

"Gabe, you remember Mary's daughter, Maggie Turner, don't you?" Janet asked.

Maggie stared up at him, watching the fleeting lift of his eyebrows. He looked at her with cold disinterest. "I remember her."

"It's nice to…see you again," she faltered.

He nodded, but he didn't return the greeting. He dismissed her without a second thought and turned back to his mother impatiently as a truck with the ranch logo purred to a stop nearby. "I won't be gone long, but I'm expecting an important call from Cheyenne. If it comes through while I'm gone, have the party call back at five."

"Certainly, dear," Janet agreed. "I'm sorry if I've…we've come at a bad time…"

"Don't you always, Mother?" he asked with a cold smile. "Isn't Europe more your style than dust and cattle?"

"I came to see you," the older woman said with quiet pride.

"I'll be back directly." He turned without another glance and walked to the truck, grimacing despite his iron control as he climbed inside the cab and managed to close the door, waving away the cowboy who offered to help him. They drove off in a cloud of dust.

Janet sighed half-angrily. "I'll never understand him," she said under her breath. "I didn't raise him without manners. I'm sorry, Maggie."

"There's no need to apologize," Maggie said quietly. "I gather that he's in some pain."

"And irritable at having to stay at home when there's work to be done. Roundup is a bad time for everyone. Besides that," she said miserably, "he doesn't like it when I come here. I have to confess that I needed you as much as you needed the rest. I don't like having to cope by myself. But truly, you'll enjoy it. He won't be around much," she added with a hopeful look. "Just until his arm will let him go back to work. Knowing my son," she added bitterly, "it shouldn't take more than a couple of days. Nothing keeps him down for long. He'll convince the doctor that strapping it will accomplish miracles."

"He isn't the most welcoming man," Maggie murmured.

"He'll be gone before you know it. Now come on and let's get settled in," Janet said firmly. "This is my home, too—even if I'm not allowed to visit it very often!"

Maggie didn't reply. She wasn't sure that she'd done the right thing in coming. Gabriel was stone-cold hateful, and time hadn't improved his old dislike of her. She knew instinctively that if his mother hadn't been around, he'd have packed her right back to San Antonio. It wasn't the brightest beginning.

She spent the next two hours reacquainting herself with the big house and getting to know the new cook and housekeeper, whose name was Jennie. She was small and dark and gay, and Maggie liked her immediately.

She settled in, changing her white outfit for jeans and a yellow blouse. She brushed her short hair toward her face and hoped that her appearance wouldn't antagonize the cattleman any further when she went down to have supper with the family.

Gabriel was already at the table, looking furious and glaring at her the minute she walked into the spacious, elegant dining room. In fact, his look was so accusatory that she froze in the doorway, flashing on a line from a dog-training manual about not showing fear and making no sudden moves. Perhaps it would work with the half-civilized cattleman whose mother was obviously kicking him under the table.

"Do join us, dear," Janet said with a glare toward her taciturn son.

"I'm sorry if I've held you up," Maggie said gently, seating herself on the other side of Janet for protection with a wary, green-eyed glance at Gabe that seemed to amuse him.

"Dinner is promptly at six," he returned with a lifted eyebrow. "I don't like being held up, in case you've forgotten." She started to speak, but he cut her off with a lifted hand, ignoring his mother's seething irritation to add mockingly, "I don't bite, Miss Turner," his voice deep and faintly amused.

"Could I have that in writing, please?" she asked with

a nervous laugh. She smiled at Janet. "The air smells so fresh and clean out here. No exhaust fumes!"

"That's right, city girl," Gabe replied. He leaned back carefully, favoring his right side, with his coffee cup in his lean hand. He wasn't even neatly dressed or particularly cleaned up. He was still wearing his work clothes, except that his dusty shirt was open halfway down his tanned chest, where a wedge of thick black hair arrowed toward his wide leather belt. That disturbed Maggie, just as it had in her teens, and she looked down at her plate, fiddling with putting the napkin in her lap.

"I would have cleaned up," he said unexpectedly, a bite in his slow drawl as he obviously mistook her expression for distaste, "but I'd just come in from the holding pens when I went to the doctor, and I'm a bit tired."

Her eyes came up quickly, with an apology in them. "Mr. Coleman, this is your home," she said gently. "I wouldn't be so rude as to criticize how you dress."

He stared at her calculatingly for a long moment—so long that she dropped her gaze again to her plate. Finally, he reached for the platter of beef and helped himself, to his mother's obvious relief.

"How did you get bitten, darling?" Janet asked him.

"I reached for a rope without looking."

Janet gnawed her lip. "It must be painful. You won't be able to work for a few days, I guess."

He gave her a cold stare. "I'm managing. If I felt a little stronger, I could ride. It's just the swelling and the pain, that's all. I won't be stuck here for long, I hope."

Janet started to make a comment, but she forced herself to remain silent. It did no good to argue with him.

He glanced from her to Maggie as he buttered a huge

fluffy biscuit. "What are you doing these days?" he asked curiously.

"Me? I'm working at a bookstore," Maggie told him. She glanced up and down again, hating the surge of heat to her face. He had the most incredible effect on her, even after the anguish of her marriage.

"Working, did you say?" His light eyes lifted and probed hers like a microscope. "Your people were wealthy."

"Times change," she said quietly. "I'm not wealthy now. I'm just a working girl."

"Have some peas, dear." Janet tried to interrupt.

He put the biscuit down and cocked his head, studying her with narrowed eyes. "It shows," he said absently. "You don't look like the spunky little kid who used to play with my sisters. What's happened to you?"

Maggie felt herself going cold. He was watching her, like a cat watching a mouse. She felt vulnerable and a little afraid of that single-mindedness. Once, she would have taken exception to his blunt challenge. But there had been so many fights, so much struggle. Her spirit was carefully buried—had to be, for Becky's sake.

She laid down her fork and stared at him. "I've grown up," she replied, her voice soft.

His level gaze sized her up. "You had money. And now you don't. Then what brings you here, Miss Turner? Are you looking for a vacation or a man to support you?"

"Gabriel!" Janet slammed her napkin down. "How dare you!"

Maggie clasped her hands tightly under the table and stared at him with a courage she didn't really feel. "Your mother offered me a visit, Mr. Coleman," she said dully. "I needed to get away for a little while, that's all. You'll have to excuse me for being so dim, but I didn't realize that I needed your permission as well as Janet's. If you want me to leave…?" She started to rise.

"Oh, for God's sake, sit down," he snapped. His eyes cut into hers. "The last thing I need is a Texas society girl out here at roundup, but if Mother wants you, you're welcome. Just keep to the house," he warned softly, his eyes emphasizing the threat. "And out of my way."

He tossed his own napkin down, ignoring his mother's furious glare.

"I won't get in your way," Maggie said, her voice, her whole manner vulnerable.

Gabriel's pale eyes narrowed as he bent his dark head to light a cigarette, watching her the whole time. "Won't you? What a difference," he added as he took a draw from the cigarette. "The girl I remember was like a young filly, all long legs and excitement and blushing fascination. How you've changed, Maggie Turner."

The comment surprised her. She looked up, feeling hot all over as his eyes searched hers. "You haven't," she blurted out. "You're just as blunt and rude and overbearing as you ever were."

He actually grinned. "Just as mean-tempered, too, honey. So look out," he added as he got to his feet. He groaned a little with the movement and murmured a curse under his breath.

"Can I get you anything?" Janet asked, frowning.

He spared her a cool glance. "Nothing, thank you," he replied formally. He nodded at the women, the brief and unexpected humor gone as he turned and went out the door.

"I'm sorry," Janet told Maggie. "It's roundup, you know.

He gets so ill-tempered, and he doesn't really like women very much."

"He doesn't like me very much, you mean," Maggie said quietly, staring at the tablecloth. "He never did." She smiled wistfully. "Do you know, I once had the most terrible crush on him. He never found out, thank goodness, and I outgrew it. But I used to think he was the whole world."

"And now?" Janet queried gently.

Maggie bit her lower lip and laughed, the sound soft and nervous. "Now, I think I'm a little afraid of him. I'm not sure that coming here was a good idea."

"Oh, yes, it was," Janet said. "I'm certain that it will work out. You'll see. I've got it all planned."

Maggie didn't ask what "it" was, but the man listening outside the door had a face that would have stopped traffic. He'd read an entirely different meaning into Janet's innocent remark, and he was livid with anger. So his mother was matchmaking again. This time she'd picked a woman he knew, although she couldn't know what he'd thought of Maggie Turner. His eyes narrowed. Well, this time his mother had gone too far. And if little Maggie thought she was going to lead him down the aisle, she had a surprise coming. A big one!

He went out the door, his eyes cold with calculation, his steps so soft that no one heard him leave.

Janet shook her head. "I was so sure that he wouldn't be around the house," she said. "He's hurting, but he won't admit it. That's why he was so rude."

"Is he like that with all women?" she probed gently.

Janet picked up a roll and buttered it carefully. "I'll tell you about it, one day," she said quietly, her eyes sad. "For now, let's just say that he had a particularly bad experience, and it was my fault. I've been trying to make it up to him ever since. And failing miserably."

"Can't you talk to him about it?" Maggie asked.

Janet only laughed. "Gabriel has a habit of walking off when he doesn't want to hear me. He won't listen. I tried, once, to explain what happened. He cut me dead and went to Oklahoma on a business trip. After that…well, I suppose I just lost my nerve. My son can be very intimidating."

"I remember," came the dry reply.

Janet smiled at her. "Yes. You understand, don't you? You know, I never even told him that you'd married. He had an odd way of ignoring me if I mentioned you, after that summer you spent some time here. You remember, when he had the fight in town with that cowboy…?"

Maggie actually blushed and couldn't hide it from Janet. "Oh, yes. How could I forget?"

"He wouldn't talk about you at all after that. He seemed preoccupied for a long time, and a little strange, in fact," she mused. "He filled in our swimming pool and wouldn't let anyone ride Butterball…"

Something barely remembered, exciting, stirred deep inside Maggie. He'd given her Butterball to ride, and she could still see him towering over her, his lean hands working with the cinch. She'd adored him in those days, despite his evident antagonism toward her. Even that was inexplicable, because he got along well with most women. He was polite and courteous to everyone—except Maggie.

"He's still not pleased to have me around," Maggie murmured.

"Well, it's my home, too," Janet said doggedly. "And I love having you here. Do have some more beef. It's our own, you know."

"Purebred Santa Gertrudis?" Maggie exclaimed in horror, staring blankly at the platter Janet was offering her.

"What?" Then Janet got the message and laughed. "No, no, dear. Gabriel raises some beef cattle as well. Purebred... oh, that's sinfully amusing. Gabriel would eat his horse before he'd eat one of the purebreds. Here, have a roll to go with it. Jennie bakes them fresh every day."

Maggie took one, savoring it, and not for the first time she had misgivings about the wisdom of coming here. Gabriel seemed to be out for blood, and she wondered if the Coleman ranch wasn't going to become a combat zone.

CHAPTER THREE

IT *WAS* VAGUELY like living in a war zone, Maggie thought as the first few days went by. Gabriel was impatient and irritable because of his arm, and he seemed to hate the whole world. Nothing pleased him—least of all, it appeared, having Maggie in the house. He treated her with a cold formality that raised goose bumps on her arms. It was obvious that he was tolerating her for his mother's sake alone. And just in case she hadn't already guessed it on her own, he spelled it out for her at breakfast three days after she'd arrived.

He glanced up coldly when she sat down. It was just the two of them, because his mother was still upstairs. She and Maggie had been up late talking the night before, and Janet seemed to sleep poorly, anyway.

"I'm sorry, am I late?" she asked, throwing out a white flag.

He smoked his cigarette quietly, his icy eyes level and cutting. "Do you care, one way or another?" he asked.

She took a deep breath. "I realize you don't want me here…"

"That's an understatement." He rolled the cigarette between his lean, dark fingers while he studied her. "What did she offer you to get you down here, Margaret?" he added suddenly, using her name for the first time since she'd been at the ranch.

Her eyes widened. "N-nothing," she stammered. "I just needed some rest, that's all."

"Rest from what?" he persisted. His pale eyes cut into hers. "You're thin. You always were, but not like this. You're pale, too, and you look unwell. What's going on, Margaret? What are you running from? And why run to me?"

Her face went white. She caught her breath. "As if I would *ever* run to you…!"

"Don't be insulting." He lifted the cigarette to his chiseled lips, watching her. "Talk to me."

She was closing up, visibly, her body taut with nerves. "I can't."

"You won't," he corrected. He smiled slowly, but it wasn't a pleasant smile. It was impatient and half angry. "I'm not blind. I know my mother, I know how her mind works. You're the sacrifice, I gather. Are you a willing one, I wonder?"

"I don't understand," she said, bewildered.

"You will," he promised, making a threat of the words. He got to his feet, more easily now than he had three days ago. He was improving rapidly; he even looked better.

"I came to visit with Janet—not to get in your way, Gabriel," she tried one last time, hating her lack of spirit.

Gabriel seemed frozen in place. It was the first time she'd said his name since she arrived. He looked at her and felt a wave of heat hit him like a whirlwind in the chest. Odd, how it had always disturbed him to look at her, to be around her. She got under his skin. And now it was worse, now that she was vulnerable. It irritated him to see her like this and not know why. Was it an act? Was it part of the plan his mother had mentioned when she'd thought he was out of earshot? He was wary of the whole damned situation, and the way Maggie affected him after all these years was the last straw.

"In my way, or in my bed, Maggie?" he asked, deliberately provoking. "Because you wanted me when you were sixteen. I knew it, felt it when you looked at me. Do you still want me, honey?"

Her face paled, and she dropped her eyes to her faded jeans, staring dully at her slender hands. The old Maggie would have snapped back at him. But the old Maggie was dead, a casualty of her marriage to a cruel and brutal man. She felt sick all over.

"Don't," she whispered, closing her eyes. "Don't."

"Look at me!" He stared down at her with his cold blue eyes until she obeyed him. Dimly, she noticed he was wearing jeans and a long-sleeved chambray shirt with worn, warped leather boots. In one lean, strong hand, a battered gray Stetson dangled. "You and Mother don't have a chance in hell of pulling it off," he said quietly. "Give it up. I don't want to hurt you."

And with that enigmatic statement, he turned and strode angrily out the door.

She didn't tell Janet about the confrontation. And afterward, she made it her business to be where he wasn't. He glared at her as if he hated her very presence, but she pretended not to notice. And around his mother, at least, he was courteous enough in his cold way.

She wondered if he'd ever loved anyone or been loved. He seemed so unapproachable; even his men kept their distance unless they had urgent business. He had little to say to them and even less to say to his mother. He seemed to dislike her, in fact, for all that he'd warned Maggie not to cause her any sleepless nights.

"He keeps everyone at bay, doesn't he?" Maggie asked one afternoon when she was strolling around the yard with Janet. The two women had just watched Gabriel walk away from a man trying to ask a question near the back porch.

Janet stared after him worriedly, her thin arms folded across her chest. "He always has," she said. "I don't think he's ever forgiven me for remarrying so soon after his father's death. The fact that he hated my second husband made it worse. He was...badly treated," she confessed, biting her lower lip as the memories came back. "Stepfathers are reluctant fathers at best. Ben liked Audrey and Robin enough, of course. They were just pretty little girls and no threat to him. But Gabe was a big boy, almost a teenager. He wound up fighting for his very life. Ben shipped him off to a boarding school, and I—" she lowered her eyes "—I was caught between the two of them. I loved them both. But I couldn't find the magic formula for making them live together. It was that way until Ben died. That was when Gabe was just out of the Marine Corps." She shrugged. "He came back and started to pick up the pieces of his father's ranch—and there were few, because my second husband was much better at spending money than making it. Gabe was bitter about it. He still is."

"That doesn't seem enough to make a man as cold as he is," Maggie probed gently.

Janet stared toward the tall man who was busy saddling a horse out in the corral. "You might as well know it all," she said quietly. "The year before Ben died, Gabriel found a young woman who seemed to worship him. He brought her here, to meet us, and she stayed for two weeks. During that time, Ben was very attentive and managed to convince her that he was in control of all the finances here and all the money." Shamefaced, Janet closed her eyes. "Ben ate up the attention. He was dying, you see. He had cancer, and not long to live. Gabe didn't know. But Ben was so flattered by the girl's attention—he was just a man, after all. I couldn't even blame him. But Gabe lost her, and blamed Ben. And blamed me. Afterward, I tried to tell him, to explain, but he wouldn't listen. He never would. To this day, he doesn't know. You see, Ben actually died of a heart attack. I didn't even tell the girls about the cancer."

"Oh, Janet, I'm sorry," Maggie said, touching the stooped shoulder lightly. "I'm so sorry. I shouldn't have asked."

"There, there, it was a long time ago," the older woman said through a stiff smile. "Gabe, needless to say, never got over it. Nor did he understand why I didn't leave Ben. After Ben died, Gabe came back from the service and stayed here, but the distance between us has been formidable. I think sometimes that he hates me. I've tried so hard, Maggie," she said softly. "I've tried so hard to show him that I care, that I was sorry, for so many things. I suppose playing Cupid was just another way of making restitution. But even that backfired."

"People don't hold grudges forever," Maggie said gently.

"Don't they?" Janet replied, and her eyes were on her son, who was just mounting his horse. She shook her head and laughed. "I wonder."

"Have you told him about Becky?" Maggie asked suddenly. "Or why I'm really here?"

"Not yet," Janet confessed. "I've been waiting for the right time."

"He doesn't want me here," Maggie said. "And perhaps I should go back to San Antonio."

"No," Janet said firmly, "this is my home, too. I have a right to invite people here. He won't stop me. Or you."

"Janet, I'm so tired of fighting...."

"We'll keep out of his way," Janet assured her. "He'll be back at work in no time, you'll see, and then we'll have the place all to ourselves."

But she sounded no more certain than Maggie felt. And her apprehension intensified when Janet hesitantly asked Gabriel the next morning if he had a horse Maggie could ride.

"Please, I don't need to..." Maggie began quickly, noticing the dangerous look in Gabe's pale eyes.

"No, I don't have a spare horse," Gabe replied with a cold glare at Maggie. "I'm trying to get my calves branded, tagged and inoculated, and my herd out to summer pasture. Meanwhile, I'm being driven crazy by new hands who have to be led around like kids, I'm trying to keep supplies on hand with my ranch foreman off on sick leave, I'm a week behind on paperwork that my secretary can't do alone... I don't have time to be hounded by tourists!"

"Gabriel, there's no need to be rude," Janet chided.

He stood up. "She's your guest, not mine," he told his mother. "If you want her entertained, you entertain her."

And without another word, he left them sitting there, arrogantly lighting a cigarette as he went.

Maggie shivered as she stared after him half-angrily. "A person could freeze to death just sitting near him," she muttered.

Janet shook her head and reached for her coffee. "I'm so sorry."

"You aren't responsible for his actions, and at least now I understand a little better than I did," Maggie told her with a smile. "It's all right. I'd like to stroll around a little, if you don't mind."

"I don't mind," Janet returned. "Just do stay out of his way, darling," she cautioned.

"You can count on that!" Maggie laughed.

She went out the back door, in fact, tugging on a yellow windbreaker over her beige blouse and jeans. It was still a little nippy, but she loved the coolness. She loved the outdoors, the land stretching lazily to the horizon, dotted with mesquite trees and prickly-pear cacti and wildflowers.

It was so different from her home in the middle of downtown San Antonio, so removed from urban traffic. Although the city was delightful and there was plenty to see and do, and colorful markets to visit, she was a country girl at heart. She loved the land with a passion she'd never given to anything else. Even now, with an enemy in residence, she could hardly contain her excitement at having so much land to explore, to savor.

She walked from the backyard down to the fence that stretched to the stables and stared over it at the few horses that were left. Most of them had gone out with the cowboys who were working the far-flung herds of cattle.

Her eyes were wistful as she stared at a huge black stallion. There wasn't a patch of white anywhere on him, and he looked majestic in the early-morning light. He tossed his mane and pranced around like a thoroughbred, as if he knew that he had an audience and was determined to give it its money's worth.

"Do you ride?"

The rough question startled her. She whirled, surprised to find Gabriel Coleman leaning against one of the large oak trees in the backyard, calmly smoking a cigarette while he stared at her.

She shifted a little. He looked bigger than ever in that old long-sleeved chambray shirt, and its color emphasized the lightness of his eyes under the wide brim of his hat. He was formidable in work clothes. So different from Dennis, who'd always seemed a bit prissy to Maggie.

"I...don't ride very well," she confessed.

He nodded toward the stallion. "I call him Crow. He was a thoroughbred with a bright future. But he killed a man and was going to be put down. I bought him and I ride him, but no one else does. There isn't a more dangerous animal on the place, so don't get any crazy ideas."

"I wouldn't dream of taking a horse without asking first," she said levelly. "Perhaps you're used to more impetuous women. I'm careful. I don't rush in without thinking."

His eyes narrowed at the insinuation, and he took a long draw from his cigarette. "Then why are you down here?" he asked coldly.

"Your mother invited me," she said.

"Why?"

"Why do you think?" she countered.

He smiled, and it wasn't friendly. He threw down the cigarette and moved toward her.

It was a deserted area. The house was hidden by a grove of oaks and pecan trees, and none of the men were around. Maggie, who'd had nightmares about physical intimacy since her marriage, began to back away until the cold bark of another oak tree halted her.

"Nervous?" he chided, and kept coming. "What of? I heard what Mother said the first night you were here. I know what you came for, Maggie. So why run away from it?"

She felt her body going rigid as he loomed over her, her eyes wide and green and frightened. "You don't understand…" she began.

"So you keep telling me," he said shortly. He rested his hands on either side of her head, blocking off all the exits, and he smelled of wind and fir trees and leather as he came even closer, favoring his right side a little where the arm was swollen.

"What is this?" she breathed.

"You're another consolation prize," he said with a mocking smile. "My mother thinks it's her fault that I'm such a lonely man. She brings me women by the gross. But I'm getting damned tired of being handed women on silver platters. When I marry, if I marry, I can choose my own bride. And I'll want something fresh and warm and sweet-smelling. A country girl—not a social butterfly who's been passed around like a plate of hors d'oeuvres."

Her lips opened to retaliate, but he pressed his thumb over them in a movement that startled her into silence. He'd always seemed like a cold, indifferent sort of man, but there was experience in the way he played with her mouth, and her surprise widened her eyes. How incredible, after all these years, to be this way with him, to see him as a man instead of an enemy; to feel the impact of his masculinity in a different way, a sensual way. Yes, he was experienced. His eyes told her so, and she wondered how she could have thought him cold when just the brush of his finger against her warm mouth was sending her mad.

"Yes, you like that, don't you, Maggie?" he whispered, his voice deep and slow and faintly contemptuous. "You didn't realize how sensitive your mouth was, did you? It can be teased and provoked into begging for a man's lips," he said softly, tracing the upper lip with the very edge of his thumb so that he could feel the moist underside and watch its sudden helpless trembling. "Like that," he murmured, increasing the pressure, seeing her face flush, her lips part involuntarily. Her body tautened, and he smiled because he knew why.

"No," she said on a sobbing breath, and even as she said it, she realized that he wasn't paying the least attention. He was powerfully made; she could feel the strength of him threatening her, the warmth that radiated from him with a leathery scent not at all unpleasant. Years ago, she'd dreamed of being touched, kissed, by him. She'd wanted him, and she'd known he was aware of it. But she'd also known, as he had, that such a thing was forbidden between them—because of her age. Her age had protected her...then. And she'd thought he was too cold to be tempted. Fool!

"Did you ever wonder?" he asked unexpectedly, tilting her chin as he bent. "Did you ever wonder how my mouth would feel moving on yours?"

Tears stung her eyes. It was fascinating that she could feel like this with him, that she could be hungry, physically, after what Dennis had done to her. She felt her own fingernails gripping the hard muscles of his upper arms, tugging gently. "Gabe," she whispered, giving in to the raging attraction.

"What did my mother offer you, Maggie?" he breathed against her mouth.

"Offer...me?" she whispered brokenly.

He moved closer, his legs suddenly trapping hers, his body demanding as his mouth hovered warmly over her lips. "She brought you down here for me. She's given up bringing me career girls, so now she's dredging up old memories. She wants me to marry you."

"Marry…you?" It was barely penetrating her hazy mind.

"Don't pretend," he said. His eyes were cold, not lover-like, as they met hers. "I heard you both plotting. Well, I'm not in the market for a wife, little Maggie," he said curtly. "But if you want to play around, I'm more than willing. You always did burn me up…."

Even as the last word faded in the air, his mouth came down on hers. But the tenderness she'd expected wasn't there. He was rough, as if the feel and taste of her had suddenly taken away his control. He made a sound, deep in his throat, and groaned as he pulled her too close and hurt his swollen arm. But he didn't let go. If anything, he was more ardent.

She felt his rough heartbeat and felt his strength with mute terror. "No!" she burst out. "Not…like this!" She tried to twist away from him.

He caught her hips with his, pressing them back against the rough bark of the tree. "What's the matter?" he taunted, lifting his mouth long enough to look down at her. "Does it take the promise of a wedding ring to get you in the mood?" His mocking voice sounded odd. Deep and slow and faintly strained.

Tears welled up behind her closed eyelids. Men weren't so different after all, she thought miserably. Sex was the only thing they wanted. Just sex. It was Dennis all over again, showing her how much stronger he was, forcing her to yield, taking what he wanted without the least thought of her comfort. She began to cry.

"Is it that bad?" he asked, his voice even and cold.

Her lips trembled. "I don't want…that," she whispered

brokenly. "I don't want anyone. I just want...to be left alone."

He scowled. It seemed to get through to him finally that she was suffering him. Just that. Just suffering what he was doing to her. He could have sworn there was desire in her, at the beginning. But now she only looked afraid. She was as stiff as a rail, unyielding, cold.

With an economy of motion, he released her. She folded her arms across her breasts, trembling as she looked at him.

"Why the pretense?" he asked calculatingly. "Didn't my mother tell you why she invited you here?"

She swallowed, clutching herself tighter against a sudden burst of wind. "Listen," she began, her voice shaking a little with reaction. "The only reason I came here was for some peace of mind. I have no inclination whatsoever to be your...your wife or your mistress or even your friend. It would suit me very well if I never saw you again!"

"Then why are you here?" he demanded coldly.

She smiled shakily. "I'm running away," she confessed. "Trying to find a way to keep my ex-husband from taking my little girl away from me. She's terrified of him, and so am I. He's remarried and has most of my money. And in a lawsuit for custody, I'll very likely lose. My daughter has a trust, you see. Dennis wants control of it."

He stared at her as if he'd been struck from behind. "Ex-husband?"

She nodded.

"Did he get the divorce, or did you?" he asked coldly.

"I did," she confessed.

"Poor man."

"He had enough women to console him, before and after," she returned, her voice empty and dull.

His chin lifted as he looked down at her. "Are you that cold in bed?" he asked, half angry and half frustrated because he'd wanted her and he'd thought she'd wanted him back.

She stared at him unblinkingly, without speaking, until he had the grace to turn away, as if his own question had shocked him.

"Where is your daughter?"

She moved away from the tree slowly, careful to keep some distance between them. He lit another cigarette and leaned back against the tree she'd just vacated to study her curiously.

"She's in boarding school in San Antonio," she said. "Janet said that I could bring her here..."

"Hell!" he ground out.

"You don't need to worry about more people cluttering up your ranch," she said with what little pride she had left. "I'll be leaving as soon as the next bus is out, and Becky won't be coming up here, I promise." She shuddered as she looked at him, feeling the force of his masculinity even at a distance. She could still taste him on her mouth. "If there's no bus today, I'll hitchhike."

His pale eyes narrowed. "Afraid of me?" he taunted.

"Yes." And it was no lie.

He took a draw from the cigarette. "And what will you tell my mother about your abrupt departure?"

"I'll think of something."

"She'll be upset," he returned. "I've got enough trouble without having her in hysterics."

"I don't want—"

"How old is the girl?" he asked curiously.

"She's just six."

"What in hell is she doing in a boarding school, then?" he demanded. "What kind of mother are you?"

Tears threatened. "I have to work," she whispered. "I was afraid to leave her at home after school and on Saturdays, afraid Dennis might try to kidnap her. He threatened that. At the school, she's protected. He'd need a court order."

He sighed heavily. "What a hell of a life for a child that age."

He ought to know, she thought suddenly, and almost said it. But she had enough on her plate without deliberately antagonizing him.

"When does she get out of school?" he persisted.

"Next week. Next Friday."

He studied his cigarette for a long moment, then those cold eyes touched Maggie's face. "All right. Bring her here. But the two of you keep the hell out of my way, is that clear?"

"I don't want to stay here…"

"You'll stay," he returned shortly. "It's too late now. I won't have Mother upset. Besides," he added, "at least you won't be running after me like her other 'guests.'"

"That's a fair statement."

He looked down his crooked nose at her, his hard lips smiling quietly. "Did I bruise you, honey?" he said in a tone that curled her toes. "I wanted to do that when you were sixteen. And you might as well not look so shocked. You wanted me to do it when you were sixteen."

She lowered her eyes. It was the truth. He'd been her very dream of perfection.

"Maggie."

She looked up again, her large green eyes sweeping his hard, dark face. "Yes?"

He shouldered away from the tree and caught her sudden withdrawal from him. His eyes narrowed thoughtfully.

"All right," he said with the first gentleness he'd shown since her arrival. "I won't touch you again. You'd better do something about your lip. I cut it when I kissed you."

She touched it with a finger and found a trace of blood there. She hadn't felt it. But she hadn't experienced so much emotional turmoil since her divorce.

He pulled out a handkerchief and offered it, noticing that she went to great lengths to avoid any contact with him when she took it and dabbed at her lip.

Her face felt hot, her knees weak. Odd that he should have such a profound effect on her. Perhaps it was just reaction.

"He hurt you, didn't he?" he asked suddenly, his gaze forceful. "He hurt you sexually."

She swallowed. "Yes."

"Then for God's sake, why have his child?" he demanded.

"I didn't have a lot of choice," she said, hiding her face.

He lit another cigarette, keeping his eyes on the match so that she wouldn't see them. He mumbled something harsh and forceful.

"It's all past history now," she said, and lifted her eyes. "I just want to pick up the pieces and raise my daughter. I don't want to trap you into marriage, honestly. I don't want anything to do with men, ever again. So I'll be glad to keep out of your way, if you'll stay out of mine."

He lifted his chin as he drew on the cigarette. "I don't bargain, honey."

"Don't call me that," she said coolly.

"I always used to. Have you forgotten?" he asked, his

voice oddly quiet. "I never tossed those words around like some men do, either. Too bad you didn't listen." Before she could pursue that, he was off on another subject. "Do you have a good lawyer?"

She shifted. "I suppose so."

"I'll make sure you do before the custody suit comes up."

"Listen here, Gabriel—"

"You were the only woman who ever called me that," he murmured, smoking his cigarette while he studied her. "I like it."

She tried again. "I don't want—"

"I'll fly you to get the little girl," he added, turning. "Let me know a day beforehand, so that I can arrange things."

"Will you listen!"

His eyebrows shot up. "To what?"

"I can arrange my own life…."

"You've made a hash of things, from what I've seen."

"I can do without your opinion!"

"Pity. You could use a few pointers. And before you jump to any conclusions," he added maddeningly, "I take back my offer to play around with you. In fact, I'll be generous and take back every damned thing I've said since you came here." He pursed his lips as he searched her puzzled eyes. "You're like a virgin, aren't you? Afraid of sex, nervous of men…"

The blush got worse. Her fists clenched beside her body. "Are you quite through?"

"For now." He pulled the hat lower over his eyes. "Stay away from that stallion," he cautioned again.

She glared after him. Overbearing, domineering… She held the handkerchief to her lip again and caught a whiff of his spicy cologne. Why that scent should make her heart race was beyond her reasoning. Before she could wonder about her reaction, however, she turned furiously and went back into the house.

She spent a restless night worrying about whether or not she should just go back to San Antonio and make a stand there, without a vacation.

Her mind laughed at that. Some vacation, with Gabriel Coleman making vicious passes at her and threatening to take over her whole life. Of course, she had to admit that he'd gotten the whole situation wrong because of Janet's past matchmaking. And what he'd overheard that first night could have sounded like a plan to trap him at the altar.

She flushed, remembering what she'd confessed about having had a crush on him. Had he heard that, too? It would have been hard to miss, though, because at sixteen her eyes had followed him everywhere. The girls had even teased her about being so taken with him, and she didn't doubt that they'd told him, too.

He'd always been more man than the average woman could handle. Something in her had always been, and still was, a little afraid of him. But underneath the cold, hard exterior, there seemed to be a surprisingly gentle man. She'd had a glimpse of that, and she'd warmed to it helplessly. Gentleness was the one thing she'd never had from Dennis, who took and gave nothing in return. Looking back, she could see his deviousness with clear eyes. But at eighteen she'd been flattered by his charming attentions and been on fire to marry and have children.

How sad, she thought as she closed her eyes, that so often what people wanted the most was the last thing that could make them happy. What was the old saying about being careful what you wished for because you might get it? She wished she'd been a little more clearheaded at eighteen. Perhaps if her parents hadn't moved to Austin, perhaps if Gabriel had really been interested in her, if he'd come courting...

She went to sleep and dreamed about that. And woke up warm all over. It seemed the scars weren't quite as deep as she'd thought—or else how could she have that kind of dream about Gabriel?

CHAPTER FOUR

MAGGIE MANAGED TO keep Janet from finding out about her disastrous confrontation with Gabe. As for him, his attitude toward her was a little less hostile. He made no more passes at her, and he stopped baiting her. But there was no drastic change in his manner. He was much as he had been before he'd learned the truth. If he felt anything at all except irritation, he hid it well. Perhaps he'd learned over the years to keep his deepest emotions hidden, Maggie thought. Heaven knew he'd had reason to.

His arm was still giving him brief twinges of pain—that was obvious—but a few days later he climbed on a horse despite the discomfort and rode out to help his men. He was kept busy, disability notwithstanding, with the separate herds of cattle, as he and his men worked increasingly long hours. Janet seemed relieved, although she didn't say anything.

The following Thursday night, Maggie was forced to wait up for Gabe. He'd promised to fly down to get Becky the next day. And it was either that or ask Janet to face the long drive into San Antonio on her behalf. Maggie laughed mirthlessly, thinking about the past, when she could easily have chartered a plane to take her. Thanks to Dennis and his spendthrift ways, that was no longer an option. If only she'd had more backbone in the beginning! If only she hadn't knuckled under! But she'd made her own bed by refusing to take action, and now she was paying for it horribly.

When Janet started upstairs about nine o'clock, Gabe still hadn't come home. Maggie was reading a book on the sofa, curled up under a lap blanket in jeans and a multicolored pullover blouse.

"Are you going to stay up for a while?" Janet asked casually.

"I'm waiting for him," Maggie said, knowing that the older woman would understand she meant Gabe. "He said he'd fly me down to get Becky tomorrow if I'd remind him. I have to see if he meant it."

"My son never says things he doesn't mean," Janet said, and actually seemed to relax. "I didn't know you'd told him about Becky, although I had a few suspicions. He's stopped cutting at you so much."

"Not noticeably." Maggie sighed. "Yes, I told him. I mentioned getting a bus, and he wouldn't hear of it. But I don't know how he'll manage time."

"Stand back and watch." Janet grinned. "Oh, my dear, I'm so glad he offered. I wouldn't have minded driving down with you…"

"But it's a tiring trip," she reminded the older woman. "It was kind of him to offer."

"I think he's curious about your daughter," Janet said suddenly. "He's not an easy man to get along with, but he loves children. It's something of a tragedy that he never married, you know. He would have been a good father."

That was surprising. He didn't seem the kind of man who would warm to a child, but Maggie knew she was no judge of men—not after the brutal mistake she'd made.

Long after Janet had gone upstairs, Maggie thought over

what she'd said about her taciturn son. He was such an enigma. He wasn't handsome; in fact, he was rather plain. And although his mother seemed to think he was unable to attract women, Maggie knew he wasn't an inexperienced man. He'd known exactly what he was doing when he'd made that pass at her in the backyard. If it hadn't been for her unfortunate marriage, it might have been difficult not to respond to his ardor. His mouth had been hard and warm and very, very expert, and something deep inside her had reacted wildly to the taste of him, although she'd kept him from knowing it.

The sound of the front door opening disturbed her thoughts. She let the book lie open in her lap and looked into the hall. The glimpse she got of the real Gabriel Coleman in that instant was fascinating.

He didn't know anyone was around, and all the mocking arrogance was gone. He was quiet and solemn, and he looked every year of his age. Dust covered him from his blue check shirt to his stained jeans and wet boots. His black hair was disheveled and damp as well, and his face was heavily lined. He tossed his hat onto the hall table and dropped the wide leather chaps he'd just discarded onto the floor. He stretched, his hard muscles shuddering a little with the strain they'd been under. Then, as he looked toward the living room and saw Maggie watching him, all the hardness returned to his face, and to his pale, penetrating eyes.

"Couldn't you sleep?" he asked with a mocking smile. "If you're looking for the obvious remedy, sorry, I'm too tired to oblige."

As she searched his face quietly, it suddenly dawned on her that he didn't really mean half the cutting things he said. They seemed to be a kind of camouflage to keep women from getting close to him, from looking beneath the savage surface. And at that realization, all the hot words poised on the tip of her tongue faded away, forgotten.

"You said you'd fly me down to San Antonio to get Becky tomorrow," she said gently. "I hate to remind you since you look so tired."

His face froze, as if the unexpected compassion had off-balanced him. "I remember."

She got to her feet. Bare feet, because she hated shoes, and hers were under a chair somewhere. "I don't know if you have time now, with things so hectic here," she continued, facing him beside the couch. "I need to know, so that I can make other arrangements...."

He had just noticed her bare feet, and it seemed as if he were having problems keeping back a grin. "Lost your shoes, Cinderella?"

Her bare toes wiggled. "I hate shoes," she muttered. "I even got Becky into the habit around the house, and when she went back to school, she got kept in at recess for it."

"Does she like it at that school?" he asked unexpectedly.

"I suppose so." Maggie hesitated. "She doesn't talk about it. She's a very shy child." She frowned. "She's so easily upset. Perhaps it would be better if I just went home now."

He cocked an eyebrow and slowly lit a cigarette, without once moving his eyes from her face. "What are you afraid of? That I'll upset her? You might be surprised at the way she reacts to my temper, city girl. Most people around here aren't that intimidated by it."

"Of course not," she agreed innocently. "That's why your men hide in the bushes every morning until you're out of sight."

That did produce a smile, of sorts. "Kids see more than

adults," he returned mysteriously. "I'll have to get things organized before I can leave. We'll get away about nine."

"You're sure you don't mind?" she persisted.

"I don't put myself out for anyone unless it suits me," he said curtly.

"Then, thank you. I'll be ready."

She started past him, only to find his strong hand on her upper arm, halting her beside him.

"How old are you now?" he asked, his eyes all too close, too searching. It didn't help that her gaze dropped to his hard mouth and remembered vividly its exciting touch.

"I—I'm twenty-five," she stammered.

He studied her quietly. "I'm thirty-eight."

"Yes, I know."

His eyes probed hers in a silence that began to simmer, until the world narrowed to the space they occupied. He turned, just a little, and the cigarette went careening into a large ashtray so that both lean hands could hold her there.

She flinched, and he shook his head.

"No," he said softly. Softly! It was the first time she'd heard that slow, tender note in his deep voice. "I won't be rough with you. Not ever again."

Her body seemed to vibrate as she looked up at him un-comprehendingly.

"I've never deliberately hurt a woman before," he said slowly. "It's just that I've had so damned many prospective brides flung at my head...." His hands slid up her arms, over her shoulders, to cup her face. "I don't like having you flinch from me, Margaret," he whispered, bending. "So I'm going to show you what it should have been like."

"But I don't..." she whispered unsteadily.

He poised there, his pale eyes narrow and flashing as they met hers. "Say my name," he breathed roughly.

"Gabe..."

As the syllable faded, he took it into his mouth. Her eyelids trembled and then closed. It was nothing like before. His lips were hard and warm but softly probing this time, brushing, lifting, savoring in a sweet tasting that was beyond her experience of men.

"That's it," he whispered against her slowly parting lips. "That's right, let me have your mouth. I won't hurt it this time."

A tiny, soundless sob broke as he parted her lips tenderly and fit his own to them with a warm, maddening pressure that made her body ache with new and unexpected sensations.

Her hands opened over his shirt, feeling muscle and the soft prickliness of hair underneath their cool palms. His heart was beating slowly, regularly, until her nails contracted, and then his chest began to rise and fall quickly.

His lean fingers stroked gently through her hair, tilting her head back, his mouth insistent as it probed hers in a rhythm that surprised a moan from her.

She felt one of his hands spread against her cheek, and while his mouth was tormenting hers, his thumb rubbed across her lips, sensitizing them, grazing them against her teeth. She made another sound, one she didn't even recognize, and her nails bit into his chest.

"Gabriel." Was that whimper coming from her lips? She was reaching up without realizing it, trying to get closer, to make him kiss her more ardently, more completely.

He obliged her with lazy indulgence, forcing her head back against his shoulder with the hungry but controlled pressure of his mouth opening on hers. She felt his tongue teasing her lips, tasting their inner softness, and her body seemed to throb where it sought his.

One lean hand moved then, easing down over her shoulder to the soft blouse, finding only softer woman beneath it, and no bra—finding a hard peak that aroused him beyond bearing. His hand slid farther down, over her narrow waist, the curve of her hip, and around to the base of her spine. He drew her hips in slowly until they merged with his, and he gloried in her sudden trembling as she felt the fierce arousal of his body.

"No," she pleaded, trying feebly to turn her head. "Oh, you mustn't!"

He didn't insist. His hand slid back up to her face, brushing away the damp hair, tilting her chin so that he could look into her misty, dazed eyes above a mouth that was parted and softly swollen from his kisses.

"Was he ever able to make you want him?" he whispered softly.

"No...oh, not ever like this," she sobbed, hating her inability to lie to him.

His fingers caressed her face gently. "There's nothing to be embarrassed about," he said, his voice deep and slow as he watched her. "You're pretty much a novice, despite your marriage. An experienced man knows how to make himself acceptable to a woman."

She was still trying to get her breath back, and his body against hers was warm and hard and welcome. "You've... had women," she whispered, searching the eyes that weren't so hard after all.

He nodded. He looked down at her yielding body, then back up at her parted lips. "And with very little effort, I could have you," he said quietly. "But that isn't what I want. This was a nonverbal apology, nothing more. I don't need the practice."

Before she could react to that, he eased her away, steadying her. "Want something to drink?" he asked then, as casually as if they'd just met.

"A...a brandy."

"Sit down. I'll get it."

She curled up in an armchair, her heart beating wildly, her eyes like green saucers in a face flushed with unexpected pleasure.

He dashed brandy into two snifters, passed her one and perched on the arm of her chair while she sipped at it with jerky motions.

"I...should go home," she burst out, thinking out loud.

"Why?" he asked. "I won't seduce you." He tilted her chin up and looked into her eyes, noting her scarlet blush, her quickened breathing. "More than likely, I'd get you pregnant," he said with more amusement than irritation.

"No, you wouldn't," she replied, her voice still a trifle unsteady. "I'm on the pill. I had a slight female dysfunction, and the doctor put me on it to regulate me. So I'm not...vulnerable that way."

His eyebrows arched and he smiled slowly. "Then suppose you come up to bed with me."

"I don't believe in that kind of thing," she said quietly.

"No wedding ring, no sex?" he taunted. "How old-fashioned of you, Miss Margaret."

"Anyway," she countered, staring at her drink, "sex isn't all that fabulous for women."

"Think so?" Again he tilted her chin to force her eyes

up to his. "I've had women claw my back raw, and it wasn't because I was hurting them."

She flushed to the roots of her hair, barely able to breathe at all.

"I could make you claw me, too," he breathed at her lips. "I could make you writhe like a wild thing under my body and scream with the need to have me."

"You shouldn't...say things like that," she said brokenly.

"You're more a virgin than a divorced woman with a child," he returned, searching her eyes. "Was there any other man?"

"No," she whispered. "Only...him."

"In the ways that count, you're untouched," he murmured. "A walking green-eyed challenge. Too bad, Margaret, that we didn't ignore the obstacles all those years ago and take what we really wanted from each other. I might have broken your young heart, but I'd have made you whole in every other way. We have an unusually potent chemical reaction to each other. We always did."

She knew that, but it didn't make her feel particularly good to have it reduced to technical terms.

He threw down the rest of his brandy and stood up, his back to her. "You'd better get some rest, honey. We'll have a long trip ahead of us."

"Yes. Of course." She finished her own brandy, put the snifter down and stood up.

He turned, towering over her. "He cowed you, didn't he?" he asked unexpectedly, his eyes narrow, calculating. "You're nothing like the woman I remember. All that sweet wildness I used to watch in you is gone."

"I got tired of being slapped down," she replied. "He got his revenge...in bed."

"Oh, God," he breathed roughly.

She looked up, searching his eyes. "You'd never be cruel that way," she said, knowing it. "You might cut a woman with words, but you'd never be physically cruel. Even that day, in the backyard, you didn't really hurt me."

"Didn't I?" he said curtly. "I cut your mouth."

It seemed to bother him that he had. She put a finger to his lower lip, where her own teeth had bitten into it in her passion minutes before. He stiffened at the light contact.

"I cut yours," she whispered.

His jaw clenched and his breathing was audible. "In passion," he whispered back. "Not in anger."

She withdrew her hand with a small laugh. "I never suspected that I was capable of passion."

She turned away, oblivious to the blinding hunger in the pale eyes of the man behind her. "Good night— Oh!"

He'd pulled her around. "Say my name, saucy girl," he whispered, teasing her. "Come on."

"I won't," she said, feeling a rising new excitement.

His lip tugged up. "Say it," he challenged, pulling her body against his, "or I'll kiss you blind."

He could have, too. She drew in a jerky breath. "Gabriel," she said.

He let her go with a faint smile. "Good night." And he walked away without another word.

Enigma, she thought confusedly. *Enigma.* She'd never known anyone like him. And her body was sending out smoke signals, begging for him. She'd never expected complications like this. And now she didn't know what to do.

At precisely nine o'clock the next morning, when Maggie came downstairs dressed in a neat gray suit, Gabe was waiting for her at the front door. He was wearing gray, too, a vested suit that made him look debonair, sophisticated, almost handsome—and every inch a very male man. He smelled of spicy cologne and soap, and Maggie wondered why she couldn't seem to stop staring at him. She gripped her purse as Janet came out to say goodbye.

"I'd go with you," she told Maggie, "but it's less crowded this way. Have a safe trip."

"I'll take care of her," Gabe said carelessly. He spared his mother a glance and walked off without even a smile.

Maggie didn't say a lot on the way to the airstrip. She was curious about him, in so many ways. She wanted to ask questions, to learn new things. And that was dangerous.

"Nervous?" Gabe asked after a minute, glancing at her wickedly as he lifted his cigarette to his lips.

"Not really. I'm not afraid of flying," she murmured evasively.

"And that wasn't what I meant, either." He pulled off the main ranch road onto a dirt track with deep ruts that led toward the airstrip and the big hangar where he kept his twin-engine planes. He had two, he explained: one for work, for herding cattle; the other for business trips.

"Don't you ever fly for pleasure?" she asked.

Gabe glanced at her. "I have women for pleasure, when I can't stand the ache any longer. That's about the extent of my recreational activities these days."

She stared out the window, embarrassed despite her age and experience. "You're very blunt."

"I don't pull my punches—about anything," he replied. "I believe in total honesty. I've never yet found a woman who did."

"Your mother told me that you…" She stopped when she realized what she was betraying.

His icy-blue eyes cut at her. "Did she tell you all of it, or aren't you that privileged?" he asked with bitter sarcasm.

"I'm sorry. It's none of my business. I shouldn't have said anything."

He took a deep draw from the ever-present cigarette and drove faster. "My God, is nothing sacred these days?"

"She thought it might help me to understand things a little better," Maggie replied quietly.

"Did it?" he asked cuttingly.

She met his brief glance. "Yes. It explained everything."

He searched her eyes quickly and then turned back to the road, slowing as they approached the airstrip. "I hated him," he said. "Even before that happened. I saw through him a hell of a long time before she did. And in spite of it, she wouldn't leave him."

"Love imprisons people, so I've heard," she said.

"Didn't you love your husband?" Gabe asked, his smile mocking.

"I thought I did," she replied. "He was charming. Utterly charming. I was shy in those days, and overwhelmed that such a handsome man would be interested in me. I was an heiress, you know. Filthy rich."

"Yes. I remember," he said bitterly. He stared at the airplane in the distance, watching a mechanic go over the large red-and-white Piper Navajo. "Our place had fallen on hard times when you were a teenager."

"I didn't know." She stared at her lap. "Dennis had fallen on hard times, too. I was eighteen," she said. "Green as grass and infatuated, and every time he kissed me, I was on fire. And then we got married." She shuddered. "My God, for all my reading, I never realized the things men would expect of women in bed!"

He scowled. "What, exactly, did he want of you?"

Maggie flushed. "I can't tell you."

"I think I can guess, all the same," he said, his eyes narrowing.

She stared at her crossed hands. Amazing how easy it was to talk to him about such intimate things. "When I froze, he accused me of being frigid. From then on, it got worse. I didn't even mind that much when he started seeing other women. It was almost a relief, except that it stung my pride. I'd planned to leave him. And then I discovered that I was pregnant."

"You stuck it out for a long time," he observed.

"My mother was still alive then," she replied. "She'd told me what to do all my life. I was afraid to go against her. She said that divorce was an unspeakable scandal, that nobody in her family had ever been divorced. So I didn't disgrace her. After she died, it didn't seem to matter anymore. The money was gone. There were no social peers to be scandalized by what I did."

"You said that your daughter was afraid of him," he reminded her.

"Becky's easily hurt," she said. "He terrifies her. He drinks, you see." She sighed. "The last time he had a visiting session with her, she did something that upset him. He left some marks on her. She's been afraid of him ever since."

Gabe said something under his breath that embarrassed her and braked to a halt beside the airstrip tarmac. "Is he suing for sole custody?" he asked, turning to look at her.

"Yes."

"We'll see your attorney while we're in San Antonio." He opened the car door. "And if he doesn't suit me, you'll use mine."

"Now, wait a minute," Maggie began as he came around to open her door.

"You wait a minute," he countered, helping her out. He held her just in front of him, towering over her slender height. "If that child is on my property, she's my responsibility. So are you, for that matter. And until you leave, I'll take care of both of you, whether you like it or not!"

"You...you... Texas bulldozer!" she accused, eyes flashing as they hadn't since her childhood.

"Go ahead, argue with me," he responded, smiling slightly. "Make a fuss. And when I've had enough, guess how I'll deal with you?"

She had a good idea, but she wasn't backing down. "That's—that's male chauvinism," she sputtered.

"I'm a man, all right," he replied without the least bit of self-reproach. "Come on, honey. Make a fuss."

He looked as if he'd really enjoy that, and Maggie remembered how it had been in the backyard that day, when he'd backed her against the oak tree and taken what he'd wanted. Her face colored.

His blue eyes sparkled with pure enjoyment. "That's exactly what I'd do, you little prude. Only this time, I'd go further than a few kisses, and it wouldn't be in anger or bad temper. I'd wear you down and lay you down, and when I got through, you'd ache for me the rest of your life."

"Conceited jackass," she enunciated clearly.

He laughed softly. "Am I? Apparently, Miss Maggie, you've forgotten how you react to me. You always did get flustered and nervous when I came too close, even at sixteen." His pale blue eyes narrowed as they traveled down her slender body, making her tingle with the frank appraisal. "You always were a beauty, to me. Especially in a bathing suit, with that long black hair down to your waist.... Why did you cut it?" he asked unexpectedly.

She sighed. "I thought it looked too girlish for a woman my age," she told him, then smiled. "And it was hot in the summer."

"Would it shock you to know that I used to dream about wrapping it around my wrist?" Gabe asked, his voice gentle. "And pillowing you on it, while I laid you down on one of those loungers that used to sit by the pool?"

Again Maggie colored, but she didn't look away. She seemed to blush all the time around him! "Did you really?" she asked.

He nodded. "It got to be more than disturbing, especially considering the age difference. I'll be blunt, Maggie, I was glad when you stopped coming here to see the girls. You caused me some sleepless nights."

"You heard what I said to Janet, didn't you?" she asked suddenly. "About having a crush on you?"

"Yes. But I knew already." His eyes narrowed, glittering. "That was what worried me so much. Your eyes were so sultry and just faintly hungry when you looked at me. I knew I could do anything I wanted to you, and you'd let me. The thought tormented me."

She'd thought about that, too; about having him kiss her and make love to her. Her heart went wild in her chest. She wondered suddenly and startlingly what it would feel like to make love with him.

"We'd better get going," he said, missing the shock in her eyes. "Come on."

He held out his hand and stood there until she took it, refusing to budge an inch. She yielded because she knew him so well. He'd die before he gave in, once he got his mind set on something. She even admired it, that stubborn streak of his. The feel of his strong hand around hers was intoxicating. She let him hold it while she wondered how she was going to keep him from taking her over, lock, stock and daughter. Odd, she thought as they approached the plane, how delicious it was to be close to him....

Then they were on their way, and she stopped thinking about it.

CHAPTER FIVE

THE EXCLUSIVE BOARDING school where Becky stayed was frantic with activity. Gabe looked around him curiously as little girls rushed down the hall outside the office where he and Maggie waited for Becky.

"Margaret, thank goodness!" Mrs. Haynes burst out as she joined them, closing her office door gingerly behind her. "I didn't know what to do. He's been here for thirty minutes. I knew you were coming since you called this morning...."

"Dennis is here?" she gasped. "Oh, Mrs. Haynes, you didn't let him have Becky?"

"Of course not, dear. He's in my office...."

Gabe moved her gently aside and made a beeline for the office, his long strides eating up the distance. Maggie, sensing disaster, rushed after him and Mrs. Haynes just stared, biting her lip.

Gabe thrust open the door and a shorter, younger, fair-haired man jerked around in surprise, his eyes wide and shocked as he stared at the formidable Westerner.

"Maggie, darling..." Dennis laughed nervously, staring past the tall man to a less intimidating presence. "I didn't expect you so early. I was just going to drive Becky over to your house for you."

"Like hell you were," Gabe said coldly. "But I can save you the trouble. I'm taking Maggie and the child home with me."

Dennis glared at the bigger man. "Who are you?"

"Gabriel Coleman."

Dennis straightened, finding unexpected new ammunition in the curt response. Gabriel Coleman... He remembered everything he'd heard about the man. And now, seeing him, it wasn't hard to believe it was all true. So this was the Texas rancher Maggie's father had wanted her to marry. Maggie probably didn't know that, but Dennis did. Her father had used it like a nagging prod every time they'd met socially. He smiled. "So, that's how it is. Living with your old lover, are you? Janice and I got married Monday, so I've really got the edge on you now, haven't I?" he added. "It won't look good in court when everyone sees what an unfit mother you are."

"You can't take her," Maggie cried. "You can't! All you want is the money!"

"She's my child," Dennis replied arrogantly. "And I've got a lot more right to her, married, than you do single and living with your...lover," he added, with a cold glare at Gabriel. "You couldn't wait, could you? Well, he'll find you as frigid as I—"

He stopped in midsentence as Gabe, imperturbably unruffled by the outburst, lifted him half off the floor by the collar and escorted him out of the office and down the hall.

"By God, that's enough," Gabe was muttering to Dennis. "How she could marry something like you in the first place is beyond me."

Becky came into the office before Gabe returned and ran into her mother's outstretched arms.

"Oh, Mama," Becky wailed. "Michelle said Daddy was here." She drew away, green eyes wide and frightened. "I don't have to go with him, do I?"

"No, darling," Maggie said softly, hoping, praying that

it would be the truth after the custody battle was over. She knelt, smiling at the young girl, brushing back the long strands of hair from the pale little face. "No, you don't have to go with him."

Becky looked past her mother and her face froze. She frowned a little. "Who are you?" she asked curiously.

"Gabriel Coleman," he said, looking down at her with narrowed eyes.

Becky's face lit up. "You're Aunt Janet's Gabe, aren't you?" the little girl asked, moving toward the tall man. She looked up at him with open fascination. "Aunt Janet says that you have a ranch and horses and cows and lots of cowboys and rustling, just like in the movies!"

Incredibly, the hard face relaxed into a genuine smile, the first one Maggie had seen yet. He went down on one knee so that he could see Becky better. "I'd love to hear the bedtime stories you tell this child," he said, amused, then looked up at Maggie.

She flushed. "Well, actually, it's the movies..."

"You'd better come home with me, Becky," he said seriously, "and you can see what ranching is like for yourself."

Becky hesitated. There was fear in her eyes—the same fear Gabe had seen in her mother—and his face hardened visibly.

"Your mother will be there, too," he said softly. "And I swear, honey, nobody will hurt you as long as I'm around."

Becky's wan little face managed a wobbly smile. "Then I guess it'll be okay."

He nodded. "Are you ready?" he asked, standing.

"Yes, sir. I have my suitcase right over there."

Gabe picked it up, glancing at Maggie over the child's head. There was an expression in his eyes that defied description.

BECKY WAS DELIGHTED with the ranch. She'd been quiet all the way back, except to exclaim at the private plane and the fact that Gabe could actually fly it. But when she got her first look at the ranch, her breath sighed out in a rush.

"Oh, isn't it just beautiful, Mama?" she asked Maggie, all eyes and laughter. "Isn't it just beautiful? Look at all the room! And cows and horses…!"

Gabe chuckled softly, smoking his cigarette without comment.

"Can I ride a horse? Oh, can I?" Becky begged.

"No," Maggie said.

"Yes," Gabe countered immediately, his eyes challenging Maggie. "She's old enough. I was four when my dad put me on my first horse. I won't let her get hurt," he added gently when she still hesitated.

Maggie bit her lip. She'd need a lot more sustenance than the rushed breakfast she'd had to take on Gabriel Coleman in that mood. But it was going to be a fight all the way; of that she was sure.

Janet was delighted to see the child and made a big fuss over her. Even the housekeeper began immediately to spoil her. She was taken off into the kitchen and then upstairs to see her very own room. Everyone was enthusiastic except Maggie, who'd had a glimpse of hell at the boarding school.

Dennis had almost succeeded in spiriting the child away, and possession was still nine-tenths of the law. If she'd been a little later, or if Gabe hadn't been with her… She shuddered to think of the consequences.

And now Dennis thought she had a lover. He was going to use Gabe, of all people, against her. How would she prove it was a lie? It might be just the lever Dennis needed to get possession of Becky, and what a hell of a life she'd have with him. If it came to that, Maggie might be forced to take the child and run. She glanced at Gabe, at the sheer magnificence of him. Perhaps they'd said something to Dennis in the early days of their marriage, something that had made him suspicious. Dennis had an active imagination, and he was good at twisting the truth to suit himself. She dreaded the thought of having him create a scandal that would involve Janet as well as Gabe.

Gabe was watching her closely over dinner. After Becky was tucked up in bed and Janet had gone upstairs, he waylaid Maggie and dragged her off into his study.

"Let's talk," he said curtly, motioning her into an armchair.

She refused his offer of brandy and sat with her hands folded primly in her lap. "What about?" she asked hesitantly.

"About that little girl upstairs," he returned, dropping into an armchair across from her. "And why she's terrified of men. What did that son of a rattlesnake do to her?"

"Dennis in a temper can do that even to big people," Maggie said miserably. She studied the hard lines of his face. "Oddly enough, I'm not afraid of your temper. Not anymore," she added with a faint smile. "I used to be. I'll never forget the day you beat up that cowboy at the grocery store in town."

His eyes darkened, narrowed. "He touched you," he said curtly, as if that explained everything. "He put his hands on you. I could have broken his neck."

She stared at him, curiously. "I wondered," she murmured, her voice barely carrying. "I always wondered if it was because of that."

He shifted in the chair, bringing the brandy to his lips

to break the spell. "You didn't know anything about men. I wasn't going to let one of my hands back you into a corner."

She studied his lean, beautifully masculine hands, wrapped around the brandy snifter. "You always were like a bulldozer."

"When I wanted something," he agreed. He studied her over the rim of the snifter. "I wanted you. But you were sixteen."

She colored softly and stared into his eyes. "You never did anything about it."

"I told you why. You were sixteen." He swished the amber liquid around, watching the patterns it made in the glass. "I might have gotten around to it, if you hadn't gone off to boarding school." He smiled slowly. "It would have been the last straw, trying to take you out with all those giggling girls watching."

Her lips trembled into a smile. "Really? Would you have?"

"I suppose I'd have come to it eventually," he said enigmatically, shrugging his wide shoulders. "You were a pretty kid. You still are, haunted eyes and all." He searched those eyes, watching the shadows in them. "You aren't afraid of me physically."

"Yes, I know." She twisted a strand of her short hair uneasily and watched him. He'd taken off his jacket and vest and unfastened the top buttons of his white shirt. Dark skin and darker hair were visible in the deep V, and she felt a thrill of excitement at the memory of being held against his long, hard body.

He laughed, his voice deep in the stillness. "Don't start getting nervous. I'm not going to pounce on you. I hope I have more finesse than that, especially after what you've been through."

She studied her hands. "I don't suppose anything frightens you. But I'm not physically strong, and I've had years of abuse, mental and physical. I carry my scars where they don't show, but they're very deep. So are Becky's."

He leaned back in the armchair, and for once he wasn't smoking like a furnace.

"Becky's young. Hers will heal. But yours won't. Not without help." He watched her with narrowed eyes, his dark head like ebony in the overhead light.

"Are you offering me the cure?" she asked, feeling bitter. "A little sexual therapy?"

He lifted an eyebrow. "I'm not that damned unselfish," he replied quietly. "And I don't need therapy. No, honey," he added, leaning forward to pin her with his pale eyes. "If I made love to you, it wouldn't be a cure—but it might be an addiction."

Heat seemed to well up inside her. She averted her eyes to the carpeted floor. Just to think of having him touch her that way made her heart run wild. Magic, when intimacy had been such a dark thing in her life.

"Shy little girl," he said with tender amusement. "Look at me, coward."

She lifted her face, hating its reddened color and vulnerability. "Stop making fun of me."

"Is that what I'm doing?" he asked. "I thought I was flirting."

She really colored then and started to get to her feet. He rose at the same time, catching her arm gently in his free hand, to hold her just in front of him. He towered over her, all steely strength and masculine dominance, smelling of tangy cologne and soap.

"I haven't spent much time around women in the past few years," he said, his voice deep and slow in the stillness. "I'm rusty at social skills, so you'll have to get used to a little embarrassment now and then. All you have to remember is that I'm no pretty boy with a line a mile long. I'm a country man with old-fashioned ideas and I'll never hurt you. Physically or emotionally."

"Are you trying to tell me that you won't seduce me if I smile at you?" she asked, testing emotions she hadn't used in over six years as she looked up at him.

He didn't move. He seemed to be holding his breath. In fact, he was. The softness in those green eyes held him spellbound. He hadn't realized just how vulnerable he was.

"That's about the size of it. You don't trust men, do you?" He touched her face with hesitant fingers. "I suppose we're alike in being wary. I thought I was in love a few times, but I got burned badly once. I guess I've forgotten how to trust women in the years since."

He sounded just faintly vulnerable, and something inside her stirred like a budding flower. She searched his face. "Damaged people," she whispered.

He understood immediately, his nod more eloquent than speech. He brushed the back of his finger over her soft mouth. "Come here and kiss me."

He bent as he spoke, and without the slightest hesitation she rose on tiptoe and kissed him. It was the first move she'd ever made of her own free will toward a man. He made everything so natural, so easy. She was sixteen again, feeling her first passion for a man. And there was Gabe, tough and hard and filling her world, her life.

"Gabe," she whispered brokenly, holding him gently as she pressed her warm, soft mouth against his and flew up into the sun with the powerful response he gave her.

She felt his hand at the back of her head, pressing her lips hard against his, and then she was free and he'd moved away, turned away, so that she couldn't see the effect she'd had on him. But when he put the brandy snifter down to light a cigarette, she noticed his hand wasn't quite steady.

"You're just dynamite," she said dazedly.

He turned, his eyes shocked, delighted. He smiled at her. "Hell, so are you."

It was a real smile, not a smirk or sarcasm. He lit the cigarette but his eyes held hers, searched them slowly. "Are you going to be that honest with me from now on?" he asked. "Because I'll have to warn you, it's dangerous."

"Telling the truth?"

"Telling me the truth about what you feel when I touch you," he told her. "My God, I've got a low boiling point with you, Maggie," he added softly, fervently. "I never dreamed it would be like that."

"Neither did I," she said, her voice soft, colored with what she was feeling so unexpectedly. "I…used to…" She stopped, horrified at what she was about to reveal.

"Used to what?" he coaxed, moving closer. "Used to what, honey?" he repeated, touching her lips gently.

"I used to daydream about you," she murmured, lowering her eyes to his hard chest. "About kissing you."

"You weren't the only one." He tilted up her chin. "The reality is pretty devastating. I gather it wasn't like that with your ex-husband?"

She shook her head. "I never really wanted him physically," she said. "I suppose he knew.... Do men know?" she asked, lifting plaintive eyes.

He nodded slowly. "I would, anyway," he said. "It's hard to fake."

"He couldn't make me want him. That made it worse. He had so many women, and I tried not to mind, but after a while, I felt like a Medusa."

"Why did you marry him?" he asked.

She shrugged. "He was a lot of fun. He'd take me places and give me things." She smiled sadly. "I'd never had a man pay me any attention. Not like that. I was a pushover."

"I could have," he said half under his breath, and the look in his eyes disturbed her. "If you hadn't been so young, honey."

"You were almost thirty," she remembered, searching his hard face. "Already a grown man. You fascinated me."

"I know." There was a world of emotion in those two words. He brushed back the hair from her temple, his fingers warm and hard and strong. "And frightened you. It was because of me that you stopped coming here to see the girls, wasn't it?"

"Yes," she confessed softly, smiling. "I knew I couldn't hide what I was feeling. I was afraid you'd see it and make fun of me or be embarrassed."

"I wouldn't have done either," he told her, his voice gentle. "I'm not sure how I would have handled it, but I'd have managed without hurting your pride too much." He pursed his lips musingly. "I lost track of you after the girls left school. I always meant to look you up again, but your family moved to Austin."

"It's just as well," she said. "You'd have wanted more than I could give."

He smoothed her hair. "No, I wouldn't have," he said firmly. "I'd have respected your innocence. I wouldn't have asked you to give it to me without a commitment." His chest rose and fell slowly. "Maggie, are you going to be able to handle a physical relationship again?"

She felt her body relaxing against his, felt her helpless reaction to his strength. Her fingers played with a button on his shirt, and she bit her lower lip, succumbing to old memories and new hungers all at once.

"I don't know," she said.

He nuzzled her cheek with his. "Shall we find out?"

Her lips parted on a trembling breath. "I'm afraid."

"No reason," he said gently. His mouth brushed over her cheek, her ear. "I'm older. It's hard for me to lose control now. I won't do anything you don't want me to do." He smiled against her cool cheek. "No sex, honey. Just some very light lovemaking."

She lifted her eyes to his. "I want to," she said, letting him see the mingled hunger and apprehension.

"Remember who I am," he breathed, touching her hair. "I'm Gabriel. I'll never hurt you. Never."

She reached up and he bent to lift her, but he grimaced and had to set her down.

"Damn," he groaned, rubbing his arm and laughing through the pain. "Damned snake! It's still sore."

"Your poor arm," she said softly, touching it lightly. "I'm sorry."

"So am I," he said, sighing. "It's slowed me down a little."

She smiled. "I think I like that. For now, at least."

He glared at her, moving into the big armchair with slow

ease. "Come here, then," he said, holding out his hand. "But watch where you touch."

"Prude," she accused, and actually laughed. It was the first time she'd been able to joke in so long.

He drew her onto his hard thighs and shifted her so that her head lay against his shoulder. But instead of kissing her, he just sat, holding her. Outside, rain was beginning to come down. The room was dimly lit and cozy. Her eyes wandered around to the heavy oak desk, the large burgundy leather sofa, the long, wide, matching divan, the huge bookcases against one wall and the wildlife paintings covering the other. It was a man's room. Gabe's room.

Closer, she heard his heartbeat, slow and heavy and regular at her ear, felt the sigh of his breath on her forehead. He smoothed her arm gently and his warm fingers felt good.

"It feels good, holding you," he said after a minute. He crossed one leg over the other, shifting her closer. "Comfortable?"

"Yes," she murmured drowsily, closing her eyes. She moved her hand experimentally on his broad chest and arm, feeling the bandage through the thin fabric of his shirt. "How long will it take to heal?" she asked.

"Not much longer, I hope," he muttered. "Damned fool, I should have looked where I was reaching. I dropped my rope behind the chute where we were working the small herd, and didn't look when I leaned over. The rattler got me right on the arm."

She studied his face curiously. "I never heard what happened to the snake. Blood poisoning...?"

He glowered at her. "The snake went the way of most snakes that come too close to me. I took my rifle and shot him."

"With a snakebite?" she gasped.

"I had the rifle right next to me," he admitted. "And just enough bad temper to do it before the poison started working. The boys got me to the emergency room, snake's head and all, and they gave me the antivenin. I was sicker than I want to remember for a couple of days. I'd just gotten back on my feet when you showed up with Mother."

"And spoiled your recovery," she recalled, smiling.

"I wouldn't say that." He nuzzled his cheek over her hair. "I have to admit that you've brightened up the place. Nothing like having a woman around to get a man well."

"You should have married," she murmured.

He lifted her left hand, noting the absence of a ring. "Becky's the one who's going to get hurt by the court suit, you know," he said unexpectedly, caressing her fingers gently with his. "From what I saw today, her father won't care who he destroys to get that money."

"Money always meant everything to him," she said. "He grew up poor. Really dirt-poor. But it warped him. He doesn't really care about anyone except himself."

"Stop feeling sorry for him," he chided. "People make their own hells, haven't you noticed? It isn't life that does the damage, Maggie—it's the way people react to it. Attitude is everything in this world."

"This, from a man whose attitude is to flatten anything that gets in his way?" she asked, eyebrows arching.

"It makes things simpler," he said, grinning.

She shook her head. "You always were too much man for any ordinary woman. I never thought you'd find a woman brave enough to take you on."

He stared at her for a long moment, his eyes thoughtful,

curious. "Plenty have tried, as you might have gathered. Mother's done her best to supply me with a wife."

"She only wants happiness for you," Maggie said gently. "She doesn't like seeing you grow old all alone."

"Neither do I, sometimes." He brushed his thumb over the palm of the hand he was holding, feeling its softness. "I want a son," he added, looking straight into her eyes.

She felt the wildest kind of excitement. He was only making a statement, she told herself, only expressing a buried desire. But the way he said it, and the way he looked at her, made her body burn to give him that child. She felt herself trembling and knew he could feel it, too.

"I wanted to talk to your attorneys while we were in the city," he said after a minute. "But I thought it was more important to get Becky out of that lunatic's reach. I'll fly back down on Monday and meet with them."

"But—"

"It doesn't do any good to argue with me," he said reasonably. "Haven't you discovered that by now?"

"I don't want to be taken over," she began.

"Sure you do, honey," he murmured, smiling gently as he folded her against his good side and eased her down in the big chair. "And this is as good a time as any to show you that you do."

"Gabri—"

The rest of his name was buried under his warm, ardent mouth. She sighed gently and closed her eyes, drinking in his strength and warmth and masculinity. He made her feel so small and vulnerable, so protected. Nothing would ever happen to her when Gabe was around.

His lean fingers trailed down her arm and suddenly, shockingly, onto her blouse.

"Don't," she whispered, catching his wrist.

"You let me do it before," he whispered back, brushing his hard mouth over hers. "You aren't going to tell me you don't enjoy it, are you?"

"It's...it isn't...right," she faltered, searching for the words that would express what she felt.

He lifted his head and looked into her eyes. "Because I'll think you're easy?" he asked matter-of-factly. "Now that's a hell of a misconception. I know plenty about you, Maggie Turner. What I know best is that you've had a rough time with men and that you're about as clued up as a pretty kid at a carnival. Do you think I'm callous enough to play around with you under those circumstances?"

The question floored her. She hadn't expected such a blunt explanation.

"No," she had to answer him honestly. "No, I don't think you're callous."

"Then let go of my wrist, sweet, and let me show you how good it feels to have my hand on your warm skin," he breathed, smiling as he bent again to her mouth.

He was a bulldozer, she thought dimly. A human, blue-eyed bulldozer with a mouth as sweet as mountain honey. He opened her lips with his and pushed his tongue gently into her mouth, feeling her stiffen at the new intimacy.

"Give it a chance," he whispered. "Deep kisses are an acquired taste. Let me."

She hesitated for an instant but then she gave in, letting his tongue invade her mouth. It was frightening, the sudden explosion of feeling that the searching motion caused in her body. She stiffened again, but not in rejection; she moaned, gripping his hard arms.

Meanwhile, one lean hand had moved the fabric of her

blouse aside and was sliding warmly under it and around her. She felt the clasp of her bra give suddenly and the cool breeze of the room on her bare flesh. Her nipple hardened even as his fingers began to search teasingly at the edge of her breast, lightly exploring.

Her breath sounded odd. It caught in her throat and sighed out in little gasps. He heard it and smiled even through his own wild excitement.

"God, you set me on fire," he murmured, lifting his head as his hands slid around her and under her breasts, holding their warm, soft weight as he stared directly into her shocked eyes. His thumbs edged up, and she shuddered as they found and tested the tiny peaks of her breasts. "I'm not hurting you, am I?" he asked softly. "I haven't touched a woman like this for a long time."

"It doesn't hurt," she said, her voice husky.

He looked down and expertly lifted the bra away so that her breasts were revealed, small and high and very firm. "Yes," he said with a kind of reverence. "Yes, this is how I pictured you, all the long years in between—sweet, pretty little breasts so soft and warm in my hands—"

"Gabriel!" she burst out, shocked by his intimate description of her.

"Don't cover them," he whispered, bending to her parted lips. "Let me look at you. Let me touch you. We're both adults, Maggie. We're hurting no one."

He had such a silky, deep voice. It hypnotized her. She stayed very still, trembling softly as he caressed her mouth with his lips. His hands cupped her, testing her softness, adoring her womanliness.

She felt her body stretching, arching upward to savor what he was doing to it. Her head fell back, her eyes half-closed. She was sixteen again, burning for him, aching for his body. Dennis and all unpleasantness was pushed to the back of her mind, while Gabe held her body in ardent bondage.

He lifted his lips from hers and looked down, watching her body plead. "Yes," he whispered. "I want that, too, Maggie."

He bent, lifting her against his arm, and softly brushed his mouth over the very tip of her breast. She whimpered. Her fingers caught in his hair, tugging gently.

"You're trembling all over," he breathed. "I've never in my life felt so hungry for a woman."

As he spoke, he opened his mouth and put it completely over one soft, pretty breast. She felt the warm, moist darkness envelop her, and she arched even farther to give him total access to her, trembling as his mouth fed on her softness, bit at her, tasted her. Her mind hardly worked at all, drowning in sensation.

His hand slid down her back to her hips and drew them suddenly under his, then he turned her in the big chair so she could feel the pressure of his arousal.

Her eyes opened to look up into his. She shuddered, but she didn't try to move away. "I hated it...when that happened to Dennis. Why is it...so beautiful with you?" she whispered tearfully.

He couldn't answer her. His mind was in turmoil, his body in anguish. He bent again to her sweet mouth and kissed it as if he'd die trying to get enough. Despite the sore arm, he lifted her close, fighting his shirt out of the way so he could feel her soft breasts against his chest.

She cried out, shocked at the sensations she felt. Never with Dennis, never like this. She wanted him. She wanted to lie down and feel his weight on her body; she wanted total union with him.

Time seemed to slow, to stand still. She was crying, and when the world came into focus again, he was comforting her with the most exquisite kind of tenderness.

"Shh," he breathed into her mouth. "Shh, calm down now. It's all right, calm down." He pressed her hot cheek against his chest and rocked her, gently smoothed his hands along her back, easing away the passion between them. "That's my girl," he whispered. "Just be still."

"I feel so strange," she whispered unsteadily.

"So do I." He laughed gently. "Would you like to know where?"

"Hush," she mumbled, hiding her hot face.

He ran his fingers through her thick short hair, testing its silkiness. "Were you frightened of what was happening?" he asked softly.

"A little," she told him.

His fingers touched her ear, sending delicious thrills through her sensitized nerves. "Eventually, I'll have to know."

"Know…what?" she hesitated.

"Whether or not you're capable of giving in to me completely," he replied. His chest, beneath her bare breasts, rose and fell heavily. "This kind of thing gets unmanageable pretty quickly, Maggie. For Becky's sake, we can't have an illicit relationship. You see that, I hope."

Things were going too fast. She stood up, tugging her blouse together, and stared down at him. "It's too soon," she said, wary.

"No, I don't think it is." He watched her fumble with buttons. He didn't bother with his own, merely sprawled back in the chair, his broad, hair-covered chest bare and welcoming, his mouth swollen and sensuous and smiling with pure male appreciation of her. "You'd better start seeing it that way, too, honey. You're going to need some help when you get into court. Especially now, with your ex-husband's scandalous opinion of our relationship."

"I'll deny it."

He lifted an eyebrow. "By all means," he suggested, and picked up his brandy snifter. "His attorney will get you on the stand and ask if you and I have ever been intimate, you'll blush like somebody's embarrassed child, and he'll have Becky."

That was true, but it didn't help her pride. She finished fastening her blouse and glared at him. "What do you propose to do about it—marry me?" she asked with faint sarcasm.

"Why not?" he replied casually, and took a sip of brandy. "You're pretty and honest, you've got a lovely little girl, and I'm a lonely man. You need money, I've got it. We're a match made in heaven."

"Those aren't good reasons to get married," she returned, but she felt as if the ground had been cut from under her. She wanted him. Physically, at least. He attracted her, and perhaps she wouldn't freeze in his arms. He was strong and powerful and rich. He'd take care of them both, of Becky and herself. And in bed, he'd give her what she'd never had with a man. But why was he offering? He wasn't a marrying man, he'd said it before. What did he expect to get out of it? Or did he just want Maggie so much that he was willing to give up his freedom to have her? That didn't make a lot of sense, either. It would be a risk, marrying him. What if it didn't work out?

The turbulence of her thoughts showed in her face as she looked at him.

"Go ahead," he said, "torment yourself with what-ifs." He finished the brandy. "You've got a little longer to play on the line before I start reeling you in." He got to his feet and towered over her. "Just remember, honey, I make a hell of an adversary. I won't give up or give in. If I want you, I'll have you."

"By force?" she demanded with a bit of her old spirit.

"Never by force, pretty girl," he replied. He bent and brushed his mouth over hers. "I want to ravish your senses, not take something you don't want to give me. Physical pleasure has to be shared, or it's selfish. You've had enough of that already."

She searched his eyes, afraid of him, hungry for him. "Can it be shared, Gabriel?" she asked in a whisper, her eyes wide and curious.

"If both partners are intent on giving more than they expect to get," he said enigmatically.

"And it...isn't supposed to hurt?"

His eyes burned down into hers. "No," he bit off. "It isn't supposed to hurt. Ever."

She dropped her gaze to his bare chest. "I didn't know. There was no one I could ask, you see. Even my best friend, Trudie. I can't talk about things like that."

"Except with me, apparently," he mused, his eyes gently indulgent. He caught her hand in his. "Sit down."

He dropped down onto the big sofa and let her curl up next to him again as he lit a cigarette. "I hope you're not sleepy. This may take a while. Don't look at me, if it helps. I'm going to tell you all about sex, Miss Turner. I think it's time, don't you?"

She looked up at him, feeling her face color. "I know..."

"Nothing," he said for her, grinning. "But you will when I'm through. Now be quiet, and listen."

It was fascinating. He might have been a university lecturer giving a cram course in sex education. He did it without vulgarity, in a matter-of-fact way that didn't embarrass or shock her. And when he was through, she knew more than marriage and having a child had taught her.

She caught her breath. "I never realized it was so complicated," she told him.

"It's a miracle," he replied. "In every respect. And miracles shouldn't be twisted into minor amusements. The only times I ever had sex with women, I was involved emotionally. I couldn't lower my pride enough to buy it."

And men were supposed to be indifferent about feelings? She stared up at him, fascinated. "Did you learn... all that...with women?"

The corners of his firm mouth curved up. "Not all of it, no. I wanted to be a doctor when I graduated from high school. I took two years of premed before I switched to veterinary science. I learned all sorts of interesting things about bodies and how they work."

"So I've noticed," she murmured.

He touched her chin, tilting it. "Sex is beautiful," he said softly. "In the proper circumstances, it's an exquisite expression of love and commitment. God must have thought so, because He allowed children to come of it."

She searched his pale eyes, smiling. He was an enigma. Such a hard, unbending man to be so sensitive. "Thank you for the lesson," she said.

"My pleasure. Hearing it might not remove those scars,

but it could put what you've experienced into perspective. You aren't frigid—you're just untaught."

"I could never talk to Dennis about sex," she recalled quietly. "He said it was my fault that it was never good."

"I'm afraid he had it backward," he replied. "A considerate lover can make it good."

Her eyes lifted. Her lips parted to ask the question, but at the last second she got cold feet and averted her eyes.

He leaned close to her ear. "What do you want to know, big eyes? How I am in bed?"

"Of course not!" she blurted.

He took her earlobe gently between his teeth and teased it, and she felt the sensations all the way to her toes. "I'm slow, and thorough, and I know where all the nerves are," he whispered.

She made a wild little sound and darted away from him, her eyes like saucers in a face burning with embarrassment.

He laughed, leaning back against the sofa to study her frenzied confusion. "Running away so soon?" he murmured. "You wanted to know. I told you."

"You were being kind, for once," she grumbled. "Now you're back to your old cutting self."

"I'm frustrated," he replied. "I should have explained frustration to you. It makes bears out of nice men."

"You never were a nice man," she told him, brushing back her hair.

"That's true," he agreed pleasantly. He winked at her. "But I'm sexy."

She smiled. "I guess you are," she agreed unexpectedly.

He lifted an eyebrow. "I'm delighted that you agree. At some future date, would you like me to prove it to you?"

"Well..."

"Chicken," he chided. "Go to bed. Tomorrow, I'm taking Becky for her first ride. You can come, if you like."

"Gabe, she's so small," she protested.

"And I'm big," he replied. "And I'll take good care of her. And her mother."

"I can't help being overprotective," she said defensively.

"It's just a stage you're going through," he told her. "You'll outgrow it. I'll help. Now, scoot. Let me drink myself to sleep, so that I can forget this swollen arm you damn near burst."

"I damn near burst?" she echoed blankly.

"Trying to take advantage of me," he replied with virtuous indignation. "Look at me, for God's sake! Shirt half off, fingerprints all over my chest, I smell of whatever kind of perfume you've bathed in…"

Her eyes widened. He was flirting with her. She'd had so little experience with flirting. But it seemed like fun.

"You took my blouse off," she countered. "Women have equal rights."

"I took more than your blouse off, actually," he mused, staring at her breasts. "The ancient Greek women used to go bare-breasted, did you know? You'd have knocked the competition dead."

And she'd always thought of herself as too small to appeal to a man. Her fascinated gaze held his. "Do you really think so?"

He laughed softly. "Yes, I really think so. Go to bed, damn it. How long do you think I can sit here calmly talking about your breasts without stripping you and throwing you down on the carpet?"

"How uncivilized," she commented haughtily.

"Exciting." His eyes glittered wickedly. "Your bare back

on that rug, and my body grinding you down into it with the door unlocked…."

She turned, catching her breath. "I'm going to bed."

"I wish I was going with you," he sighed, reaching for his brandy snifter. "Maggie…"

She paused, her hand on the doorknob. "Yes?"

"I want a few days to see how Becky adjusts. Then, if she likes it, you and I will talk and come to a decision about what needs doing."

She stared into his narrowed, quiet eyes. "I don't understand."

"Oh, I think you do," he said, and held her gaze until her heartbeat shook her. "I think you know exactly what I mean, after tonight."

She held on to her nerves with shaky control. "I may not be able to give you what you want," she said. "Dennis… changed me. What we've done is sweet, and I like it. But…"

"But you aren't certain you can give yourself to me, is that it?" he asked with quiet perception.

"That's it exactly," she said miserably.

He pursed his lips to search her eyes. "Maggie, if it helps, I'm not insensitive to what you must feel about intimacy. But I think you're overlooking one important factor."

"What?"

"I'm not your ex-husband," he said. "I've never hurt a woman deliberately. I'm not a sadistic man."

"Oh, I know that," she told him. "I've always known that."

"Then give me credit for a little sensitivity," he replied. "Trust me."

"Trust is hard."

"Tell me about it." He chuckled darkly. "Or have you

forgotten that I've had some hard knocks of my own in that department? Mother told you that I got hurt, but I'm the only one who knows how badly. I loved her. Or thought I did," he added, and for the first time he wasn't really sure. It all seemed very far away now, with Maggie here, lovely and tempting.

"I'm sorry about that."

"I'm sorry about your rough time, too, honey," he said softly. "But that's in the past. You and I have Becky to think about. If we don't do something, you may lose her."

"I know," she murmured.

"Don't worry," he said. "He'll have to go through me to get her, court or no court. But maybe there's an easier way. I've got an idea. I'll tell you if it pans out. Good night."

"I haven't even thanked you," she said suddenly, "for all you've done."

His eyes traveled slowly to her mouth. "Haven't you?" He raised the snifter, smiling as she turned, flustered, and left him there.

CHAPTER SIX

BECKY SEEMED LIKE a different child on the big ranch. Despite the demands of his position, and his sore arm, Gabe found time to help her get used to her new environment.

He put her on a horse the day after she arrived, while Maggie stood with her hands clenched, murmuring soft prayers.

"It's all right, honey," Gabe told the nervous little girl as he helped her onto a small mare, grimacing as he forced his arm to perform the minor task. Becky was light, but any pressure still caused him some problems. "She's old and gentle. Your mother used to ride her, in fact," he added, glancing toward Maggie with a grin. "Remember Butterball?"

"That isn't Butterball!" Maggie exclaimed. "But, Gabe, she'd have to be twenty-five years old."

"She's twenty-six," he said. He checked the cinch and put the reins in Becky's hands, teaching her how to sit the horse, how to hold it in check, how to keep her knees and elbows in and guide the horse with the faintest pressure of her legs.

"You sure know a lot about horses," Becky said with shy admiration, her soft green eyes glancing off his.

"I've worked around them all my life," he replied. "I love animals. I took courses in veterinary science in college and almost had a degree in it."

"I like animals, too," Becky said enthusiastically. "But we never got to have any," she added, looking away sadly. "Daddy was allergic. And when we came away, Mama had to work and I had to go away to school. They don't let you have dogs at school."

"Do you want a dog?" Gabe asked her, ignoring Maggie's frantic signals and head shaking. "Because Bill Dane down the road has a litter of registered collies. If you want one, I'll get it for you."

Becky's face was fascinating—a study in admiration, excitement, surprise and pure delight. "You would?" she whispered.

Maggie shut up. She'd let the dog sleep in the parlor. She'd buy it a house. Whatever she had to do, it would be worth it to see that young face so happy. She hadn't even known Becky wanted a pet.

"I would," Gabe said, and grinned. "If your mother doesn't mind," he added belatedly, cocking an eyebrow at Maggie.

"Of course her mother doesn't mind," Maggie murmured, and made a face at him.

He laughed. "I thought you wouldn't. Closing the gate after the bull gets out, don't they say?" he added.

"I like dogs," she said.

"Me too!" Becky burst out, her ponytail bobbing as she stared down at Gabe. She started to reach out but abruptly brought her hand back to her reins, and her small face closed up all over again.

Maggie felt tears sting her eyes. She'd have to tell him, later, how great a step that was for Becky, who avoided any physical contact with people she didn't know—especially men. Just the inclination to reach out was a milestone in the child's life.

But he seemed to know, because when he looked toward Maggie he wasn't laughing. And the eyes that met hers were dark with a kind of pain.

"Can we go now? Right now?" Becky asked excitedly. "Can we get a puppy today?"

"First we go riding," Gabe said. "Then we'll see."

"All right," Becky sighed.

"Becky," Maggie chided. "Where are your manners?"

"In my back pocket." Becky grinned. "Want to see?"

It was a sharp and delightful change to see her shy little daughter so vividly happy and outgoing. Maggie smiled up at Gabe, the sunlight turning her eyes as green as grass.

He winked at her before he turned to give her the reins of her own mount. "Can you get up all by yourself?" he asked in a gently mocking tone of voice.

She glared at him. "I know how to ride," she replied indignantly—and then ruined everything by missing the stirrup.

He caught her arm with his good hand and kept her upright. "Pilgrim," he accused. He steadied her while she got her booted foot into the stirrup and threw the other leg over gracefully. The steely hand on her arm wasn't doing a lot for her nerves, but she didn't refuse the offer of assistance.

He gathered the reins of his own horse and stepped easily into the saddle, looking so much at home up there that Maggie just stared at him.

"Stay right with me, honey," Gabe told Becky, moving into step with her horse. "There's nothing to worry about. I'll take care of you."

"All right," Becky said. Her small hands gripped the

reins just as Gabe had taught her to. She glanced at him to make sure she was doing it right, and he nodded.

Maggie trailed along beside Gabe on the wide farm road, drinking in the beauty of vast horizons and grazing cattle and the feel of the warm spring breeze in her hair. There had been other times like this, long ago, when she and his sisters had gone riding. Sometimes they'd meet him unexpectedly on the trail, and her heart would run wild. It might have been only a schoolgirl crush, but it had hurt when she hadn't seen him again. Her eyes adored him unconsciously, admiring the powerful length of his body, the straightness of his carriage, the lean hands so deft and strong on the reins. He was exceptional. He always had been. And she might marry him....

The thought disturbed her. She'd been wrong about Dennis. What if she was wrong about Gabe? It was different, living with someone. You never knew people until you lived with them.

He turned his head, studying her in a somber silence. "You're too quiet," he said. "Say something."

"She's always quiet," Becky told him. "She doesn't talk much."

"She used to," Gabe returned with a grin. "She never shut up, in fact."

"I only blabbered because you made me nervous," she shot back, and then cleared her throat when she realized what she'd confessed.

"Your mama had a crush on me," Gabe said arrogantly, lifting his chin at a cocky angle as he studied Maggie with knowing eyes. "She thought I was the best thing since buttered bread."

Becky giggled, and Becky's mama ground her teeth together. "Why didn't you marry my mama, Uncle Gabe?" Becky asked suddenly.

Maggie wanted to get under the horse. She bit her lower lip while Gabe stared at her under the wide brim of his hat and pursed his lips thoughtfully.

"I was afraid she wouldn't be happy with what I had to offer her, back then," he said matter-of-factly and without embarrassment. "We weren't always well-to-do, young lady," he added with a gentle smile. "We had some hard times here for a while. It was during those hard times that I lost track of your mother."

Maggie stared at him, fascinated. Was it just for Becky's benefit—a little white lie—or was he telling the truth?

He caught her intent scrutiny and grinned, his pale eyes making a joke of it. She smiled back, but something inside her closed up like a flower in the darkness: she'd wanted it to be true.

"Down this way," Gabe said suddenly, turning Becky's mare. "I've got something to show you."

There was a little path down to the creek, and near it were several cows with calves.

"Baby cows!" Becky burst out. "Could I pet one?"

"Oh, Gabe, no, those are longhorn cows!" protested Maggie, who'd once been chased by a mad mama longhorn.

"These are old pets," Gabe replied easily, dismounting. "They won't hurt her. Come on, baby."

He reached up his arms. Becky hesitated, but in the end she let him swing her to the ground. And this time he made sure she didn't see him grimace.

"These are just a few weeks old," he told her, keeping between the young girl and the old cows. "Go easy, now.

You can win over most any creature if you're just slow and careful and talk soft. Ask your mama."

Maggie blushed furiously as he glanced over his shoulder with a mischievous grin.

Mercifully, Becky didn't understand what he was saying. Her wide eyes were on the calves. She moved close to a young one and touched it between the eyes, where it was silky. It tried to nibble on her hand, and she jerked back with a delighted laugh.

"Oh, isn't she pretty?" Becky cooed, doing it again.

"He," Gabe corrected. "That youngster is going to grow up to be a good young bull."

"Not a steer?" Maggie asked.

"Not this one. See the conformation?" he asked, gesturing toward the smooth lines of the young animal. "He's already breaking weight-gain ratio records. I want to breed this one."

"How do you keep up with so many cattle?" Becky asked unexpectedly.

"I have a big computer in my office," he told her. "I have every cow and calf I own on it. Ranching is moving into the twentieth century, honey. We don't use tally books too much anymore."

"What's a tally book?"

He explained it to her, about the old-time method of counting cattle, about the days when every ranch owner would send a rep to roundup to make sure none of his cattle were being appropriated.

"That's still done in these parts, too," he added, leaning against a tree to smoke a cigarette while Becky stroked the calf. "We have quite a crowd here when we start branding and moving cattle, and at the end of it I throw a big barbecue for the neighbors. We help each other out, even on a ranch this size."

"Do you really use those airplanes to round up cattle?" Maggie asked.

"Sure. The helicopter, too. It's a great time-saver when you're moving thousands of head." His pale eyes moved slowly down Maggie's body, over the white knit short-sleeved sweater and the neat jeans that hugged her rounded hips and long, elegant legs.

"It's hard work, too," she said, burning under his frank appraisal.

"Very hard." He lifted the cigarette to his mouth, glancing at Becky, who was talking softly to the calf while its mother watched with indulgent interest. "I get ill-tempered this time of year."

"I did notice," Maggie began.

He turned, crushing out the cigarette as he started toward her. "Did you?"

She backed up. Surely he wouldn't...not with Becky watching!

He intimidated her back against a large oak tree and kept her there with just his presence. "What was that," he asked politely, "about noticing I was ill-tempered?"

"You would have sent me packing, but for your mother," she reminded him.

"Not really." He smiled at her gently. "You started getting under my skin all over again, that first day. I might have let you get as far as packing, but I'd have found an excuse to keep you here."

Her heart began to run wild. Becky wasn't even watching.

Gabe moved a little closer, leaning one arm, the uninjured one, beside her head against the tree. The action brought him so close that she could smell the tobacco on his breath, feel the muscles cording in his powerful legs and chest.

His eyes dropped to her mouth. "I can almost taste the coffee on your breath," he whispered. "And if Becky was a few yards down the creek, I'd ease my body down on yours and let you feel the effect you have on me in those tight little jeans."

Her breath caught. "Gabriel!"

"Don't try to pretend you don't know it, either," he continued. His eyes dropped. "That sweater doesn't hide what you're feeling."

Maggie frowned slightly. Her eyes followed his, and she could see the tautness in her nipples even through the flimsy bra and knit top.

"You know, don't you, that your body reflects desire that way?" he whispered, searching her wide eyes. "Why do you think men get so stirred by a woman who isn't wearing a bra?"

"I... I am wearing one," she began.

"It doesn't cover much, does it?" He frowned. "Don't go around the men that way," he added suddenly. "I can't afford to fire anybody this week."

Her eyebrows arched. "But—"

"You have pretty breasts," he whispered softly, holding her eyes.

She tingled from head to toe. Her breath wouldn't let out. Gabe's eyes were drowning her, she couldn't get to the surface. The whole world was pale blue, and her body was trembling slightly, burning up inside. Her lips parted, and she made a soft, barely perceptible movement toward him.

"You shouldn't talk that way to me," she breathed.

"You shouldn't let me," he whispered back. "If you keep encouraging me, I'll make love to you."

"You can't."

"Sure I can." He nuzzled her nose with his. "So can you. I don't mind if you sleep with me."

"There's Becky."

He smiled. "Becky is quite a girl. She'll make a rancher before she quits."

"That isn't what I meant," Maggie replied. She touched his chest, liking the feel of hard muscle under the warm shirt. "You're very hairy there," she said absently, and caught her breath when she remembered how his chest felt against her bare skin.

"You always seemed to like that," he murmured, watching her. "At least you sure stared when I stripped off my shirt while I was working."

She swallowed. "You...you're very nicely built."

He smiled. "So are you."

Maggie smiled back. She felt shy and giddy, all at once.

They stared at each other for a long moment, eyes meeting eyes, curious and then quiet and probing and intense. She felt her breath quicken, saw his chest rise and fall heavily.

"I'm on fire," he whispered huskily. "I want your hands on my bare skin."

She trembled because she wanted it, too. "We...aren't alone."

"How fortunate for you," he replied curtly. "Because if we were, I'd lay you down, so help me."

Her body reacted to his threat in a wildly responsive way. She tried to get a deep breath and couldn't.

"No comment?" he asked. "No urge to cut and run? Or doesn't the thought of having sex with me frighten you anymore?"

"It would be…more…than that," she whispered. "Wouldn't it?"

"More than you can imagine, honey," he replied evenly, searching her soft eyes. "You and I would go up in flames if we got in bed together."

Her mind was seeing that. Seeing his long, nude body stretching against hers on cool, striped sheets, feeling his muscles ripple as her hands smoothed over them and savored their warm, rough strength.

"My God, don't look at me like that," he cried harshly, and actually shuddered. "I can read your mind!"

Her lips parted on a trembling breath. "So beautiful," she murmured. "That…with you."

Gabe caught her arm with his hand, holding it with such fierce ardor that she welcomed the discomfort. Her head tilted back, her mouth invited his.

"I can't kiss you like that with Becky here," he said in a hoarse undertone. "God, I couldn't even stop once I started! I'd devour you."

"I'd let you," she whispered softly. "I'd let you do anything…."

He turned away with a hard groan, letting go of her arm. "Becky, want to see the wildflowers?" he called. His voice didn't seem quite normal but Becky didn't notice. She was still petting the calf with fascination.

"Sure!" she called back, laughing.

Maggie eased away from the tree on shaky legs. She wasn't at all sure how to handle these new, explosive emotions. Gabe was wearing her down without even trying.

And now she wanted him, as she hadn't even in her youth. She couldn't think what was best anymore. She wasn't at all sure that she could leave him.

"Come on, slowpoke," Gabe called to her, smiling, although his eyes were blazing as they met hers. "Let's get going."

She waited for him to boost her into the saddle after he'd helped Becky up. But he was towering over her, so close that she could feel the warmth of his body.

"I've got to," he whispered sharply as Becky turned her horse away from them. "Just for a second!"

His mouth crushed down on hers, hungrily, roughly. She opened her lips, but he drew back immediately with a visible shudder.

"Oh…" she whispered on a sob.

"I'll be on my knees by tonight," he ground out, helping her into the saddle. "My God, I'm already shaking like a boy."

"So am I," she told him with an unsteady smile.

"Pretty soon we're going to have to settle this thing, honey," he said, his eyes steady and intent. "I can't handle what I feel."

Her face colored. "I can't be sure—"

"I won't rush you," he interrupted as Becky came back toward them. "Good girl," he called, striding toward his horse. "You're beginning to look like a cowgirl!"

"Am I really?" Becky asked enthusiastically.

"You really are," he assured her. "I'm going to show you a sea of wildflowers. Texas meadows look like fairyland in spring."

He led them back toward the farm road, then turned to

the south. They were facing a field that looked as if it had been paint-splattered. It was alive with color.

"The blue is bluebonnets, our state flower," he announced, sweeping his hand toward the distant horizon, where dust clouds told them men were massing cattle. "The orange and red is Mexican hat and Indian paintbrush, and there are daisies and some blooming thornbushes mixed in with it. All this used to be prairie," he added with a wistful look. "Black with buffalo herds, unspoiled. It's a pity what we have to trade for progress."

"Will the buffalo come back?" Becky asked.

Gabe leaned his forearms over the pommel and shook his head. The leather creaked with the smooth motion of his body. "Afraid not, honey. They're gone, like the pioneers and the Indians. Gone in a rage of passion called westward expansion."

"Reactionary," Maggie accused gently. "You'd like to tear up the cities and start over."

He turned toward her. "Sure I would." He grinned. "I'm a cattleman. I like plenty of space and no fences."

"You were born a hundred years too late."

"Amen to that," he agreed. He sighed, glancing toward the dust. "Well, I hate to do it, but I'll have to get you two home so that I can go back to work. Becky, we'll go over to Dane's late this afternoon and see about that pup. What do you say?"

The child grinned. "I think you're terrific, Uncle Gabe."

"Do you like it here, honey?" he asked, suddenly serious.

"Oh, yes," Becky sighed, her face radiant as she stared around. "I wish I could live here always."

He looked over her head at Maggie, whose own eyes dropped. She didn't know if she could give him what he'd demand if she married him. Marriage terrified her, he had to know that. *Please,* she thought, *please don't back me into a corner.*

He seemed to understand what she was feeling, because he didn't say another word about it. Instead, he began talking about puppies again, and on this happy topic Becky kept up an enthusiastic monologue all the way home.

The days went quickly after that. Gabe always found time to spend with Becky and her mother. He bought the collie puppy for Becky and convinced her that they had to wait until it was weaned to bring it home. It was only for a few days, and he kept the little girl busy with all sorts of adventures.

He found a bird's nest for her to explore one day. The next, he drove her and Maggie in the truck to a small creek that ran right across a dirt road, where Becky could wade and chase butterflies that lifted in swirls of color from the damp sand. He always had a surprise for Becky. And like any child, she responded to his attention with slow but genuine affection. As time passed, she relaxed and actually seemed to trust him. Maggie, whose own feelings for Gabe had fluctuated wildly from anger to affection, was having trouble adjusting to his sudden switch in attitude toward her. Becky was getting all the attention now. Gabe hadn't made a move toward her physically since the day they'd gone riding. He seemed to be deliberately letting things cool off between them. He was gentle with her, and he teased her and picked at her in a roughly affectionate way. But he hadn't made another pass at her, and although it was a kind of relief in one way, it was a bitter disappointment in another. Maggie couldn't begin to understand herself these days.

Things were going along fine when a phone call came for her one day while Janet and Gabe were out. It was from her attorney in San Antonio, telling her that Dennis had initiated the custody suit. And as she'd dreaded, he'd named Gabe as her lover, claiming that she was unfit to raise a child when she was openly living with a man in an illicit fashion.

Maggie was devastated. She didn't mention it to the family, but Gabe seemed to sense something was wrong. He watched her as they went to get Becky's pup, his eyes narrowed and thoughtful.

"He's filed, hasn't he?" he asked under his breath when Becky cuddled the pup on the way back home.

"Yes," she said miserably, glancing over the seat of his Lincoln to the happy little girl in the back seat. "I don't know how to tell her."

"Leave that to me," he said gently. "I'll handle it. Just relax, Miss Turner. You're going to be fine. So is Becky." And he began to whistle as if he hadn't a care in the world. But Maggie was beginning to understand him now. And she knew he had something up his sleeve.

Becky carried her collie into the house with almost comical care, cuddling it and telling it not to be afraid. It was a sable-and-white female, and Becky was on top of the world. She showed the tiny animal to the whole household, delighted when Janet asked to hold it and cuddled it warmly. She could hardly bear to put it down long enough to have supper. It was fascinating, the change that small animal was making in the shy, withdrawn child. In fact, Maggie mused, watching her, the change Becky and Gabe had made in each other was amazing. The cold, taciturn man and the shy child had lit candles each for the other.

They were both changing, day by day; opening up, warming. Janet had mentioned it to Maggie, who was seeing it at even closer range.

Becky walked up to Gabe when it was time for her to go to bed and looked at him with worshiping eyes.

"I wish you were my father," she said with such wistfulness in her voice that Gabe's face actually softened.

He hesitated for a minute, studying the delicate little face with a curious, searching expression. He glanced at Maggie and seemed to come to a decision about something.

He went down on one knee, so that he could see Becky's eyes. "I'm not always going to be pleasant," he said matter-of-factly, talking to her as if she were an adult. "I have a temper. I lose it. Sometimes I get impatient with people, and there are times when I want to be alone. I may hurt your feelings sometimes without realizing it. You might wish you'd never come here."

Becky nodded, clutching the puppy to her chest. "I have bad days, too," she said very somberly. "But I like you even when you're mad."

He laughed softly. "I like you, too. So how do you feel about staying here?"

"You mean, like a vacation?"

He shook his head. "I mean permanently."

Becky stared at him while Maggie held her breath. "Would you be my daddy?" she asked softly.

Gabe's jaw tautened. "Yes."

Becky nibbled on her lower lip. There was a little fear left. But even as Maggie watched, it seemed to drain away. "My daddy was bad to me," she whispered. "He made me afraid. But I know you wouldn't ever hurt me."

"Oh, God," he breathed huskily, emotion in his voice, his whole look. "No, I'd never hurt you, precious."

Tears spilled over Becky's eyes. "Oh, Uncle Gabe, I love you!"

She threw her free arm around the big man's neck and nuzzled her little face against his. Gabe held her, but he didn't speak. Not for a long time.

"I'll take care of you, Becky," he said at last, his voice oddly taut. "You and your mama. Nobody will ever hurt you again."

Becky kissed his hard cheek. "I'll take care of you, too," she promised, smiling. She drew back and frowned. "Uncle Gabe, your eyes are wet."

"I guess they are," he said without embarrassment, and grinned. "It isn't every day that a man gets a new daughter."

"Could I call you Father?" she asked.

"Anytime at all."

Becky glanced at her mother, whose eyes were also a little wet. "Can we stay with my new daddy?" she asked softly.

"Darling, of course we can," Maggie said with feeling. She met Gabe's eyes. "Of course we can!"

He nodded, his eyes never leaving hers. "Mother!" he called.

Janet came out of the living room in a rush. "What is it! Is something wrong? I was just watching a movie—"

"Maggie and I are getting married," he told her without preamble. "How about arranging everything?"

Janet looked as if she might faint. "What?"

"We're getting married," Gabe said curtly.

"We really are," Maggie assured her, smiling. She turned

to Becky. "Darling, go on up to bed, and I'll be right there to tuck you in. Oh, the dog…"

"It's all right," Janet said. "I had Jennie put a nice wooden box with a blanket by the bed." She smiled warmly. "Becky, I'm going to be your grannie!"

"I'll be so good," Becky promised, going close to her grandmother. "You'll be proud of me, I promise."

"I always was," Janet laughed. She stared from Maggie to Gabe, all smiles. "What a delightful surprise!"

"Surprise, my eye," Gabe said disgustedly, glaring at her. "But you got your own way. As usual." Janet's pleasure dissipated a little with that cutting remark. Gabe brushed by Maggie on his way back upstairs. "We'll talk later," he said. "Come on, Becky, I'll go up with you."

"Yes, sir," Becky said smartly, and ruined it all with a large, mischievous grin. She cuddled her puppy and giggled as it licked her cheek.

"Oh, Maggie, I'm delighted." Janet sighed, hugging her. "If you knew how your mother and I hoped for this day."

"It isn't all what it seems," Maggie said gently. "It's mostly for Becky. Gabe says I wouldn't have a prayer in court as things stand. Dennis has remarried."

"I know. But it will work out for the best. Really it will. I only wish my son could forgive me for the past," she added wistfully. "Maybe it will happen someday."

"Of course it will," Maggie assured her. "Janet, am I doing the right thing?" she added, glancing worriedly up the stairs. "For Becky, of course it is. But I…don't love Gabe. And he doesn't love me."

"Love comes after marriage sometimes," Janet said. "Give it time, darling. Just give it time."

Maggie nodded, but she was worried, and not just about

the distant future. Gabriel was going to want a physical commitment from her. And despite the desire she felt for him, she wasn't at all sure she was going to be able to give in to him—marriage or no marriage.

She occupied her mind by taking a minute to call Trudie in London, with Gabe's permission, to tell her the news.

Her boss was delighted for her, even though she hated losing her only employee. She made Maggie promise to write her all about it, then launched into delightful details of her European trip. She added that it must be nice to marry a man who could allow his intended transatlantic phone calls.

Maggie agreed that it was, but all the while she was talking about how wonderful it would be for Becky, she worried about what she was walking into. Gabe had been so good to Becky, and to Maggie. He deserved more than gratitude. He deserved a wife who could love him and take care of him and be everything he needed in bed. Would she be able to live up to all that, ever? Or would he regret his impulsive decision to marry her?

CHAPTER SEVEN

GABE HAD TO go out with one of his men to see about a sick bull—a purebred one, apparently, from the worried look on his face—and he still wasn't back when Janet went up to bed, humming delightedly.

Maggie curled up on the sofa in the living room, tucking the full skirt of her candy-striped shirtwaist dress around her slender legs and bare feet. She was halfheartedly watching television when he returned, and her eyes were drawn immediately to the sight of him standing in the doorway.

He always looked different when he was in casual clothes. His denim jeans clung lovingly to the powerful muscles of his long legs. The chambray shirt outlined every hard contour of his chest and arms. The wide-brimmed hat he wore gave his face enticing shadows, and the boots made him even taller than he actually was. Maggie could never get enough of just looking at him. He was so virile, such a—a *man*.

"I hoped you'd still be up," he said, closing the door behind him. As an afterthought, he locked it, then, with a wicked smile, stood watching Maggie's disturbed expression as he shucked off the thick leather gloves he was wearing and tossed them aside, along with his hat. "Nervous of me, Margaret?" he taunted gently.

She felt her breath lodge in her throat as he came closer.

"A little," she said. Why try to deny it? Those pale, narrowed eyes saw altogether too much.

"Why? Because I locked the door?"

"Everyone's gone upstairs...to bed," she faltered.

He stopped just in front of her and searched her green eyes quietly. "I don't want to be interrupted while we're talking."

"What are we going to talk about?" she asked hesitantly.

He pursed his lips and reached for a cigarette. "Why you're afraid of me, for one thing."

"I'm just nervous," she corrected. "Not afraid."

"They're usually one and the same." He went to the television and switched it off, then came back and dropped down beside her, pulling an ashtray forward on the chrome and glass coffee table before he leaned back.

He smoked his cigarette in silence for a minute, and she began to relax when he didn't seem intent on pouncing. She hadn't realized just how strung-up she was until then.

"That's better," he said, glancing at her. "Now, suppose you tell me what's got you so upset."

She clasped her hands in her lap and stared down at them. "Dennis has accused me of being an unfit mother. He's stating in his custody suit that I'm having an affair with you."

"Well, honey, we knew he was going to, didn't we?" he asked reasonably.

"Yes, but he's done it! It will make headlines, don't you see?" she asked, her eyes wide with apprehension. "Janet will be hurt!"

His face hardened. "You overestimate my mother's capacity for pain."

"And you underestimate it," she countered. "She's a sensitive woman, and her health doesn't seem all that good, Gabe. I don't want to do this to her. Becky's so young, she won't even understand it, but other people will."

He studied the tip of his cigarette. "It bothers you, what other people think?"

"I know you don't care what they say about you," she muttered. "But I'm not a man."

"Thank God," he drawled. He lifted the cigarette to his mouth and took another draw, stretching lazily. "I'm tired," he said unexpectedly. "I hadn't realized how lazy I've gotten since I've been hanging around the house this past week."

"You, lazy?" She laughed. "That'll be the day."

He draped a long arm across the back of the sofa and stared down at her. The shirt pulled taut across his chest, revealing a patch of dark skin and thick hair at the wide opening. Maggie averted her eyes.

"I like that," he said under his breath. "I like the way you react to me. You can't even hide it. I can see your heart beating from here."

She swallowed a surge of panic. "You're a very attractive man," she said evasively.

"No, not really," he replied. "Just to you, I expect. But as long as that interest is exclusively for me, I won't complain." He finished the cigarette and stretched back toward the arm of the sofa, his powerful body covering almost all of its length except for where Maggie was sitting.

"Did you mean it, what you told Becky?" she asked, turning her head to look at him.

"Of course I meant it," he replied. "She needs a stable environment, a family, a place to grow up without pres-

sure. She can have that here. I can give her damn near anything she wants."

"She loves you," Maggie said gently.

"I know. It's a pretty big responsibility, being loved," he
replied, leaning forward to crush out his cigarette. "That's
why I was honest with her. There will be bad times as there
are in any relationship. She had to choose for herself."

"She's so different around you," Maggie told him, standing up and staring down at him. "She's always been frightened of men. But she's opened up with you. She laughs and
plays—she's not the same shy little girl I brought here. And
all this has happened in just over a week."

"She wasn't happy," Gabe replied. "She told me. She
was afraid her father would take her away from you. Now
she's not." He grinned at her. "I told her what I'd do to him
if he tried."

She relaxed even more, her weary eyes seeking his. "You
told everybody we were getting married."

"Yes, I did, didn't I?" He stretched, easing his back
against the arm of the sofa. His pale eyes narrowed, searching her slender body in the colorful dress. "Come here."

She hesitated. He looked…very sexy like that. Dangerously male.

"Come on," he coaxed. "I'll let you play with my chest."

She colored feverishly and glared at him. "Of all the
masculine arrogance I've ever seen…"

"You haven't seen anything, yet," he laughed softly. He
reached up unexpectedly with his good arm and jerked,
landing her squarely on top of him with such delicious
force that it winded her. He held her there with both hands
on her waist.

"Let go of me," she muttered.

"Stop wiggling, Maggie," he whispered at her ear.

All at once, as her hips came into contact with his, she began to feel what he was talking about. Stiffening, she tried to move away, but he held her there with one large, lean hand at the base of her spine. After a moment her eyes came up to meet his, finding there a wry acknowledgment, and a kind of quiet pride.

"I'm more of a man with you than I've ever been with a woman," he murmured, holding her shocked gaze. "You can arouse me by walking through a room, for God's sake. I don't even have to touch you."

"Isn't that...the normal thing with men?" she asked bitterly.

"Not with me, it isn't," he replied. "I'm thirty-eight. I've reached the age when I have to work up to arousal, as a rule."

She hadn't realized what an intimate turn the conversation had taken until he said that, and she bit her lower lip. It was vaguely flattering to have him admit such a thing, but it added to the subtle doubts she already had about being able to satisfy him. Love play was one thing; it was delicious with him, and she enjoyed it. But love play wasn't sex.

His lean fingers brushed lightly under her ear, making sweet shivers where they touched. "Relax," he whispered. "You're all tensed up. There's no need to be defensive with me. I won't take you like this."

She colored, feeling sixteen again with this devastatingly masculine man. Her fingers pressed lightly against his shoulders as she tried to keep her balance.

"Come on," he coaxed. "Just relax. It won't hurt to let your body go soft against me, will it?"

"You're..." She hesitated, trying to find the words.

"I'm...?" he teased. He nibbled softly at her earlobe. "I'm aroused? And it embarrasses you to feel it?"

"Yes," she burst out, burying her face in his throat.

His lean hands spread against her back, smoothing her against him with easy, stroking motions. "Give in, honey," he whispered, his voice deep, silky. "Just relax. Lie against me and let me feel your heart beating."

"Gabriel..." Was that her voice, sounding so weak and helpless?

"That's it," he murmured. He could feel the tenseness going out of her, feel her breasts softly cushioned on his hard chest, feel her legs like silk over his. He reached down to the very base of her spine and moved her softly against his hips, loving the surge of pleasure it gave him.

"Oh, you...mustn't!" she cried. Her body felt hot. Blazing hot.

His face nuzzled against hers until he found her mouth. In the raging silence of the room, the only sounds were her frantic breathing and the slide of cloth on cloth as he brought her even closer and thrust his tongue hungrily into her mouth.

She couldn't breathe, couldn't think, couldn't fight. She gave in all at once, her mind in limbo, her body one long throb of exquisite sensation as his lean hands explored it with a delicious lack of restraint. He touched her in ways he never had before, learning all the soft contours of her body, brushing at her breasts, easing up her dress so he could caress the long, graceful line of her legs.

"Gabriel," she gasped.

He bit her mouth, his teeth tender, his breath warm and smoky on her swollen lips. "I won't hurt you," he whispered, turning her ever so slowly under him. His voice was husky with passion, his body vibrant with it. His mouth drew slowly, passionately, over her parted lips, letting her feel every texture of it.

Her body ached. It was a new sensation, different from the other times he'd kissed and touched her. She felt a kind of throbbing excitement all over, as if her skin were wide-awake and every nerve were being stimulated.

Her eyes opened as his lean hand began to work at buttons and fastenings, faintly accusing, faintly shy.

"You have a beautiful body," he whispered tenderly, holding her eyes. "I want to look at it."

Her lips parted. "I'm frightened."

"Yes, I know." He bent and kissed her with exquisite gentleness. "There's no reason to be. We're going to make a little love, that's all. Just the way we did once before."

That relaxed her. Yes, she trusted him. He wouldn't hurt her. He wasn't Dennis.

She looked at his shirt, wishing it were out of her way so she could put her hands on his hair-roughened chest and explore its hardness. Her brows drew together in puzzlement. She'd never wanted to do that with anyone.

"What do you want?" he asked as he began the slow, sweet process of separating her from her dress and slip.

"I...want to touch you," she said dazedly.

A corner of his mouth curved up. "Where?"

She lowered her eyes quickly. "There," she whispered, brushing her fingers over his shirt.

"Take it off, then," he murmured dryly.

She'd never done that before, either, but it wasn't so hard. Her slender fingers worked at buttons, struggling them out of buttonholes. Slowly his chest was revealed, all hard muscle and thick black hair and tanned skin. She almost caught her breath at the masculine perfection of it, right down to the firm muscles at his belt.

One of his long legs rested between hers. He shifted her a little, his hands moved, and suddenly she was bare to the hips. She stopped breathing and tried to grab the fabric, but his hands, warm and strong, caught her upper arms and eased her back down.

He shook his head slowly. "None of that," he whispered softly. "You don't have a single reason to be afraid of me, and I'll never give you one. I only want to kiss your breasts, Maggie."

Her face flamed. She never would have imagined that sultry look in his pale blue eyes, on that hard face. He smiled as he bent his head to her body; then his mouth opened over her whole breast and took it into the moist, warm darkness.

She trembled. Her hands clasped the back of his head, and as the magic worked on her she pulled him slowly closer. Her body began to move helplessly. She arched a little, her hands tugging.

He lifted his head, and she guided his mouth to the other breast, pulling him down with only a little shyness. The feel of his mouth on her was intoxicating. It made her breath come quickly, it made her body throb. She liked it.

His hands swept slowly down the silky length of her body while his mouth moved to her shoulders and back up her throat to her mouth. Insistent now, he divested her smoothly of the rest of her clothing and began to stroke her in the most unexpected and shocking way.

She started to protest, but his mouth slowly overcame hers, his tongue probing deeply, his hands moving again and finding wildly responsive flesh. She moaned sharply, her nails biting into his shoulders. Then she gasped and opened her eyes.

He lifted his dark head to look down at her with eyes that were as possessive as they were observant of all the exposed cream-and-mauve flesh. "What sweet little noises you make, Maggie mine," he whispered, smiling into her eyes as the movement of his hands produced some helpless writhing. "That's it, sweet, just lie back and let me show you. No, don't try to get away. I won't hurt you. I won't hurt you, little one. I know exactly what I'm doing."

And he did. He did! Once, she almost bit through her lower lip as an explosive spasm of pleasure rocked her. Tears sprang to her eyes, and she looked up at him in mute wonder, her body suddenly trembling all over in a fever so hot she couldn't bear it.

He bent and kissed her with exquisite tenderness. "Softly," he whispered. "So softly, Maggie."

The kiss echoed his words, was a tasting of mouths that transcended sexual arousal. There was a reverence in it, an unexpected beauty.

He stood up, every movement slow and calculated, and looked down at her helpless trembling as he stripped off his shirt and removed his boots. He turned, letting her see him as he removed everything else as well.

Her eyes possessed him, devouring all that glorious masculinity in a kind of shocked delight. He was tanned all over, hair-roughened muscle rippling with every movement he made. He took a deep breath at the blatant pleasure in her fixed stare and felt himself bristling with pride.

She didn't protest when he lay down beside her. Her slender hands reached for his face, drawing it down until she could give him her mouth.

She trembled as his hands found her soft body and slowly teased it again into the fierce, throbbing submission he'd won from her before. But this time he didn't draw back. He shifted over her, giving her his full weight for an instant before his forearms caught his weight. His sore arm felt the pressure, but he didn't flinch. His body was aching, throbbing, on fire to bury itself in hers. It was an anguish to hold back, to go slow. But he had to. He couldn't frighten her—not now.

His leg coaxed hers to move, to admit the hard shift of his hips against shocked softness. Her eyes opened, and she gasped as the reality of what was going to happen washed over her and brought back all the old fears.

But he sensed that. His hands framed her flushed cheeks, and he kissed her eyelids closed. "God made man and woman to join this way," he whispered. "Not in animal lust, but in exquisite sharing. I want to give you pleasure. Let me have your body. Let me give you mine."

She trembled at the tenderness in his deep voice, at the slow, exquisite probing. "Gabe, I'm…frightened!" she cried, her voice a keening mixture of apprehension and desire.

"I won't hurt you," he breathed. He moved—tenderly— and held her eyes at the same time. "Watch me. That's it, watch me. Feel me, feel my body cherishing yours.…"

It was the most incredibly intimate thing she'd ever felt. Never like this with Dennis, who had hurt her and forced her and never taken the slightest care of her body. But it was Gabe, now, Gabe's quiet, hard face above her, Gabe's body so warm and powerful over hers, his skin as hot as her own, his hips gently moving down, his body…penetrating!

Her mouth opened, her breath stopped, at the feel of him. Her eyes mirrored her frank astonishment. It didn't hurt.

It didn't hurt at all, it was… Her eyes closed on a moan. It was…tender and slow, and he was…filling her…his body, locking, interlocking, moving, stopping, rising, probing…

His hand moved down her side, his thumb working at the hard nipple on one breast, his mouth tender on her face, adoring it, cherishing it, while his body made a miracle of this unexpected intimacy.

He was breathing as roughly as she was, but every movement was tender, calculated, unselfish. He smoothed back her damp hair as she trembled under him, straining upward, her arms holding him, her voice shaking with tiny, pleasured noises.

"It isn't sex, is it?" he whispered at her ear.

"No," she agreed in a voice high-pitched with building pleasure. "Oh, Gabe…it's…not!"

His hips moved now in a slow, building rhythm, his skin gently abrasive against hers, his dampness clinging to hers, the sofa cushions shifting beneath them with the hard, sharp movements.

"When it…happens," he whispered urgently, "don't…cry out. Bite me, claw me, but don't…cry out, they'll hear us."

"Gabriel." She was weeping, her voice thick with tears she didn't understand. Her body was like a puppet's, manipulated by his, possessed by his. She followed his movements with desperate abandon, blind with pleasure, her nails scoring him, her teeth against his hard shoulder, her tongue tasting his damp, salty flesh.

It was sudden. Like a flash of lightning, like summer hail. All at once, blinding colors came rushing down on her in a hot, sweet flood, and she threw back her head, arched her body in a tension that had to be fatal as it curled up inside her like locked steel. She made a sound she couldn't hear, burying it against his skin, and her body began to echo the sudden feverish, rough motions of his.

Crashing together, she thought in the back of her mind. Crashing together, we'll hurt each other!

Somewhere in the middle of the thought, her body burst into sweet flames. She heard his deep voice, biting back a harsh groan, felt him over her, felt him convulsing. Her mind welcomed the sudden oblivion that washed over her, the sweet pulsing aftermath of something she didn't even understand.

She was damp all over. It was hard to breathe. Her heartbeat was shaking her, like his, and she was so tired. So tired.

Her arms curled around his neck, and she began to kiss him languorously. On his chest, his shoulders, his chin, everywhere she could reach. Brief, adoring kisses that tasted salt and cologne and pure man.

"You made love to me," she whispered. She sounded and felt awed.

"Yes." His hands drew her with him as he shifted onto his back with a heavy, shuddering sigh. "Never like that, Maggie. Never in my life."

"I thought we were going to hurt each other, at the last," she murmured drowsily. "It was so...violent."

"Violence, out of such tenderness," he mused, giving a shaky laugh. "Oh, God, I cherished you," he breathed fervently, crushing her against him. "Cherished you with every part of me!"

She trembled at the emotion in his hard voice, at the feel of him, the scent of him. She clung, nuzzling her face against his with tears staining her cheeks. "I don't mind anymore."

He frowned. "Mind what?"

"If Dennis accuses us of being lovers," she whispered at his ear. "I feel like shouting it to the world, telling everyone what a wonderful lover you are."

He nipped her ear. "My mother would be shocked. She didn't raise me to seduce women in her parlor."

She lifted her head and looked around, dazed. "Oh, my goodness," she faltered, glancing down at him.

"Shocking, isn't it?" he murmured with a smile, looking down at the scattered clothing. He looked back up at her. "Shocking. And good. Right. Like marriage is going to be."

"You don't have to marry me," she began.

"I want to be with you," he said simply. "Night and day. What we've just done is going to color our lives from now on. Lovers are pretty transparent," he added quietly. "I'd lay odds the whole household, except for Becky, will know the minute they see us what we've done together."

"Oh, no," she moaned, hiding her face.

"Don't be embarrassed," he said, smoothing back her thick short hair with a gentle hand. "It isn't proper to be ashamed of something that beautiful. You're my woman now. My wife. I'm going to take care of you and Becky as long as I live. And you and I are going to build a good life together."

"It's asking a lot, for you to take on a ready-made family," she said softly.

"I like my ready-made family." He laughed. "Becky's a spunky little thing. I'll enjoy being her father. Just as I'll enjoy being a father to our other children," he added, tilting her face up to his. "Do you want that, to have children with me?"

Her eyes widened. It seemed natural, now, to discuss

such a thing. She found the thought not at all distasteful and wondered why. She didn't love him. She was attracted to him, she liked him. He didn't love her. He felt a sexual attraction and affection for her. But the way they'd loved... it had felt like loving.

"Yes," she said simply. "I want to have your child."

The words sounded so profound coming from her lips that he trembled. The involuntary movement of his body shocked him, and he frowned. This was getting out of hand. He'd wanted her; he'd had her. But he still wanted her. And that question about children had been an impulse, not something he'd consciously thought about. But it was exciting to consider making her pregnant. Deliberately...making her pregnant. His heart began to shake him.

She saw the look and didn't understand it. Her eyes searched his curiously.

"Is something wrong?" she asked softly.

"I was thinking about making you pregnant," he said, his face growing taut. "It...arouses me."

She smiled delightedly. That must be a good sign. "I'm still on the pill."

"And I didn't mean I wanted to start a new family tonight," he said, recovering his senses. He chuckled as he sat up, drawing her next to him. "We need to get married and get used to each other before we take that step. Becky will adjust better if she has us to herself for a while."

Amazing, how perceptive he was. She touched his face gently. "You were like her, as a child, weren't you?" she asked. "Shy and alone and a little sad."

His jaw tensed. "Yes."

"I didn't mean to pry."

He sighed, drawing her palm to his mouth. "I'm not used

to sharing things," he said. "Especially not emotions. Give me time. I've been a pretty private person up until now."

"So have I," she confessed. Like caressing fingers, her eyes moved over him with sudden possession. "I never liked looking at him," she said absently, and then flushed when he chuckled.

"I like that scarlet blush," he murmured, drawing her against him. "I'll miss it."

"You sound as if you're planning a cure for it," she teased.

"Oh, when I get through with you, Mrs. Coleman-to-be, you'll be shockproof." He bent his mouth to her ear to whisper something, and she gasped. He took the sound into his mouth, twisting it sensuously, and she gripped his arms with helpless pleasure.

He drew his mouth away, the expression on his face both explicit and reluctant.

"I want to have you again," he said quietly. "But I don't think it's a good idea."

She stared at him, waiting for him to tell her why, the question in her eyes.

He touched her mouth gently with a lean forefinger. "I didn't plan this. I was going to make a little light love to you, but it got out of hand. I wanted everything to be perfect when we married, complete with a wedding night. I've robbed you of that."

"Men aren't supposed to feel guilty about seducing women," she reminded him.

"I feel as if I've seduced a virgin," he whispered, searching her shocked eyes. "And one lapse is all there's going to be, Margaret. I won't take you again until you're wearing my ring. And I think, deep down, you like that."

Deep down, she did. She stared at his hard, craggy face with new eyes. He saw so much that was buried beneath the surface. He seemed to read her thoughts.

"I like very much what you did to me," she whispered. "And I... I'll like it if you...if you do it every night after we marry."

He bent to her mouth, kissing it with soft reverence. "No more fears?"

She shook her head. "How could I ever be afraid, after... that?"

"Because I won't always be that tender," he said matter-of-factly, his eyes quiet and narrow. "Eventually, I'll want you to match my own passion. I'll want something a little wilder and hotter than tonight. This time was expressly for you. I loved it—don't get me wrong. But it isn't what I like."

She colored. "What do you like?"

He searched her eyes. "After we're married, I'll show you."

She felt a little apprehensive then. Would he be demanding? Cruel? Would he want to hurt her?

"Damn it," he snapped, glaring. "Not like...that! For God's sake, I'm talking about lovemaking, not torture!"

She bit her lip. "I'm sorry. I know very little about it."

"Yes, I know. I'm sorry, too. I'm so damned hungry!" He turned her, ignoring the twinge of pain in his arm, and jerked her over him so that she was facing him in his lap, her hips pressed blatantly against his. "Feel me," he said in a rough whisper.

Her lips parted. "I don't mind—"

"Well, I do." He lifted her away and got to his feet, bristling with masculine frustration as he jerked up his clothing.

Maggie watched him as she slipped into her own things,

admiring the fluid grace of his body as he dressed with deft, sure motions.

"You're very good to look at," she said absently.

"I'm in a temper," he grumbled. "Don't push your luck."

"Why? What will you do?" she teased softly, smiling.

He glared at her. "Do you really want to know?" He leaned down, his shirt unbuttoned, and put his hands on either side of her. With his hair tumbling over his forehead, his mouth swollen, his eyes narrowed, he was so sensuous that she wanted to reach up and kiss that hard mouth senseless.

"Yes," she challenged.

"I'll throw you on the carpet," he whispered with mock fury, "where I'll strip you and ravish you until you scream for help."

"Ravish me how?" she whispered back, her lips parted. "Show me."

His breath caught in his throat. She had potential. There was passion in her. It had been crushed out, but he could revive it. He could make her burn for him. He knew he could.

He bent and rubbed his open mouth against hers in a rough, inciting caress. "Like that," he murmured. "And this." His tongue teased around her lips, probing in quick thrusts until she lifted toward him with a tiny moan.

But he drew back, smiling rakishly. "Next time," he said, watching her, "We'll have to have a radio beside us, to drown you out. You're noisy."

"If I am, it's your fault," she shot back, and laughed. Her hair was in a tangle, her makeup gone, but she was still a dish. "You did all those shocking things to me."

"Were they shocking?" he asked curiously.

She lowered her eyes to his broad, sexy chest. "I felt

pleasure. That was shocking," she corrected. "I loved it. Every second of it. I didn't think women were supposed to really enjoy it."

"My God, he was a basket case, wasn't he?" he asked curtly.

"Emotionally, I guess he was. And is. I feel halfway sorry for his wife." She looked up. "He'll hate the idea of Becky being here. He'll fight it with every dirty trick he can find. He was always jealous of you, even though there had never been anything between us. My parents adored you. They were always talking about you."

He smiled. "I liked them, too. Let me worry about your animal of an ex-husband." He pulled her to her feet and held her close to his lean, relaxed body. "You just worry about me."

She slid her arms around his neck. "I want to make love to you," she said with unexpected passion, searching his eyes. "I want to give you as much pleasure as you gave me."

"You did," he said, stunned. "Didn't you know?"

She colored a little. "You were...very quiet."

"I always am," he replied softly. "But I felt it all the same. You felt it just before I did," he added with a gentle smile. "I don't imagine you had the presence of mind to notice what was happening to me. I felt your body shuddering...."

"Don't," she whispered, pressing close.

"It shouldn't embarrass you to talk about it," he said at her ear, smoothing the dress against her back.

"I'll get used to it," she promised. "But it's all so new."

"Yes." Everything seemed to be, with her. He closed his eyes as he rested his cheek against her hair. It smelled of flowers. So did she. Her body was soft and warm, and his began reacting to it all over again.

And this time, when she felt it, she laughed delightedly.

"You witch!" he cried, shocked into laughing himself. "I thought you were too shy to talk about it."

"I'm only shy, not numb," she teased, and moved even closer. "Gabe, I love it when…this happens. I love being a woman."

His chest expanded until he thought it was going to burst. "We'd better say good night before I lose my head again." He lifted his face and searched her eyes. "I'm sorry if I forced this on you. I want to marry you. But I didn't mean to back you into a corner."

She touched his shirt. "Actually it wasn't a corner you backed me into, it was a sofa you laid me down on…."

"Stop that," he murmured darkly, and pinched her.

"You stop it," she returned with pert defiance. "I'm a big girl now, I could have said no if I'd wanted to."

"Bullfeathers," he snorted. "You were half out of your mind. I'm the one who should have—"

"Bullfeathers?" Her eyebrows arched.

He glowered down at her. "Well, there's Becky," he said, glancing away. "I can't very well use my regular words around her, can I?"

Maggie laughed delightedly. He made the sun come out, he made her whole and free and so happy. "Oh, Gabe," she breathed, and embraced him suddenly, holding him, hugging him. "You're wonderful."

He knew instinctively that, like Becky, she avoided physical contact most of the time. The fact that she was relaxed enough with him to initiate it now was devastating. He held her, ignoring the anguish of his body.

"Honey, I'm glad you think so," he murmured against her hair. He smoothed it, admiring its silky texture. His arms contracted gently, and he smiled. "I never imagined it would feel like that," he said absently, and nuzzled her cheek. "I used to dream about undressing you, touching you. Long after you left here, you'd invade my dreams. I should have realized then…"

"Realized what?" she murmured dreamily.

He stopped, shocking himself with what had popped into his mind. He ignored it, put it away quickly. No, that wasn't going to happen; he wouldn't let it.

"Nothing," he said. "I was just thinking back."

She stared across his broad chest to the window beyond. "Gabe…was it like that with her?"

He stiffened a little. "'Her'?"

"The woman you were so much in love with."

He drew a quick breath, hesitating. He didn't want to talk about it, to remember it.

"I shouldn't have asked," Maggie said when she realized how personal a question she'd asked him. She lifted her head. "I haven't the right to ask you such questions."

"Haven't you," he replied quietly, "after the intimacy we've just shared?" He touched her face with oddly explorative fingers. "Maggie, it's never been like that with anyone," he said at last. "Not even…with her."

She blossomed in front of his eyes, her face suddenly radiant, unexpectedly beautiful.

He laughed nervously. Imagine, feeling nervous with Maggie. He bent and brushed her mouth with his. "Go to bed. We'll talk again in the morning, in broad daylight. You're very seductive at night, and we've already committed one big blunder, thanks to my sudden lapse."

"It was a very nice sudden lapse," she whispered.

"I thought so, too." He let her go. "Get out of here, will you? This stoic front is going to shatter if you keep looking at me like that."

"One can hope, can't one?" She sighed theatrically, looking at him like a lovesick puppy.

He glared, and she grinned. "Good night," she said pertly, and left him, without even realizing the sudden, sweet difference in her manner. But Gabe noticed. And his eyes began to glow with a soft, budding light. He felt the first tingle of possession.

And it wasn't at all unpleasant.

CHAPTER EIGHT

BECKY WAS UP at dawn, bouncing on her mother's bed with her dog in her arms. "Wake up, Mama!" she laughed. "Look, the sun's out!"

"Well, tell it to go away," Maggie mumbled, and put the pillow over her head.

"You have to get up!" the little girl persisted.

"Why?" her mother said from under the pillow.

"Because we're going fishing," came a deeply male voice from above her. The covers and pillow were suddenly torn away, leaving Maggie exposed and defenseless in her pale blue gown, staring up into Gabe's laughing face.

"Fishing?" She gaped at him through sleepy eyes. He was already dressed in jeans and a print shirt, looking fresh and rested and vibrant. And she felt like an oversqueezed cloth.

"Fishing," he replied. "Honey, go downstairs and tell Jennie we all want a big breakfast, then tell your grandma that we'll be leaving before she gets up. Okay?"

"Okay!" Becky jumped down with the puppy clutched tight against her pale blue shirt and ran off, ponytail flying.

"But I'm so tired," Maggie moaned. Then she came fully awake and realized that she wasn't only tired, she was sore, and knew why, and blushed.

"My, my, no wonder you're tired," he murmured with a devilish grin. He sat down on the bed beside her and leaned over her on his forearms. "Mmm, aren't you a pretty thing when you wake up?" he mused, studying her disheveled dark hair and flushed oval face.

"You're pretty, too," she said, her huge green eyes staring at him admiringly. "Good morning."

"Good morning, sunshine," he teased, and bent to her warm, soft mouth.

There was a new tenderness in him, one that radiated from him like spring sunshine. She sensed it and delighted in it, reaching up to bring his chest down against her breasts.

"That's risky," he whispered at her lips. "You're barely covered. I can feel you, even through the cloth."

"I can feel you, too," she whispered back, reaching to press her hand over his hard, broad chest. "I wish…"

"You wish what?" he asked gently.

"I wish we were alone on a desert island, just for a few hours," she replied. "And there'd be no one to see us or hear us, and I could be with you the way we were last night."

"Desert islands are in short supply around here," he said with a smile, brushing her hair away from her face. "But I'd like that, too. You're sweet to love."

Her body tingled at the sound of the word, and she remembered how he'd put it, whispering that it wasn't sex at all. And it hadn't been. Sex was just a physical coming together, a brief pleasure. What they'd shared was deeper, somehow. Almost…reverent.

She searched his pale blue eyes, noticing the tiny lines fanning out from their corners, and the length and thickness of his black lashes. His brows were heavy and dark, and impulsively she ran the tip of her finger over them. It was heady, touching him that way, and he seemed not to mind. His eyes closed.

"Go ahead," he murmured. "Explore me if you want to."

She did. It was exciting, too, to run her fingers over his lean cheeks, the place where his nose had been broken and was the most crooked, the chiseled line of his hard mouth, his stubborn chin. He wasn't handsome—not technically. But he had an inner attractiveness that made his looks irrelevant. And his body was just magnificent, she thought with a sigh.

"I like that," he murmured as she worked her way down to his chest. "I like the way your fingers feel."

"I like touching you," she confessed, finding the realization fascinating. "I've never wanted to touch anyone else," she added vaguely. "It's odd, how I can't seem to stop doing it with you."

His eyes opened, searching hers. "That sounds serious."

"Does it?" She returned his scrutiny. "You don't have to look so worried," she told him, and smiled. "I'm not going to fall madly in love with you and start clinging like ivy."

"That's a relief," he said, saying the words without really meaning them. He grinned. "I'd hate to have a lovesick woman hanging on me all the time."

Her eyes dropped to his chest so that he couldn't see how much his careless remark had hurt. But why should it matter? She didn't care about him. "Well, there's no danger of that," she told him firmly.

He wondered why he felt irritated by her remark. Did he want her to love him? He drew back, a little disturbed.

She looked sad. Her face had lost its lovely color, and she seemed oddly taut.

"Hey," he said gently, tilting her chin up until her eyes met his. "What's wrong?"

"Nothing," she said quickly. "I was just wondering if we should marry…"

"I like you," he said at once. "Don't you like me?"

"Yes!" she said with smiling enthusiasm. "Very much!"

He chuckled. "And together, physically, we create something beautiful and lasting. So why shouldn't friends marry?"

She couldn't think of a single reason why not. There was always the hope that love would come, that he'd learn to care about her; of course there was.

She sighed, watching him, thinking how devastating he was, how masculine and appealing. And he was going to be all hers. No other woman would know him again as she did. He'd be her man. Completely. She felt a wild hunger for possession. She wanted him to wear a ring; she wanted everyone to know that he belonged to her. Her own bold thoughts startled her.

Her green eyes searched his hard face and she thought, I love him. I always have.

She felt the shock to her toes. Yes, she did love him. Otherwise she couldn't have given herself as she had the night before. Especially not when she carried the scars from her first marriage so close to the surface. Why hadn't she realized that before? A purely physical coming together wouldn't—couldn't—have been so profound.

"You're worried," Gabe repeated, frowning.

"No!" She sat up, pushing back her hair, forcing a smile. "Truly I'm not. I just don't know if I remember how to fish!"

"I'll teach you. That, and more," he promised, and bent to touch her mouth carelessly with his.

Maggie gasped at the soft contact. It was suddenly so exquisite to know how she felt and have him touch her. She moaned a little and opened her mouth for him.

He caught his breath at her unexpected submission. His heart began to beat wildly. He lifted his head and looked at her, feeling all man and a yard wide—and frankly hungry.

His lean fingers took hold of the strap of her gown and slowly tugged it down, baring one taut, pretty breast to his glittering eyes.

Her lips parted. Her head fell back. She watched him, glorying in the way he was looking at her, in his obvious hunger for her.

"Touch me there," she whispered huskily.

His heart leapt into his throat. She was going to be a handful. He hadn't expected this. He didn't know what he'd expected anymore. His fingers trailed down her shoulder, her arm. To her ribs, up, but just enough to tantalize. He watched the nipple grow harder and harder at his teasing, heard her breath turning shallow and quick.

"Is it my hands you want, or my mouth?" he whispered, brushing his lips softly against hers.

Her nails gripped his shoulders helplessly. "Anything," she whispered back, her voice shaking. "Anything!"

"Only for a second, then," he breathed, bending slowly. "We can't start something now."

But he wanted to. He cupped her breast in his palm and savored its soft weight as he bent to tease it gently with his lips and tongue and teeth. Maggie was whimpering. The sound excited him almost beyond bearing, but he had to keep his head, he had to be gentle, he had to… God!

He threw her back into the pillows and followed her down, his face hard with passion, his hands pinning her.

"Do it," she challenged. Her eyes were wide and hot, and behind them was the first spark of a blazing need for possession. "Do it. I dare you."

He shook all over with the effort to control it. She was a siren, lying there with her eyes daring him, her body yielded, promising heaven. Becky. Becky would be back any minute.

He eased his grip on her wrists. "Becky," he whispered. "She'll see."

She blinked, as if she hadn't really been lucid. Then she caught her breath as she stared up at him with slowly dawning comprehension. "Oh."

"Oh, indeed." Gabe sat up, drawing her with him, faintly amused even through his own frustrations at the look on her face. "I wasn't the only one who got carried away," he insinuated devilishly. "What did you want me to do, for God's sake? Take you right here with the door wide open?"

She went beet red. He made it sound like a quick tumble in the hay, and she hated him for it. She didn't consider that he was frustrated and eaten up with desire. She only knew that he was hurting her.

"Sorry," she said, trying to sound unaffected by it. "I guess I forgot. I'd better get dressed."

He let her go with reluctance and watched her tug up the shoulder strap of her gown. The light had gone out of her, even before she went to her closet and started pulling out jeans and a green print blouse.

He got to his feet slowly and went to stand just behind her, not touching. "Don't draw into a shell," he said gently. "I told you, I'm rusty at this. It…surprised me. That's all."

It had surprised her, too, but she'd only just realized that she was in love with him. And how could she admit that, when he was only marrying her for Becky's sake? He'd said so. The physical magic was a fringe benefit. He didn't love her. He didn't want to love anybody.

She forced herself to act casual and turned with a smile. "It surprised me, too," she confessed, her tone light and superficial. "No harm done."

He searched her eyes. "I didn't mean to hurt your feelings."

"You didn't," she said quickly. Too quickly. "I'll get my clothes on. Where are we going?"

"Down on the pond," he replied. "I keep it stocked with game fish."

"You'll have to bait the hook if you use spring lizards," she murmured. "I don't mind worms, but I don't like lizards."

"Okay."

She turned, holding her clothes, and stared at him.

He got the message, belatedly. "I'll go see about the gear." He paused at the door and looked back with steady blue eyes. "I won't leave the room after we're married. I don't think married people should be embarrassed to undress in front of each other."

"Neither do I," she agreed calmly. "But we're not married yet."

"We will be by Friday," he told her, and went out the door without another word. And that was the first she'd heard of her wedding date.

She was surprised to learn after breakfast that they were going to fish with cane poles instead of rods and reels.

"What?" she exclaimed, staring at the old, enormously

long pole he extended toward her. "You want me to catch a fish with *that*? Where's the safety? Where's the spool? Where's the—"

"It's all one unit, see?" he said reasonably. "Hook, sinker, float, thirty-pound test line and a box of worms. Here."

She took the worms and the pole and gaped at him. "This ranch is worth a fortune, and you can't afford a spinning reel?"

"I'm not doing it to be cheap," Gabe began.

"A spinning wheel is how you make cotton thread," Becky said importantly, looking up at them. "We learned about that in school."

"No, no, darling, a spinning reel," Maggie told her. "It's a kind of rod and reel that doesn't backlash."

"City slicker." Gabe glowered at Maggie. "What's the matter, can't you catch anything without expensive equipment? I guess you're used to that scented bait, too, and the electronic gadgets that attract the poor old fish—"

"I am not!" she shot back. "I can so catch fish with a cane pole!"

He crossed his arms over his broad chest. "Prove it."

"All right. I will!"

She grabbed the pole and stalked out of the house, off toward the pond that was several hundred yards down the dirt, ranch road.

Becky giggled, holding her own pole over her shoulder as she and Gabe followed at a respectful distance. "Mama never used to get all funny like that," she told Gabe. "She sure is different."

"Yes, isn't she?" Gabe grinned, watching Maggie's straight back as she marched ahead of them.

"Can she fish?" asked Becky.

"I'm not sure," he replied. "I think so. We'll find out, though, won't we, honey?"

"You bet!"

They sat on the banks of the pond for over two hours. When they returned to the house, Becky had a fish. Gabe had a fish. Maggie had wet jeans and a broken line.

"Poor Mama." Becky sighed. "I'm sorry you didn't catch anything."

"She didn't have an expensive rod and reel," Gabe said, straight-faced.

Maggie aimed a kick at his very masculine seat and fell flat on hers when he whirled, anticipating it, and side-stepped.

The look on her face was comical. He grinned and extended a hand to help her up.

"Next time, don't put so much spirit into it," he murmured, delighted at the show of spunk. "You're going to have a hard time sitting down. Again," he added with an innocent glance.

She colored at the insinuation and fell quickly into step beside Becky, ignoring him.

"Isn't this fun?" Becky said, holding up her stringer of one fish. "Just like a real family. I'm so glad I can stay here."

Gabe glanced at her. "Me too," he said. "It's kind of nice, having my own daughter."

Maggie felt warm at the thought of it. But she knew Dennis, and she was frightened. Gabe was formidable; but what could he do with a man like Dennis, who wouldn't fight fair?

She worried at the problem without finding any resolution. She thought about mentioning it to Gabe but knew he wouldn't listen. He wasn't even taking the custody suit seriously, he was so certain of winning. Maggie wasn't that certain. And she was afraid. Becky was her whole world. She'd do anything to keep Dennis from using her as a key to the trust. Anything!

Gabe made blood-test appointments for himself and Maggie, and the next day, after they left the doctor's office, the couple applied for a license at the county courthouse. Then the waiting began.

Janet helped with the invitations, which were extended by telephone because there wasn't time for anything elaborate.

"It will be fine, dear," she assured Maggie. "We're just inviting some friends from Houston—John Durango and his wife, Madeline. They've been married four years now, and have two boys. At first they thought their sons would be identical twins, but they're very different. They don't look anything alike."

"That might be a blessing," Maggie commented.

"I agree." Janet studied the younger woman. "Are you and Gabriel going to have children of your own?"

"Yes," Maggie said, smiling.

Janet nodded. "I'll like that. I'll like that very much." And she went back to telephoning.

"What do the Durangos do?" Maggie asked Gabriel the next day just before he left to help finish the branding.

"Do?" He stared at her. "Hell, John owns an oil company."

"Excuse me, I don't read minds very well," she muttered, glaring at him.

"Madeline is a mystery writer. She did *The Grinding Tower*, which ran as a miniseries on television," he added.

"That was one of my favorite books! You actually know the writer?"

"Well, I guess I do," he said. "She's just a person."

"She's a writer!"

"Just a person," he emphasized, "with a marvelous talent and a lot of sensitivity. Writing is what she does, not what she is. You'll see what I mean when you meet her." He pursed his lips. "She threw a pie at John and dumped spaghetti on him. She stranded him on a country road with a broken-down car—my God, he was lucky to have survived until she agreed to marry him."

"Sounds like a rough courtship," she remarked.

"It was. He made her pregnant," he said softly. "And she tried to run, thinking that he'd only want her out of misplaced responsibility."

Her eyes searched his. "And did he?"

Gabe smiled. "He'd loved her for years. She didn't know, until then."

"What a nice ending."

"They thought so. John's brother, Donald, was sweet on her, but he gave up with good grace, went off to France and married a pretty young artist. They have a daughter now." He brushed back her hair with a gentle hand. "Stay out of the sun. You're getting blistered."

Maggie made a face at him. "Look at yourself."

He grinned. "Like leather," he murmured. "My skin doesn't burn anymore."

She wanted to reach up and kiss him, but then she remembered that he didn't want her love. It wasn't going to be a love match. She had to keep that in mind.

He ruffled her hair affectionately. "See you later." And he moved off the porch to light a cigarette, every step vibrant and sure. She loved to watch him walk. He was so graceful. He looked all man, delicious.

She turned with a hard sigh. She had to stop making love to him with her eyes. God forbid he should notice. That wasn't what he wanted from her, after all.

And in the days that followed, it did seem that he wanted nothing more than companionship. The night before they were to be married in a quiet ceremony at the small country church nearby, Maggie was living on her nerves. Gabe hadn't even touched her since the morning he'd taken her and Becky fishing. He'd been roughly affectionate and polite, but nothing more.

"When do the Durangos get here?" she asked him after supper, when Janet had taken Becky upstairs to read her a story and Jennie had left.

"In the morning," he told her. "They'll fly up and back the same day. John's in the middle of some financial manipulating. Oil's about hit rock bottom, you know. He's had to diversify pretty quickly."

"Too bad," she murmured. She sipped her coffee, oblivious to the quiet, steady look he was giving her.

"Suppose I lose everything one day," he asked suddenly, leaning back in his chair. "What would you do?"

Her eyebrows shot up. "Get a job, of course."

He burst out laughing. "Always the unexpected." He shook his head. "Get a job. Would you leave me?"

"No, I wouldn't leave you," she said reasonably. "Why should I?"

"Forget it. I suppose I'm thinking out loud." He drained his coffee cup and stood up. "You'd better get some rest. Tomorrow's the big day. Got the rings?"

He'd given them to her the day before, a small diamond and a matching gold band. Nothing fancy at all, and she'd been a little disappointed because he'd only given her the box and walked off without bothering to put the engagement ring on for her.

"Yes," she said, her voice sounding hollow. "I have them."

"You aren't going to back out on me, are you, Maggie?" he asked suddenly, pausing at her chair.

"No." She looked up. "Are you having second thoughts?"

"Not at all. Why?"

"I just wondered," she said, staring at her mauve slacks. "You don't seem to..." She hesitated, glancing up at him. "Well, to want me anymore."

"Not want you!" The words were half amused, half angry. "Why?"

She was embarrassed now, shy of him when he looked at her with that vaguely superior, very adult expression on his hard face. What was she supposed to tell him? That since he never made any advances, she'd decided he was regretting his decision? She couldn't!

"Why?" he repeated.

Her face went rigid. "You don't touch me."

"Sure I do," he argued gently. "I touch you all the time."

"Well, not like you did before," she muttered.

"You haven't been all that approachable," he said. "I thought you didn't want it."

She threw up her hands. "Since when did that ever stop you? Weren't you the one who was backing me up against trees when I'd barely gotten here in the first place?"

His eyebrows arched. Maggie in a temper was a new and tantalizing proposition. He tilted his chin up, pursing his lips as he gazed down at her. "My, don't we sound frustrated, though?"

"We aren't frustrated." She threw her napkin down and got to her feet. "I think I'll go to bed."

"So early? It's barely seven o'clock," he remarked with a glance at his watch.

"I'll need plenty of rest to cope with tomorrow," she said, turning.

"Maggie."

She stopped with her back to him. "Yes?"

He moved closer. He didn't touch her, but she could feel the warmth of him behind her. "If you want me to make love to you, all you have to do is tell me. Not even that. Cut your eyes around, smile at me, flirt with me…. Men need a little encouragement. We don't read minds."

"I've done everything except take my clothes off for you," she said through her teeth.

"No, you haven't. You've managed to keep right out of my way all week. I haven't been avoiding you, honey. It's pretty much the other way around."

She drew in a slow breath. He was right. She hadn't realized it, but he was right. "I'm sorry, Gabe," she murmured. "I've been worried—about Dennis, and if we're doing the right thing to marry…. I've been worried about a lot of things."

"Want to talk?" he asked gently.

She nodded without turning her head.

"Come on, then. The cattle can live without me for a while." He caught her hand in his and led her into his study, closing the door behind them. "I won't lock it," he said dryly, letting go of her hand. "Does that make you feel more secure?"

"I'm not afraid of you that way," she told him, surprised that he should think so. "You're nothing like Dennis. I know you won't hurt me."

"I suppose that's something," he said gently. He held her gaze for a long moment, feeling the electricity all the way down to his toes. He laughed because it disturbed him, and he turned away to perch on the edge of his desk and light a cigarette.

He'd cleaned up for supper but was still wearing denims and a green print shirt. He looked very Western, completely masculine, and Maggie's fingers itched to run through his thick black hair.

He was doing his own share of looking at the picture she made in loose mauve slacks and a taupe blouse, both silky and very sensuous. With her short dark hair framing her face and her green eyes wide and soft, she was a vision.

"You look more and more like your mother," he remarked unexpectedly. "She was a beauty, too."

Maggie flushed. "I'm not pretty."

"You are to me," he replied. "I like the way you look."

"Thanks." She sat down on the long leather divan and folded her hands in her lap.

"You wanted to talk," he said, waving his cigarette in her direction. "What about?"

"What if we lose the court case?"

"For God's sake, we aren't going to lose," he said shortly, impatient with her. "I won't let him have Becky."

"If the court says so, we'll have to."

"The court won't say so." He lifted the cigarette to his mouth.

"I can't help worrying." She sighed. "Becky and I have had some hard knocks because of him. She's worried, too."

"Well, I'm not," he told her. "Everything's under control. There's no need to dwell on it."

"That's right, just tell me. Like you tell everybody." She got to her feet, lashing out at him for the first time. "You're Tonto and the Lone Ranger. Nothing bothers you, you can beat the world...."

"I can sure as hell try," he agreed, smiling. "Come here, saucy little woman. You're just frustrated, and I can take care of that."

"Oh, can you? How?" she asked with a cold, level stare.

His eyebrows arched. "Ouch," he said. "You want to bite, don't you?"

"I hate men," she muttered, glaring at him.

"I figured it would come out sooner or later. I guess it's a good thing it was sooner." He crushed out his cigarette, slowly and deliberately, and came off the desk into a posture that made her heart race.

"Don't you touch me," she challenged, backing up. "I'm not in the mood to be subdued by the superior male."

"Oh, I think you are," he said with a slow, devilish smile. He moved toward her, holding her eyes, backing her toward the divan she'd vacated. "I think that's exactly what you want—to be shown that I still find you desirable."

"I won't beg for your exclusive attentions!"

"I wouldn't beg for yours, either," he replied easily. "I don't think people need to be put in that position." He stopped when she'd reached the divan and, watching her, began to unbutton his shirt with slow, careless motions of his lean fingers.

"What are you doing now?" she asked breathlessly.

"Getting comfortable," he murmured. "Lie down, Maggie."

"You said we wouldn't…!"

"And we're not going to," he promised. "But I think you need some reassurance. Maybe I need it, too. Marriage is a big step."

"Yes, I know."

"Come on, lie down," he coaxed. He took her by the waist and eased her down onto the wide divan, sitting up long enough to strip off his shirt.

His chest was broad and brown and covered with a thick wedge of hair, and she stared at it helplessly, remembering how it felt to run her hands over it, to experience the touch of it against her breasts. Her lips parted on a wave of remembered pleasure.

He saw that, and something in him began to burst with delight. Her eyes were sultry. He loved the way they devoured him acquisitively. She wanted to touch him. He wanted that, too.

His ribs swelled with a deep breath. "Go ahead," he whispered. "Touch me there."

She didn't need a second invitation. Sitting up, eyes glowing intently, she tangled her fingers in the liberal growth of his chest hair and caught her breath, loving the wiry feel of it, the play of muscles beneath it, the sudden quickness of his breathing.

"You make me burn when you do that," he whispered above her head. "I don't think you realize how expressive your eyes are when you look at me."

"You have a very sexy chest," she murmured, pressing her hands flat to savor its warm strength.

"I could return the compliment," he said dryly. "You're a sweet sight, too."

His hand had worked its way between them. His knuckles were drawing gently over her collarbone, her shoulder. He ran them slowly down to the soft swell of her breast and farther, to the nipple that grew swiftly hard at the tender abrasion.

"Wouldn't you like to lie against me with your shirt off, Maggie?" he asked at her ear. "And feel my chest against your bare breasts?"

She trembled. He made it sound sinfully delicious. Yes, of course she wanted it; but why did she have to admit it?

He laughed, as if he could read her mind. "Unbutton it," he whispered, moving his hands down to her waist. "It's more exciting if you let me watch you take if off."

It was. She trembled at the impact of his eyes when she let the silky fabric fall from her shoulders. She wasn't wearing anything under it, and he had a delicious view of firm, pink-tipped breasts that were just slightly swollen with passion.

"Like...this?" she whispered, needing reassurance. She felt inadequate; she always had since Dennis's cruel needling. But Gabe wasn't laughing. He reached up, lightly touching one perfect breast, and found it cool and soft and wonderfully responsive.

"I don't know why," he said absently, watching her with a rapt expression that was totally male, "but I've always liked women who were small, like you. Not that you're all that small. But my God, how perfect!"

She felt herself swelling, as much with pride as desire. Her back arched just a little, a helpless response to his voice, his touch.

"I'm going to lift you against me," he said, taking her waist with both hands. "Feel you. Absorb you."

He brushed her against him, watching where they

touched, his eyes on the pink flesh that buried itself in the thick dark hairs of his muscular chest.

"How does it feel?" he whispered.

"Exquisite," she whispered back. She arched her spine, letting her head fall back so that she pushed against him.

His hands contracted. "Is this what you want?" he whispered, and bent his head to her shoulders.

"Yes," she sighed, holding his head. "Only...lower."

"Where?" he teased softly. "Tell me."

"You know."

"Tell me, or I won't do it."

"Yes, you will." She laughed, feeling him laugh, too, feeling his mouth go warm and moist down her bare arm, over to her ribs, her waist, and then back up to tease around the very edges of her breasts.

Her breath came in tiny gasps. She was burning up, on fire for him. She moaned.

"Lie down so that I can do it properly," he breathed, easing her onto her back. He knelt beside her, one hand lifting her back, the other cradling her head. And his mouth worked on her, explorative, deliciously thorough. He did things to her with his lips that she'd read about and heard about but had never really experienced. He made her shiver and burn, his mouth fierce and demanding on her warm body, his breath coming as fast as hers.

"Maggie," he whispered. He moved, rising, holding her eyes as his body lowered slowly over hers.

She shivered a little as he approached, because he was fully aroused. "Are we...going to?" she asked helplessly, because if he said so, she would. She couldn't help herself; she already wanted him.

"No," he said softly. "Not until we're married. I just want to feel you."

"You want me," she whispered recklessly. "I know."

"It would be hard to miss," he agreed with pained humor. His mouth explored her nose, her chin. "Open your mouth...."

She did, meeting the probing kiss with headlong delight. She reached up and held him, twisting her mouth under his with blind pleasure. He was all man. He was hers. He was the whole world, and everything in it.

"This," he whispered at her mouth, "is stupid."

"Yes."

"Stop agreeing with me."

She moved under him. "I want to make love with you."

"I want it, too. That's why I've kept my distance," he groaned. "You little fool, it wasn't lack of desire keeping me away, it was just the opposite. I haven't slept all week. I've worked myself half to death to keep my body from aching all the time."

"Oh, my goodness," she said unsteadily, looking into his narrowed blue eyes. "I never realized... Well, Dennis never wanted me, you see. Not really. He had to force it, and because of that, he was cruel."

"I can't imagine a man not wanting you, Margaret," he said gently, looking down at the soft breast cupped in his palm. His thumb caressed it, and she jumped. He glanced up again. "Pleasure?" he whispered.

"Delicious..." She laughed, shivering.

"Tomorrow night," he said, moving his hips deliberately against hers while he looked at her, "I'll do everything you want me to. We won't sleep at all, and when we do, it will be in each other's arms with nothing between us."

She caught her breath at the passion in his eyes. "Oh, Gabriel," she whispered softly. "I can hardly wait...."

He groaned, getting reluctantly to his feet, and looked down at her with a shudder. "Get your blouse on," he said, turning away from the beauty of her. "You're going to be the death of me, Maggie."

"Oh, I hope not," she murmured as she sat up and fastened her blouse, warm all over and delighted with herself. "You can't die before our wedding night."

He groaned again and shouldered into his shirt, fastening it before he tucked it back into his jeans. She was standing by the door when he finished.

"Will you please go to bed now?" he asked, joining her. "If you want a husband, that is...."

"I want you," she replied with an impish grin. "You hunk, you," she added, batting her eyelashes.

"For God's sake, Maggie—!" he burst out, exasperated.

"I know, stop it and go to bed. I'm going, I'm going. Turn me out into the cold, a poor little frigid woman...." She was joking about it! It was the first time.

He knew it, too. Tenderly, he bent and kissed her. "You aren't frigid," he whispered. "Tomorrow night, I'll prove it to you beyond a shadow of a doubt. Now, good night!"

He walked past her with a grin, and she floated on up to bed. Things were definitely looking up.

The next morning, Janet and Becky were up at the crack of dawn, helping Maggie get her things together.

She was wearing a silky oyster-white dress with a full skirt, a spray of lily of the valley in her hair and several sprigs woven into a bouquet. It was only going to be a simple affair, but she was excited all the same.

"What are you going to wear?" she asked Gabe in the hall as he went up to start getting his things together.

"Oh, jeans and a sweat shirt..." he began, his eyes laughing at her.

"Gabriel!"

"My gray suit, I guess," he replied. "Will that do?"

"You look very nice in gray," she said, smiling up at him. "You look nice in jeans, too."

He winked at her. His eyes darkened a little as they searched hers. "No second thoughts? No cold feet?"

She shook her head. "None at all. And you?"

"Same here." He lifted her hand and slowly removed the dainty diamond ring from her finger, his expression unreadable.

"What are you doing?" she asked.

"What I should have done when I gave it to you," he replied, disturbed by his guilt. It had bothered him, not making a production about giving her the ring. Now he was going to remedy it.

He slid the ring gently onto her finger and lifted it to his lips. He brushed it softly and looked into her shocked eyes. "That's the way I should have done it, Maggie," he whispered. "That's the way I meant to do it. I made it feel like a merger, didn't I?"

"I—I didn't mind," she faltered.

"Sure you did. And so did I. It may not be the world's greatest love match, but it's no business arrangement, either." He bent again, probing her lips lightly with his. "Now, go and get dressed, little one. We're going to be invaded by people any minute. Tonight, we'll start where we let off in my study last night."

She smiled against his mouth. "Until tonight!"

He laughed and went upstairs with a quick wink. Maggie stared after him, sighing. It wasn't at all like her first marriage. She wasn't afraid of him. Becky loved him, and he was going to be the ideal husband and father. Only one thing was missing.

If only he could love her…

CHAPTER NINE

MAGGIE DIDN'T HAVE time to get cold feet before the wedding. The Durangos showed up early that morning with their toddlers in tow, and she became so involved with company and wedding preparations that it was impossible to brood.

John Durango was huge—a tall, broad-shouldered man with a mustache and thick black hair. His eyes were slate gray, and Madeline was his exact opposite. She was slender and had reddish-gold hair, which she wore long, and pale green dancing eyes. The boys took after their father but they had Madeline's green eyes, and their parents obviously doted on them.

"This is Edward Donald," Madeline told Maggie, nodding toward a plump little boy in a sailor suit, "and this is Cameron Miles," she added, indicating another son in shorts and a striped shirt. "I guess technically you could say they're twins, but they aren't identical, thank God."

"When do you find time to write?" Maggie asked.

Madeline grinned. "At one in the morning, usually. John and Josito try to spare me by looking after them in the evenings when I'm on deadline, and we have a nanny who comes in when we need her. It works out. I still manage to spend enough time with them. I've cut back on the number of books I write, and that's helped, too."

"Writing must be fascinating work," Maggie mused.

"Motherhood is even more fascinating." She glanced out into the hall, where Gabe was introducing Becky to a charmed John Durango.

"We were shocked and delighted to find out that Gabe was getting married," Madeline remarked, watching the tableau. "John was just his age when we married," she added. "He's forty-three now, and I'm thirty-one. Time does fly, doesn't it?"

"All too fast," Maggie agreed. "Becky loves him."

"Yes. It shows." She turned, searching the younger woman's eyes. "So do you."

Maggie blushed, dropping her eyes. "He doesn't know," she said softly. "He thinks it's for Becky."

Madeline frowned. "Shouldn't you tell him? He might feel the same way."

Maggie shook her head. "He's already said that love isn't something he wants. We're friends. That suits him."

"I thought it suited John and me, too," came the dry reply. "Until one night in a storm I lost my head and said yes instead of no. And just look what happened." She sighed delightfully at her sons. "What a simply beautiful reminder they are." She glanced up. "Sort of like human love tokens, don't you think?"

Maggie laughed. "Yes."

The older woman watched her curiously. "Gabe doesn't say a lot about you, but I gather that you're having a bad time with your ex-husband."

"Really bad," Maggie replied. "He wants my daughter—only because she has a trust."

"Rat," she muttered. "Well, don't you worry. Gabe will take care of him!"

Probably he would, Maggie thought later as she stood

beside Gabe in the small church, repeating her wedding vows. She tried not to betray herself by crying, but it was hard. Becky was the flower girl and John Durango, towering over everyone, was best man. Janet served as matron of honor. And a few local people had turned up for the brief ceremony.

Afterward, there was a reception at the ranch and Maggie felt her nerves going raw from all the excitement.

"Calm down, now," John Durango told her as she filled a plate beside him. "All these party animals will go home soon, and you'll have him all to yourself—Edward, stop shoving cake down your brother's shirt!" he called to one of his sons.

"Boys look a bit harder to manage than girls," Maggie commented playfully.

He glanced at her with a charming smile. "Think so? Look what your daughter's doing."

She turned around, and was horrified to find Becky sitting in the middle of the floor with a big green frog in the lap of her taffeta dress. "Becky!" she gasped, her hands going to her mouth.

"Where did she get a frog, for God's sake?" Gabe asked from behind her, staring.

"Oh, I gave it to her," John Durango said nonchalantly. "It was sitting on the porch eating flies, and it looked pretty lonely to me. I thought it needed a friend."

Gabe glared at him. "Wait until your sons get to be her age. I know your own fatal weakness, *son,* so look out."

"You wouldn't," John said.

"Oh, wouldn't I?" Gabe grinned at him.

"Go and take the frog back," Madeline told her husband.

"I can't! It would be cruel," John muttered. "Look, she's kissing it."

"Animal," Madeline accused, hitting at him.

"Wait, now," Gabe said, holding Madeline back as she started past him. "Wait a minute."

"Why?" she asked.

"I want to see if he changes into something better-looking."

Maggie gave him a hard look and moved past them to her daughter.

"Isn't he sweet?" Becky sighed. "Mr. Durango gave him to me. Do you suppose Cuddles will like him?"

"Your puppy will like him very much, especially with catsup," Maggie replied, smiling. "He'll eat the frog."

"He won't," Becky argued, glaring.

Gabe solved the problem. "I've got some flies for him," he said, reaching down to take the frog from his new daughter. "You can visit him later."

"Am I really going to stay with Grannie while you and my mama go on a honeymoon?" Becky asked Gabe.

He sighed. "Sweetheart, it won't be much of a honeymoon. Just overnight, in fact, but I think Grandma's got a special cartoon movie just for you to watch on the VCR."

"For me? What is it?"

"Go ask her," he said gently.

She jumped up, forgetting the frog. Gabe studied it and Maggie, then grinned as he offered it to her.

"I already have one handsome prince," she whispered, reaching up to kiss his chin. "But thanks, anyway."

He smiled at her gently and went off with the frog.

That night, after Madeline and John and all the guests had gone, they drove to Abilene and checked into a luxury hotel, where Gabe had reserved the bridal suite. He carried her across the threshold and stared wickedly at the huge king-size bed.

"That's sure as hell going to beat the sofa in the parlor," he told Maggie with a grin. "My back still hurts from it."

"Maybe there's a vibrator built into this one," she suggested, although she felt a little shy about saying it.

He put her down and went to check. "So there is," he chuckled, and glanced at her with raised eyebrows. "Want to try it?"

She stood in the middle of the room in her demure off-white shirtwaist dress and tried to affect a sophistication she didn't feel. "If you like," she said weakly.

He turned, frowning. In his gray vested suit, Maggie couldn't help admiring him. He looked marvelously handsome. "What's wrong?" he asked, coming over to her. "You aren't afraid of me, surely?"

"No," she replied quickly. She stared at his vest. "We haven't spent a lot of time alone, that's all. It's a little strange, now."

He sighed, taking her by the arms. "I should have thought of that. But I was too afraid of losing my head with you. I guess I went overboard the other way."

"It will all work out, won't it?" she asked, really worried, her eyes wide and soft as they looked up into his.

He searched them, feeling wild shivers of pleasure all over. "Sure it will," he murmured. He drew her closer, loving the exquisite sensation it gave him when he felt her tremble. "I'm going to take a long time with you tonight," he whispered at her lips. "It may not be our first time, but I'll make you think it is."

She reached up to his mouth, felt it move slowly over

hers, minty and smoky and softly penetrating. And she trembled because this slow ardor was so much more shattering than violence. Drawing closer, she moved her body against his in a gentle rhythm.

His tall, lean body vibrated at the contact. His breath quickened, and he bent, lifting her, his pale eyes darkening as they searched hers. He carried her to the bed, laid her down and stretched out beside her.

The lights were on but Maggie never noticed. The bed was large enough to give them plenty of room, and they needed it. He was insatiable, his body first over hers, then under it, his hands touching, touching hers, guiding. She learned the warm, hard contours of his powerful, hair-roughened body in a new way, a shockingly bold way that made him laugh and shudder all at once.

"Come on, touch me," he chided when she drew away. He brought her hands back, holding her shocked gaze. "We're married. It's all right."

"I know, but it's new," she whispered. "It's still new."

"I hope it always will be," he whispered back. He smoothed his lips down her body as he spoke and felt the sweet, slow trembling start all over again.

He took an eternity arousing her, until she was moaning and crying and writhing like a wild thing. And then he took her—he was patient even then, despite the storm and fire of it—in a rhythm that was slow and deep and demanding.

Maggie never felt afraid, not even when the tenderness reached a peak that threatened to tear her apart. She felt the mattress shudder beneath them, heard his tortured breathing at her ear. Her nails bit into his back, and she couldn't even help it. She reached up with her legs, catching his hips, holding them, her body arched like a bow. Tears streamed down her cheeks and she trembled uncontrollably, crying out in exquisite anguish as the pleasure slammed into her.

Above her, Gabe was feeling it just as intensely. His voice broke at her ear, his powerful body crushing down on hers, shaking her as it convulsed. His hands on her hips dug in and hurt, but even that was sweet.

She heard him hoarsely whisper her name. And then he relaxed, his full weight settling damply over her, his heartbeat almost frightening in its heavy, hard quickness.

She touched his hair, exhausted, sated. Part of her, she thought dazedly, loved him until it was pain. Her eyes closed and she drew him even closer, her arms loving.

He felt that surge of possession and it aroused him all over again. He was tired, so tired, but her body was tormenting him with its exquisite softness, its eager submission. He trembled and his hands moved under her hips, lifting them into his again.

"Gabe?" she whispered, stunned.

"Shh," he whispered back. His mouth found hers, tenderly. "Shh, it's all right." He moved, and she trembled. His head lifted, his eyes searching hers. "Is it all right if I do this again?" he whispered softly. "I won't hurt you?"

His consideration made her cry. "Of course you won't," she whispered. She reached up, touching his face, her eyes so filled with emotion that he had to look away.

He didn't want gratitude. That was what this was, he convinced himself. He was saving Becky, he was giving them both a home and security. Maybe she was attracted to him, too; but the rest was all sacrifice and submission. That wasn't at all what he wanted.

When he turned his face back to hers, Maggie saw that the light had died in him. "What is it?" she asked softly.

"What do you want that I'm not giving you? You'll have to tell me. I know very little about this."

He lifted his face, hard now, and taut, and looked into her eyes. "I think you know what I want," he said half under his breath. "But part of you is afraid to give it to me."

She searched his eyes slowly. Yes, she knew. He wanted passion. He wanted more than submission. He wanted… this.

She let instinct guide her, forcing down the fear of violence that had consumed her for so many years. She reached out and touched him, stroked him, relishing the feel of his body shuddering against hers.

"I can be anything you want," she whispered. She lifted her hands to his face and tugged. "Anything, Gabriel." Her mouth opened against his, and she thrust her tongue gently inside his mouth, twisting her body up against his in quick, hard advances.

"God!" he cried.

It was the last thing he was capable of saying. He trembled like a boy, hurting her without meaning to in the violence of passion she aroused in him. He held her, gripped her, took her in as sweetly primitive a way as he'd ever dreamed of doing. And she went with him eagerly, every step of the way, matching the hard, sharp motions of his body, matching the ardent hunger of his mouth, holding him, encouraging him, her soft voice whispering things that drove him out of his mind.

Suddenly everything exploded in a spasm of color and back-breaking pleasure, a convulsion of joy that made him cry out against her, that drowned out the sounds of her own savage ecstasy. He saw, felt, heard, knew nothing except the drumming crash of onrushing oblivion. For the first time in his life, he came close to a faint.

He was staring up at the ceiling when her face blocked it out. She looked down at him with pure pride, smiling into his exhausted face, his faintly surprised pale blue eyes.

"What an expression," she murmured demurely. "Didn't you think I had it in me?"

"No," he said flatly. He was still trying to breathe.

"Well, now you know, don't you?" She bent and kissed him very gently. "I'm famished," she sighed, stretching lazily, unconscious of his appreciative gaze. "I think I'll order a steak. Do you want something?"

"Liniment," he groaned. "For my aching back."

She grinned as she got out of bed. "I'll rub it for you, later," she offered enticingly.

He sat up, watching her open the suitcase and take out a gown and peignoir before she waved at him and disappeared into the bathroom. He felt poleaxed. He'd expected a nice little night of lovemaking and had found himself in bed with a wildcat. What a sweet, unexpected surprise. He watched the door, frowning slightly, and then he smiled. As marriages went, this one was starting out well. He rolled over on his back and lit a cigarette, conserving his strength. He felt he was going to need it before morning.

In the bathroom, Maggie was feeling pretty smug herself. She'd surprised him. Good. Maybe it would start him thinking. She loved him utterly and completely. Now all she had to do was show him, with her own actions. And perhaps, in time, he'd be able to return her love.

But once they were back at the ranch, Gabe was caught up in business. Phone calls, out-of-town trips, a thousand-and-one daily irritations that she couldn't share or prevent.

In business, he was still like a stranger—all cold, shrewd logic and hard-hitting determination; a real bulldozer.

In bed, everything was wonderful—and it got better all the time. But it seemed to be their only meeting place. And when the custody suit came up in court, Maggie was more nervous than she'd ever been, because she felt alone again.

Becky stayed behind with her grandmother while the adults all met in court for the first time.

"Don't be nervous," Gabe told Maggie quietly. "He won't get her. I promise you, he won't."

But that didn't reassure her. She loved Becky so much. The child had blossomed at the ranch; she was like a different little girl, and she worshiped her new father. She delighted in showing him off to people in town or in Abilene when they went shopping together. And they were like a family, even though Maggie felt more like a housekeeper than a wife. Gabe shared nothing with her except his body. His body was magnificent, and they'd achieved a beautiful peak of pleasure together, but Maggie wanted so much more: she wanted his love. And that seemed to be something he wasn't capable of giving her.

The judge was a woman, Black and very beautiful and very young. Maggie's heart sank; she would have felt a little more secure with someone older, perhaps someone with children of her own.

It was just as bad as she'd expected it to be. Worse. Dennis sat beside his attorney, smiling at Maggie with open contempt. His new wife was sitting beside him, more intent on her nail polish than she seemed to be with winning the case. Dennis jabbed her, and she glared at him, blonde and beautiful, as she put up the polish and assumed a bored look.

Dennis's attorney accused Maggie of carrying on a long-standing affair with Gabriel Coleman. He added that despite their subsequent marriage, Maggie had been more interested in her own sensual satisfaction than in the welfare of her daughter. He even added a tidbit about Becky's stay in boarding school, which he claimed was obvious evidence that Maggie didn't want her child with her.

Maggie felt sick all over. How like Dennis to twist the truth. She sat there, dying inside, grateful that Janet hadn't been forced to come and hear so many vicious lies.

"Stop looking so terrified," Gabe whispered in her ear, and actually grinned. "It's our turn now. Just listen and you'll find out what we've got on that smiling jackass over there."

She looked up, shocked. Her attorney was on his feet now, a nice elderly man with a voice that carried like that of a Shakespearean actor, deep and rich and authoritative. He had a folder in his hand, which he opened.

"We would like to acquaint the court with Mr. Blaine's most recent activities," he began, glancing at Dennis, who'd just assumed a wary posture. He read from the folder. "On the evening of March 15, he and his...wife...hosted a party that was subsequently joined by two plainclothes policemen. Mr. Blaine and his wife were arrested for possession of cocaine," he added with a bland smile in Dennis's direction. "On the evening of March 18, Mr. and Mrs. Blaine attended a party at a neighboring home. They were observed using cocaine, and participating in a...how shall we put it, Mr. Blaine?" he added, turning toward Dennis. "Orgy?"

"Your Honor," the other attorney broke in, rising, "this is nothing more than a deliberate attempt on the part of the defendant to discredit my client. I feel—"

"I have the arrest record right here, Your Honor," Maggie's attorney said blithely. "Along with a detailed report of Mr. Blaine's activities for the entire month of March, prepared by one of the most respected private detective agencies in Texas." He moved forward. "Your Honor, the defense maintains that Mr. Blaine has no interest in his daughter other than control of a million-dollar trust left for her by her late grandfather. We can show beyond a reasonable doubt that Mr. Blaine is continually in debt, that he gambles, that his amorous activities are not confined to the home, that he uses illegal drugs... In short, we feel that to allow the child to live with him would be nothing less than condemning her to a day-to-day hell!"

"Lies!" Dennis shot to his feet, pale. "It's all lies! It's just her, trying to make me look bad!"

Gabe started to get to his own feet, feeling a red-hot urge to tear Dennis apart for what he'd done to Maggie. His own Maggie. But her hand restrained him. He glanced at her and, miraculously, calmed down. He sat but didn't let go of her hand.

"One more outburst, Mr. Blaine, and I'll hold you in contempt of court," the judge said with majestic dignity. "Continue, please, Mr. Parmeter."

Mr. Parmeter nodded. "Thank you, Your Honor." He put the file folder down. "Your Honor, my client, Mrs. Coleman, was recently married to Gabriel Coleman. He owns the very successful Coleman Santa Gertrudis Ranch, the C-Bar Cross, just outside Abilene. He is rather well-known in these parts as an honest, responsible, highly respected businessman. He and my client have taken excellent care of the child, Rebecca, and Mr. Coleman is prepared to adopt her—"

"Over my dead body!" Dennis raged.

"Sit down, Mr. Blaine!" the judge said sharply.

Dennis sat, glaring at Gabe and Maggie.

"—as soon as the legalities are finalized," Mr. Parmeter continued. "Your Honor, a little girl's only hope of a happy future lies with you. We entrust her fate to your hands."

Mr. Parmeter sat down. Maggie clung to Gabe's hand, her face white with horror.

The judge studied a paper on her bench and then lifted her head, pursed her fingers and studied both sides of her courtroom. "I don't approve of divorce, as a rule," she began. "I prefer it when people try to work things out, especially if children are involved."

Maggie's eyes closed. Here it comes, she thought.

"However," the judge continued, surprising Maggie, "in this case, I can understand very easily why a divorce was necessary. Mr. Blaine—" she looked at the stiff man beside the fluffy blonde "—having gone over the records provided by defense, I am certain that remanding Rebecca to your care would be a mistake. Your entire history is one of deception and selfishness and self-indulgence. Once you acquired control of the child's inheritance, and went through it, you would have no more interest in her welfare than you would in a blade of grass.

"Now, I've spoken to Becky," she added, surprising everyone except Gabe and Mr. Parmeter, "and asked her where she thought she'd be happiest." She glanced at Gabriel and smiled. "She told me she wants to live with her new daddy, because he's kinder to her than anyone else in the whole world except her mama."

Gabe bit his lip and looked away. Maggie leaned close to him, her hand clinging to his.

"On the other hand," the judge continued softly, "when I mentioned letting Becky go with her real father, she turned white as a sheet and had hysterics." Her dark eyes narrowed as she looked at a now pale Dennis. "She told me a great deal about you, Mr. Blaine, including some things that she hasn't even told her mother. And you are indeed fortunate that you haven't been charged with child abuse. In fact, if the Colemans would like to press charges against you and pursue them, they would be well within their rights to do so."

"Oh, hell, I don't want the kid, anyway," Dennis growled, standing. "I've got a job offer in South America. We're going down there to live."

And smuggle drugs, Maggie thought bitterly. It was just his style, and he'd always threatened that it was an easy way to make money. But someday his own deceit would do him in, she felt sure of it.

"Custody is awarded to the Colemans, with my blessing," the judge said. "And due to the circumstances, visitation rights are denied. Case dismissed."

"She's mine," Maggie whispered, and put her arms around Gabe. "She's mine."

He stared at her for a long moment. Hers, she'd said. He felt left out, as if he didn't even matter. And there was that blond jackass glaring at him across the room. Suddenly his temper flared again. "Excuse me, Margaret, I've got something to do." He started to stand up, staring at Dennis with an expression that meant trouble.

"No," she pleaded gently. "Please don't."

"I need to," he said between clenched teeth. "I want to break his damned neck!"

Dennis caught his look and seemed almost to hear the

words, because he grabbed his blonde attachment by the arm and half dragged her out of the courtroom in a faintly comical exit.

"Must read lips," Mr. Parmeter mused dryly as he collected his papers. "Lucky man. I know that look. I've defended it in murder trials," he added with a meaningful glance at Gabe.

"I wouldn't have killed him, exactly," Gabe muttered, glaring after him. "But I'd have enjoyed breaking his arm."

"Good job that detective agency did," Mr. Parmeter said. "I'm glad we could afford it."

"So am I," Gabe told him, shaking the older man's hand. "Thank you."

"Yes, thank you so much," Maggie added fervently, and hugged him.

"My pleasure, and I mean it. Be happy," he told them, winking as he left the courtroom. Maggie stared after him, wondering if he realized how difficult that might be. Gabe had turned to solid ice, and he hardly thawed all the way home. Worst of all, Maggie didn't even understand why.

Janet and Becky were standing on the porch, waiting for them with nervous apprehension.

"We won!" Maggie called out even as she opened the door. "We won!"

Becky burst into tears, running straight toward them. But it was Gabe she ran to first, and he threw her up in his strong arms, laughing delightedly, hugging her with rough affection.

"How's my girl?" He grinned. "And I do mean my girl."

"I'm fine!" Becky laughed. "Oh, Papa, I knew you'd win!"

He kissed her warmly. Janet came forward to embrace Maggie, who felt oddly left out.

"I'm so happy for you." Janet sighed. "We were so afraid."

"So was I," Maggie murmured. "But Gabe pulled it off. He hired a private detective agency," she added with an accusatory glance at him, "and didn't even tell me. As usual."

He cocked an eyebrow. "You didn't ask."

She turned away. "We won, Becky mine," she said, holding out her arms.

Becky hugged her, too, and planted a happy kiss on her cheek. "I'm so glad I can stay with you and my papa," she sighed against Maggie. "I was scared to death, Mama."

"I know the feeling." She kissed the dark head. "How about some cake? I'm hungry, aren't you?"

"Starved," Becky said, and holding on to her mother's hand on one side, and her grandma's hand on the other, she led them all inside.

That night, Maggie thought it was time she melted the ice between herself and Gabe. He'd hardly looked at her since they'd come home and seemed to draw into himself even more with each passing minute. She couldn't know that her careless remark about Becky being hers now, had cut him to the quick, made him feel used. His old suspicions about why she'd really married him had surfaced, and he was sure she didn't care about him. She'd only wanted him because he could help her keep Becky.

She put on a slinky peach silk negligee after the household had gone to bed, then walked into the bedroom to wait for him. He was a long time coming up: it was well after midnight when she heard his step outside the door.

He opened it, pausing when he saw her draped across the bed in a seductive attitude.

"What is it, payoff time?" he asked with cold sarcasm and a smile she didn't understand. He closed the door with a thud, looking dusty and tired and as if he'd worked himself into exhaustion. There were hard lines in his face, around his mouth.

She sat up, blinking. "I don't understand."

"I got Becky for you," he said. "Is this what you've thought up to reward me? The sacrifice of your body?"

"Gabriel!" she cried, horrified. "It's never been that! Surely you know better!"

"Do I?" He took off his hat and gloves and threw them onto a chair, running an angry hand through his hair. "I need a shower, and some rest." He glanced toward her coldly. "Thanks for the offer, but you're more than welcome. Becky's mine, too, now. I don't need gratitude from you."

He went into the bathroom and locked the door, leaving Maggie shocked and speechless. For a long time she heard nothing but the sound of running water, as she sat quietly on the bed, her mind whirling with unexpected thoughts. Did he really think that she'd sold herself to him, just to enlist his aid in keeping Becky? Apparently he did. Then she remembered what she'd said in court. "Becky's mine." When in fact, Becky was theirs....

She got up and paced the floor, puzzling out what to do, how to convince him. She remembered so many little things, then. His anger on her behalf in court, the careful way he put her feelings first, his gentleness in bed. Maybe he didn't know it, but he'd come to care for her. He had to care: why else would her careless remark have had the power to hurt him? And he thought...he thought she was only using him! It was almost comical, when she was dying of love for him!

But how to convince him of that? She paced some more. The water stopped running. She had only a few seconds left. If she let that cold wall come down between them, she might never be able to get it up again. Gabriel wasn't an easy man to convince.

And then she found the perfect way. The best way. The most loving way. With a tender smile, she went to her jewelry box and took out a small round pillbox. Clutching it in her hand, she turned to face him when he came out of the bathroom with a towel draped around his hips.

His hair was still damp and mussed, falling onto his brow. His face was dark and hard and formidable. When he glared at her, she saw the old Gabe, the intimidating stranger she remembered from her adolescence, the cold man who never seemed to smile. He looked utterly ruthless but she wasn't backing down. She had her spirit back, now that the fear was gone. And he wasn't winning this time.

She held out her hand. "Do you know what these are?" she asked quietly.

He cocked his head a little, his eyes narrowing. "They're your birth control pills."

"That's right."

She went to the trash can and, holding his gaze levelly, dropped them into it.

There, she thought to herself with a primitive kind of triumph. *See if that ties in with your theory, big man.*

CHAPTER TEN

GABE DIDN'T SEEM able to breathe properly after she'd thrown the pills away. He stood rigidly, watching her.

"What was that all about?" he asked, his tone curt. "Is that some other way of showing your gratitude, telling me that you want my children? Well, you don't have to go that far. You're welcome, is that enough?"

She hesitated, and while she was hesitating, he whipped off the towel and turned to the mirror to blow-dry his hair. He saw her watching him, but he didn't seem to mind.

Her eyes adored him. He was so good to look at. All muscle. All man. She smiled as her possessive gaze traveled from his dryer-blown black hair down to his very shapely masculine feet.

"Take a picture," he muttered, because her look was bothering him. He wished he hadn't taken off the towel. She was going to get a real eyeful in a minute.

She already had, in fact, and her lips pursed in frankly amused delight. "Well, well," she said, folding her arms across her chest, "and I thought you weren't interested."

He glared at her. "Stop that. Women aren't supposed to notice such things."

She grinned. "Then put your clothes back on."

"I'm getting ready for bed." He put down the hair dryer and reached for a comb.

"So I noticed," she commented dryly.

He slammed down the comb and jerked a pair of pajama bottoms out of his drawer. Pulling them on with an economy of movement, he snapped them up with a violent flick of his fingers.

"Prude," she said softly.

He glared at her. "What in hell's gotten into you?"

She moved toward him with a sinuous grace, watching the way his eyes were drawn to her breasts, which were already taut and hard-peaked. The material was so sheer that with the light behind her, he could see right through it. "I want you," she said, smiling demurely. "Doesn't it show?"

"Well, I don't want you," he shot back. "Not this way."

She lifted her eyebrows. "For a man who isn't interested, you sure do have a visible problem."

He actually flushed. "Will you quit!" he cried. "For God's sake, Maggie!"

"Am I embarrassing you?" She clicked her tongue. "Sorry, I thought you wanted me to be a little more aggressive."

"I did. I thought." He scowled at her. His heart was beginning to race. She could see his pulse throb under the dark, hairy mat of his chest. "I don't want gratitude from you. Not when I know that's all you can give me."

There was a deep note in his voice that made her tingle all over. "You sound as if that's not all you want from me," she murmured, smiling gently.

He ran a hand through his thick hair and sighed in angry frustration. "I don't know what I want anymore," he said. "It was all cut-and-dried, wasn't it? We'd get married and keep Becky, and I'd take care of you both. We'd be…friends." He looked up, his eyes possessive, exciting. "But we don't make love like friends, Maggie. What happens to me when

I love you…isn't sex. And I don't ever want it to be just physical." He took a slow breath, his pale eyes troubled as he looked at her. "I thought a convenient marriage would be enough. Until today, in court, when you laughed and said that Becky was yours. And I felt like an outsider looking in, like a convenience."

"I know—now. I didn't mean it that way. I'm sorry I hurt you. Because I did, didn't I?" she asked gently, and moved toward him, stopping when she could feel the heat and strength of his body. "And I did it again, today, when I told Janet that you hadn't told me anything about the detective. But it was true. You share nothing with me except your body. You don't want to let me that close."

His pale eyes narrowed. "You don't know how close I want you," he said huskily, with fierce emotion in his voice. "You don't have the faintest notion."

Her lips parted. "Don't I?" She slid the peignoir down her arms, watching his eyes fall to it.

"Not sex," he bit off.

"It won't be," she whispered. "I promise. Watch me, Gabriel."

She slid the straps of the gown down her arms, too, and slowly, seductively, bared her body to his glittering eyes. He started to reach for her automatically, but she held his hands gently at his sides, shaking her head.

"Shh," she whispered. "I…need to show you…that I'm whole again. I think you need the proof."

As he held his breath, her cool hands reached for the snaps of his pajama bottoms and undid them, letting the fabric slide down the length of his powerful, hard-muscled legs. She moved close to him then, just barely touching, letting him feel every texture of her skin as she brushed against him.

"Maggie," he groaned, his eyes closing.

"I want all of you," she said, putting her mouth to his chest, sliding her hands down the warm, smooth silk of his back and hips, around to the hair-roughened skin of his flat stomach and thighs.

He bit back a harsh groan and his muscles convulsed, but he didn't try to stop her.

"Oh, Gabriel," she breathed against his skin, her eyes closed, her hands adoring his body, loving the freedom of touching him as she'd always dreamed of doing, arousing him, giving him everything there was of passion and love in her whole being.

"Let me lie down," he whispered, "before my knees give way."

He went to the bed and stretched out, his body arching in sensual expectation, his eyes open. "Come on," he whispered, his eyes glittering, challenging. "Do it."

She'd invited him once in exactly those words. And now she took the invitation. All the things he'd done to her, she did to him. Exploring. Touching. Drawing the very tips of her fingers over skin so sensitive that he began to make odd, hoarse sounds.

"And you say I'm a noisy lover," she teased at his lips as she smoothed her body completely down the length of his and lay over him. "You're noisy, too."

He looked up into her soft, loving eyes and suddenly didn't need words; suddenly knew. His hands slid to her hips, holding them lightly to him. "That pill..." he whispered. "Did you take it today?"

"No." She smiled. "And if you miss even one—" she

bent to his open mouth "—it can be very, very dangerous."
She bit his lower lip. "I feel absolutely primitive. I want to
bite you all over."

He burst out laughing, although it was a sound laden
with passion and delight. He held her hips. "Sit up," he
whispered, daring her. "I'll help you."

"I don't know how," she said.

"Shh." He sat up against the headboard, drawing her
over him, facing him, her body close and warm against
his as he eased her onto his hips and watched her lips part
on a breath as he deepened the contact into stark intimacy.

Her nails drew sensuously against his broad, dark shoulders. She looked into his eyes as she lifted and fell, and
trembled a little at the newness of what they were sharing.

"I've never done this deliberately," he whispered.
"Knowing that a child could come of it, and not minding."

"Neither have I," she whispered back, catching her
breath as she saw the depth of emotion in his eyes. "Becky
will...like...having a baby in the house."

His lean hands smoothed her hips down against his.
"It may take a while," he told her. "Sometimes it takes
months. Years."

She smiled through the building passion. "I'll like that.
Won't you?"

He shuddered as she moved again, his fingers biting into
her. "Don't. I'll bruise you."

"I don't mind," she whispered at his lips. "I'm not afraid
of passion anymore. Not with you."

He took a deep breath. "Tell me this isn't some new
way of showing me how grateful you are about Becky," he
said, his movements beneath her growing sharper, quicker.

"It isn't," she whispered. She lifted closer, watching

his face grow taut at the sensuous brushing. "It's simply a new way...of showing you...how very much I love you," she murmured, and found his mouth, and moved suddenly, sharply.

His mind exploded. He wanted to ask her, to make her say it again. But she was showing him. Her body was telling him everything she felt.

He groaned hoarsely under the flame of her twisting body, and his back threatened to give way as the frenzy of trying to get as close as possible threw it into convulsive spasms. He cried out something he didn't hear because the blood was beating in his ears. He was vaguely aware of her own voice, then the world seemed to go dark and warm and gently trembling around him, and he buried his face in her throat and shuddered.

"I love you," she whispered against his shoulder. She kissed his face, his closed eyes, his warm mouth. "I love you, I love you...."

"Keep saying it," he whispered, his voice weak with exhaustion. "Say it until I die. I want to hear it all the time, all my life."

She smiled against his lips. "You love me, too," she murmured smugly. "You said so. You said so, just before your body went wild. I heard you."

"Said it? God, I screamed it!" He held her closer, wrapping her up, cherishing her. "I didn't even know it, until today. I'd always wanted you, cared about you. But I didn't realize it was love until that blond jackass started telling lies about you, and I wanted to kill him. Because you were my Maggie, and he was hurting you."

She smiled, her heart bursting, on fire with new delights. "I knew it the night after you made love to me on the sofa," she told him. "All at once I realized why I'd let you. I couldn't have done it without loving you."

"I didn't even think about that. I tried not to think of you, it disturbed me so. Every time I went in the living room afterward, I'd see your body lying in exquisite positions on those cushions and I'd bend over with pain."

She laughed, looking into his pale eyes lovingly. "Me too," she confessed.

His hands smoothed over her, his eyes adoring every soft curve. "I thought my legs were going to give way when you threw those pills in the trash can," he said dryly.

"Mine almost did," she told him. "I could hardly walk by the time I started undressing you. And you just stood there and didn't even protest." She cocked her head. "I didn't think you'd let me make love to you like that."

"I wouldn't have stopped you, no matter what you'd done to me," he chuckled. "That was so damned exciting, my heart stopped beating a time or two. I never thought I'd hold off until you stopped torturing me long enough to take me."

Her eyes widened with delight. "You really didn't mind?"

"Honey, lovemaking is give and take," he said gently. "It's as exciting for a man to be aroused as it is for a woman. I don't feel any less a man because I give you that kind of freedom with my body. In fact," he added with a wicked laugh, "I feel a lot like a man with his own private harem, intent on his pleasure. I loved it."

"I'm glad. We'll have to take turns from now on."

He eased her down onto the bed, his body still locked with hers, and moved over her, resting his weight on his elbows as he looked down into her soft eyes.

"Do you think it could get any better than it just was?" he whispered.

"I don't know," she replied, her voice husky with excitement.

His hips moved experimentally as he bent his dark head. "Let's see."

She closed her eyes with a faint smile. Her arms reached up. Heaven was so close, she could feel it....

The next day, while Becky was playing with the ducks near the small pond, Maggie decided it was time Gabriel heard the truth about his stepfather. Janet had been quiet since the wedding and was already talking about going back to Europe. Gabe hadn't protested; if anything, he'd been even more indifferent to his mother. It was breaking her heart, and Maggie wanted more than anything to help heal the breach between them.

"I want to tell you something," she said softly, lying in his arms under the big oak tree.

"You're pregnant already?" He grinned down at her.

She hit him. "It would be a miracle if I wasn't, after last night. But that's not what I meant." She touched his mouth with gentle fingers. "I want to tell you something. About your stepfather."

His face closed up. Grew hard, as it had in the time before they married. "I don't want to hear it." He tried to move her aside but she clung.

"No," she said firmly. "You're going to hear me if I have to sit on you!"

His eyebrows arched. "Aren't we daring today?"

"We'll get more daring by the minute, now that we're loved and happy and secure," she returned. "So look out, cowboy, I expect to be a sexy shrew in no time. Now, listen. Your stepfather had cancer. He was dying. Your mother knew that. It's why she didn't leave him when he had his fling with your mercenary little intended."

"He what!" He sat straight up, almost unseating her. "And she never told me?"

"You wouldn't listen, as usual," she said. "She did try."

He drew in a slow breath and let it out again. "Damn. All these years I've blamed her, hated her for shielding him. She said he died of a heart attack."

"Mercifully, he did," she told him. "It was bone cancer, you see. He had very little time to live, and the woman was attentive to him, and he was reliving his youth. And it's just as well that he did," she added firmly, "because the last thing in the world you needed was to be tied to some greedy little girl with dollar signs in her eyes!"

"Amen," he said, his voice husky as he looked at his Maggie with exquisite love in his eyes. "I guess I've been blind."

"You might tell your mother that."

"And shock her to the back teeth?" he asked. "She doesn't expect me to be nice to her. I'd hurt her feelings."

She studied him quietly. "Gabriel."

He grimaced. "All right. I'll make my peace with her. I can afford to be generous now—what with my new family and all."

"This part of your new family loves you to distraction," she whispered, lifting her lips to his warm mouth. "And would love to prove it to you all over again, if she had the strength."

He chuckled against her soft lips. "I'll be sure you get two portions of everything at supper."

"You'd better eat seconds yourself," she said, smiling. "I feel primitive again...."

His mouth was moving hungrily over hers when a soft, excited young voice broke through the illusion of privacy they'd created.

"Papa! Mama!" Becky called them, hands on her hips, looking indignant. "Oh, do stop that, and come quick! The ducks have laid an egg! You have to come and look, it's much more fun than what you're doing. Why people like all that kissing is just beyond me, anyway. Yuck!"

Gabriel got to his feet with his lips compressed, his eyes shimmering, trying not to burst out laughing. Maggie followed suit, biting her lips with the effort to remain sober.

"You bet I'll never kiss any boys," Becky muttered as she turned back to the bushes where the ducks had made a nest. "Not me, no sir. My goodness, you'll give each other germs!"

That did it. They broke up. Gabe took Maggie's hand in his and lifted it to his mouth, laughing against the soft palm. "You contagious little thing, you," he teased as they followed their daughter. "I've already come down with a bad case of you, and I hope never to recover."

"I'll guarantee that you'll be properly reinfected if you try." Maggie pressed close to his side, happier than she'd ever expected to be. Becky was kneeling beside a nest in the brush, her eyes fixed wide and fascinated on two large oval eggs that rested there. Maggie smiled at her daughter. Like the eggs, happiness seemed to be hatching all around them. She glanced up at Gabe's vibrant face and found him watching her, his eyes tender with love.

Something he'd said once came back to her as she glanced toward the flowered pastures that stretched to the wide horizon. Something about the pioneers coming, claiming the new territory in a rage of passion. Her eyes turned toward Gabe, and she felt it all the way to her toes. And she smiled.

* * * * *